Praise fo

GIRL AMONG CROWS

"Vayo's gripping debut . . . is an entertaining thriller that will keep even seasoned horror fans guessing." *—Publishers Weekly*

"Vayo's debut novel combines sinister pagan rituals with a fast-paced, compelling mystery reminiscent of a James Patterson best seller . . . The twists come fast, and the characters' decisions lead to brutal consequences. Share with fans of Stephen King and Riley Sager." *—Library Journal*

"Brendon Vayo has crafted a pagan potboiler that is equal parts mystical and mysterious, profane and profound, blissfully existing at the intersection of horror and whodunnits." **—Clay McLeod Chapman, author of *Ghost Eaters***

"Brendon Vayo's heroine in *Girl Among Crows* is as relatable as she is enigmatic. A woman who seeks to right the wrongs of history while unraveling her own family secrets, Daphne Gauge soars triumphantly from these pages right into the reader's heart." **—Rudy Ruiz, award-winning author of *The Resurrection of Fulgencio Ramirez* and *Valley of Shadows***

"*Girl Among Crows* drew me into a dark world of ritual sacrifice and tantalizing mystery so completely that I lost all track of time. This immersive thriller is haunting, enigmatic, and utterly gripping to the very end . . . one of those wonderful debuts that cannot easily be put down." **—T.O. Paine, author of *The Excursion***

"Brendon Vayo's debut thriller is eerie, mysterious, and addicting." **—Brooke L. French, author of *Inhuman Acts* and *The Carolina Variant***

"*Girl Among Crows* is an eerie page turner rich with Norse Mythology, cult rituals, and creepy twists to rival Stephen King, Shirley Jackson and Stephen Graham Jones." **—MQ Webb, author of *When You're Dying* and *How to Spot a Psychopath***

GIRL AMONG CROWS

GIRL AMONG CROWS

BRENDON VAYO

CamCat Books

CamCat Publishing, LLC
Fort Collins, Colorado 80524
camcatpublishing.com

This is a work of fiction. Names, characters, places, and incidents are either products of the author's imagination or are used fictitiously.

Hardcover ISBN 9780744306552
Paperback ISBN 9780744306590
Large-Print Paperback ISBN 9780744306613
eBook ISBN 9780744306637
Audiobook ISBN 9780744306668

Library of Congress Control Number: 2023934022

Book and cover design by Maryann Appel
Family tree illustration by Maia Lai

5 3 1 2 4

FOR YEN, WHO BELIEVED.

GERARD GEDNEY (1986-)
DOMINIC GEDNEY (1981-)
DAVID GEDNEY (1976-?)
DAPHNE GAUGE (1977-)
ELIDA "ELLIE" GAUGE (1979-)
LORETTA NEWTON (1955-)
RON ABISH (1958-)
GEORGE GEDNEY (1948-)
COURTNEY GAUGE (1973-)
BRADY PAUL GAUGE (1981-?)
BRANDY GAUGE (1971-)
CHASTITY DRANE (1953-1988)
BRANDON GAUGE (1954-2010)
DOUGLAS DRANE (1918
MISSING DONNIE SOBASKI
SCOTT WILSON (1978-)
CHARITY (1922-1979)
DEBORAH WILSON (1959-)
MATHER WILSON (?-?)

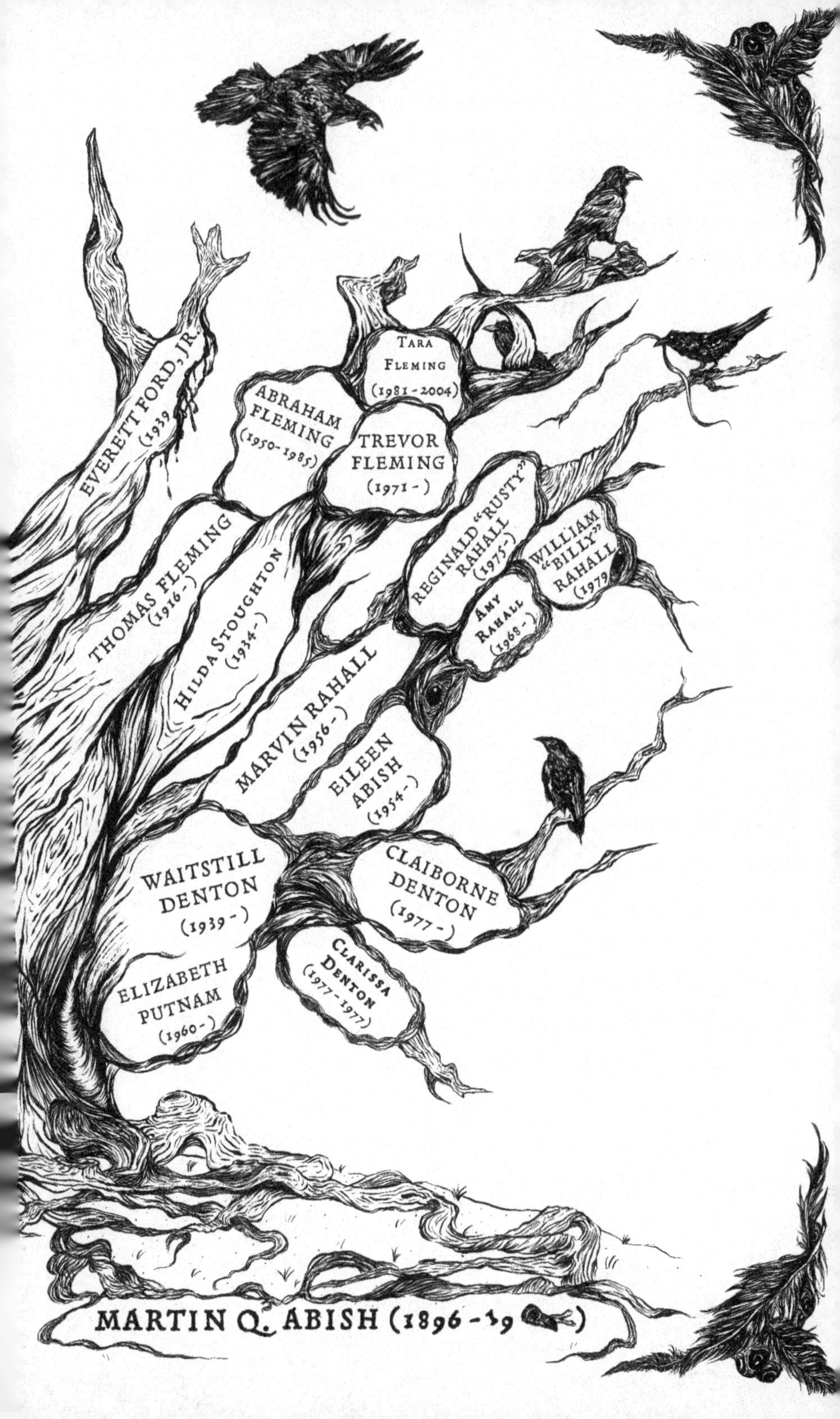
Tara Fleming (1981-2004)
Everett Ford, Jr. (1939
Abraham Fleming (1950-1985)
Trevor Fleming (1971-)
Thomas Fleming (1916-)
Hilda Stoughton (1934-)
Reginald "Rusty" Rahall (1975-)
William "Billy" Rahall (1979
Amy Rahall (1968-)
Marvin Rahall (1956-)
Eileen Abish (1954-)
Waitstill Denton (1939-)
Claiborne Denton (1977-)
Clarissa Denton (1977-1977)
Elizabeth Putnam (1960-)
MARTIN Q. ABISH (1896-19

EXHIBIT A

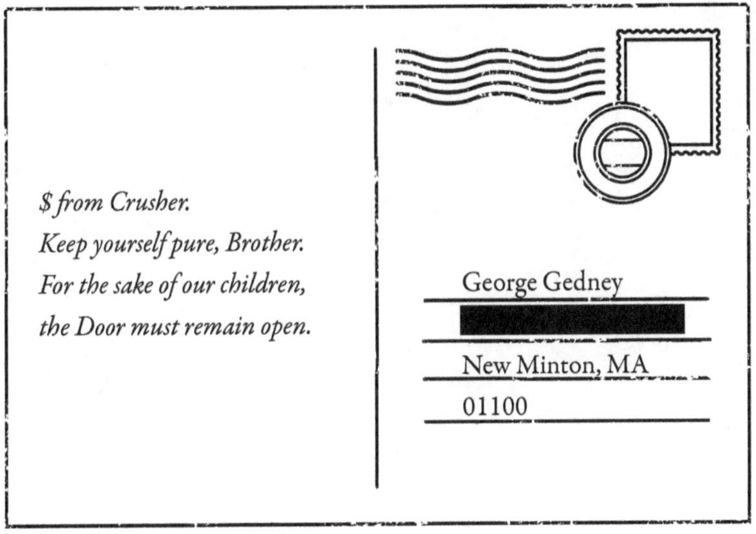
$ from Crusher.
Keep yourself pure, Brother.
For the sake of our children,
the Door must remain open.

George Gedney
[redacted]
New Minton, MA
01100

—Postcard in Gerard Gedney's possession, postmarked October 20, 2020.

CHAPTER ONE

April 22, 2021

My husband Karl shakes hands with other doctors, a carousel of orthopedic surgeons in cummerbunds. I read his lips over the brass band: *How's the champagne, Ed?* Since he grayed, Karl wears a light beard that, for the convention, he trimmed to nothing.

The ballroom they rented has long windows that run along Boston's waterfront. Sapphire table settings burn in their reflections.

The food looks delicious. Rainbows of heirloom carrots. Vermont white cheddar in the macaroni. Some compliment the main course, baked cod drizzled with olive oil. My eyes are on the chocolate cherries. Unless Karl is right, and they're soaked in brandy.

At some dramatic point in the evening, balloons will drop from nets. A banner sags, prematurely revealing its last line.

CELEBRATING THIRTY YEARS!

Thirty years. How nice, though I try not to think that far back.

I miss something, another joke.

Everyone's covering merlot-soaked teeth, and I wonder if they're laughing at me. Is it my dress? I didn't know if I should wear white like the other wives.

I redirect the conversation from my choice of a navy-blue one-shoulder, which I now see leaves me exposed, and ask so many questions about the latest in joint repair that I get lightheaded.

The chandelier spins. Double zeroes hit the roulette table. A break watching the ocean, then I'm back, resuming my duties as a spouse, suppressing a yawn for an older man my husband desperately wants to impress. A board member who could recommend Karl as the next director of clinical apps.

I'm thinking about moving up, our careers. I'm not thinking dark thoughts like people are laughing or staring at me. Not even when someone taps me on the shoulder.

"Are you Daphne?" asks a young man. A member of the wait staff.

No one should know me here; I'm an ornament. Yet something's familiar about the young man's blue eyes. Heat trickles down my neck as I try to name the sensation in my stomach.

"And you are?" I say.

"Gerard," he says. The glasses on his platter sway with caffeinated amber. "Gerard Gedney. You remember?"

I gag on my ginger ale.

"My gosh, I *do*," I say. "*Gerard*. Wow."

Thirty years ago, when this convention was still in its planning stages, Gerard Gedney was the little boy who had to stay in his room for almost his entire childhood. Beginning of every school year, each class made Get Well Soon cards and mailed them to his house.

We moved before I knew what happened to Gerard, but with everything else, I never thought of him until now. All the growing up he must've done, despite the odds, and now at least he got out, got away.

"I beat the leukemia," he says.

"I'm so glad for you, Gerard."

If that's the appropriate response. The awkwardness that defined my childhood creeps over me. Of all the people to bump into, it has to be David Gedney's brother. David, the Boy Never Found.

My eyes jump from Gerard to the other wait staff. They wear pleated dress pants. Gerard's in a T-shirt, bowtie, and black jeans.

"I don't really work here, Daphne," says Gerard, sliding the platter onto a table. "I've been looking for you for a while."

The centerpiece topples. Glass shatters. An old woman holds her throat.

"Gerard," I say, my knees weak, "I understand you're upset about David. Can we please not do this here?"

Gerard wouldn't be the first to unload on what awful people we were. But to hear family gossip aired tonight, in front of my husband and his colleagues? I can't even imagine what Karl would think.

"I'm not here about my brother," says Gerard. "I'm here about yours." His words twist.

"Paul," I say. "What about him?"

"I'm so sorry," says a waiter, bumping me. Another kneels to pick up green chunks of the vase. When I find Gerard again, he's at the service exit, waiting for me to follow.

Before I do, I take one last look at the distinguished men and a few women. The shoulder claps. The dancing. Karl wants to be in that clique—I mean, I want that too. For him, I want it.

But I realize something else. They're having a good time in a way I never could, even if I were able to let go of the memory of my brother, Paul.

The catering service has two vans in the alleyway. It's a tunnel that feeds into the Boston skyline, the Prudential Center its shining peak.

Gerard beckons me to duck behind a stinky dumpster. Rain drizzles on cardboard boxes.

I never knew Gerard as a man. Maybe he has a knife or wants to strangle me, and all this news about my brother was bait to lure me out here. I'm vulnerable in high heels. But Gerard doesn't pull a weapon.

He pulls out a postcard, its edges dusty with a white powder I can't identify. The image is of three black crows inscribed on a glowing full moon.

"I found it in Dad's things," says Gerard. "Please take it. Look, David is gone. We've got to live with the messes our parents made. Mine sacrificed a lot for my treatment, but had they moved to Boston, I probably would've beat the cancer in months instead of years."

"And this is about Paul?" I say.

"When the chemo was at its worst," says Gerard, "I dreamed about a boy, my older self, telling me I would survive."

I take my eyes off Gerard long enough to read the back of the postcard:

> *$ from Crusher. Keep yourself pure, Brother. For the sake of our children, the Door must remain open.*

Crusher. Brother. Door. No salutation or signature, no return address. Other than Crusher, no names of any kind. The words run together with Gerard's take on how treatment changed his perspective.

Something presses my stomach again. Dread. Soon as I saw this young man, I knew he was an omen of something. And when is an omen good?

"Your dad had this," I say. "Did he say why? Or who sent it?"

An angry look crosses Gerard's face. "My dad's dead," he says. "So's Brother Dominic. Liver cancer stage 4B on Christmas Day. What'd they do to deserve that, huh?"

"They both died on Christmas? Gerard, I'm so sorry." First David, now his dad and Dominic? He stiffens when I reach for him—of course, I'm the last person he wants to comfort him. "I know how hard it is. I lost my mom, as you know, and my dad ten years ago."

The day Dad died, I thought I'd never get off the floor. I cried so hard I threw up, right in the kitchen. Karl was there, my future husband, visiting on the weekend from his residency. I didn't even think we were serious, but there he was, talking me through it, the words lost now, but not the comfort of his voice.

I looked in his eyes, daring to hope that with this man I wouldn't pass on to my children what Mom passed down to me.

"Mom's half-there most days," says Gerard. "But one thing—"

The rear entrance bangs open, spewing orange light. Two men dump oily garbage, chatting in Spanish.

"Check the postmark, Daphne," says Gerard at the end of the alleyway. He was right beside me. Now it's a black bird sidestepping on the dumpster, its talons clacking, wanting me to feed it. I flinch and catch Gerard shrugging under the icy rain before he disappears.

The postmark is from Los Angeles, sent October last year. Six months ago, George Gedney received this postcard. Two months later, he's dead, and so is another son.

What does that mean? How does it fit in with Paul?

Though he's gone, I keep calling for Gerard, my voice strangled. Someone has me by the elbow, my husband. Even in lifts, Karl's three inches shorter than me.

"Daphne, what is it? What's wrong?"

"Colquitt. I need Sheriff Colquitt or . . ." Voices argue in my head, and I nod at the hail swirling past yellow streetlamps. "Thirty years ago, Bixbee was a young man. He might still be alive."

"Daphne, did that man hurt you? *Hey*."

Karl demands that someone call the police, but I shake him.

"It's fine, Karl," I say, dialing Berkshire County Sheriff's Office. "Gerard's a boy I knew from my hometown."

Karl's calling someone too. "Some coincidence," he says.

Though it wasn't. Here I am trying not to think about the past, and it comes back to slap me in the face as though I summoned it. Paul. The little brother I vowed to protect.

The phone finally picks up. "Berkshire Sheriff's Office."

"Hello," I say, "could I leave a message for Harold Bixbee to call me back as soon as possible? He is or was a deputy in your department."

"Uh, ma'am, I don't have anyone in our personnel records who matches that name. But if it's an emergency, I'd be glad—"

I hang up. Damn. I should've known at nine p.m., all I'd get is a desk sergeant. I'd spend half the night catching him up to speed.

"Daphne." My husband lowers his phone, looking at me as though I've lost my mind. "I asked Ed to pull the hotel's security feed. You're the only one on tape."

"What? No."

"It shows that you walked out that door alone," says Karl, gesturing, "and I came out a few minutes later."

The Door must remain open.

Dread hardens, then the postcard's corner jabs my thumb. I'm about to show Karl my proof when I realize that now there are only two crows in the moon.

"How'd he do that?" I keep flipping it, expecting the third one to return, before I sense my husband waiting. Distantly, I hear wings flap, but it could be the rain. "Gerard wanted me to have his dad's postcard."

"So this boy Gerard comes all the way from Springfield to hand you a postcard," Karl says. "And he can magically avoid cameras?"

"I'm not from Springfield," I say, shaking off a chill. *Magically avoid cameras.* And Gerard can turn pictures of crows into real ones too. How?

"You seem very agitated," says Karl. "Want me to call Dr. Russell? Unless . . ." Karl's listening, just not to me. "Ed says the camera angles aren't the best here. There's a few blind spots."

"I said I'm not from Springfield, Karl. Any more than you're from Boston."

My husband nods, still wary. "Boston is more recognizable than Quincy. But how does your hometown account for why Gerard isn't on the security footage?"

I lick my lips, my hand hovering over Karl's phone.

When we first met, I wanted to keep things upbeat. Me? I'm a daddy's girl, though (chuckling) certainly not to a fault. In the interest of a second date, I might've understated some things.

"Here," I say, "it's more like I'm from the Hilltowns. It's a remote area." My lips tremble, trying to force out the name of my hometown. "I was born and raised in New Minton, Karl."

Somewhere between Cabbage Patch Kids and stickers hidden in a cereal box, the ones Paul demanded every time we opened a new Crøønchy Stars, is recognition. I can tell by the strange flicker on Karl's face.

"The New Minton Boys," he says. "All those missing kids, the ones never found." Karl is stunned. "Daphne, you're from there? Did you know those boys? God, you would've been a kid yourself."

"I was eleven," I say. And I was a kid, a selfish kid. I came from a large family. Brandy was seventeen, Courtney fifteen, Ellie nine, and Paul seven.

The day before my brother disappeared, I wasn't thinking that this night was the last time we'd all be together. I wasn't thinking about the pain Mom and Dad would go through, especially after the town gossip began.

No. I thought my biggest problems in the world were mean schoolboys. So I ruined dinner.

"Daphne?" Now Karl looks mad. "That's a big secret not to tell your husband."

If only he knew.

CHAPTER TWO

March 30, 1988

Muddy green hills pitched and rolled as far as I could see from my window. This time of year, the bare trees looked like thousands of needles stuck together.

We lived halfway up Hangman's Hill, about a mile from church. Our house had masonry and stone on the first floor, wood shingle panels on the second, a stone-end chimney on the gambrel roof. Six bedrooms, two baths, and a kitchen with teak countertops. Oh, would Mom talk your ear off about those teak countertops. *My design*, she bragged. Back when her friends came over.

While we waited for Dad to come home, I read Florence Parry Heide's *Brillstone Break-In* over and over in the room I shared with my younger sister, Ellie.

Liza and Logan were siblings who investigated crimes committed against their neighbors. No matter if evil relatives tried to swindle a lonely old man out of his inheritance, they'd solve it, no problem. I planned to do the same thing, except I'd solve mysteries all over the world for free.

Each time the hills reddened, I paced with Liza and Logan tucked under my arm. If the sun was a birthday candle, I'd blow it back up into the sky, keep us frozen in time forever. The end of today meant that tomorrow was Thursday. Thursday meant Rusty Rahall and David Gedney were back in school after a two-week suspension, and I was dead. Like totally, pond scum dead.

"He needs to . . ."

"Move out of the way, Court."

I followed voices to the bathroom. With all the drama I could muster, I placed my hand against my forehead and groaned. "I don't feel good," I said.

No reaction. No *Get Daphne some lemon water. Here's a warm cloth, dear. Now stay in bed for the rest of the week.*

Dang. I wasted my award-winning wooziness on Brandy and Courtney, my older sisters, who tucked Paul's shirt under his chin to reveal his bulbous belly. I could've backflipped into the bathroom and expected the same response.

Brandy unsnapped a button on Paul's pants. "*There* you go, Paul," she said. "It was just *stuck*." When she talked or laughed, Brandy sounded ditzy.

My brother's name was actually Brady, though only Mom called him that. Despite being the youngest and the only boy, Paul was perfectly capable of dressing himself and brushing his teeth. Not that you could explain that to Brandy and Courtney, who did everything for him.

"Where's Mom?" I said.

"You got legs, don't you?" said Brandy.

I whined against the doorframe. "I'd sell my soul not to have school tomorrow," I said.

"Don't say that, Daph," said Courtney, tugging at her hair. When she hit puberty, it sprang into a copper-red bush unlike anyone else's in the family.

"What?" I said. "It's a joke."

Though Courtney's words dug in. How come when the other kids said it, everyone laughed? They did when Rusty was clowning.

Brandy frowned as though she could do a better job of urinating for Paul. When he finished, Paul snapped his underwear.

"Wait, honey," said Brandy. "You don't want to touch your face or anything until after you wash your hands, okay?"

"Germs are bad, right?" asked Paul, his voice raspy and thin. He watched Brandy turn on the faucet while Courtney lathered his hands with soap, mouth agape.

"Actually," said Courtney, "urine is sterile."

"No, it isn't," said Brandy to Paul. "Don't listen to her."

"I read it in a book, Bran. Urine doesn't have germs. That's why you can drink it."

Mom's voice bellowed from the kitchen. "What are you telling my only son to drink his pee-pee for?"

Brandy denied involvement. I took advantage of the melee to find Mom slamming the fridge, muttering that she had enough problems.

Mom had black hair and a low stomach bulging from her Levi's. With oval-rimmed glasses, she resembled a librarian, which she was part time, except her face was dotted with black scabs. They looked like bug bites, but she said they were from chicken pox.

"Mom," I said, "my stomach hurts."

An armload of trash bags plopped on the kitchen tiles. My heart quickened as Dad patted my head, his hands cold. He was finally home, though he didn't pause for long.

"Girls?" he said, headed for the master bedroom. "After you finish your homework, think we could stitch a few pants and shirts for the penitent and less fortunate?"

Mom eyed me. "Was that your father?"

I turned into Brandy, who brushed me aside, Paul in tow.

"Hop up, big boy," she said, helping Paul into his seat. Then Brandy opened cabinets with no apparent purpose. "So, practice was totally awesome." She meant basketball practice. Brandy was the team's power forward. "Friday, Elkshire is toast."

That got Mom's attention, when I couldn't. "Friday," she said, "not Saturday?"

"Yeah," said Brandy, "I kinda . . . forgot?"

She snapped a carrot and Mom held her breath, as she did every time some tragic flaw manifested in her daughters. A cooking pan clinked onto the back burner. "Ahhh," said Paul after each glug of juice. Outside, branches sliced the wind into a whistle.

The front door slammed. Loud footsteps transformed into Ellie hopping over Dad's garbage bags. "Ta-da," she said, speckled in neon paint and nearly euphoric since her headlong plunge into drama this year. She chased us until Mom issued a decree.

"Only children recognizable as my daughters and son are allowed at the dinner table."

"She hasn't showered in four days at least," said Brandy.

"Maybe I'm going for the record," said Ellie, reaching for Mom.

"Maybe my soiled children could be civilized for one night," said Mom. Momentarily ignored, Paul rocked in his chair as if hoping to gallop toward us.

My sisters set the table. A prism danced on their backs. I traced the glow to a crack in the patio door, a thin line bone cold to the touch.

I never noticed before, but the crack pointed right to the church. Above it and the tree line, the moon floated, an unpolished white stone.

Now back, Dad flurried Mom's sweaty neck with kisses. "I missed you," he said.

Though his arms and legs were thin, Dad was naturally potbellied, which his simple white robe, untucked and unbuttoned, revealed as a smooth mound. He had deep dimples that, in the morning light, would make him look gentle and even boyish.

"Supper was ready twenty minutes ago, Brandon," said Mom. "It's just me and the kids." When a flushed Courtney walked by, her Walkman rumbling with classical opera, Mom snatched the headphones. "Unless you brought home some more transients."

"Hey," said Courtney. Halfway through his apology, we smelled the reason for Dad's haste to the bathroom. Courtney gagged. "Pee-*you*, Dad! Gosh!"

Dad shrugged. "Stink over substance," he said. "Happens when you get older."

Collective disgust kept us silent as Mom resisted Dad's affection. Seeing them together again was still a little disorienting. Kids called it a trial separation, the months Mom lived with a friend in Hyannis. The week after Thanksgiving, Mom came back with a suitcase, crying only when she held Paul.

We asked what was wrong. Were they fighting too much? Was one parent unhappy, or both?

All Mom and Dad said was that they loved us very much. Of course, some more than others.

Some dots I could connect. Mom made her distaste for New Minton well-known. Ten years later, she still didn't appreciate the way Dad moved us here.

Dad was the minister of Second Unitarian Universalist. Before his calling in 1977, he owned a wildly successful marina in Hyannis. He sold fast boats to playboys, living like how you might imagine the Kennedys in the 1960s.

Dad was forthcoming about the drinking, the partying. The arguments he had with Mom. One day, he told Mom that he had a vision about becoming a minister in New Minton, a town in desperate need of a functioning church.

Mom, though, was dismissive. Dad often had spontaneous impulses that he termed visions, sudden gusts of energy to change the world. Once, he proposed the family single-handedly clean the Blackstone River. Mom probably assumed Dad would forget about New Minton, and a few days later he'd chase another of his "visions" the way a dog chased the next car in the neighborhood.

Instead, Dad came home to announce that he'd sold the marina. He planned to build a Unitarian church in New Minton, the only Christian branch that accepted him and his ideas. And he would be known as Reverend Gauge. So long as we stayed, I wondered if Mom and Dad would be forever pitted against each other.

"Daphne," said Mom. "Sit."

Everyone was ready to eat but me. I stood in front of the crack, my forehead hot, though maybe more because I kept rubbing it.

"May I please be excused?" I said. "I'm not hungry."

Brandy closed an eye and blew at a strand of hair. "Pumpkin's trying to wiggle out of school tomorrow," she said. "In case no one got that."

Pumpkin was Dad's nickname for me, a constant reminder that when I was born I was seventy percent head. Brandy was Bean, Courtney was String, and Ellie was Peel.

Dad smacked on potatoes. "You like school, Pumpkin," he said.

"Well," said Ellie, "school doesn't like *rats*."

"Ellie, don't say that word."

"I didn't rat out anyone," I said.

True, Rusty and David got a two-week suspension in part because of me. Someone broke into Mrs. Patowski's desk. All the tests and grades were gone. Chief Boyd even dusted for prints. It was actually an easy case to solve. And it set me up to thinking I might be good at detective work.

Early one morning, I sneaked into Mrs. Patowski's room. Everyone paid attention to the desk, but I noticed all these short red hairs in the teacher chair's wheel ruts. My first thought was this older boy Rusty Rahall who scratched his eyebrows a lot. I also recovered a string that belonged to a talking Pee-wee Herman doll, which got David in trouble too.

"Eat, Brady," said Mom, flustered that Paul was burying green beans under his lemon chicken. "Look, Mommy's eating. Yum, yum, yum."

Paul shook his head. "Yuck, yuck, yuck."

"Please," I said. "I'll do all the dishes. I just need to lie down."

Mom slammed a knife flat on her plate. "You know what?" she said, and now my stomach really did hurt. "Daphne, you can go to your room. All of you can go. Brady's only like this because you girls baby him. He can't even pee by himself, and with Ellie's nighttime problems . . ." Sweat bled from Mom's forehead. "The breast was fine half an hour ago. Now it's a brick. So how about Mommy gets some time, huh?"

Mommy gets some time. Mom said the same exact thing last year. Two weeks later, she was gone, her perfume fading, all the wedding photographs facedown. We found Dad reading a letter left on the kitchen table, wiping his eyes.

No other moms we knew were like Mom. The kind who always kept us terrified that she would erupt again.

Now we looked again to Dad, who folded glasses into his breast pocket. Shadows accentuated the glacial depth of hurt in his eyes, but he didn't say anything to comfort us or to contradict Mom. If he did, he'd have to choose one over the other. So Dad chose to complete his work in the basement.

The others retreated to their sanctuaries. Brandy had basketball, Courtney the violin. Ellie went off to do whatever weird thing she was into. Paul crashed cars.

Thinking she was alone, Mom pushed the plates aside. She moved a gold-plated vanity mirror from the breakfast bar to the dinner table and stared into her reflection, her gaze as hard as Brandy's. Then she dug her thumbnails into her cheek.

Her hands shook, but Mom did not wince. She moved methodically across her face, leaving bright dots of blood to glow.

Glass shattered, jolting me from my blankets. It sounded like all our windows were exploding.

What began as terror soon faded into annoyance. Awake now, I realized that, once again, Ellie woke me with grinding teeth. Each time I rolled, my bladder throbbed.

Heat lightning fizzed in the night sky, lighting shadows on the floor. They were Ellie's clothes, I knew that, but I hesitated on the bunk bed's ladder, wanting to be extra careful before I climbed down. The shaking caused a bubble to blow from Ellie's nostril.

"You breathe so *loud*," she said.

"Go back to sleep," I said, and headed for the bathroom and relief.

Something dropped, a pen maybe, in the purple velvet hallway. I followed bursts of heat to the fissure on the patio door. I was prepared to run if Mom was out there, still upset that I'd disrespected a meal, but it turned out to be Dad bent over a coffee table. He scratched an idea into a journal while his glass rattled.

"It's rude to watch people in the shadows, Pumpkin," he said.

"I'm sorry, Daddy," I said, though neither his words nor his face were sharp.

Since the patio light was on, I didn't feel like I was spying. I *peeked* to see who was up so late. "Are you writing Sunday's sermon?" I asked.

"I'm tired." Air whistled through Dad's nose. "God tires me out sometimes. Come here, Pumpkin. We just got to be sensitive with your Mom, okay? It's not your fault. Being here isn't easy for her."

"I know," I said, feeling too wide for Dad's lap. Capillaries of oaks glinted at the edge of our backyard. "Mom doesn't like it here. But if she just gave it a chance . . ."

"See," he said, "some people think if you come from a bad family, you're bad too."

My breath caught on Dad's lie. "I thought Mom was from Hyannis," I said. "Like you."

Nor was Dad's admission the first time I'd poked a hole in Mom's supposed ignorance of New Minton. Three years ago, a man whistled me to his car and asked if Mom was still a *looker* like she'd been in high school.

I was stunned. Mom's looks were so legendary, they knew her on the other side of the state?

Of course not, I realized. Mom grew up in New Minton. We were the only town for miles. So how come everyone knew Mom's family and we hardly knew anyone but Grandpop?

The sky rumbled. "I've never been afraid of a storm, Pumpkin-head," said Dad. "Have you?"

"No," I said, though I was. Screens swelled against their frames. The earthen odor of beechnut rolled into the room. "Why would Mom lie about where she was from?"

"Phew," said Dad, as if the effort to yawn drained him. "I'm tired but I feel close. One of these days, we'll know how to atone."

I held my breath because his was terrible. Again, Dad yawned, and again he needed a moment to recover from it. He set me down, toward his open journal. Normally, I'd never dare touch his work. But maybe he was writing about Mom. I slid his bookmark over so I could read, only to realize the bookmark was more like a flashcard, the kind we used to study for an exam.

You may hear the steer's bell at the Idol some night soon, Churchman, it read, *but this is your only warning. Do not interfere.*

The Brotherhood of the Raven.

A postcard, addressed to Dad. Under it were his notes.

Don't know who they are because they all wear Raven masks. Once the moon is full, they lay the steer at the base of the Idol.

Seven of them pick seven candles. Six blue, one red. Whoever chooses the red candle guts the steer and drips blood on the Idol. And for another year, the Door remains open. They call it Blót.

In the margins, Dad wrote a question: *How do you save these people, if they still do this*?

"Seems like He's trying," said Dad, "to communicate. Like—in that flash right there."

"Daddy?" I said, a tingle running up my legs as I tapped *Churchman*. "What does this mean?"

Something struck the house, knocking out the lights. I reached for Dad in the dark, my hands stretching across the empty cushion for what felt like infinity. Dread crawled into my throat. Dad was gone, yet I heard his voice.

"He's trying to tell us . . . something we can almost . . ."

A bloody chunk of flesh smacked the patio window. With a few wisps of hair, it looked like a scalp, though that made no sense. Pressure filled my ears. Stones formed a smoky pyre in our backyard. Above all, Dad's church blazed in the night.

CHAPTER THREE

May 2, 2021

I'm being shaken.

Karl snaps on the nightstand lamp, leaving my heart to gallop. "Daphne," he says, "you were babbling like crazy in your sleep."

"Why didn't you let me finish?"

"What?" says Karl.

I hold my head, wanting to twist it until it pops off my neck. I don't remember rocks piled in our backyard, but the night before Paul disappeared, Mom really did send us to bed without dinner. And she picked imaginary pimples, which was obviously a compulsion, a way to deal with her unhappiness.

Not that Mom was a fan of psychology. She was too high-strung—insecure and yet a know-it-all—to accept help, a byproduct of being shunned by New Minton and by everyone outside its limits. She had the perfect personality to be the town's scapegoat.

And gosh, Dad used to be so young and vibrant back then, his hair brilliantly russet. The only person on the planet who understood me.

Now our bedroom seems alien. The king bed, flat screen, even my body pillow looks like it doesn't belong. Or I don't belong with it.

Then I see pictures of my children, Zachary and Stephen. I watch them, reminding myself to breathe. "What was I saying, Karl?"

"Bird being blotted out, I'm not sure."

I use too much force, ripping out my nightstand's drawer. Karl yelps as I kneel on the carpet and rifle through holiday cards with sweet messages from my husband, but Gerard's postcard isn't there. I'm sure I left it on top too.

"Where is it?" I say.

"Where's what?"

"The postcard," I say, hearing the impatience in my voice. "Gerard's postcard. I left it in here, and now it's—"

I turn to Karl, who's holding it defensively between us. What did my husband do, hide the postcard from me? Hope I'd forget? Normally, we're the kind of couple who say please and thank you, but today I snatch it from him, and bury my irritation in our bedroom carpet.

$ from Crusher. Keep yourself pure, Brother. For the sake of our children.

"The Door must remain open," I say, reading the last line.

Dad talked a lot about finding God in the trees, hearing His words on the wind. Once I believed everything Dad said, his word as literal fact. Just as I believed in Dad's calling to know "God's language." Dad's journal was something else. And it was already fading.

Brotherhood guts steer, I write. *Drips blood on Idol. Door opens 1 year. Blót.*

Whoever sent the postcard called George Gedney a "Brother." Gerard sure didn't act like it came from an estranged uncle.

One member of the Brotherhood of the Raven communicating with another. It has to be.

They were writing with Dad too. Threatening him to stay away from whatever they were doing on Hangman's Hill, less than a mile from where his children slept.

I click on the light to my office. The closet's hinges growl. Doesn't make sense. Our house is three years old.

A tarp covers a stained cardboard box with the name of an old law firm I worked at before I met Karl. Back when I was a paralegal whom everyone expected to be the coffee girl for all the big corporate clients. Free from its wrap, the box's must spreads.

Inside are hundreds of files about my brother, Paul, and the other children who disappeared in 1988. The newspapers called them the New Minton Boys.

Law enforcement, journalists, and private investigators compiled hundreds of clues and pursued dozens of "credible leads." All their effort distills into an archive of explanations, some redundant, many contradictory. Maybe that's why Karl suggested I give up on piecing through it, for my psychological health.

Files are missing, others destroyed in the Great Roof Leak of 2017. Looking over my family history is like rereading a journal I wrote as a teenager.

Desperate for approval. Knowing no one will ever give it, so I keep to myself. My preteen angst rails against the mimeographed bars that forever imprison it.

Even though I don't have any journals. I wrote dozens, a habit I picked up from Dad, but none survived.

Paul disappeared on March 31, 1988. He was seven years old, and the youngest of five children. His parents were Brandon and Chastity Gauge.

That day, Paul had soccer practice after school. Mom was supposed to pick up Paul, but she couldn't. Mom called Dad. Dad never got the message.

Paul wasn't the only child to slip his parents' minds that day. The other child's name was Dominic Gedney, one of Gerard's older brothers, the one who died last Christmas. Of course, neither Paul nor Dominic told Coach

Brody their parents forgot to pick them up. At 4:45, Paul and Dominic were seen leaving the elementary school's gymnasium together.

For the next half hour, they passed a diner, video rental, and pharmacy. Witnesses recalled seeing the boys unchaperoned, but in 1988, no one thought it unusual. Not even with news arriving earlier that day that Clai Denton had run away. New Minton was a simple Hilltown, where life moved slower. At 5:15, the boys stopped at Lincoln Bridge. To get home, Dominic would go left, Paul straight. Instead, they decided to keep playing under the bridge. Then Paul vanished. Others would follow.

Nothing about a Brotherhood, steers, or Blót.

I stretch my neck, rolling blindly until I bump into a bookcase. Years ago, Karl sanded and stained it for our anniversary. The bookcase is eight feet tall and looks like something you'd find in a medieval library.

Light winks from a glass case on the top shelf, which houses a bleached leather book bound with a drawstring. *Journal of Reverend Gauge, '86–'88*, it reads. I haven't thought about Dad's journals in years. I wonder if Dad's postcard is still tucked in there.

I flip randomly, hoping that I'll jar it loose. "Where is it?" I say to myself.

"Daphne." Karl's at the doorway as though he's been watching for a while. "It's been two weeks since you found that letter. I really think Dr. Russell can help."

It was a postcard, and Gerard Gedney gave it to me, not that I want to have the discussion again. My husband was very meticulous in interviewing dozens of people who attended the banquet, all of whom deny Gerard's existence. He probably thinks I pulled random junk mail out of the trash.

"Dad received one too," I say. "When I was a kid. Darn it. I could've gone to the police."

"With a postcard?"

My eyes are bugging before I can control them. "With two postcards," I say, "sent thirty years apart. But . . ." I hear my whiny eleven-year-old self bubbling up, and I hate it. "It's not here."

The postcard was thirty years old. With all the moving and shuffling, it could've fallen out. Or maybe Dad ripped it up like he did with some of the journal's pages. I don't see his notes about the red candle either.

My hands stop at Dad's tiny chicken scratch. I'm going to need my glasses, though I read the heading just fine.

THE INITIATION

A cold hand grips my heart. Yes, here's something.

Karl's on his knees, cleaning around my feet. I guess I broke some glass and carried it from the bedroom to my office. The black dots on the carpet must be blood then. He tries to hug me, and I smile in his face. In his eyes, I see how fake it is, fake as my teeth.

"I was having a bad dream, Karl," I say. "About the night before."

"Night before what?" Karl rolls a Band-Aid on my feet. I'm about to tell him the glass doesn't even hurt when my heart stops at seeing Zachary at our doorway. A wet stain blackens the crotch of his jammies.

"Oh, what happened?" I say, pushing Zachary's bangs out of his eyes. He has a big bush of auburn hair, with my brunette genes to thank. "Did you have an accident?"

He's three, old enough to say complete sentences, but Zachary has his scared face. He'd never admit to peeing his pants.

"It's okay, Bud," says Karl.

I strip Zachary and take him into the bathroom. Karl brings clean clothes. Zachary's eyelids flutter while I rinse, which is good. I'd love for him to hit the pillow and start snoring because his daycare won't accept kids past nine a.m. But soon as we get to his bed, a turbo race car, Zachary's eyes spring open.

"Can we watch *Bread Bowl*?" he asks.

I look at Karl. "The one where animated toasters race for trophies made of butter," he says. I can barely stand, but his dry delivery warms my heart. I haven't been fair to him these last few weeks. He's borne the brunt of all my frustrations.

Watching the blankets on the other twin turbo car stir, I decide that maybe *Bread Bowl* is what everyone needs right now.

"Come out, Stephen," I say. "We're watching a movie."

"Yay!" the boys exclaim in unison. Stephen explodes from the covers. Zachary runs to the TV. The five-year-old and the three-year-old choose their profile on Amazon Prime and find the movie before Karl comes back with a bowl of popcorn, the junior technophiles. We sit on bean bags, the boys between us, while they cackle as if seeing it for the first time. Karl squeezes my hand three times. I send the message back.

Two hours later, with my family breathing deeply in slumber, I grab clothes and slip downstairs to read Dad's journal.

EXHIBIT B

THE INITIATION

Deliver your child to the base of Hangman's Hill. He may be groggy and afraid, ***but you must tell him nothing.*** All boys climb to the summit alone.

Fathers, prepare the circle for the boys' arrival. The tunic must be made of wool and bear the triangles of Wodan. The Raven headdresses must be three feet tall, sit comfortably on the shoulders, and be consecrated with feathers ~~from the Idol~~. **From near the circle.**

Seven men will draw to wear the Raven headdresses. They will form a circle ~~around the Idol~~ and read from the Book of the Brotherhood:

The first Blót is the offering of a steer. It must come when Arcturus begins its move back to Earth, as it does this year. Then on Lammas Day, we shall give thanks for Arcturus's return with a second Blót.

The second Blót opens a Door to the Elementals. It is not as we had in the old lands, but it is the only way for us to offer them our gratitude, and for them to give us wealth and power.

Each father will teach his son how to use this power. It is your bond to the Elementals, the connection you and your family have shared since time began.

In a moment, our gothi, *our priest, shall bring out the steer for the first Blót. Any boy who does not wish to celebrate in this tradition may leave Hangman's Hill the way he came. No harm shall come to you.*

If you choose to stay, you commit yourself to the Brotherhood.

You commit yourself in the Book with an oath in blood.

—Pages 46–49 from the 1986–1988 journal of Brandon T. Gauge, Unitarian Universalist Minister, Second Unitarian Church of New Minton

CHAPTER FOUR

May 3, 2021

No rain, never any rain, but gloom descends on Pittsfield Barracks, swirling clouds just over our heads. I slip into a corridor of sweaty yellow brick, and shake my hair.

"Can I help you?" asks a redheaded officer behind glass.

The interior looks more like a cramped 7-Eleven than a police station. A metal box appears for us to exchange materials, which is where I slide Gerard's postcard and Dad's journal. To think, I was eleven, arguing with my sisters about who had dibs on the hair dryer, and Dad was in his study, working out a strategy to convert people so they wouldn't harm any more livestock.

How many people is the question.

And why did they kidnap my brother if all they wanted was a steer? Goodness, so many questions.

"May I speak to Harold Bixbee?" I say.

According to their website, he's the barracks commander. Maybe someone familiar with the case can serve as my way in. And help me avoid the Hilltowns altogether, hamlets in the foothills of Western Mass. There's no exit from the Pike, no highway, no reason to be there if you're not local. Someone gets lost in the Hilltowns, and it's hard to find their way out. The woods run deep and the mountains run high.

"And what should I tell him this is?" The officer holds Dad's leather-bound book.

"A warning," I say.

He asks me to wait under fluorescent lights. While I wait, I call in sick, which is somewhat true. I spent the night reading and researching, and now it feels like an air-raid siren is blasting in my head. Until a month ago, I never missed work, not in seven years. Now I've used up all my paid leave.

Karl says being an ethics investigator is perfect for me because of my moral inflexibility. *That's a joke*, he says, but I'm not always sure. Even though the Enforcement Division wasn't my childhood dream job, I've grown to love it. I love the commute to Boston. I love background checks. A builder is awarded a contract, and I make sure no one received any preferential consideration. That might sound nerdy, but it's interesting to learn about family trees, and how the roots connect. You could say my childhood prepared me for a position like this.

Are you okay? texts my supervisor.

They escort me to Bixbee's office before I can answer. I find him with his feet on a desk, turning the pages of Dad's journal, his hand shaking at *The Initiation*. His hair is patchy. Dark liver spots dot his skull.

"No one's reported missing cows that I know of," he says to the darkened window, "but we'll keep a lookout, Ms. Meraux."

"Missing children," I say, swallowing the edge in my voice. Bixbee doesn't turn. "Dad's journal mentions farm animals, I realize that, Deputy, but last time it was children who went missing. You know. You were there."

So was I. Maybe it's the fact that I haven't seen Bixbee since I was eleven, but I feel a childish need for him to explain everything that happened, from Paul's disappearance to now. As though Bixbee could validate my memories. Or help them come back. They're still so blurry, no matter how hard I try to remember.

"Captain."

Bixbee's correction hits like a slap. I hear myself stammering but can't stop it. "C-Captain Bixbee," I say. "I'm sorry."

Bixbee finally turns, and meets me with sad blue eyes. "I haven't been a deputy in thirty-two years, Daphne," he says. "Because your mom got me fired."

"I know. I'm very sorry." Repeating the words only makes them hollow.

"She blamed me for not being able to find your brother," says Bixbee. "There were hundreds of officers working that case, but she chose me. You know why?"

"My mom was very confused," I say. I could share more—like how Mom fixating on a deputy who played a minor role in investigating Paul's abduction was just another thing she did that is impossible to explain—but a flush turns his liver spots purple.

"Instead of retirement on a county pension, I'm a 'captain' with half the pay. At this rate, I'm working until I'm eighty."

"Please, Captain Bixbee," I say. "Arcturus began its planetary shift yesterday. The first Blót might be tonight. A new initiation for the next generation of boys who would sign their names in blood."

A line from Dad's journal burns between us.

It is the only way for us to offer them our gratitude, and for them to give us wealth and power.

Power.

What power?

That was one glaring hole in Dad's work.

"So what is it you want, then, Daphne?" asks Bixbee.

"Any files you have on my brother's disappearance," I say. "Or on the other New Minton Boys from 1988. If there's something you recall after all these years—"

"Our files won't help." Bixbee snaps Dad's journal closed and gathers the other folders I brought. "After 2000, we computerized our records. A flood wiped out the rest."

He returns my belongings with a promise that someone will get in touch. They never do.

A letter waits in our mailbox. The United States Postal Service has concluded its review of Gerard Gedney's postmark.

The postcard originated from a processing station in Los Angeles. The PVI strip was part of a bulk mail package distributed in the Fresno area sometime between August and September 2020 by a publisher called PPMPrint. They apparently handle junk mail for Catholic charities.

I pull into our driveway and idle, not sure what I'm supposed to do with that information. Brown birds dart from flat-top bushes to the brick walkway. We live in a single-story Cape house in my husband's hometown of Quincy, about five miles from Boston and a few blocks from the shore.

Compared to my parents' house, our home is much more modest. Definitely no teak countertops. Gabled roof, shuttered windows. Double doors we can open for a nice salty breeze.

A whiff of the neighbor's smoky clambake hits me, and I realize how warm it is, with temperatures in the seventies. Stormy in Western Mass, but here the sky is a deep blue that piles on top of itself. My breath is easier now. A flat land can't hold secrets.

Karl's on the deck. Zachary and Stephen push tow trucks around our stone garden. Unlike Zachary, Stephen was born blond. They both have their father's mouth, so their lips hang low while they mimic hydraulics. "Stop it," says Zachary.

"I didn't do it," says Stephen. They circle around and around.

The boys are already too old for Mommy's kisses. I chase them only to get foreheads, then I sit where the sun tickles my legs. Karl hands me the *Boston Globe*. This is nice. Exactly what I need.

"She's recovering from shoulder surgery," says Karl. "I was thinking, we should send a card."

I nod, vaguely remembering he mentioned some top surgeon at Beth Israel, and stop at an all-too-familiar headline.

BOYS VANISH IN NEW MINTON

Yesterday, May 2, Grant and Roderick Nolan, aged ten and eight, were tenting at the edge of their family's property. At three a.m., the boys' mom, Theresa Nolan, woke to see the flashlights were still on. Believing Grant and Roderick were horsing around well past their bedtime, she went outside to find the tent fly open and the children gone. The sleeping bags were crumpled as though any minute they would return from a bathroom break.

Under the photo of a New Minton police officer is a caption: *Police say they found no sign of foul play.*

Their address is the Wilsons' old house, which has a nice view of Corvus Pond and Hangman's Hill. A boy who used to live there picked on me when we were kids. A lot of the boys picked on me. Funny that childhood bullies keep being my first thought.

I squint at the barn behind the officer. Someone spray-painted two sentences across the double doors.

The Door must stay open. The Wheel can't be allowed to turn.

Needles tickle my hands and feet. It's shock, I think, a phrase that should be unfamiliar echoes in stereo. Well, almost. *Stay open*, not *remain open*. I don't know what the change means. Gerard's postcard is just one more mystery I couldn't solve in time, and now two more boys are missing.

"Those kinds of gestures can really go a long way," says Karl.

"Kids," I say. "Go inside."

"But *Mom*."

"Go inside right now."

I didn't mean for them to drop everything and run like a hurricane is on top of us. One tow truck's wheel is still spinning after they slam the door.

Our junipers catch a breeze I don't feel. Green trimmings sprinkle the deck and itch where they touch my skin.

Karl keeps those annoying cautious eyes on me. "You're always saying they should be outside more, Daphne."

"Let them play video games," I say, not wanting to deal with the fact that I sounded like Mom just then. An outburst of anger, which I ignore, then double down. "Just keep them inside. Where it's safe."

Gerard's postcard set some gear in motion, something large enough I can't wrap my arms around it. Too few details, and not enough time to process them.

The Door must stay open.

They call it Blót.

Each father will teach his son how to use this power.

One juniper tree pitches forward. I grit my teeth against the splintering of its base. I hear squawking too. Ear-piercing and desperate like I've never heard before.

"One heck of a squirrel fight," Karl says. He shaves the junipers thin specifically so squirrels wouldn't build nests there, or so I thought. I can't see them, but buried in my head is a memory, like a coin at the bottom of a lake.

You want to be one of us or not?

Rusty Rahall asked me that question more than thirty years ago. We were behind the elementary school. Paul would disappear later that day, but Clai actually went missing first.

Clai Denton was a sixth grader, like me. Rusty wanted to show us something he called Blót, which his dad taught him. Blót and something else. *You want to be one of us or not*? he asked, and before the strange thing happened to Clai, I almost said yes.

CHAPTER FIVE

March 31, 1988

Sixth graders whooped around the swings. Fifth graders stomped down the rolls of a massive hill. Teachers patrolled with arms crossed and mustaches twitching, clearly disgruntled that the year's first outing made us delirious.

I stayed on the blacktop, telling myself I didn't like to play with others. I said they don't like girls with mousy brown hair and a body she was growing into. My legs were, after all, uneven.

Even though I tried. I smiled at a group of irradiated girls with pigtails and asked if I could be their friend. They took one look at my red corduroy overalls and snickered. I baked treats and dressed like them, forcing myself into pastel pleated skirts, and they laughed even harder.

They mocked the way I talked, my lack of athletic ability. Gym was a never-ending nightmare. They had no patience for any piece of information that wasn't about New Minton, which they gossiped about constantly. And when I got higher grades, they accused me of cheating.

I blamed my four siblings too.

Being a middle child was tough. Always stuck between warring nations. The mediator no one respects. Accepting those excuses was easier than dealing with years of rejection.

Of course, tattling on Rusty Rahall and David Gedney only widened the gap. All day long, they whispered how I was going to get it. No one ate with me.

Soon as recess began, I sat on the sidewalk and read *Brillstone Break-In* for the millionth time. I read until a shadow darkened the page.

Rusty stood in my light, his hair fiery red. *Here it comes.* I was a rat. Two-faced pond scum. When I finally looked up, Rusty snatched my book.

"Hey," I said.

Rusty grinned through freckles. "Come and get it," he said. "Come and get it."

I tried to get my book from Rusty on the baseball diamond. And again behind the backstop. The teachers were no help, as always. They were too busy shouting at David Gedney halfway up the basketball pole. At least that was one less bully to worry about.

"Rusty," I said. "Give it back."

"I will. For a kiss."

"Gross."

Rusty shrugged and joined some kids passing under a fence. Cranberry thorns cross-stitched a sign that warned the boys they were leaving school grounds. I backed into a marshmallow of a boy who wouldn't budge. It was Scott Wilson.

"Where are you going, Preacher's Kid?" he said. "Rusty said dweebs can't stay on the school side."

"Dweeb?" I said. What the heck was a dweeb?

"Girl's got a California Raisins poster on her wall," said Scott. The other kids snorted, and I felt myself flush. "Dweebs think the California Raisins are cool."

Actually, Ellie loved the commercials with the Claymation raisins singing "I Heard It Through The Grapevine" . . . wait a minute. How would

Scott know about the poster in my bedroom? No way would I ever let him into my room.

Unless Ellie told him. How did the subject come up then?

Not that it mattered anyway. They brought me here so I could beg. Let's get it over with.

"You want an apology for ratting you out, Rusty?" I said. "Fine, I apologize. Okay? Stop it."

They didn't. After a brief game of keep-away, Rusty tossed my book right over the fence.

I chased after it, burrowing through the leaves. On the railroad tracks, I wiped dirt off Heide's cover.

"Unbelievable," I said, and looked up.

The others weren't Rusty's friends. They were the boys with leaky ears. The outcasts. The dweebs. Rusty and Scott thought I belonged with them.

"*Zap*!" David Gedney tapped the fence with a stick, his Pac-Man shirt already stained with mud. I guess he got tired of basketball. "Now, if anyone touches the metal? You'll be electrocuted and die and the birds will pick your bones."

David wasn't kidding about the birds. They hopped alongside Rusty and his friends, their beaks open, following like chickens. In the middle of the ravens, Scott pounded a stick into the earth.

Others inscribed circles around a large oak, though that's the last spot I'd choose. People had dumped a bunch of garbage all over the place. Pictures of a wild man in pelts holding a spear and skull, others of the sun, and a stone tower in flames.

It was disgusting.

"What's going on?" I said. More ravens rustled in the canopy. "Guys?"

"Just do what we say, Preacher's Kid." Scott shook his head as I shrugged.

What they said was to lay rocks in a circle. Wood lice flailed under each one we lifted. In late March, the earth should be muddy. But I saw how dry the dirt was after a long winter with little snow. Pebbles clung to our hands, stubborn as ticks.

Geoffrey Olsen whined. "It's the wrong time of year to open a Door," he said, one long canine tooth resting on his bottom lip. "Arc-Arctris is traveling on the Wheel as we speak."

"*Arcturus*," said Scott. "And no, it's not."

"What's a Wheel?" I asked.

"The Wheel turns every year," said Clai Denton.

Others joined him. "Closing all doors and restoring balance to dark and light." They said it in the same tired way my sisters recited hymns at Sunday Service. Weird.

"Guess you didn't hear the steer screaming from the Idol last night," said Scott. He jabbed a stick on the boulder, and squealed. "There was blood and guts all over. And they smeared it. And on Lammas Day—"

"She's going to run home," said Geoffrey, "and tell her dad."

"Pssh," said Scott. "Like I care."

I thought Dad might already know. The seven candles, six blue, one red thing. Animals slaughtered by the Brotherhood of the Raven.

On Lammas Day. I remembered banners hanging from the city's streetlights, though we'd never been to the town's festival. Dad always took us to Dark Harbor in Maine in the late summer instead, citing a retreat. We didn't complain because we got to swim all the time. Dad told us what it was, though.

"Isn't Lammas Day like donating food and clothes to charity?" I asked. "Big whoop."

Though someone had warned Dad. *Do not interfere*.

"You should go." Geoffrey turned to Scott. "Just leave her alone."

"*You*?" I said. "Don't you mean *we*?"

"Any move under the fence is going to scrape the metal, though," said Clai.

"The fence isn't really electrified," Geoffrey said. "They're just saying that."

Clai polished his glasses. "Follow the tracks, Daphne," he said. "In like a mile, they'll take you right to the front of the school. This winter, Dad and me hunted all over these woods."

"All right," said Rusty, leading his friends back to us. "Let's do the preacher's kid next."

"Cool."

"Too late," said Clai.

"Do me how?" I asked. Clai didn't answer. I turned to see why.

Rusty had grabbed Clai by the collar. Clai flushed but he didn't fight Rusty. That was probably smart. Rusty stood a good foot and a half taller.

"You and your dad get to skip Hangman's Hill," said Rusty. "But that doesn't stop you from running your mouth, huh? You want to show her Blót, Clai? I don't see a steer around. Guess we gotta make do with you."

My chest tightened. "What?" I said. "You're going to stab Clai? With what?"

Scott held up a pointy stick and grinned.

"Guys," I said, "this is sick."

"Sometimes," said Rusty, "the steer is stubborn. So what you do is freeze him out."

Some kids laughed. "Freeze, freeze, freeze," they chanted.

I frowned. Didn't Rusty mean *chill*? Like, chill out? Geoffrey and the other boys watched, their eyes vividly blue despite the oak's long shadow.

Clai whimpered, but didn't open his mouth. "En. En."

"For that," said Scott.

He reached into the hollowed-out square of the oak and pulled out something. A box, maybe, mottled brown with streaks of white. Other boys were in the way.

I didn't recognize it as a book until Scott opened it. A book that looked a thousand years old. What was it doing in a tree?

"You're going to need," said Scott, tapping a page.

"I got it," said Rusty, scowling in concentration. "My dad showed me how already."

"Freeze, freeze, freeze."

Clai's collar still in one hand, Rusty raised his other.

A hush fell over the boys. I never saw Rusty this serious about anything before. I never saw the boys this quiet. Not even on test days.

My stomach tightened, though I couldn't say why the air darkened. Maybe it was the wind picking up.

"Hey, Rusty," I shouted. "Let him go."

"En. Nn."

Rusty blinked before grinning. "What was that, Clai?" He released Clai's shirt and pointed his middle finger at Clai's Adam's apple, forming a crude Y-shape with his arms.

Run, Clai, I thought. *Get out of here.*

He was free. But instead of running, Clai took large gulps of air as though drowning, his collar an upturned lip.

Rusty's eyes were on the book Scott held out for him, reading something. I couldn't hear because the ravens cawed and branches shook. I peeked over Rusty's shoulder, and saw the top of the page.

Freeze Spell.

I remembered the boys whispering about this nonsense like they were trading their dads' latest *Playboy*. Who brought this stupid book to school? No one could say. Seeing it made me furious.

"Stop right now," I said and reached out. Even though I was forty pounds lighter than Rusty, I brought my arm down as hard as I could.

Rusty dropped his hand, almost as if he decided to do it before I could touch him. This close to the oak, black flies swarmed piles of rotten plums and oranges packed in the tree folds. I covered my mouth, trying not to gag. Clai did the same thing.

"Daphne Gauge." Rusty shook his head as though still unaccustomed to the sound of my name. "Ever since we was kids, this girl's been trying to be like us."

"If you're so tough, Rusty," I said, gasping, "why are you always picking on us?"

Rusty winced. Or smirked. If anyone didn't belong in the sixth grade, it was Rusty Rahall. He was thirteen, two years older than us because they held him back in third grade, and last year, suspended him for bringing a knife, leaving his parents no choice but homeschool.

"You're not like us, Daphne. You'll never be. We're Ravens and you're worms."

"I'm a Raven," said Scott.

"I'm a Raven," echoed the other boys.

Which made me the worm, or the rat. Thanks for the reminder. That was me, the outsider. The girl who couldn't fit in.

Dad said that eventually the other kids would mature, but the loneliness was already a part of me long before I ever knew why. Every time I tried to convince Rusty or anyone else of the fact that I was born here in New Minton, they didn't believe me.

It was true. So were my younger sister and brother, Ellie and Paul. The only ones from Hyannis were my older sisters, Brandy and Courtney.

Everyone except maybe Clai, who liked me okay. Clai whose face was beet red. Who kept waving at a black dot glowing on his neck.

"Clai," I said. "What's wrong?"

He opened his mouth. Nothing came out.

"Clai won't speak until I take it back, Daphne," said Rusty with mucus in his mouth. "Now bring her to me."

"Why can't Clai talk?" I said, stepping on something. "What's this freezing thing? And no way I'm kissing you. Not in a million years."

"Kiss you?" Scott breathed into his sleeve as if on life support. "That's gross, dude. I thought you wanted to do the moon thing."

"I *do* know all you *dudes* are pussies," said Rusty. "Come on. I bet every girl in our grade's been to first base but her."

Geoffrey Olsen and others scurried from trunk to trunk, but my focus was on the lumps under the leaves. Alarm spider-walked up my back.

Barbie dolls, dismembered and charcoaled. A purple T-shirt similar to Clai's, this one torn at the collar.

"Say something, Clai," I said. "If you're pretending, say something now."

Clai was gone. Piles of leaves to the left. Crooked trees to the right. That left Rusty, David, Scott, the ravens, and me under the oak.

"You have to get her ready. The quarter moon is almost set. If you intend to bind yourselves for all eternity . . ."

The voice sounded deeper than everyone else's. Was there someone else?

"Just one more thing," Rusty whispered, though not to any of the boys. They kept glancing at a shape behind the trees. Maybe someone's shoulders. The day moon floated above them, hollow as an eggshell.

"Who's back there?" I said. "What's a moon thing?"

"Daphne." Even though we were in the shadows, Rusty's hair burned with fire. "You want to be one of us or not?"

I don't know why I didn't run. Maybe it was Rusty closing in, white film on his lips, the ravens, too, nowhere to run to, and I was scared. When a black fly scrambled over a cragged vein on Rusty's forehead, he puckered, and my legs buckled.

"Get up, Daphne." Rusty yanked my arm. "Clai's fine. I barely touched him."

"Get off," I cried. My clothes ripped, just like that purple T-shirt. Who else did they bring back here? What happened to them?

The boys stood over me. David shook black bangs out of his beady blue eyes.

"If she doesn't want to join us," he said, "we should take her to the Idol now."

Rusty grinned. "No more little kid stuff," he said. "A real Blót with people, like the olden days."

Rusty lifted the book into the sun. How would it feel if he struck me with the spine? Was Blót blood smearing like Scott said? I prayed for answers until a twig snapped.

And I woke on a slab of powdered rock. The stone was ice cold.

I could feel it leaching heat from my body. I sat up, looking over my muddy knees. Roots stuck to my palms.

Sunlight broke through crooked birches. It felt later in the day, long after our normal recess, though I couldn't say what the time was. I couldn't say where I was either.

Then I saw the concentric circles Scott had drawn. I had to be on the other side of the tree. How did I climb onto this slab anyway? It was as tall as I was.

As I looked for a way down, I heard a rustle of wings. A black bird foraged under dry leaves, triggering a prickle in my throat. Its yellow eye caught on me, then it flew with a *caw-caw-caw*, right over a group speaking in hushed tones.

They were teachers. Four or five, but I couldn't see who they were because they had their backs to me. Like their brown coats, their words blurred together.

"They ran away from school to pile up rocks?"

"White Stone forms the Wheel. It's the first step in opening a Door."

"Christ, those boys get younger every year."

"If you live in New Minton long enough, you learn to just clean it up and forget what you saw."

Actually, the lunch ladies were the ones cleaning up. I rubbed my eyes while they bagged rotten fruit and shooed the birds, cigarettes hanging from their purple lips. They left the feathers, which sprang from the ground like black spikes.

No one seemed to notice I was on the slab, not until the janitor, Mr. D., pointed at me, then at each of Rusty's posse sulking at the fence line. Scott had a hand clamped on his bottom, having soiled himself. They must've rounded up everyone who went into the woods.

I tried to ask what happened, and gagged. Something moved in my mouth like a worm. My stomach tightened, the queasiness building, then I spit it out.

A mangled feather.

Blech. Had it fallen into my mouth while I slept, like spiders do? Kids say you eat eight a year, and I didn't want to add feathers too.

"You fainted, Daphne," said Mrs. Patowski, our science teacher. With me still sitting on the slab, I was about her height. Dozens of reddish birthmarks swam just under the surface of her milky skin. "But you're fine. Keep your eyes on the ground, so you won't get dizzy."

I flung the wet feather, hoping no one else saw me do something gross. I never heard of staring at the ground to get over a spell of dizziness, but I didn't remember being dizzy in the first place. When I dared look up, I saw Mr. D. breathing heavy, his brown shirt stained with sweat.

"She makes eight," he said.

"There were nine truants from recess," said Mrs. Patowski, counting the boys. Then she fixed on me. "Where's Clai, Daphne? Where's Clai?"

I last saw Clai right before Rusty and David were talking to a shoulder behind the trees, but the panic in her voice filled my mouth with sand. I kept shrugging, the light blinding.

Mrs. Patowski held up her hands. "Everyone stop, please," she said. "The boys went too far this time. We've got to call some parents."

CHAPTER SIX

May 3, 2021

Karl's voice sounds underwater; his words don't make sense until he gets to the last two. "That dad," he says. I shake my head at the deck, wanting to touch it to make sure it's real, and he raises his eyebrows. "Jay Nolan? Something's off about him."

Gradually, the gray melts back into dappled sun on our patio. A warm, sugary breeze still carries the clambake. Everything's the same, yet I feel torn from the fabric of a different time.

I was daydreaming about Rusty freezing Clai right before Clai disappeared. Now the newspaper's left ink on my fingers. *Boys Vanish in New Minton.*

On top of the newspaper is one feather long enough to be a quill, the tip of its hollow shaft shaved to a sharp point.

"Karl," I say, "how'd this get here?" I have the urge to check Gerard's postcard to see how many ravens are left in the full moon.

"He was all over TV today," says Karl. Six hours I wasted in Pittsfield, and something awful happens. "His kids could be anywhere, and he's slurring about how he's been out of work since he broke his back, and they moved there because they need machine operators real bad."

"The Nolans are outsiders. Like we were." I watch the junipers, one split in half, trying to understand. Makes sense. New Minton only has like six or seven surnames. "They think he did it? Kidnapped his own kids?"

The article concludes, *While police are not naming Jay Nolan a suspect at this time, unnamed law enforcement officials acknowledge that he is the only person of interest.*

"Read this, please," I say, showing him Gerard's postcard from my purse, after I confirm the two ravens haven't moved. "Okay, now look."

Karl lowers his eyebrows at the Nolans' barn. "Doors something," he says.

"Must remain open. It's the same phrase. And look." I notice a new detail, an arc carved around the Nolans' driveway in the shape of a semicircle. "Half a Door, Karl. Dug into the lawn."

"Someone spun a donut," he says.

"Scott Wilson carved the same shape thirty years ago behind the school."

If there ever was a moment in our marriage when I wish my husband would trust my judgment, it is now. Instead, Karl shrugs. "Who's Scott Wilson?"

I reread the *Globe*'s article. *We're not going to indulge in any rumors at this time,* said the officer. New Minton needs workers because people know to stay away. They heard stories, the same whispers Mom and Dad exchanged when they thought us kids couldn't hear. Those dark secrets only a few families keep.

What about everyone else? Thirty-three years since we had a headline about missing boys. Memories fade with age. Pills block the rest.

And we're so busy now, angling for promotions so we can remodel shining kitchens. I go into ours, bringing the hand towel to my mouth. I smell cheese and soap, the smell of my family. Inhaling, it seems like the police and my husband are right to suspect Jay Nolan.

Grant and Roderick have nothing to do with Blót or a Door.

There is no connection to Paul's disappearance thirty years ago.

Upstairs, I smell the box with my brother's case files. My palms sweat, hearing it breathe.

Again, I lay out the files. Next to them are a glass of wine and a sticky with five words.

Crusher. Los Angeles. Door. Blót.

Still no cases of animal slaughter anywhere in Western Massachusetts, though the Brotherhood could've hidden the carcasses somewhere no one could find them.

"Daphne." My husband stifles a *Jeez*. "I've been looking all over."

I hold back a scream at his sudden appearance, my eyes sliding from Karl's concerned face to the open door. Hadn't I locked it? Did Karl have another key?

"Honey," I say, trying to turn on the charm and failing when he leans around me. I can tell because his smile wavers watching the wine I spilled stain my papers violet. Like most of Dad's journals, the pages are impenetrably purple. Fatigue settles in, and I wonder how long I've been sitting here.

"You've got to slow down, Daphne," he says.

"Yeah," but I can't think of what else to add. I'm distracted by my lack of progress. I've been through the files a hundred times and found nothing about a Door, Blót, or Crusher. Not that I expected much there. The Brotherhood of the Raven would not last long if they didn't know how to camouflage themselves.

"Have you seen Zach and Stephen for more than five minutes?" asks Karl. "They miss their mother."

They were playing alone most of the afternoon. They play by themselves, as I did when I was their age. I meant to get back to them. But time got away from me.

"I'm checking on them right now, Karl," I say, hoping he doesn't hear my words slur, and wait for him to leave before I dry everything out.

The phone rings. Karl grabs the cordless from the office wall. "Hello," he says. He exhales into the phone, the way Karl does before he gets angry. Before it sets on his face, a new emotion takes hold. The same look Karl had when he was on the phone with Ed. "It's your friend Gerard."

Elation swells in my chest as I take hold of the receiver, though of course I knew I didn't imagine him. "You're a difficult person to reach," I say, holding the mouthpiece tight.

"Did you see the article?" he asks.

"About the Nolans? Yes. Does this have something to do with your dad's postcard? Fresno, by the way. The postmark is from Fresno."

Karl crosses his arms. "Tell him to stay in sight," he says.

"In the business section," says Gerard.

"No." I hurry downstairs and outside, scanning so quickly I can't read.

"Vulcan bought some equipment," says Gerard, "from a defunct mine in New Minton."

"Vulcan Inc. Completes Sale?" I ask. No wonder I overlooked the headline, but okay. Six months ago, Vulcan Inc., based in California's Central Valley, bid for the rights to Fleming Quarry. Fresno's in a valley, isn't it? The same area where, ten months ago, someone mailed the Gedney postcard. "The purchase includes the Flemings' crusher," I read aloud.

$ from Crusher.

I stare at a seagull floating in the sky, my mouth parched. The jagged pieces of this puzzle finally snap into place.

Crusher wasn't a person. It's equipment owned by the Flemings.

"By Trevor Fleming," I say. "Ever since his father got sick, he's been liquidating company assets, including the crusher. Gerard, why'd you make me go through weeks tracking down clues from your dad's postcard? Why not just tell me that Trevor and the Brotherhood of the Raven were planning to kidnap Grant and Roderick Nolan? That's what you're saying, isn't it?"

"He is the Brotherhood, Daphne," says Gerard. "He's killed or exiled everyone else, including my dad and brother. I don't know who else is left, or who to turn to. When I saw your job profile on a website, I thought, 'Here's a cop who will listen.'"

"I'm an ethics investigator. It's not the same thing." A gust of wind sprays dust in my eyes, though I can't say where it came from. "How'd Trevor kill your dad with liver cancer?"

"I told you, Daphne. Last year, Dad's liver is fine. I have the test results. Christmas Eve, he collapses. New tests show advanced angiosarcoma. It spreads fast, but the doctor says he's never seen it spread that fast to a father and son aged thirty years apart."

I don't remember any of this, though given his childhood sadism on animals, I shouldn't be surprised for Trevor's name to pop up again. He's Brandy's age, seventeen then, fifty now. Old enough in 1988, and young enough in 2021, to kidnap children.

"The cops laughed me out of the station," Gerard is saying. "They said the postcard doesn't threaten anybody. The fingerprints don't match Trevor's, and neither does the handwriting."

The white powder. Gerard convinced local police to fingerprint and analyze the postcard, leaving residue behind, and got nowhere. He's been on the hunt for Trevor much longer than I could've imagined. Hunting the man he believes murdered his father and brother.

In desperation, Gerard turned to me, hoping I could find in the paper trail a link to Trevor Fleming. Hard evidence.

Vulcan Inc. sending bulk mail might be the key. Maybe the PVI strip was mislabeled, but I don't think so. I think someone in the Brotherhood made a mistake.

"Why is Trevor selling his family's assets?" I ask. "Where is he now?"

"I think Dad knew," he says. "Ever since Trevor came back from Harvard, he's been talking crazy."

"Harvard," I say, going back in the house. "Hm." My two degrees come from UMass Lowell. Money was a lot tighter then.

Under the sink, we keep cleaning supplies and Devil Mountain, the strongest coffee in the house. Karl used to drink this every night while in school. I'll be up half the night, but I need to be clearheaded.

"Trevor wanted to expand beyond New Minton," he says. "Like the Brotherhood was a franchise. He wanted more Blóts, and not just on Lammas Day. On every solstice and equinox. 'The Elementals will shower us with riches,' he told us."

It is the only way for us to offer them our gratitude, and for them to give us wealth and power.

Riches wouldn't hurt the pocket either, would they, Trevor? If, say, your dad's business was going bankrupt. Though not even the Elementals can salvage the construction business right now.

"I realized they don't Blót because they still believe," says Gerard. "They Blót because they're killers."

I reach for a pad of paper, my fingers ice cold. "Slow down," I say. "Blót is when you kill a steer and drip its blood on an altar. So why does the Brotherhood kidnap children?"

A real Blót with people, Rusty said, *like the olden days.*

"There's many different gospels," says Gerard, "so it's difficult to say which version your dad translated in his journal. Sometimes, it's a steer on the first Blót and a boy on the second. If you go way back, each family Blótted. This second Blót will include the Nolan boys."

"Gerard." My breath catches. "How do you know about my dad's journals?"

How did Scott know about my California Raisins poster? The precision with which those boys ridiculed me, always with the scoop on something embarrassing I said or did at home. I realize that I unconsciously blamed my sisters, not seeing any other way for them to get the information.

Gerard doesn't blame my sisters, though.

"The ravens see all," he says.

"And they tell you somehow? In between popping out of postcards." I hold up the feather, which indoors takes on a purplish hue.

It creeps me out, twists my stomach, but I have to admit, the feather is beautiful.

Soft. Even comforting.

"The first Blót opens a telepathic link to our companions," says Gerard. "They gift us with what's called the Knowing, and they know so much because they assume many forms. But companions are more than that. They help you channel the elements as you recite the Word. It's not simply memorization. The journey is dangerous. Bodies burn out. Gothis go insane."

The feather is suddenly hot in my hands. I have to throw it in the garbage so that I can concentrate on Gerard. "Channeling the elements," I say, "allowed Rusty to freeze Clai and you to evade cameras."

"My grandfather taught me how to dim myself so that unless you were looking directly at me, all you'd see is a shadow, or blur."

Companions, I write. *Dim*. Rusty needed the book, the Book of the Brotherhood, because he was still learning the spell. Gerard didn't because he'd learned to master his power.

"The Door facilitates that telepathic link, doesn't it?" I say. "So long as the Door remains open." I don't give Gerard time to answer before another question bolts out of my mouth. "Gerard, how many Doors are there?"

"Opening one Door was hard enough for our ancestors, Daphne. Maybe it's the White Stone, but Blót doesn't work outside of New Minton. Of course know-it-all Trevor thinks he figured out how to work around that little problem."

Little problem. Trevor can have that little problem for the next thousand years so far as I'm concerned.

The coffee's ready. I down too much in my first gulp, and it feels like someone made me shotgun hot lead.

"Gerard," I say, suppressing a cough, "can I set up a time for us to meet with the police?"

"Daphne, I told you. They won't listen."

"A deposition is different. I can give you the name of a good lawyer I know." I scratch a few notes, but my fingers are already tweaking. Maybe I can set something up next week. "And we need to find Trevor before he or anyone else in the Brotherhood kidnaps more children."

"Ten years ago," he said, "we had a falling out. I haven't seen Trevor since he moved away."

Ten years ago, Dad died. My sisters turned against each other too.

"What about his friends?" I say. "Rusty, Scott Wilson, Derek, and Jeremy?"

"Funny you should mention Scott," says Gerard. "You see the agent listed?"

Again, I skim the article before I find it. "Deborah Wilson," I say, "Commercial Real Estate. Scott's mom brokered the deal between Trevor Fleming and Vulcan Inc.? Did she also sell her old house to the Nolans, I wonder?"

I pass through the living room. The small space amplifies my words so it sounds like I'm shouting. This time of day, the sunlight is heavy enough to weigh down my clothes.

"Deborah sold her house after Scott became a Lost Boy," says Gerard, a name for those kicked out for not following the rules. I want to ask what rules Scott broke, but Gerard's talking fast. "Rusty too. Ever since then, Scott's been a small-time dealer in Worcester. These kids just don't have the skills to live outside New Minton."

"A dealer," I say, hoping my kids can't hear. Who do I know in the drug world? Only one name pops up. I haven't spoken to my younger sister in years.

Zachary and Stephen, now overstimulated, crash through toys in their bedroom. "Cool it, guys," shouts Karl to the ceiling, but my concentration's on my laptop. I barely register his warm breath on my neck. Devil Mountain works fast.

Deborah Wilson's website is easy to find. Wilson Real Estate, based in New Minton. I dial the number, hoping my job title is enough to impress her.

"My name is Daphne Meraux," I say, "and I'm an investigator in the State Ethics Commission, Enforcement Division. May I speak with Mrs. Deborah Wilson, please?"

"Speaking." Mrs. Wilson has a pleasant masculine voice. I don't remember any detail about her. To me, she's a woman with a bleached face and red lipstick.

"Mrs. Wilson, I'm investigating a complaint against Vulcan Inc." Companies frequently receive ethics complaints, so it wouldn't be uncommon for my office to request information from people Vulcan has done business with. A phone call is unusual. Normally, our lawyers would draft a letter. "Now, this has nothing to do with any of your business dealings, but it'd be very helpful if you could forward any transactions you brokered with Vulcan Inc. to my office." And, say, any contact info of Trevor Fleming's.

"Well." Mrs. Wilson clears her throat. "That doesn't sound right. What'd you say your name was?"

"Investigator Meraux, Mrs. Wilson," I say, feeling myself redden. "You're not in any trouble. The complaint is against Vulcan Inc. only, and we're trying to amass."

"Without a warrant," she says, "you can talk to my lawyer."

Slam. The line's dead.

Karl's looking at me. "Doesn't sound like that chat went too well," he says.

I try a social media search of Scott Wilson and Worcester, but don't turn up anything. If Scott's as maladjusted as Gerard says, his absence online makes sense.

If I had Scott's fingerprints, I could run them through Worcester's arrest records. All I can settle for is checking CORI, court arraignment records. If anyone by the name Scott Wilson appeared in court, then I can track his address.

Twelve matches for that exact name, all for drug possession or selling illicit substances. Better than nothing. I turn to Karl.

"Ellie can narrow the list," I say, verbalizing the end of a conversation with myself.

Karl watches me getting ready, confused. "How?" he asks. "What about tonight?"

Was it something for the kids?

No. Fifteen minutes later, I'm merging onto Neponset Avenue when I remember that Karl had a double date planned. A double date with that surgeon at Beth Israel.

The town of Roxbury features gothic row houses amid thin trees. I follow GPS to a dilapidated brick tenement.

As I wait, I try to remember who got the surgery, the surgeon or her wife.

My sister Ellie gets into my car and barks at me to go. She used to be the only girl in our family with blond hair. Now it's black, parts of which stick to her forehead, the girl she used to be stepped on and walked over and beaten up. She fixes her bangs, revealing white scars on her wrists and angry red sores on her face.

"You have my birthday money?" she asks, her nose leaking.

It's the drugs, I tell myself. The same ones that gave her Hep C. That's why Ellie looks like Mom.

"I sent a check last month, Elida," I say.

"Birthday money" is Ellie's term for the money I give her. Forty-two, and she still expects a hundred dollars for being born. I'm trying to find my way out of Roxbury and onto the freeway, but I'm only driving faster. The car's tires squeal. Winos and addicts shuffle across hard-packed lots, land they cleared but never did anything with.

"Oh, I lost it, Daph." Ellie's arms jerk like her clothes are on drooping coat hangers. "You know I'm always losing things."

Not according to bank records. She's retold the same lie a few times now, that she never received any of my checks or that she lost them. I send it again, they all get cashed. Part of my penance for surviving Mom better than her.

My sister's come a long way from the girl who had the bottom bunk. Five years ago, Ellie was institutionalized. We found her in the bathtub with her wrists slit. She wrote a letter about the night Mom locked Ellie in the bathroom. Ellie said she saw the Devil, who sent birds to pick her flesh. The Devil told Ellie that she belonged to him.

A week of "evaluation" stretched until May 2019. Now the skin on her wrists looks like melted wax and Ellie drifts from one fleabag apartment to the next. Or she sleeps on the streets, for all I know.

Ellie must be sensing my thoughts, for she reaches for the door. "Fine," she says. "I'm out."

"Do something for me," I say, grabbing her arm. "Please?"

"And I get an advance? A super big one?"

The teenage way in which Ellie's lip twitches tells me she's already spent whatever I'll give her. I'm enabling my sister to buy drugs. Despite all the money Dad spent on rehab.

"Scott Wilson," I say. "Know where he is? I know you dated him, El."

"For like," Ellie lights a cigarette, mumbling, "a minute."

I open the windows and explain about Vulcan Inc. Freezing air pours in. Ellie squirms, embarrassed that she shacked up with a boy who was overweight and uncool. Every girl's been there before. Or done worse.

"And that led me to Trevor Fleming's crusher," I say, handing Ellie the printout of twelve addresses for Scott Wilson. "If I could find Scott, or Rusty."

"Well," says Ellie, smoking. "Rusty Rahall's in Framingham MSP for pimping a girl. Like a preteen girl."

MSP. Massachusetts State Prison. In the rearview, I see my face twist. "Ew," I say. "A total creep."

"Scott won't know where Trevor is," says Ellie. "One shell company's not going to lead you to Trevor either."

"How do you know Vulcan Inc. is a shell company, Elida?" The rumble strips vibrate up my legs, but we're a few feet from the guardrail before I jerk us back into the right lane. "Because Scott told you." I jab the printout in Ellie's hands. "Any of these familiar?"

Ellie raises her eyebrows at it. "Okay-ee," she says, "but your job's going to fire you if you abuse it."

I turn sharp onto the highway. "You're so worried about your birthday check, you haven't asked about Grant and Roderick Nolan. You know what people are saying about *our* family?"

Ellie slaps the paper on my chest. "Grove Street," she says.

I look down, trying to read and drive at the same time. "Twenty Grove Street?"

"If you bring up Mom or Paul again, Daph, I'm jumping out of the car."

"Okay," I say. "Thank you, Ellie." All I have to say is people are talking about us, and Ellie knows who I mean. We should have a frank talk about Mom, but I don't want to risk losing Ellie. Best to keep my sister upbeat. "It's going to be an hour drive to Worcester. You need anything? A drink? Bathroom break?"

"I need my check," she says.

I glance at her scratching a new wound above her eyebrow, repeating the word *check*, *check*, *check* like a prayer.

Being an ethics investigator is rewarding and stable. But it's funny. All these files and notes I'm taking make me remember something I completely forgot. When I was a kid, I wanted to be a detective.

When Mom separated, Dad brought home dozens of boxes earmarked for the Christmas charity drive. In one of them we found stacks of *Boxcar Children*, *Encyclopedia Brown*, and *Nancy Drew*. My sisters frowned at their musty covers, but that winter I joined forces them and with Trixie Belden and Beverly Gray. They weren't interested if Johnny the football captain asked them out.

They used their wits to put bad people away. Solving crimes was my dream job. For the first time since I was eleven, I feel like I'm an amateur sleuth again. Following a lead in the night where streetlights are scarce.

"There," says Ellie, pointing at a weak yellow bulb that suggests a porch.

I pull under the closest streetlight. Grove Street has large gaps of darkness between closed-down factories and triple-deckers. This place is even more run-down than Ellie's Roxbury apartment.

"Maybe I should go in alone," says Ellie.

"What?" It's more like a honk, outrage that my little sister would act as my protector.

"No offense, Daph, but you have this nice bourgeois Quincy life, and Scott isn't the most stable guy. Once, he burned the delivery guy for being late with a pizza."

My eyes snap to the alleyway. Either people or statues watch us in the shadows. "Burned him?"

Ellie stares, too, but I can't tell if she sees anything. "The kid thought he was on fire," she says. "He was screaming, trying to put himself out, but nothing was wrong. No flames. Scott asked if the kid liked *the family specialty*."

"Scott made the kid hallucinate," I say. The Gedneys dim. The Rahalls freeze. The Wilsons are illusionists. Each family specializes in a certain power, like Dad's journal said.

"And if you piss him off," says Ellie, "he'll lock you in place. Your crucifix won't stop it. Neither will prayer."

"I get it, Ellie," I say, getting out of the Prius. The boys can channel elements, leaving you powerless. I hope the gusts of wind will help me think. Since the sun set, the temperature's dropped into the low fifties.

There has to be a way to protect ourselves. Because if Trevor figures out a way to open another Door . . .

Ellie guides me tightly across the street. "Hey, don't let them touch you," she says. "And please, don't leave anything behind."

A group of people roll dice against a brick wall. It doesn't look like street craps. Whatever they're playing, it involves interlocking circles.

Circles like the kind Scott Wilson drew behind the elementary school when we were kids.

Once in the alleyway, wind beats the buildings that glow like large, jagged teeth. Stairs lead to apartment buildings on the second floor, situated above various businesses. At the top step, I see the weak yellow light is affixed to a cobwebbed pole.

Someone taped a yellow envelope to Twenty Grove Street. Red letters sear the darkness: Eviction Notice.

"No," I say, reading that Scott got kicked out three months ago. "No, damn it."

I try to pull up CORI, but it denies me access. With double verification, the system should work on a phone. Unless it's something else. Deborah Wilson terminated the call pretty quickly.

That leaves me with my backup plan: knocking until Ellie pushes me out of the way. With her trademark eye roll, Ellie opens the unlocked door. Something metal gives way and clatters on kitchen tiles. Fluorescent tubes wink alight as though they'd been on the whole time.

"It's a trick," I say. Though Ellie did tell me about the Wilsons' power.

"Beats Jehovah's Witnesses harassing you all the time, doesn't it?" says Ellie, brushing through Christmas lights. They're killing children because they don't want someone knocking on their door? Seems so petty.

"El," I say, hesitant to enter a stranger's house, loathe to leave my sister behind. She got ahead so fast. "Ellie?"

The kitchen is piled with dishes and Diet Coke bottles, a yellow I can smell. The living room throbs with reddish light emanating from a maze circle.

"It's okay, Scott," says Ellie around a corner somewhere. "We're just trying to find information about those missing kids."

I find Ellie, acne shining red, standing in front of a sweaty man on a couch. Scott Wilson, who went from calling me a dweeb to one of New Minton's Lost Boys, now has dyed white hair and twin brass ear gauge plugs. He shakes his head like a kid being force-fed medicine, then sees me and snarls.

"That little prick," says Scott. "Gerard told you everything? I'll kill him."

"Don't hurt him, Scott," I say, the threat to kill Gerard like a hot brand on my chest. Gerard told me the ravens feed the boys secrets. I waltz into Wilson's lair anyway, with every seed of knowledge I gathered waiting for him to pluck.

When he gets up, I see Scott's lost a lot of weight. Not the healthy way. The way a drug user does. The way Ellie did. So that wrinkled skin hangs off the bone. His nose is a lot more hawkish than I remember, like he mangled it, and the nasal bone never healed right.

"Trevor will eat Gerard's soul when he finds out," says Scott. "He'll eat mine, too, if I do nothing. You think I'd rat him out to you?"

School doesn't like rats.

"Scott," I say. "Grant is ten and Roderick is eight. They're scared out of their minds. If Trevor abducted them, I need to know where he is." Scott still doesn't say anything. "I know your mom sold Trevor's crusher."

"Fuck her." Scott turns to Ellie. "Fuck you, too, for bringing her." His eyes slide to the coffee table. "Doing his dirty work for peanuts. Think I need this?"

"What's Trevor paying you to do?"

I look to where Scott's eyes went. Between ash trays and pizza boxes is a leather-bound book. Maybe not leather. Its texture is velvety, more fragile. It pulls me in with icy hooks.

"No copyright page," I say, flipping. "No author. No publisher information. This is the book, isn't it? The one from the tree with the square hole when you were going to Blót Clai. The one Everett Ford asked for before he died?"

"Christ," says Scott, "you went right for it." He paces, chastising himself. "If Rusty wanted Clai dead, he would've kept him frozen. What you're talking about is the Quarter Moon Binding. You can't become a man without a bride, right? Rusty wanted you. Turn the preacher's daughter. On Lammas Day, there used to be mass weddings."

You have to get her ready, someone whispered to Rusty thirty years ago. *The quarter moon is almost set. If you intend to bind yourselves for all eternity . . .*

I manage to swallow my disgust. Never would I be Rusty's wife. The same guy who pimps children? Never. Ever. Ever. Ever.

Though Ellie dated Scott. Brandy loved Jeremy White. Was seducing a preacher's daughter a Lost Boy fantasy?

Scott left a bookmark. I pull it out, remembering Dad's postcard, and my stomach clenches. Sure enough, it's another postcard. First to Dad, then to George Gedney. Now a third one to Scott.

Your part will be the Book of the Brotherhood, it reads. *Keep yourself pure, Brother. For the sake of our children, we must keep the Door open.*

Los Angeles postmark. Sent in October. Almost identical to the Gedneys' postcard, with the exception of nine digits scratched under the address. A phone number, area code 559.

"This was a call," I say, slipping the postcard into my back pocket. "To all you Lost Boys. Trevor's planning another Blót. He wants to open another Door outside of New Minton, and he'll use the blood of Grant and Roderick Nolan to do it."

Scott's inches from my face, right eye lower than the left, reeking of cat urine. I hold my breath, pulse thudding in my neck, wondering if he saw me pocket his postcard.

"Trevor says we can't have just two Blóts anymore," he says. "To restore us back to the old ways, we need more Blóts. A lot more."

They Blót because they're killers. Then I cock my head. "Restore you?"

"One thing they don't tell you when you're a kid on the Hill is the more you use the power, the more you become like them. The psychic link becomes so strong you can't cut it."

Scott holds up his forearm so I can see scars symmetrically placed on either side.

"They inserted two rods in my arm," he says, "because my ulna and radius have broken four times in the last three years. Four frigging times."

"I'm sorry, Scott," I say, at a loss to come up with anything better, and not really caring if I'm at all convincing. Kidnapping and murdering children outweighs a few broken bones, in my mind.

"I've lost almost half of my bone mass." Scott's face flickers. For a moment, his features sharpen into a beak. I blink, and he's back to normal. "I got air pockets too. Let me show you this."

"Birds have air pockets, Scott," I say. "Not people." I turn to Ellie, convinced for a moment that he's making an inappropriate joke. Or maybe he's crazy.

Scott lifts his shirt, revealing his bony, hairy back. Gross.

I'm about to look away when I see what he wants me to see. Dozens of spines poke about an inch out of Scott's back. Each one has a black bud, as soft and oily as the feather that fell on my lap earlier today.

"Let me tell you," says Scott, "growing feathers hurts like a bitch."

"Oh, God," I say, the revulsion buzzing under my skin. "Souls of the damned."

Scott screws up his nose and lips. "What?"

"An old Norse legend. Ravens are imprisoned souls of the damned."

That's why they eat carrion. Like Cain, they roam the earth for eternity. And they do the bidding of the Elementals for the next generation of the Brotherhood.

I fall back, like Scott might be contagious, and something topples in the kitchen. A minute ago, it was empty. I don't remember closing the front door.

Compared to the harsh red light, the kitchen is dark as a cavern. Something's moving in there. A shadow hops across the table. "You have a roommate?" I say.

"When I die," says Scott behind me, "I die. I'm not going down that route, becoming a familiar, forever bound to serve."

My hand finds the light switch. And I gasp.

Black feathers and blood smear the table. They lead to two ravens, who look like they were in one heck of a fight. The larger raven won. It stands over the prostrate loser, eating its left eye.

"Get away from me," Scott screams at the raven, which chews with a blank expression.

The ravens aren't just links to the Elementals. They're manifestations of the boys' thoughts. Scott's clearly conflicted. One side of him is fighting the other to the death.

"Let me help you, Scott," I say, though something pricks my insides at the thought of doing so. Dad's altruism pits against the wrong these boys did to me and to my family. "Trevor's lying if he told you more Blóts will restore you. Trevor wants money. He thinks another Blót will reverse the bankruptcy on his family business."

"Maybe you're right." Scott sniffs and nods.

"Tell me where the Door is. And how you close it."

Scott wipes away tears and looks up at me with a vulnerability I never saw from him before. "You've always been so kind to me, Daphne. And there is something you can do." Despite everything, I gulp, eager to please. "You remember that day at Mountains with a View? You saw me with my grandfather. My dad wasn't around, so the initiation's responsibility fell to him."

My fingers absently trace the raven's head on the book cover, my stomach queasy again. Grandpop stayed at Mountains with a View before he died, a retirement home in New Minton. After Clai disappeared, Mom and I visited him. I remember being with Grandpop, and someone was talking in the background. *Abraham offered his only son to speak with God.*

"Good," says Scott. I snap back to beads of sweat glowing on Scott's forehead. I was going to help Scott, and he'd tell me about the Door, but we got lost too quickly. "That tickle in your stomach. That's just the Elementals working through you, but you know that. You felt that way around your mom sometimes, too, didn't you? That Drane blood in her veins. I think that's why Rusty thought you would join us."

"Scott, don't," says Ellie.

I feel them. Alien fingers on my skin. They know I'm afraid, but I don't have to be.

"It's okay," says Scott. "You don't have to call it the Devil anymore. You know the truth."

It's more like sleep paralysis. I feel air from Scott's vent, and I smell his BO, but I can't move, I can't speak. I'm locked in Scott's living room, wanting to run. Ellie told me not to let Scott touch me. I wish her warning had been more specific.

"Your mom showed you the Elementals," Scott's saying. "They're hungry for you. You feel it in the tremors."

Mom showed you. How would Scott know?

Because of the ravens, who see all. I hear their whispers, hundreds of voices, each with the supernatural knowledge of a demon. The Knowing.

That's not what they're saying though. *Ellie*, they squawk, *Ellie*, *Ellie*. Her betrayal hacks an open wound in my chest, releasing me from Scott's vile grip.

"You told Scott what happened in the bathroom?" I say to Ellie. Turning toward her is more difficult, my muscles stiff and uncooperative. "Him, but not me?"

"She lied to us, Daph." Ellie's eyes drain from blue to black. "About who she was. I was so messed up. I thought Scott was the only one who could understand."

"Mom knew Blót." Scott's maze plunges toward me, or I fall into it. The fiery walls singe my face. "And you never mentioned it?"

A memory flickers. Bright lights from downstairs. Mom's strange voice. She showed Ellie something awful, Ellie and not me, but I can't. I need to be alone to process.

"Why don't you give me the book, Daphne?" says Scott. "And I'll show you life eternal. Power eternal. Maybe we don't even have to Blót the Nolans. Restoring the Drane blood might be all the regeneration our families need."

I have no reason to hold on to Scott's stupid old book. It's his. It's really hot. I'm sweating, too, and I'm a guest in his home. I'm about to return it; I don't want to be here anymore. But I keep turning into Scott, who loses patience.

"Give me it," he says, ripping the book out of my hands.

"*Hey*." Ellie slaps his forearms. "Don't you touch her."

"He will eat my soul if he doesn't get the book back, El," says Scott. "It's the only way out now." I'm like a rag between two snarling dogs, being pulled back and forth. Acid races up my throat.

"I said, *leave her alone*," says Ellie.

A gust of wind knocks me down. I should be springing to Ellie's defense. She's holding her own against Scott, impressive for someone who weighs a hundred pounds, maybe, and drives him out of the room. They get swallowed in the hall's bright light. Somewhere deeper in the apartment, a shower curtain screeches.

I'm dizzy as I roll onto the book, which got lost in the scuffle. Now it's on the floor, flipped to the inside cover. Scott or someone else scrawled five words there, sending spikes of heat and ice through my body.

KNOW THIS BOOK IS CURSED.

Adrenaline jump-starts my heart. "Ellie?" I yell. "Ellie, where are you?"

My sister grabs me from the dark hallway, and I yelp. "Come on," she says, rushing to the front door.

"Where's Scott? What happened?"

"Never mind that," says Ellie. A long shriek nearly drowns her out. It's coming from somewhere behind us.

I break free, my head foggy, and follow vibrating walls to the blasting phosphorescence of the bathroom. Steam blankets the mirror. The bathtub's faucet screams at full blast.

Somehow, Ellie got ahead of me. "Don't, Daph," she says, eyebrows pleading. Moving her by the shoulders, I see why she blocked my view.

Scott bobs in the green bathtub, one foot sticking out, a maniacal smile on his lips. He's got another smile on his neck, this one gushing red. Blood fills the tub, spreading like tentacles across the water's surface.

"Oh, God," I say.

"I didn't do it, I swear." Ellie's cheeks tremble. "I couldn't stop him."

"Right in front of you?" I shout. The horror weakens my legs. I hunch over, wanting to vomit. "Why?"

"He told you." Ellie rocks, her welts as red as the bathwater. "Trevor will kill him."

That's not what Scott said, but the light winks out for a second. Then an inky shadow ripples across the foggy bathroom ceiling. I don't see the raven until it lands on Scott's shoulder, the larger one that killed the smaller one. It sidesteps over the open wound, eyes fixed on Scott's face.

"No," I say, knowing what it wants, my stomach clenching. Before I can shoo it, the raven pecks Scott's eye.

The iris cleaves and deflates. Milky pink liquid bubbles out.

The raven's next peck plucks out the whole eye. It tilts its head back to fit the gummy ball in its beak, everything but the severed optic nerve. If I could read a bird's expression, I'd say this one's happy we can watch him eat.

I feel myself slipping, unable to block out the sound of the raven's beak smacking. Scott dead in the tub. The spines on his back. Ellie's betrayal. Blót. All leading back somehow to Mom.

CHAPTER SEVEN

March 31, 1988

The principal called for Mom hours ago. She wasn't home, and she wasn't at work. Mr. Corwin dismissed my story of how I ended up on the slab. Instead, he interrogated Rusty, David, Scott, and me about the whereabouts of Clai Denton.

"It was the Parsons Witch, the Parsons Witch," cried Rusty.

From the principal's office, Rusty recounted that after Clai headed to the tracks for no reason, Mary Bliss Parsons slipped out of her skin and dragged Clai somewhere deep into the woods. I heard them argue as I sat in the hall, my head spinning.

Daphne Gauge says you grabbed Clai's neck.

"I laid one finger on him," said Rusty. "Ask the other kids."

Why couldn't Clai speak?

"He was just goofing around. To prank Daphne."

No, Clai looked genuinely scared. Didn't he?

So why'd Clai run away?

"The witch called him. We seen it."

I saw something, but obviously it wasn't a witch. As hard as I turned it over in my head, the memory only got muddier. It had to be a tree or a shadow.

No, it was definitely a shoulder.

How could I know someone by a shoulder?

One by one, everyone's mom arrived, except Rusty's and mine. Finally, at 3:20, Mom showed up in a dress made of doilies. It marked the first time I'd seen Mom since she sent us away with no supper.

Every time she went anywhere, Mom's nervous energy was like a weight in the air. The secretaries stiffened at Mom's entrance, feeling awkward because Mom was awkward. Usually, they exchanged one word, then busied themselves with files on the other side of the room. I wished today would've been no exception.

"Daphne did *what*?" Mom shouted.

Everything in the office stopped, and so did my heart. Before kids piled on with their impersonations of her and the phones went back to ringing, Mom's look withered me to ash. Clai was missing, and Mom blamed me. That was fairly standard. Runaway or not, so far as Mom was concerned, the fact that I was one of the last kids to see Clai was proof enough of my guilt. Now Mom apologized to the principal for the millionth time. "I didn't raise my daughter like this, Mr. Corwin," she said, her glasses fogging, desperate for the principal's approval. That's one trait I wished Mom hadn't passed on. "If there's anything I can do?"

Mr. Corwin chewed gum, his hazel eyes following me. "She's a good kid."

My brother Paul waited for us in the hallway, his hair combed in a Beatles fop. This close, it smelled like parmesan cheese.

He went to school on the old side where the middle grades weren't allowed. I never liked it there. The splinters were as long as fingers. Spiders hung from the one long beam. And it was always freezing.

Seeing Mom tight-lipped, Paul gave me his slimy hand and said nothing. Even he knew punishment awaited me, soon as we got home. I dreaded it so much that I didn't notice Paul had changed into a wool jersey and athletic shorts.

We didn't head for the van. Instead, Mom followed a growing crowd into the gym. I don't know how I forgot that on Thursdays, Paul had soccer practice.

Kids dribbled soccer balls, a sound that drilled into our teeth. A few of the moms noticed Mom and her dress.

"Sue Ann," said Mom with a smile. "Hulda."

The women raised eyebrows at one another. "Hasn't changed at all," said Mrs. Willette. Another person who knew Mom's past. Before I could confront Mom, my legs buckled for the second time today, and I tumbled to the floor.

"Dorks Express. Going *down*."

My sister Brandy stood over me, chewing on a banana, pleased with herself. She was obsessed with having blown-out hair like Kelly LeBrock from *Weird Science*, and she'd kicked the back of my short knee to make me lose my balance. Whatever Brandy saw on Mom's face made her frown.

"What's Pumpkin in trouble for?" asked Brandy.

"Daph was on her knees," said Courtney, loud enough for everyone to hear, "talking to God about birds."

"What?" Brandy laughed. "You're such a loser."

I looked down, blushing not of embarrassment but of outrage. My collar kept slipping down my collarbone, proof Rusty had grabbed me, not to mention my copy of *Brillstone Break-In* was ruined, and no one cared.

My sisters kept giggling. Doughy and freckled, it was hard to believe Courtney was Brandy's sister, who everyone admired for her gristled frame. They both went to the high school half a mile away.

Mom's eye swerved to Brandy. "I spoke to Mrs. Sommerson," she said. "She told me about last week's report cards?"

"Yeah," said Brandy, tucking a hair behind her ear. "Did she tell you my GPA now qualifies for a Duke scholarship? Oh, and I am a *lock* for UConn. U*Conn*, U*Conn*, U*Conn*."

She cajoled Paul to dance with her. All I could think of were the boys chanting, *Freeze, freeze, freeze.*

"I don't want to practice," said Paul, hand to his lips. "My head hurts."

"Maybe we could skip this week," said Courtney. "Let things settle."

"It's fine," said Brandy, boxing me out. "Kids run away, like, all the time."

"I smell tires," said Paul, watching boys stumble like drunk sprinters.

Mom's lips whitened until we stopped talking. "Mrs. Sommerson said you have a B minus in anatomy and trigonometry."

The cheer evaporated from Brandy's face. A flush filled the void.

"Anatomy's, like, the *hardest*," said Brandy, glancing at the eavesdroppers. "Literally no one gets an A. A B's a really good grade in that class."

"The tutors are rich," said Mom, "but still she can't do math and science. Because you're doing the *minimum*. What do you think, Brandy? Will the top schools *in the country* accept a student who does the *minimum* in math and science?"

Humiliated, Brandy kept her head down. She shrugged off Courtney's attempt to comfort her. Then Coach Brody clapped at the kids, saying, "All right," to anyone nearby. He was easy to spot, a hairy man in a red ball cap.

"And it's lipstick, honey, not teeth-stick," said Mom. On her way by, I got a whiff of burning tires. "Daphne, let's *go*. Grandpop's been acting up."

The first day, she and Dad watched practice. But today all the parents were off to their cars or to the drugstore for an hour, Mom included.

Last thing I wanted was to visit Grandpop. I knew if I pouted, though, I'd only get in more trouble later. So I tried not to think about how much life stunk that I was the only kid who had to go for Mom's million errands.

In town, the land flattened and fog settled in. New Minton's buildings sprang from the white mountain pine, including the white-latticed General Store. Mom pulled in there, in front of the Passerine Diner. She parked too close to another car, its antennae-like side mirrors blocking me in, and resumed her lecture on all the ways I would need to compensate for being a girl; this in response to Rusty's attempted Blót. In closing, Mom threatened me.

"You better hope they find Clai real soon, Daphne."

"Mr. Corwin hardly asked any questions about Clai, though," I said, even as I struggled to remember. He had no patience for Blót either. The more I mentioned it, the angrier he got. *Anyone says they're killing steers is lying*, he'd shouted. *And that's the last I want to hear about it.*

The principal also acted like he'd never heard of Dad. I mentioned the food drives, clothing drives, the time Dad donated personally so the band had uniforms instead of a maroon shirt? All Mr. Corwin did was shrug.

You're one of them Unitarians?

Is Unitarian a Christian religion, dear?

Between questions, Mr. Corwin's finger swirled around a picture frame. He had twelve or so around his office. Each frame held the photo of the same albino Siamese, distinctive because of its overbite.

Strangest thing, though—I was pretty sure Mr. Corwin's eyes were black. The whole time in his office, I could barely breathe.

"I tried telling him about the dolls and a torn shirt," I said. "Like a girl's T-shirt."

"It was probably trash someone dumped." Mom slipped on white gloves to choose a white lily from the flower store's outdoor rack. "You don't have to be so nervous all the time, you know."

"You're right, I guess." Having the principal question me didn't happen every day. Not like I was seasoned, like Rusty and his friends. The shape was probably just a shadow, like everyone said. "But how could Rusty freeze Clai with only one finger?"

Mom's eyes narrowed. "He did? Which boy?"

"Rusty, Mom." Had she even been listening?

"The Rahalls," said Mom with disgust.

That was the last word on the subject. At the double doors to Mountains with a View, Mom shushed me. She checked her face in the mirror and smoothed her dress. Then she yanked my headband until my eyes burned.

"Now if I can only get your sister Courtney to wear one," said Mom. They gave Courtney a headache, but Mom whisked me into Grandpop's retirement home.

We passed rows of wrinkled women and men slumped over in wheelchairs. The walls turned peach, Grandpop's wing.

His room reeked of armpit and dysentery.

A nurse was getting visibly flustered with Grandpop, who fumbled under the bed for his shoes. His clothes were spread all over the floor.

"Mr. Drane," she said. "Mr. Drane."

Grandpop only stopped dumping his clothes when he saw us. "I've been waiting three hours, Charity," he said.

"It's Chastity, Dad." Mom led him back to bed. After tucking the blankets across his chest, Mom planted a kiss on Grandpop's forehead with a dramatic gurgle of her throat. "You look so good."

"Where the hell have you been?" His arms and legs worked under the tight sheets, then he squinted. "You're not Charity. You're too old. What happened to your face?"

Charity was my grandmother, though she died several years before I was born. Soon as I thought these thoughts, Grandpop begged me as though I was in charge, his blue eyes bulging.

"Not safe here," he said, "not safe. We've got to get out."

"Blót didn't stop the dry spell," said Grandpop's roommate, nodding. "Everyone gets nervous."

The roommate reached for a cup of water on a bookshelf. I went to get the cup, but Scott Wilson beat me to it. I held my breath so that I wouldn't scream at his lumpy white orderly clothes a million sizes too large for him. Where had he come from?

"I'm visiting my grandpa," he said, as though I'd invaded his territory, his cheeks burning.

I shrugged. "Me too?"

"The real problem is their Bible," said Scott's grandfather. "Stories stolen from the Sumerians. Hm."

Scott held the straw so his grandfather could drink, but his white tongue lolled around the cup's lip, as blind to the bendy straw as his eyes. I hadn't moved. Never in my life had I heard someone be so mean.

Criticizing our beliefs, Dad's work. Why would they make him Grandpop's roommate? I looked to Mom, but she was refolding Grandpop's shirts.

"Gothi found the truth. Abraham offered his only son to speak with God." Scott's grandfather was the source of the armpit smell. This close, I also saw a tattoo on his forearm. A crow with black wings. "Call it bread and wine all you want, but they don't speak to their God without Blótting neither. So we're not so different." His smile was toothless. "Pray your own way, huh?"

The sun formed blistering crescents under Mom's eyes. "I wouldn't know," she said. Grandpop muttered and again Mom tried to get him to sleep.

CHAPTER EIGHT

June 2, 2021

I *wouldn't know.*

Scott's grandfather mocked the Bible's story of Abraham. Then he asked Mom a direct question, and she denied knowing a thing.

She lied to us, Daph, said Ellie. *About who she was.* With all her drug problems, Ellie remembers better than I do.

How come I don't remember Mom and Dad the same as she does?

Something in my past, some memory, is gnawing at me. I fill journals, the ones from preteen years I never got to keep, ramming into the same dead ends. There's an answer here, somewhere. Something not in the case files. Then I wonder if I'm losing my mind.

One thing's for sure. I have no direction.

Rusty's in jail. Scott's dead. Trevor's been clean since a 2002 arrest for the killing of three dozen chickens. After losing arguments for religious freedom, he agreed to pay a fine. None of their fingerprints match the Gedney and Wilson postcards. No luck with handwriting analysis either. The author of the postcard was left-handed, and Trevor is a righty.

The Flemings' New Minton address is abandoned. According to the post office, Trevor has no current address. I keep reaching out to his friends and family, but most hang up. Word spreads not to cooperate.

If only I could get Trevor to come to me. I just need to figure out what he wants, other than to kidnap children.

Three packages are on the table when I get home. They're piled behind wrapped foil, my dinner. Nothing creaks or shifts in our house. Somewhere upstairs, my husband and children sleep.

I could tiptoe into my office, but Karl doesn't like me in there after midnight anymore. Too much temptation. We haven't had a lot of trust since he found me hiding gin.

If there was a night for a Fog Cutter, this would be it too. Yesterday afternoon, New Minton police arrested Jay Nolan for drunk and disorderly and assault of a police officer. He's got a whole spread since they recovered the charred remains of Grant's and Roderick's pajamas in Corvus Pond.

Pictures of the police escorting Jay Nolan around the pond, pointing at various landmarks.

Articles about Jay Nolan's temper. Witnesses claim he was abusive toward his wife and sons, including an occasion when the family had a "screaming match" in a grocery store. Every time, Karl repeats the same thing: *innocent people don't act like that*.

The first package is a copy of the coroner report on Scott. Seeing the papers causes me to relive the moment I found him dead in the bathtub.

Right in front of you? I shouted. *Why*?

He told you, said Ellie. *Trevor will kill him*.

No, Scott said Trevor would eat his soul.

What did Scott mean exactly? He was afraid of Trevor, I get that. But did Ellie kill Scott before Trevor could eat Scott's soul? Did she assist in Scott's suicide because he didn't want his body to degenerate any further?

How did everything happen so fast?

The police have no follow-ups. Soon as they confirmed Scott Wilson's long list of priors, they fell back to X-ing boxes. *You were conducting a welfare check*? they asked, and I found myself nodding. I left with Scott's postcard and book without so much as a raised eyebrow.

Patient recently diagnosed with Gorham-Stout disease, reads the report. It's when a person suffers bone loss, though never at the rate Scott claimed. Also, Morgellons disease, where fibers grow out of slow-healing sores. I wonder when was the last time a patient had two extremely rare diseases at the same time. After reading the whole thing, I let out a giant whoosh of air.

Suicide, certified by the medical examiner. Judging by the angle of the wound pattern, the blade had to be in Scott's hand.

Thank goodness.

Not that Ellie agrees. She used her birthday money for everything but rent and got kicked out of her Roxbury apartment.

The second package is from the Department of Justice. A letter notifies me that I am among those invited to 201 Maple Street in Chelsea, Massachusetts for the week of July 26-30. Two months after the Nolan boys' disappearance, the FBI finally gets involved.

The FBI wants something: me. I'd be a big catch for them. Thirty years, and my family has been tight-lipped to law enforcement. Question is, do they want to talk to others from New Minton too?

Because I want something as well. A chance to get in the same room as Trevor Fleming. Maybe Trevor wants something. The same as anyone in hiding. His testimony in exchange for a plea deal.

If this works, I'll have to open myself up to a lifetime of my family's dirty laundry. I wonder if, in time, my sisters will forgive me.

The third package is the Book of the Brotherhood I sent off for analysis, followed by a vague note. *Custom made*, it concludes. That's the seventh rare book dealer who rebuffed my questions about Scott's book.

Touching the cover makes whispers come from the living room. I open to the foreword.

KNOW THIS BOOK IS CURSED.

It is written by madmen and harridans. That's what they called those who communed with the Elementals and met axe and stake. Their blood boiled in the bonfire so you could know the true teachings of Wodan.

Honor their sacrifices by learning to bend the elements to your will, but also know this. Each spell found in these pages is fraught with danger. The Elementals are unpredictable. They can reward as well as punish.

Beware.

Unpredictable except when they're slowly turning you into a familiar.

The prologue details a long allegory. Apparently, the world began as a chasm of fire and ice. No balance. Wodan, a sky god, discovered that if he combined the Elementals, he could fill the chasm and create water. Land. The universe.

But soon the Elementals would separate, and it would be just fire and ice in a chasm again. So Wodan created the Wheel. A way to keep the Elementals in motion and hold all life together. Each generation, the Brotherhood of the Raven maintains this balance, keeping the Wheel in motion.

Yet part of that balance includes kidnapping children. They have to be a certain age, between eight and twelve, with seven-year-old Paul a notable exception. All have their clothes burned. Next is a long history:

In the old lands, there was no need for a Door. Our ancestors lived with the Elementals, who cared for them the way a father protects his son. They taught our people how to use Air to live in the sky. And they gave us the White Stone, a combination of all the elements, that towered from the highest hilltop all the way to Valhöll.

But a great evil came from the south. The new way, they called it, monotheists who murdered our sisters at Torsåker. They salted the old land and destroyed the White Stone.

The Torsåker witch trials of 1675, seventeen years before panic would strike Salem. Seventy-one Swedish people beheaded and burned, nearly all of them women. I keep reading.

Cut off from the Elementals, our people suffered greatly. Many died of hunger and disease, for the new way's technology was primitive, their knowledge backwater. We had to abandon the old land, never to return.

Years later, the dozens that were left founded a settlement in the Hilltowns. Long winters left scant supplies. Murderers from Salem wiped out whole families. We almost didn't make it. The only reason you're here now is because of one man's courage during a great storm at our darkest hour.

The storm exposed the top of a hill, the very hill you are standing on now. Wrath, they said, from the god who would be one.

I pause, repeating the line. *The god who would be one.* Is the Brotherhood referring to God, the Christian God?

The man could've fled, as others had done, but he crept up the hill. He explored the destruction. And he discovered, beneath this black soil, a gift from the Elementals. More White Stone.

With his ear to the Stone, the man heard the Elementals speak for the first time in thousands of years. He transcribed their wisdom into a book of prayers, the same book you hold now. Thus, he became our gothi. And as gothi, he taught our ancestors how to excavate the White Stone, and how to rebuild it as the Idol. This is how New Minton was born.

Born on the blood of two Blóts. Sacrifices that open a Door to the Elementals and grant them wealth and power. Next is *The Initiation*, but something tells me to wait.

I open Dad's journal to the Book of the Brotherhood. Along the left-hand line is a repeating pattern, the three interlocking triangles of Wodan Dad tore in order to painstakingly glue *The Initiation* into his journal.

I sit back in the chair, wondering how Dad got a copy of the Book of the Brotherhood. Maybe he didn't get a true copy, for some details are different. This text calls them cows, not steers, and they come from each family, who is expected to donate one for the first Blót.

If you go way back, each family Blótted, said Gerard.

The next section is titled "Spells."

It is by far the largest in the book, though the quickest for me to skim because I can't read the language. Old Norse is written in Runic, and so is the book, just with an alphabet that predates the second-century CE. It's some extinct Norse language that runs pages and pages for the Brotherhood to memorize so that they can invoke the Elementals' power. No wonder it takes years to master.

Scott also has cards. Not postcards. They have images of a seven-headed dragon. A kind of Huldra, a beautiful woman except instead of a cow tail I'd say it's more of a horse tail. Scott wrote symbols under the images. They almost look like . . .

"Prayer cards," I say. Catholics don't pray to God for everything, but rather to patron saints. I wonder if these creatures are drawings of different Elementals.

Not that I can prove anything. It's mere speculation.

The last five pages are in English and, I kid you not, instruct the initiate on how to care for your raven.

> *They share a personal bond to all who celebrate Blót. Ravens are drawn to help the elements transfer safely from the Door to the Brother, so we must provide them with a delicious and healthy diet.*

Not surprisingly, ravens prefer salty eyeballs, but being carrion and all, they're not too picky. Gives a whole new stomach-churning meaning to the eye of newt. Ravens have other powers too. They have the power of divination, what Gerard called the Knowing, the ability to see the future and to read people's minds.

Where would they hide Grant and Roderick? The book doesn't say. Neither does Scott's postcard. Gerard could be a really big help here. Since I pressured him on cooperating with the police, he won't return my calls.

That 559 number taunts me. Again, I dial. It services Fresno, California, about two hundred miles from LA. But the number's disconnected.

I toss the phone, which spins Scott's postcard. Upside down, 559 reads as 622. I've stared at Scott's postcard a million times, but never with the ceiling fan lighting this angle; after the numbers comes a scratch I couldn't see before. It looks like someone wrote a *Z* but ran out of ink. There's more. I fiddle with the postcard to read the rest.

Zenia. 1 a.m. Corvus. Flip 559, read the whole thing together, and you get . . .

"622 Zenia Lane," I say. My skin flushes. "Holy shit. The Wilsons' house." Deborah and Scott's.

Not anymore. The Nolans live there now.

Someone wanted Scott at Corvus Pond at one a.m. On May 1, that would place Scott less than a mile from Grant and Roderick Nolan two hours before they disappeared. Looks like Scott's part had to do with more than just the Book of the Brotherhood.

My fingers shake, scanning the yellow pages. *Call the police*, I tell myself, but instead I find the Nolans' number. Maybe a plea from Theresa will carry more weight than one from me.

I dial, doubt growing with each ring. No way they'll pick up, not after midnight. You want to contact someone these days, you send a text. And what would I say?

"Hello?"

I hop to the countertop, nervous energy commanding me to wipe it. New Minton is like stepping back thirty years, when people still answered landlines. "Theresa Nolan?" I ask.

"Yes."

She's as nervous as I am. Hopeful that a strange woman on the phone means her sons are safe. In one breathless word, Theresa reminds me of all the times Mom begged the sheriffs for the same good news.

She never got it. Mom never heard Paul's voice again, never knew what happened to him. Look how that awful fact twisted Mom into a monster, at least in Ellie's eyes. Knowing that makes me want to do anything for Theresa.

"Mrs. Nolan, my name is Daphne Meraux. I'm so sorry for what you're going through."

"I can't, Ms. Meraux. I can't talk to no writers."

"I'm not a reporter, Mrs. Nolan," I say. "I'm from New Minton. The same thing happened to our family. Thirty years ago, my brother, Paul, was abducted."

Silence. She hangs up before I can finish.

The counter's quartz soothes my forehead. I want to help. Please let me help. Otherwise, what's the point of Gerard Gedney tracking me down? Finding out about the Door, Blót, and this book? It can't be for no reason.

There's something else, a selfish need. I want to let Theresa know that she's not alone. Then maybe I won't feel so alone either. If we work together, I know we can solve this thing.

The phone buzzes in my hand, making me jump. A 508 number. I answer quick as I can. Please, let it not wake Stephen and Zachary.

"Hello?"

"My boys were a hundred yards away, Daphne," says the person on the phone. "I look outside, I still see their flashlights bobbing."

"'Bobbing,' did you say, Theresa?" I ask, pleased to ease into a first-name basis. It's like she never hung up on me at all.

"The trees weren't moving," says Theresa, "but it was like hurricane-force winds outside. Next thing I knew, my husband, Jay, was shaking me, saying, 'Where are the boys? Where are the boys?' I couldn't breathe. The smoke was so thick."

Theresa's words strike me cold. Not ten seconds in, and she's given me more information than I gathered in a month.

My notepad's on the kitchen table, but the fridge is closer. Papers droop over the Meraux Message Board. I pull so hard, a magnet tears them.

Hurricane winds, I write. *Fire*. Wind like the kind that bowled me over in Scott Wilson's apartment?

"So your husband was right next to you?" I say. If Theresa places him in the house, then why would he remain a person of interest? Then the problem clicks into place. "Theresa, did you tell the police your memory is blank?"

"They asked if I was drinking," says Theresa, "but I wasn't. I swear. I wasn't dreaming neither."

"I believe you," I say. A thousand needles prick me while I write one more word: *Fugue*. Detectives probably think Theresa contradicted herself. Sometimes Jay Nolan is in the house, and sometimes she can't remember, which opens the door to doubt.

Theresa reminds me of something I just read. I flip Scott's book to "Freeze Spell." No, this is the wrong entry.

"It's so hazy," says Theresa, "but I think those lights. I think they were another set."

"Another set of what?" I ask, tearing my eyes from a list of items. *Incense. Salt. A chicken's heart*. I pray I didn't miss something crucial.

"Flashlights," says Theresa. "Coming from the lake. Right after midnight."

1 a.m. Corvus.

Flashlights coming from Corvus Pond. The abduction happened near the water, just like Paul's. But the police don't believe Theresa because of her memory lapses. Just like the ones I had thirty years ago when I woke on a slab behind the school. And still have today.

"Theresa, it could be a forgetting spell." Took long enough to find. The book's entries aren't in alphabetical order.

"A what?" Theresa asks like I recommended a new sex position.

"A forgetting spell," I say, rushing my words, "cast so you can't remember who was there when your boys were kidnapped. Just the other week, another guy from New Minton put one on me, I think. I felt wind. Dizziness. There's a gap in my memory."

No, that's not right. The Wilsons specialize in hallucinating, not forgetting. Someone else knows the forgetting spell. Who?

Theresa takes in a breath. "I think I should go," she says.

"Think hard, Theresa. Maybe you didn't see anyone, but did you hear a car, or a van? This smoke. Was someone burning leaves off-season? Are you sure your husband was home the whole time?"

Flipping the torn paper, I forget my questions. The front side is Stephen's math test, dated today. *Mad Max says you can count to ten!*

100%. A+. The smiley face fills me with horror.

"No, no," I say, smoothing Stephen's test. What was I thinking, with my notepad three steps away? It was closer than my briefcase.

Stephen must've shown it to Karl, who put it up so Mommy could see when she got home. I didn't notice because I'm an awful mother, something Theresa confirms with hurt in her voice.

"They warned me about a preacher's daughter," she says. "Said she might stir things up with voodoo nonsense. I didn't want to believe someone could be so hateful."

"Not voodoo, Mrs. Nolan."

A crease keeps covering Stephen's name. Maybe I can steam it?

If I could just ask one or two more questions, I can help her. I know I can help find Grant and Roderick before it's too late.

Scott's book contains a section titled "Opening a Door." At the bottom of the page is Trevor's signature.

Trevor Augustus Fleming. Under that is Thomas Fleming, Trevor's dad. Others beneath it are so old they've faded. *Opening a Door* is the Fleming specialty.

"Have you ever heard of the Brotherhood of the Raven?" I ask. "Or Trevor Fleming?"

I go back to Scott's book. The next page is "Dim." George Gedney signed his name, as well as half a dozen Gedneys before him. "Binding Spell" has Jonathan Rahall and Eileen Abish. "Herbane," a type of hallucinogenic plant, includes Mather Wilson. Deborah Wilson. Scott Wilson.

The book flips, seemingly on its own, to "Forgetting Spell." That's definitely creepy. I know I didn't touch it. The air isn't on either.

A forgetting spell purges selective memories. Unlike the other spells I've seen so far, the caster doesn't need a lot of preparation. Concentrate on who you'd like to forget. Recite some lines with a quartz crystal, which holds the memories. After you memorize the words, it's simply an act of will.

Charity Drane. The name leaps off the page, constricting my breath.

I recognize that name, though we've never met. My grandmother, who's been dead forty years.

Okay, so forgetting is the Drane specialty. But how could someone cast my grandmother's spell in Scott's apartment? It was only me—

And Ellie.

No. Air comes in so tight, my heart thumps to catch up.

Please, not Ellie. Anyone but Ellie. She's been through enough.

"I know all about your family, Daphne," says Theresa, "and we're nothing like you. We're good, hard-working people. Not criminals."

"Theresa, please," I say. Decades later, and the same accusations cause the same wounds to bleed.

"And I didn't murder my children."

The phone slams in my ear. It rings, and so do Theresa's words.

I didn't murder my children.

Neither did we. I swear, neither did we.

CHAPTER NINE

July 20, 2021

I idle at the corner of Massachusetts Avenue and Melnea Cass Boulevard. The homeless call this intersection the Methadone Mile. They're humps along endless lines of fence, huddling if not for warmth, then for a few hours of peace.

Five thirty a.m., rays strike the tops of brick tenements. And they stir. The second woman I pass by is my sister Ellie.

"Want a ride?" I ask, holding out fresh clothes.

Ellie's hunched over, walking with two fistfuls of plastic bags. "Daph?" she says as though nearsighted. "How'd you find me?"

"Your blond hair stands out," I say. "Last time, it was black."

Actually, three weeks ago, I bribed a volunteer at the homeless shelter. Ever since news broke of the CARD Commission's announcement.

Once in the Prius, I see how my joke was made in poor taste. Ellie's hair is falling out. She smells of urine and vinegar. Parenting websites would inform me that the latter might be trace amounts of heroin.

My poor sister.

We stop and sit in the car at Peters Park, where people are on their phones and dogs intermingle. Ellie takes one bite of chicken teriyaki, which the boys love, and sets it back in the foil.

"So you tracked me down," says Ellie. "Guess you're here to offer me another ninety days in sunny Malibu, huh?"

"Would you go if I did?" I stare at her rough profile. "God, Ellie, I thought we'd be best friends. Gossiping about our families, retelling childhood jokes. But I can't remember them, and I think you know why." From the driver door, I pull out the Book of the Brotherhood.

Ellie doesn't look particularly surprised to see Scott's book on the console between us. "I thought I hid it better than that," she says. "I was going to burn it."

When did Ellie hide it, before or after Scott's suicide? How much time did we spend in his apartment before she rushed me outside?

Beats Jehovah's Witnesses harassing you all the time, doesn't it?

How come I couldn't see through Scott's illusion, but Ellie could?

"Our grandmother signed her name in that book, El," I say. "Charity Drane. But you knew that. Just like you know the Dranes specialize in forgetting, an ability Mom apparently passed down to her daughter." A question pulses deep in my stomach. Did Mom ever use her family's power, especially after her only son disappeared? "Which is the reason I can't gossip with you about the past. The reason I can only recall a few scant details of my childhood, is you."

When Ellie closes her eyes, two fat tears run down her face. They crack the rough gray exterior of grime that has built on her cheeks. Unlike me, Ellie doesn't get to wash Boston's air pollution off her face every night before going to bed.

"I was trying to protect you," she says.

I'm the older sister. I'm supposed to protect you. And what a good job I've done.

First Paul, and now Ellie.

"Did you cast a Forgetting Spell on Theresa Nolan too?" I ask.

"You think I'm involved?" Ellie flushes. "After those assholes lied about taking Paul?"

"So now you think people abducted Paul," I say. Though the point feels cheap. "I spoke to Theresa Nolan. She has a memory gap when Grant and Roderick went missing."

"Are you sure she's forgetting?" asks Ellie. "Because in a hallucination, you *mis*remember."

The distinction gives me pause. Ellie might be right. Theresa says she saw two sets of flashlights and empty sleeping bags, smelled smoke, then her husband was shaking her. Maybe the contradiction lies in at least one of those details being untrue. How could I ever figure out which one?

First thing I need is all my memories back.

"How long have you been placing Forgetting Spells on me?" I ask.

"Not counting the other night at Scott's apartment," says Ellie, leaving muddy smears across her face, "seven years ago. So it makes sense the seal's wearing off. Scott's suggestion didn't help."

Gerard's, too, with the postcard.

Her nose is clogged. "This was a few weeks before you got married. Karl called because you were obsessed with Dad's journals. He was worried about your mental health. I told him I could make it all better."

Outrage smolders under my skin. Thus began my tenure with the soft voice of Dr. Russell, appointments on Mondays and Thursdays. How much of my life have I missed? All those special memories we're supposed to cherish. My sister sealed them in a well, and my husband helped.

"None of this makes sense," I say. "I thought you could only cast a spell if you participated in two Blóts on the Idol on Lammas Day, 1988. In '88, we were in Hyannis. Nowhere near New Minton."

Those awful days when no one would get out of bed. I remember that. Or someone mentioned it, and I appropriated the memory.

"And what about Rusty?" I say. "He froze Clai months before Lammas Day, after only one Blót. How could he cast that spell? Where was his prayer card?"

"A rune card," says Ellie, "is for beginners or something." She takes a long, hitching sigh. All these people playing tennis and flirting, and we're in my Prius, discussing ritual murder. "You're talking about an echo."

"What else did Scott tell you?" Before he slit his throat.

Ellie wipes soot off her eyelashes. "Kids get them sometimes, if their families have been Blótting a long time. It's like a free trial. No expiration, but it's not full power either. It's . . ."

Just an echo. Strong enough to freeze a scared child and impress his dim-witted friends. Of course, the Elementals want to hook the kids as early as possible. Give them a taste of the powers to come.

"You still have the Drane echo," I say. "Maybe we find Trevor, and you make him forget about Blót?"

And stop them. But Ellie bugs her eyes.

"You think I'm any match for Trevor?" she yells. "Or Rusty? They'd cremate me on the spot." Ellie rubs her face. I remember what Scott Wilson said about Trevor eating his soul and wonder how literal my sister is being. "God, I wish I could make myself forget. Be like everyone else. Like you."

A spell doesn't work, so Ellie turns to drugs. She's been on the streets for a month, limping from her problems. Her and a thousand others. All because some parents wanted their kids to shake hands with ancient bloodthirsty deities.

"What about the commission?" I say, pulling out the FBI letter. "It starts next week. We expose their lies, you and me."

Ellie shakes her head. "You think you can dab some eyeliner on me, and the police will suddenly care what a homeless addict has to say?"

"El, please."

"There's no point," says Ellie. "The FBI can literally do nothing to help the Nolans. And isn't the dad already in jail for kidnapping his kids?"

"Jay Nolan got arrested for punching a policeman," I say, conveniently omitting the burned evidence found in a nearby pond. "Thirty-three years ago, the police made some false arrests too."

"Maybe they didn't, Daph."

Ellie's jab hurts, but I try to ignore it. "I can't find Trevor on my own," I say. "But if I can find witnesses who say he's a person of interest in the case, the FBI can depose him. At the very least, we can get tabs on him."

So far, my suggestion to offer Trevor immunity in exchange for a deposition hasn't lured him out of whatever rock he's under. But the chairman was very nice in an email, saying he would do his best.

"Go back to your family, Daph," says Ellie.

"I can't." My nails dig into the armrest.

Who can say if it was the sight of my office covered with case files, or if it was the smell of mildew blowing into Zachary's and Stephen's bedrooms. That was the moment Karl and I agreed that I should live in a hotel. *For now.*

My supervisor used that same phrase when he showed me Deborah Wilson's complaint. Extended leave *for now*. I'd take leave over termination, and I'm thankful he's that nice. For the last month, I'm living on savings with no idea how to fix my life.

Ellie grabs my hand. Again, that sense of morning sickness grips me. When Ellie mentioned a seal, I assumed she was being metaphorical.

But I feel it. Like someone loosening rope around my throat. I gasp for voices and smells I haven't thought of since childhood, even as they smoke.

It's like Odinism, right?

When the Wheel turns again, he'll hold the Door open.

You don't know this place. Not like I do.

"El," I say.

Veins thud against my skull. Too much. Slow it down. I just need to breathe.

I reach for her, but my fingers only touch the passenger seat. Ellie's outside, peering in.

"I can't go to the police," she says. "But I can take it back. Just give me time, Big Sister. Please?"

A cruiser blasts a horn at some jaywalkers. When I turn back, I see homeless headed for treatment at Boston Medical Center. I pray to see

Ellie disappearing with the others into long triangles of shadow. That might mean she's ready for rehab, too, but despite her thinning blond hair, I can't find my sister in the crowd.

CHAPTER TEN

July 26, 2021

Federal Officers motion me through security. After inspecting my carry-on, they run a metal detector down my back. I still feel like I finally woke from the last clutches of a long dream.

A horrific dream. I write about so many instances in which my marriage disintegrates that my fingers wither to stubs.

Even if, as a high-functioning mother of Quincy, I could not recall all the details, I remained protective of my past. I never wanted Karl to know it because I didn't want him to treat me the way we treat Ellie. First, his voice soft and full of understanding. Then angry, then afraid, but that's our summer. That's been so many summers.

The first thing that attracted me to Karl was his confidence. All my life I wanted people to listen when I spoke. I wanted someone to say they understood and I belonged.

I didn't get that at home, school, work, or even in a book club. Product of a broken home, a therapist said. Not until I was thirty-three, and I met Karl.

He had all the qualities I wanted for myself. And he used all of them trying to help. But I took that from him. Seeing over and over again that he couldn't fix me took that confidence away. Now Karl is murky, a purple spot in my mind.

If he were sitting on a long bench in an FBI field house with me now, though, he'd see our matrimonial problems aren't even in the top ten of worst things to happen to a husband and wife.

To my left, a feather-haired couple runs fingers around a picture frame. To my right, a bald man clutches frayed toys, eyes lost like a refugee's in the corridor's blue light.

This isn't the first time the police had them wait. They've waited since that first awful phone call. As they wept over an empty casket.

Now they stretch down the hallway, orphaned parents who received the same letter I did. They're waiting to say the names of the sons and daughters who never came home. Waiting to know why their prayers for a safe return went unanswered.

For the sake of our children, the Door must remain open.

So many. I can't believe this many.

"Daphne Gauge?"

My turn. "Yes," I say, gathering my things.

A pretty brunette keeps a door open with her ankle. She has a look of pity for us, though I'm not like the others. I didn't lose a child. I lost a family.

"Meraux actually. Gauge is my maiden name."

"Ah," she says, raising her eyebrows. "This way."

I don't know why I told her that, and the brunette doesn't either. Millennial attitude with FBI credentials swinging around her neck. She's probably an intern and thinks maiden names are for grandmas.

The anxiety churns, entering the conference room that looks more like a classroom. Rows of chairs lead to a semicircular table, where six agents in bland suits tower over us.

Their eyes leave me every time I glance at them.

Only a few occupy the chairs. I recognize some of them, despite not stepping foot in New Minton for thirty years. No one in my family, though. No Nolans. No Theresa. No Gerard Gedney. No Trevor Fleming either.

"Is that her?"

"How does she live with herself?"

Behind them, a long window dissolves into patchy clouds. From where we stand on the third floor, brick row houses sketch the horizon. Maybe that's where Boston begins.

"Ms. Gauge?"

"Yes," I say. Fine, Gauge it is, the girl I was.

The girl who wanted nothing more than to help the FBI solve a case like a sleuth might, if the feds were stumped.

The girl trapped in 1988.

"I'm Bradley Reeves," says a man, leaning forward to shake my hand. Whatever he expects to see, I'm not sure he finds it.

"It's good to meet you, Mr. Chairman. Thank you for the invitation."

Despite how handsome he is, or perhaps because of it, worms crawl in my stomach. So much of my past and present set to collide in front of these people, and my name might as well be Hitler or Stalin.

"You are Daphne Gauge. The date is July 26. The time is." The chairman looks under the desk. "Very early."

A slight chuckle from the committee. The intern directs me to a blue chair with dark stains. She drags a microphone to my lips. Its foam cover smells like coffee.

"Thank you, Vikki. And what is your occupation, Ms. Gauge?"

"I am an ethics investigator for the commonwealth," I say, fishing for a nod, a sign they see my cause as worthy. "I was."

"From the look of your reports," says the chairman, "I would've guessed law enforcement."

I redden, trying to figure if he's insulting me. "No, sir," I say.

"This is a special convening of the Child Abduction Response Deployment," he says, addressing the others as well, "a.k.a. CARD Team, whose purpose is to streamline information from the public. Given the urgency of our situation, let's get right to it."

"Yes, sir," I say. "My brother, Brady Paul Gauge, disappeared on March 31, 1988."

"I'm sorry, Ms. Gauge," says Bradley Reeves. "My understanding is that you have evidence regarding the abduction of Grant and Roderick Nolan. Suspicious postcards, is that right?"

"Postcards," I say, "that signal coordination between George Gedney, Scott Wilson, and someone else. I don't remember if my family knew of any postcards back in 1988. But—"

"Ms. Gauge." Bradley Reeves exhales into the microphone. Already, I can tell this isn't going how he planned. "Isn't that case closed? Obviously, we're aware that in the 1980s, three boys disappeared in New Minton, Massachusetts. One was found alive, one dead, the whereabouts of the third boy remain unknown. But the case is closed. We have a confession, do we not?"

I didn't murder my children. Theresa Nolan's words still sting.

"Police charged one man for the boys' abductions," I say, "but they never secured a conviction." Anxiety becomes a flush as I unpack my carry-on. "Four boys that we know of, sir, including my brother. Not three. Paul actually disappeared second."

"Abductions thirty years apart." The chairman glances at the stenographer. "What's the connection?"

"I have police reports, sir," I say, watching the men flip through notes. "Newspaper articles, photographs dating back to the 1800s, my journals, the postcards."

Last is the seven of us in a Sears family portrait. I shake handing over the five by seven. They don't really need it, but I want the CARD Team to see us before Mom died. Before my sisters ran away or attempted suicide.

"Let's admit these as Exhibits A through F." Bradley Reeves frowns with my family in his grip. "How do they help, exactly, Ms. Gauge?"

They help because they are my life. They are every moment in our ten years of marriage that I spent apart from my two kids and husband, whose last words to me were not to come here today. Actually, Karl's last words were, *How come you care more about two boys you never met over your own children*?

I hate that Karl thinks that. I hate myself if Zachary and Stephen think that as well. Those boys are the loves of my life. No one and nothing is more important than them.

But how can I do nothing when Theresa Nolan suffers at home? Every time I close my eyes, I think of her in the Wilsons' house. I may not know a mother's pain for a missing child, but I know a sister's.

Here's my contribution, these documents, which I see them marking as Exhibit A, Exhibit B.

"They're all the information I have," I say, "on who took my brother, and why. See, the abductions weren't a simple crime. Usually, a parent's responsible, a relative, or a stranger, but not then. And not now. The whole reason you convened this CARD Team Commission is you must have contradictory evidence on Jay Nolan's guilt. Evidence that's difficult to explain."

Soon as I say it, I regret speculating. Of course the FBI isn't going to comment on the New Minton Police Department's investigation. Bradley Reeves carries a strong poker face.

"If not a parent, relative, or stranger." He lowers his eyebrows. "Who else would it be?"

I nod at what he's holding. "Exhibit C, Mr. Chairman."

"A book," he says, examining it behind the plastic. "An old book?"

"A book that belonged to Scott Wilson," I say. "It contains the Brotherhood's history and the names of families who can cast spells." Sweat breaks on my lip. Names of families including mine. "If they participate in ritual murder."

EXHIBIT C

OPENING A DOOR

Our most ancient practice. And the most dangerous. It is not for the impure of heart.

The Brotherhood is pure. We know that while the Elementals appreciate the steer, their hunger burns for a greater offering. That is why, when Arcturus aligns with the Wheel, a true unspoiled unleashes the SPIRIT of the ELEMENTS. And thus portals to the chasm are paved with blood.

You will need:
White silk robe (for each unspoiled)
Raven's head (for each Brother)
Athame Flint Dagger
Sea salt
Six blue candles
One red candle
Access to the White Stone

Very important. Each Brother must be sanctified before Blót. Failure to do so can cancel the entire ritual.

—Surviving page from a sheepskin journal, author unknown, date unknown

CHAPTER ELEVEN

July 26, 2021

"Ritual murder?" echoes Bradley Reeves. "You came here today, with your postcards and exhibits, to allege that the motive for abducting Grant and Roderick Nolan was"—he shrugs at Scott's book—"Blót? Is that some sort of witchcraft?"

More people have wandered into the conference room. They take seats behind me, blinking at us, sleep lines on their faces. Their snickers burn my skin.

"I don't know if witchcraft is the right word," I say, not sure if the chairman is mocking me. "The Brotherhood of the Raven dates back to the birth of Jesus Christ."

"What is Blót, Ms. Gauge? And this *Spirit of the Elements*?"

"Blót refers to an ancient Nordic practice of ritual sacrifice, Mr. Chairman. The Brotherhood believes that two Blóts of 'unspoiled' children will open a Door to the Elementals, their gods. And those Elementals will unleash the *Spirit*, a spell unique to each family. With the help of raven familiars and rune cards, some families dim their frequency to visible light.

Others make you hallucinate. But the more they summon the spirit, the faster they transform into ravens. The ravens are literally their ancestors."

Bradley Reeves beams a large smile to the crowd. "I've always been curious how magic works," he says, to a few chuckles. "By its very definition, if you can explain it, then it's not magic, right? So thanks for that. It'd be helpful to know if these spells are all-powerful as well."

That's what Ellie thought. Yet I broke Scott's hold on me, didn't I?

Maybe my resistance had nothing to do with the deep, soul-burning pain of Ellie's betrayal. Maybe it was Ellie. She had history with Scott. The chairman's question strangely mirrors my own.

"And how did a"—he consults his notes—"'Nordic practice' manage to supplant itself in New Minton, Massachusetts?"

"New Minton was rebuilt on the town of Minton in 1734," I say, "following the abrupt collapse of a settlement some years before, believed to be Danish or Norwegian. Rumor is, some kept the old ways."

Bradley Reeves taps his pencil. "Ms. Gauge, do you recall the first time someone used the word 'Blót' in conjunction with the New Minton Boys?"

"That would be Rusty Rahall, sir," I say. "When Clai Denton disappeared."

A white-haired man on the commission interrupts me.

"Beg your pardon, Mr. Chairman," he says. "Clai's running away falls outside the scope of the commission regarding the so-called New Minton Boys. And the deponent has long overrun her allotted fifteen minutes."

No. They can't kick me out. I haven't gotten to the others, the suspects. The subject of my mother.

Bradley Reeves and the white-haired man whisper while my heartbeat quickens. I've learned to spot them, vintage black ties pinned at the chest, metal crowns when they speak. Who is he? How did he get on the commission? Thankfully, my cell provides a distraction. Henderson's texting me. He's a PI I hired back in May. In two months, he's made little progress on Scott's postcard and book. He probably wants to know when he's getting paid. A gray box slides up.

559 # back online.

559 number. The 559 *phone* number? Like I touched a live wire. He has three dots blinking, but my thumbs are forceful.

What?

Henderson responds.

Call themselves the Crusher Group.

My God. They've come full circle.

Someone sent that 559 phone number to Scott Wilson in October, 2020. Trevor sold the Fleming Quarry's crusher to Vulcan Inc. Months later, somewhere in Fresno, California, the number went active. And they call themselves the Crusher Group. Why do I get the feeling they sold the property back to themselves? Some magical way to recycle their wealth, Trevor's driving ambition for expanding Blóts.

Gerard might answer that question, along with some others. If only I could get him to respond to any of the twenty voicemails I left over the last month. The beginning of a sentence floats, barely audible.

"You have to understand she . . ."

What, is a liar? Nothing but a crazy bitch? I hear others whispering again. The dead boy. The one never found.

She had to know.

Maybe she helped.

I finish my text.

Find out everything you can.

"Okay, Walter, um." Behind circular frames, Bradley Reeves's eyes are watery. "Although time is so precious to the ongoing investigation, the committee is concerned about the relevance of Claiborne Denton, especially since we have no documentation on him."

I balk. "Uh, you should have police reports, interagency memos, and Clai's medical file I submitted. Exhibit D, sir, though as I said, some info has been lost or destroyed."

Vikki blocks the chairman, delivering my documents. Why did she wait? He talks as he reads. "Claiborne has no memory of where he was between the hours of 10:30 a.m. and 4:19 p.m. When asked if he was abducted, Claiborne responds, 'I don't know.' No mention of black magic in the report. Nothing about doors or wheels."

Walter shakes his head. *See? Told you.*

"Clai was found in the mud near Corvus Pond, Mr. Chairman," I say, "about a mile from the Nolans' house, covered in raven feathers. His core temperature was seventy-nine degrees. He couldn't speak for several days because of Rusty's freeze spell."

The chairman flips indiscriminately. "And that's what Claiborne told the police after he escaped?"

"That page is missing, sir," I say, "but the report says Clai had ligature marks on his wrists."

Bradley Reeves sees it too. He shows the rest of the committee. *Ligature marks indicating the victim had been tightly bound.* Behind me, the people rustle.

"Could Reginald Rahall have done it?" asks the chairman. "When he grabbed Claiborne by the shirt collar, perhaps he squeezed his wrists too? And it was Reginald who made those marks and not rope?"

Wow. He read that deposition quickly. Just a minute ago, it seemed like Bradley Reeves had no idea who Rusty and Clai were.

"The last time I saw Clai," I say, "he had a mark on his neck, sir. Not his wrists. Any injury on his wrists or arms had to occur after recess. After Rusty's assault."

"When Clai was found, where were you? Where was your brother?"

"Mom and I finished her errands."

"Your mother," he says, "Chastity Gauge."

Mom's name cuts through me. It's like they use it as a swear, or as a curse.

"Paul's soccer practice was over," I say, "and he should've been home with Dad and my sisters, but . . ." My lip trembles.

Bradley Reeves mulls over Exhibit E, a cassette tape, as though it's an artifact. I've had the tape in my attic for twenty years.

"This is the 9-1-1 call to New Minton Police?"

I nod. My eyes heat up.

"Can we play the tape? Let's . . ."

Speakers occupy corners of the room, our very own surround sound. At the first click, they screech. The second click, and nothing. The volume creeps up. For thirty seconds, my heart pounds to the hungry sound of static.

"I'm sorry," says the chairman. "We seem to have technical difficulties."

No. Someone deleted the call. They didn't want the FBI to hear it, but why? What was on that tape? I have a copy back in my hotel room, though it's been a while since I listened to it.

"Ms. Gauge? Could you recount the night of March 31, please? There was a cross-up, you said, where your mom thought your dad was going to pick him up, and vice versa."

I hesitate, wondering if, hoping I'm being paranoid. When did I tell the chairman about a cross-up?

Maybe he read it somewhere.

"Ms. Gauge?"

"After some calls," I say, "Dad learned that Paul was with Dominic Gedney at Lincoln Bridge." A bubble forms in my throat, hoping that after all this I don't betray Gerard's confidence and expose him to Trevor's wrath. "That's where we raced."

CHAPTER TWELVE

March 31, 1988

Panic dug under my fingernails as we rocked in the van, Brandy, Courtney, Ellie, and me in the back, Dad driving, no Mom in case Paul came home. When we left, I saw Mom pressing a box of matches in her hand. She set it down, picked it up again, and pressed. Streetlights whomped over our heads.

Before Lincoln Bridge, the trees lit up. Brandy pointed. "What is that?" she asked.

We tried to see around the parked vehicles, vans leaving and cars arriving. Dad skidded into the curb, and we hopped out. A dozen trucks congregated a few hundred feet down a bald gully, engines growling in idle.

It was just after eight p.m., though search parties first began at seven. We couldn't believe how many people had mobilized so quickly. Men in overalls, the most ardent members of Dad's congregation. Bloodhounds howling when their owners jerked them. Teenagers and a dozen police officers with a map spread over the hood of a squad car. Their cigarettes burned my throat. One man, not dressed in uniform, traced a long line on the map.

"The trail goes for another fifty miles," he said. "That doesn't include all the fishing holes and side trails."

"George?" asked Dad.

The man turned, and so did the police. He was a bank manager with a full sphere of dark hair.

"I don't believe we've met," said the man, shaking Dad's hand. "George Gedney. Dominic's father." Our eyes went to the back of a squad car, where behind a fogged-up window, seven-year-old Dominic lay asleep. "I got here as soon as I could."

"Thank you, George," said Dad, nodding earnestly. "Dominic was the last to see Paul, is that right?"

"Dominic knew to come home right after practice," said Mr. Gedney. "Instead, he says the boys came here to throw rocks at fish. About sixty yards down that way."

Mr. Gedney pointed where the Little Housic River burbled and the trucks' headlights thinned. In New Minton, the river wasn't much more than a green stream that housed tires and old appliances, black shapes in the darkness. Visibility ended at maybe twenty feet.

I went back to Dad's van and grabbed his measuring tape. Mr. Gedney said sixty yards, and I decided to measure it like a detective reconstructing the crime.

Since the tape only went twelve feet, I marked the end with a rock. From that spot, I measured again. Twelve times fifteen was sixty yards.

"Stop being a dork," said Brandy, trying to smack my behind.

Mr. Gedney looked pained. "Brady knocked Dominic down," he said. "He spit on Dominic, then ran down a gravel road. That's another eighty yards toward the gate. Dominic went to check, but Brady was just gone. I'm so sorry, Mr. Gauge."

The measuring tape snapped with a growl. Why had Paul and Dominic fought?

No one else questioned the statement. Dad covered his mouth, his eyes glowing.

"Okay," said Brandy, nabbing a man's flashlight. "Let's go."

"Bean," said Dad.

"Dad." Brandy stomped. "How come I'm still being treated like a child? I've got, like, *the* most endurance of anyone here. And if anyone's qualified to travel a rugged wooden path, it's definitely me."

"Well," said Courtney, reaching for another person's light, "I want to help too."

"We don't even know where we're going yet," said Dad. "Let's get all the information first before we traipse into the woods, okay?"

The police assigned grids. One of them, a short man with a comb-over, oversaw the whole thing—Chief Boyd. As he worked, Chief Boyd tugged his felt uniform.

"Last night, I dreamed about the woods," he said. "Suppose that's what they call a hunch? It's my first one, to tell you the truth, and I'm not sure how I feel about it just yet."

The people chuckled while Dad prayed with the men in overalls.

"'No one can come to Me unless the Father who sent Me draws him,'" quoted Dad, holding hands, "'and I will raise him up on the last day.'"

I was glad to see the conviction in the other grownups, for rather than search for Paul, the men looked ready to burn a girl for being a witch.

Miffed at being rejected, Brandy and Courtney complained to the other kids. One of them was Brandy's boyfriend, Jeremy, a boy with heavy eyelids and a scruffy neck. He asked what they were doing later, and Brandy shook her head.

"What, babe?" he said.

"I think it's wicked sick, what they do," she said.

"It's just some candles and a pendulum," said Jeremy.

"It's like Odinism, right?" Courtney beamed like Jeremy was captain of the football team. "But I heard the Brotherhood predates all those groups. They get their beliefs from German and Norse mythology and stuff."

Brandy wasn't impressed. "I heard Trevor used a knife on squirrels," she said.

"They hurt squirrels?"

Mr. Gedney pointed to more markers near the river and relayed the distance between them. An inverted image of him swam across Courtney's lenses.

"We're really not supposed to like talk about the Blót stuff anymore?" said Jeremy. Instantly, my ears pricked. The Brotherhood and now Blót. I veered toward them, still measuring. "Look at her, Junior Detective."

"I have to live with her," said Brandy.

"But hey," said Jeremy. "No one's hurting anybody. Okay? It's just people exploring themselves in nature, like what you do on Sundays."

"Is Derek gonna be there?" asked Courtney.

"Ick," said Brandy. "He is nothing but pimples and shaggy hair."

"I like his hair."

"It's revolting," snorted Brandy.

"Guys," I said, "what's Blót?"

The kids shushed me. Many shook their heads, glancing nervously at the adults.

"Don't you say that word ever again, Daph. It's a bad word."

Courtney was stern, but I persisted. "Like a swear word?"

Their stares were unblinking, which was fine because everyone was saying something different.

Scott said Blót was stabbing a steer and smearing its blood on Hangman's Hill. Rusty wanted to Blót Clai, and he and David mulled Blótting me where they killed the steer the night before.

For Brandy's boyfriend and company, Blót was *exploring themselves in nature*? Why shift and rub their necks, like the subject of S-E-X came up?

One thing Jeremy and Scott agreed on, though.

Whether squirrel or steer, Blót involved stabbing someone with a knife.

Near the municipal trucks, Dad handed out candy bars, filled canteens, and argued with Chief Boyd.

"Lookit here, Reverend." Chief Boyd gestured to the river, the sand, the rocks. "If a stranger comes up on your son, he's going to fight, right?

Kick up some dust, tear clothes, leave something behind. You see any of that here, sir? Boys just ran away separate, I'm telling you."

Boys. Chief Boyd must mean Clai and Paul. They didn't know each other. Who was saying they might run away together?

Pondering the scene only made Dad more flustered. "He's been missing *five hours*, Randy. Without food, or water, or shelter?"

Dad's question was loud. Mr. Gedney had finished, and another officer, Officer Mercer, consulted his clipboard. "*Before* we fan out, we have the boy's father, who wanted to say something."

Dad shook his head at the ground.

Chief Boyd held up a folder. "We got some pictures," he said. "Of Brady Paul somewhere." He passed the photographs to the men, who glanced for a moment before handing them off to the next.

"Once you get a look," said Officer Mercer, sounding out of breath, "fan out. Follow your officer, and please follow his every instruction."

Chief Boyd patted Officer Mercer on the back. "Good, son. Real professional sounding." Grizzly men rumbled downhill with metal tanks and flippers, and Chief Boyd hollered, "What'cha gonna do with that, snorkel? Hell, the river ain't more than four feet deep here, gentlemen."

Each group, armed with dogs and flashlights, trucked down their assigned path, their lights pitching like a boat caught in a tempest. My sisters pouted that everyone, including high school kids, got to search and they had to stay. Our brother's name echoed until they passed the gate. One sister had no problem being excluded. Ellie sat on her haunches, clouding the river's floor with a leaf's stem. She watched me lay a new rock at the muddy banks of the shoreline.

A pink wrinkle looked like it had sliced the furrows of Ellie's forehead all the way through an eyebrow. Unlike the rest of us, Ellie didn't mind wearing Brandy's hand-me-downs, mostly oversized T-shirts that featured one basketball camp or another.

"That is so *bor*ing," she said, then reached for the measuring tape. "Wait, I want to try."

Height was one of my few advantages over my younger sister. I raised the tape, and Ellie hopped on her toes, her heart beating hard against my arm. "When Bran and Court aren't here," I said, making sure they were indeed out of earshot, "I'm in charge, El. Fine, I'm a sleuth-for-hire, and you're my assistant."

Ellie bent the measuring tape, liking the warbly sound it made.

"But you have to keep count, okay?"

"Fine," Ellie mumbled.

Our sixth rock brought us to a steep cliff, impossible for a child to ascend. Dominic's account had been so measured and concise. Why would it be off now? That wasn't the only thing that didn't make sense. Last year, Paul pushed another boy for kicking an anthill. He wouldn't hurt a fish.

I went back to the municipal truck and measured again, careful of the glass. Kids had thrown bottles against the concrete walls, where a spotlight made them glitter under a goat's skull like the broken teeth of old men. Another search party formed back there.

They tightened straps, grumbled about mosquitoes. One of them was kicking something. I peered around the truck's bed. Sand, as it turned out, lines in the sand whose points went under the truck. It looked like a faded star. Another tried to stuff something into his pocket. When the man saw me, he held it up. A black sock.

"See how each tine of the star points to an element?" he said, shotgun under his arm.

I didn't answer. Even though Dad was pretty close by and these people were nice to help us find Paul, I didn't feel comfortable with a stranger addressing me so boldly. Like he was challenging me.

Or knew me.

The man gestured to where one "tine" ended at the Little Housic. "Water," he said. "Earth." He pointed to the rocks rising up the embankment. "Air."

Ten feet away, someone had laid rocks in a circle. Clai and I were forced to make that shape this morning. Kids called it the Door.

"And fire."

Men bumped past me. I didn't think I screamed, but one glared with white-blue eyes. Their campfire still smoked. They were kind enough to join the search party, but watching them fade into twilight, my stomach clenched.

"The fifth element is the unspoiled," said the man who remained. "On the second Blót, he goes here, on the White Stone."

He stomped the ground he'd overturned. Where he picked up the sock.

A long sock, large enough to fit a shin pad. Like that torn purple T-shirt behind the school.

"Go ahead," said the man, sliding a hat over his face so that I could only see his mouth. "Tell the preacher I said the unspoiled needs to be starved pure. You won't see him again till Lammas Day. See if he'll act surprised. See if anyone believes you."

When he walked away, I could breathe again. And think.

Four elements. Plus a fifth for the unspoiled. And that long black sock.

"Hel*lo*," said Ellie. "I'm asking you like an important *quest*ion."

In the back of my brain lay a thought my sister punted into a crack. I reached in, searched, fumbled. Dad called for us, and I snatched it.

"Daddy, Daddy," I said, and ran toward him. "Paul was wearing soccer clothes. Wasn't he, Daddy? Wasn't he wearing soccer socks because of practice?"

I pointed, but the men were already at the gate, veiled in shadow.

Starved pure. You won't see him again till Lammas Day.

"Ooh, *soccer*." Ellie kissed the air as they did on daytime television. "I love you so much, *soccer*."

"Uh, okay, Marnie," said Chief Boyd, lowering his BE4370 radio. The joking demeanor was gone. "George, Missus Gedney called the station worried sick. David isn't at home."

Mr. Gedney blinked, his face stretching to process what that meant. "N-no," he said, sounding like Clai behind the school. "No, no. David's in his room because I grounded him for causing another ruckus at school. He had to pick up his brother Gerard, then he was to be in his room until I got back home. Is Loretta sure?" Mr. Gedney looked up. "David's not just hiding under the bed or in a closet?"

Dad grasped Mr. Gedney's shoulder, exuding an aura of sympathy. Dad was the kind of man who never wavered in helping the lost, the tired, the unfortunate.

And the less devout the better, for Dad nurtured his faith the same way he might strengthen his immune system by stepping into the mist of a sick man's sneeze.

As Chief Boyd spoke into the radio, Officer Mercer updated another officer in a whisper. "Mrs. G heard a thump," he said, "and checked to find David gone along with his backpack and some clothes." I wondered how much of this the general public was supposed to hear.

"Say again. Marnie, say again."

Static. Then a woman's voice.

"Mrs. Gedney says the bedroom window's busted. Two sets of tracks leaving the house. And a neighbor says he saw an adult male prowling in the Gedneys' backyard."

"No," said Mr. Gedney, his breath clouding. "That's not right. David's not supposed . . ." He trailed off, squeezing his eyes shut, the news crashing over him. Fire burned through my veins. I swore Mr. Gedney was about to say, *David's not supposed to go missing.*

If not David, who was supposed to disappear?

"*Daddy*," I shouted. Seeing how upset Mr. Gedney was, I thought the sock mattered more than anything.

Dad grabbed my hand and frowned at me, black hair sprouting from his nose. If my demands made him impatient, given the stress of losing Paul and his dissatisfaction with Chief Boyd's answers, he didn't let it show. He never gave a mean look to his daughters, but he hadn't wanted us to come. He'd wanted us to stay home, protected against poison oak and rocks and all the dangers he said slouched in the forests of a small town like New Minton.

Even when we begged to go, we weren't sure he'd relent. We had to be good, he said. Had we been good? Without active supervision, I wasn't sure.

"We have to get back, Pumpkin." His voice was soft enough to make me cry. "The sheriff's waiting at home for Daddy."

CHAPTER THIRTEEN

April 1, 1988

The first glimpse I got of Sheriff Colquitt was a white-haired man with topographic maps. He told Dad the search had to be called off after a boy broke his ankle, the whole time surveying the ceiling as though we called about a leak in the roof. Again, I asked Dad about Paul's soccer socks. He told us to search the house. For Paul's socks?

"For Paul," he shouted.

We checked the washer and dryer, all the cubby holes. My labored breath lifted spider webs in the darkest recesses of our home. Paul wasn't hiding, not anywhere we could see. My sisters collapsed in the living room, making posters to help find Paul. I was in the middle of telling them the story when Brandy took all the glitter.

"Because some man kicked up some *dirt*?" asked Brandy. "He must be a criminal then."

"It was a star," I said. "In the sand. And the fifth point was for Paul's sock because he's an unspoiled. They're hiding him until Lammas Day. Does anyone know when that is?"

"Doesn't prove anything, Pumpkin, even if you're right. Which I *highly* doubt."

"In the dark," said Courtney, sticking a piece of scotch tape to each finger, "obstructed view, everyone blabbing about Lammas Day. You combined all the town talk in your mind because you have a tendency to exaggerate, Daph. Remember last time?"

Now, wait.

"*Whoa.*" Ellie waved over Brandy's sign. *Find Paul Gauge,* it read in thick swaths of glue. "You can't do that."

Brandy indirectly acknowledged Ellie's protest by pelting the glue with glitter. That was it. Nineteen signs complete, leaning against the spinning jenny in the corner, and no more bright colors.

"I saw it, though," I said. "Ask El." Though I couldn't think of what the man looked like, let alone describe him.

Ellie wasn't interested in coming to my defense anyway. She slammed the carpet, upsetting my design of popsicle sticks. "We're supposed to share, Bran. Mom? Didn't you say we're supposed to share the glitter?"

Mom and Dad were speaking to a group in the kitchen.

"How about we start in the Flemings' backyard," said Mrs. Kouts, who owned the General Store along with her husband.

"The Leeds' backyard, right?"

"That way the reverend can . . ."

"Work on his speech," said Mom, a bandanna across her forehead.

"God's sending signs in threes," said Dad, "and you want to cancel Easter Sunday?" The others looked down, as uncomfortable as I felt hearing Dad sound desperate.

"It's always the same with you guys." Ellie gloomily inscribed a smiley face in the *P* of Paul's name. "You gang up on us and you cheat."

Courtney proofread as if her sign was experimental medication. Brandy's marker squeaked.

Mr. Mellinger, the town librarian, adjusted his spectacles over our posters, his hair brown and prim. "Very nice, girls," he said, taking them.

"A child is missing," said Mom, "and I left him. That's the mother I am."

"We're going to find him," said Dad, holding the front door for Mr. Mellinger and his armload of our crafts. "Boyd said there's programs now." The screen door clattered, then it squeaked. "They teach kids to leave something behind, like a shoe or something."

Or a sock. Maybe it really belonged to that man and his . . . did he have a mustache?

Yes. A white one.

How many people in town have white mustaches?

A really annoying creak wouldn't let me think. It was a long, agonizing sound like a mouse unscrewing brass mounting. Just when I glanced at the patio's doggy door, something shiny flopped onto the welcome mat. Everyone else kept coloring.

If I made a big deal about what just happened, Brandy might dismiss me. But she also might take over, so I played it casual. "Does anyone have the blue marker?" I said.

"Mom took it."

"I need that glue, Bran."

I hopped up, my butt asleep.

On the mat lay a white envelope. That was odd. We usually didn't get deliveries via Badger's old doggy door. Inside the envelope was a typed note:

According to George Gedney's initial statement, a black truck with dark windows followed Dominic and your son Brady to Lincoln Bridge. Dominic claims the truck was driven by a fireman who told the boys "they shouldn't be out without their parents."

None of this information is included in the investigative report. And the police are not following up on it.

The first tip comes free of charge. If you'd like more of my services, please make out a check for fifty dollars to Zebra Investigations and leave it in your mailbox this Sunday.

I am so sorry for your troubles.

"Uh, Mom?" I said.

The patio was empty, the room a gritty brown. Compared to it, the kitchen sparkled, though the piles of lilies and roses suggested Mom hadn't gotten to the breakfast counter yet. Just two nights ago, Dad and I watched heat lightning with me on his lap.

"But Brandon," said Mom, following Dad outside, "the Denton boy was hysterical. The bruising on his arm."

"Didn't you say the hill kids were neglected?" asked Dad. "Neglected, not abducted. So let's not even go there. Okay, Chastity?"

Mom's retort got lost with a knock on the door.

So did that mean Paul had been kidnapped? What happened to Clai's arm?

The phone rang. Instinct took over my spinning thoughts, for I greeted the caller as Dad instructed: "Good morning, this is the Gauge residence, how may I help you?"

"What are you *doing*, Daph?" said Courtney.

"Who is calling, please?" I said, squirming from Brandy and her grabby hands. No need to shout. Or topple the art supplies.

I couldn't hear a thing, then the caller's voice hissed in my ear.

"Daph, who's Baja Buggy?"

"Baja Buggy," I said, my eye twitching. How did this weirdo know my name? "That's my brother's favorite toy. Why would you ask about that?"

"Is someone on the phone?" said Mom, blazing from the stairs. The hair on my arms rose as her footsteps quaked. "Who's on the phone? *You're not supposed to be on the phone.*"

"He keeps crying for it," said the phone. "Says it will help him sleep."

My stomach hardened. "You're with Paul?" I said. "Where?"

On the other end of the line, some metal spun like a top. "Blót's a secret I can't tell, Daph. But when the Day Star returns, he'll hold the Door open."

Mom ripped the phone out of my hands, flinging my sisters and me into the cabinets. Had Mom meant to push us so hard? Maybe the floor was still wet from when she mopped.

"Who is this?" she said.

Courtney pointed from the kitchen tile. "He's got 'im. He's got Paul."

"The Bad Man's back maybe," said Ellie, cradling her skinned knee.

"What did he say, Pumpkin?" Brandy shook me, black eyeliner running down her face.

"I. I." I was hiccupping, copper filling my mouth, the PI's note trembling in my hands. Black truck. Fireman. Police *not following up*. "Baja buggy. Blót and doors. Paul crying."

Mom's face darkened. "You hand him over," she said, "you hear me, you sick son of a bitch? I swear to all holy—"

The line went dead. Mom crumpled under the stools, blubbering. No one could understand her. A tissue, did you want a tissue? She batted it away, her face broken. What, Mom, what? Her dress rode up, flashing her fearsome bush. We lay in a heap until Dad found us, trying to nurse wounds that couldn't be closed.

CHAPTER FOURTEEN

April 2, 1988

Who abducted Paul?

What was Zebra Investigations?

Why didn't the sheriff tell us about a fireman driving a black truck?

A world-famous sleuth would answer the questions in no time, but all night I wrestled with them. Then all morning. No one left their rooms. No one ate. No one told us to get out of bed.

In the afternoon, a dozen policemen set up camp in our living room to tap the phones. They unbuckled industrial suitcases, zipped wires across the living room as if to keep a lion at bay. Mom trailed the men, a bucket of bleach in hand.

"Daddy doesn't have time to look at drawings, Pumpkin," Dad said, ignoring the note I shook. In all the confusion yesterday, I accidentally held on to it, and now its type had tattooed my skin, smudged words running in reverse. "They have to check your room, too, girls."

"It's because only two percent of missing children involve a nonfamily member," said Courtney, plucking the bottom of her shirt so that it wouldn't accentuate her stomach. "Investigators can't take our word that we searched the house already."

"And how do you know all this?" asked Brandy, and Courtney shrugged.

A suitcase lay open on Mom and Dad's bedroom floor, half of Mom's clothes pulled out. The scene looked a lot like Grandpop's from yesterday.

Because Mom packed up.

If Grandpop hadn't been so upset, and if Paul hadn't run away, would Mom be gone again? Maybe that was why no one could find her when Mr. Corwin asked me about Clai.

"Pumpkin," said Dad, "this is Sheriff Colquitt. He has some questions, okay?"

They divvied us girls and took statements. One deputy with peppered stubble, his nameplate reading Bixbee, appeared uncomfortable interviewing Brandy, who was swaddled in contraband: lipstick, mascara, and a shirt advertising her midriff.

The sleuth books said that you could tell if someone was trustworthy by looking into their eyes. But I felt like Sheriff Colquitt's milky blue irises gleaned much more information from mine than I could from his.

"You were the child present at the break-in," he said, "and you're the one who answered the phone, is that right?" I nodded and his pen clicked. "What's your name, little lady?"

"Daphne Gauge."

The break-in. Ellie mentioned the Bad Man, but I completely forgot about the burglar. What Mom might call a *transient*.

As the sheriff wrote, I recounted that, two weeks ago, I came in from walking our old dog, Badger, and found the Bad Man rummaging through Dad's desk. When Mom saw him, a smile quivered as though the Bad Man tried to be cute with her. "Oh Bad-ger?" she said. "Free meee-eat." She sang it, like a hymn.

Then the Bad Man panicked and slammed into the patio door, leaving the crack on the window I pointed to, and he disappeared into the woods. But what did the Bad Man have to do with Paul?

Dad glanced nervously at the sheriff's notepad. "I'm sure your mother didn't say it like that, Daphne," he said.

"Bad Man?" asked the sheriff.

"Ron Abish." Dad scratched his forehead. "It's, ah, all there in the report."

"The Clifton firefighter you mentioned," said Sheriff Colquitt. "Do you know what kind of vehicle he drives?"

Dominic claims the truck was driven by a fireman who told the boys they shouldn't be out without their parents.

My mouth went dry. Ron Abish was a fireman for the next town over.

"Ron hasn't been in shape to be a firefighter in decades," said Dad. "When I picked him up, he was living on the street."

But Ron Abish could still own a T-shirt with a fireman logo. He could've been wearing it yesterday at Lincoln Bridge.

Where he spoke to Paul and Dominic.

"I mean, lots of people could want to hurt our family." In the living room, Brandy played with her necklace. "We're very wealthy *and* Ron Abish's, like, mentally unstable."

I frowned. He is? And we are? I knew Mom and Dad didn't work, and yeah, that was odd, but we had a thirteen-inch TV with one rabbit ear.

My eyes swept the table, where the note was hidden somewhere in the piles. If only I could get my hands on it again. Maybe I overlooked some detail. Did anyone see Paul get into Ron Abish's truck? Was Paul forced in?

Sheriff Colquitt looked up. "And yesterday's phone call?"

"Hm? Oh, he said there were Doors and Blót. And Baja Buggy, my brother's favorite toy. The kidnapper could've known about it only from Paul." A metal clang, too, but it was difficult to remember clearly.

"Good," said Sheriff Colquitt at my story's conclusion. "Very detailed, Sweet Pea."

Despite my reservations, I felt a tingle when he called me Sweet Pea. I liked his breath too. Coming from his mouth, the spearmint coffee smelled heavenly.

"The day Mr. Abish broke in," said Sheriff Colquitt. "Did he say anything to you, Daphne, or . . ." He glanced into the living room, where Mom knelt. While the police worked around her, Mom sprayed Glory rug cleaner over the carpet. "To your mom?"

I shook my head.

"Then how did you recognize the voice as belonging to Mr. Abish?"

Sheriff Colquitt waited patiently as my cheeks burned. Dad said it was the Bad Man, not me. But each time I tried to speak, my throat clicked. In front of me was an upturned lip of mac and cheese. It was one of fifteen pods of tin foil stationed across the table, drop-offs of cheese broccoli casseroles and carrot cakes and the like from our neighbors, Mrs. Leeds and Mr. Mellinger, some as far as ten miles away. Because no one refrigerated them, rainbows now formed in the hazy pool at the bottom of each plate.

Sheriff Colquitt scratched a long line across his notepad. "Okay, now. Okay, Sweet Pea. Did you speak with Brady? Did the caller make any demands? Ask for money?"

"Mom yelled at him," I said.

"Okay," said Sheriff Colquitt, and he nodded at Dad.

"Go wait with your sisters, Pumpkin."

I excused myself to the kitchen, where Courtney and Brandy debated whether the call was a crank. Ellie told an officer Badger was in a farm upstate now, one we'd never seen before.

"That's helpful, right?" she said, twitching her nose. "I knew it would be."

In the dining room, Dad's interview continued in a hushed tone.

"We know Ron Abish landscaped for the Gedneys," said the sheriff. "Would he know the Rahalls-sez too?"

What about the Rahalls? Did he mean Rusty's family?

Dad shrugged. "I hate saying anything bad about Ron. He lost his wife to booze, his kids to drugs, you know?"

"He has an open warrant for kidnapping, Mr. Gauge. From back in '82. The child was under sixteen."

"Sheriff, what?"

He leaned in close to Dad. "The Rahalls-sez son, William, was last seen playing in his backyard. And now he's missing."

"Oh God." Dad covered his eyes.

"You see how this changes things?" said Sheriff Colquitt. "Yesterday, the assumption was, we were strictly on a recovery mission. Now we got three missing boys, and at least one unidentified adult male."

"I was trying to tell Chief Boyd a million times," said Dad. "I said, 'No way these kids ran away at the same time.'"

Four, if you included Clai. It was like they forgot him for some reason. And who was the second unidentified man?

An accomplice. How else could Ron Abish coordinate the abduction of four boys in a period of seventy-two hours?

"What that means is," said the sheriff, "all the boys went willingly with their captor or captors. Was your son Brady friendly with Mr. Abish? If Mr. Abish came up to him and said, 'Mom and Dad asked me to pick you up,' would Brady go with him?"

My stomach tightened. Paul was that trusting.

Downstairs, the screen door groaned to a close, the living room empty of everyone but Mom, a bull's-eye of sweat growing on her chest.

"I saw him last week." Dad shook his head, the weight of the news paining him. "Ron. Didn't seem right, him getting in trouble for taking a few bucks. I didn't know he was a kidnapper."

"Some real weird shit about doors and a Day Star," said Deputy Bixbee. He was talking to a policeman who buried a necklace under his collar, an orb and two half crescents. "Trying to scare them. You ever hear that before?"

"Ron was on Hangman's Hill," said Dad. "I believe he wanted to pray one last time, but . . ." Dad tapped the table. "Not in the church."

Sheriff Colquitt shook his head. I felt the question but couldn't hear it. *Where*?

"You ever been up there, Sheriff? Opposite the church. They say it's a harmless tradition, but you ever seen it, what's left?"

Sensing the intrusion, Sheriff Colquitt nodded at me. "Don't frown, young lady," he said. "Voice analysis can tell us the ethnicity of the caller."

He was stunned the phone rang. Amplified by speakers, it echoed for a long time.

"Bad Man calling back?" said Ellie, frowning. "Didn't see that one coming."

One policeman donned giant headphones. Others scrambled behind him. They flicked switches. The tape rolled.

"Okay," said Sheriff Colquitt, "in these scenarios, there's usually a ransom. You do the talking, but we'll guide you through it."

Dad nodded, his face grim. He squeezed my hand so hard he could break my bones.

"This is Mountains with a View. Will you accept a collect call from . . . ?"

We glanced at each other.

"Douglas."

Dad closed his eyes as though he would cry. The officers sighed. It was Grandpop.

"You'll know the Day Star is coming," said Grandpop, "when they wet the Fulcrum. They will feed the boy's blood to the White Stone at the Fulcrum. You hear them screaming for it down the halls. Charity. Charity, come back for me, *please*."

Charity, my grandmother. Mom always said how smart Grandpop was. He wrote a book on Aleister Crowley, once dubbed the Wickedest Man in the World. But he sure sounded crazy.

"Yes, accept call," said Dad. He quietly assured Grandpop as Mom rose from the carpet. She removed her bandanna, leaving her black hair matted.

"No. You're still not listening." Mom's face trembled as though cockroaches crawled under her skin. "Between eating overcooked manicotti and drinking our coffee." Deputy Bixbee blushed at his mug. "You're really focused on us as suspects, isn't that right?"

The sheriff's face clouded.

"Now, Mrs. Gauge, I can assure you everyone in my department's going to treat you without prejudice. What a mother did or did not do twenty years ago is irrelevant to—"

"Well, it might be," said Deputy Bixbee, shrugging. "If someone in the Sobaski family feels like they got an axe to grind."

I looked to my sisters. What were they talking about?

"Honey," said Dad, hanging up the phone. He looked sadly at the tennis bracelet that sparkled from Mom's wrist, a gift following the break-in. "They're here to help."

"You don't know this place." Mom's eyes turned glassy. "Not like I do. All the children who never get heard from again, whose last name isn't Denton. No one cares, and no one remembers. It's not just wine they're spilling on the Idol at Litha. I was three, but I remember. Of course, the police call you crazy or they're in on it. Will you help me, Brandon? Will you help me find our son?"

Mom searched Dad's face, her will pitted against God's, everything they couldn't acknowledge or resolve. Other than taking her hand, nothing formed in Dad that would return Mom's gesture.

CHAPTER FIFTEEN

April 3, 1988

Police took two days to canvas Hangman's Hill.

They began in the unusually thick red spruce and circled upward. In wetter years, they might see waterfalls, but that spring, all they found were ledges of stone swept clean. Shelves where the roots gave way. At two thousand feet, the church nestled in the false summit. And the true peak inscribed with a chalky circle of bald rock where the Idol once stood.

Dad's church had a wood frame and a steeple sixty feet high. On a clear day, Main Street's pedestrians could view it as an ignited strip of magnesium. Average weekly attendance hovered around forty. Sometimes the loudest noises were the parishioners scuffing their shoes.

He was optimistic that, given time, he could attract half the townspeople. But the audacity of its size, and its obnoxiously sapphire murals, mainly drew tourists, skeptics, the desperate, those who believed Dad was eccentric, even slightly mad.

To build a Georgian cathedral was one thing, but who would come to a gaudy megachurch buried in the Berkshires?

The Sunday after Paul disappeared, the answer was five hundred.

The Gedneys and Wilsons sat in front, baking in the murals, part of the largest congregation we'd ever seen eager to hear from a man who spoke with God. Mr. Rahall draped his arm around Rusty in the back. Though laid off since Christmas, Mr. Rahall still wore his auto body uniform, A–F Collision Repair. I shook my head. They couldn't be bothered to dress up even for church. Dad ascended the pulpit, glowing with casual ultraviolet magnificence. He set a brass chalice on the podium and flicked a lighter. Outside, we heard flashbulbs and police speaking low out of respect.

You'll know the Day Star is coming when they wet the Fulcrum.

My sisters dismissed Grandpop's phone call. Agitated state, they said, but his words haunted me.

We learned about fulcrums in Mrs. Patowski's class, one of the earliest machines. What fulcrum did Grandpop mean? How did one "wet" it?

"How do we reunite with ones lost?" boomed Dad. "On this day, Jesus Christ reunited. 'He has risen, just as he said. Come and see the place where he lay.' Gospel of Matthew 28:6. Jesus reunited with life because he is the Word become flesh. He is the son of God and a man. What does that mean?"

We snapped to attention like an army, ready to hear a wise answer.

"Jesus is of many elements. He is the rolling stone. He is the angel whose 'appearance was like lightning.' Jesus is earth, water, wind, and yes, fire." The flame's waxy scent floated to us, and a few chuckled. "Jesus is proof that God wants the elements to unite."

Dad's imperious stare latched on to Mom. She had craned her head to meet him, and her attention did not shift. She seemed to follow Dad's every word, like someone who listened to a child's nightmare but didn't believe a monster lurked in the closet. Whatever Dad saw in her eyes caused him to lose his place, and he needed a moment to review his notepad.

"As you leave today, ask yourself, how can I help reunite those elements so dear to us? God and man, parents and sons. We hope wherever our boys are now, they will be returned to us safe."

Usually, Dad's sermons were lighthearted, telling how his children brought him closer to God. Rarely did he use a prop.

But today was different. With that last suggestion, "wherever our boys are now," Dad meant *whoever* has our boys now. Both parents essentially believed the same thing.

Ron Abish's accomplice was in our church.

The awkwardness of being a Unitarian minister and distressed father was not lost on Dad. He stood in his black robe at the open double doors as he always did after a sermon, shaking the hands of those who departed. At the Gedneys, Dad had trouble keeping his eyebrows still.

"George," said Dad.

"Mr. Gauge," he croaked, extending a hand. Strange that he didn't address Dad as Reverend. His hair, four days ago so thick and full, was now a silver wisp. "This was never supposed to happen. You understand?"

Dad acted like he did. "The Lord tests us, George. We have to put faith—"

Mr. Gedney snarled, ripping his hands away.

"George," cried Mrs. Gedney.

"*What*?" George turned on his wife. "What are they going to do?"

Both he and Dad grimaced at the sight of Deputy Bixbee, who didn't seem to know if he should get in line or wait. Mrs. Gedney bounced the bundle in her arms. Stirred by his daddy's voice, it babbled cutely.

"Anything, Deputy?" asked Dad.

Deputy Bixbee shook his head, though the Gedneys didn't wait for the deputy's answer. Mr. Gedney hobbled across the parking lot as though his hips might give out.

I narrowed my eyes. Dad basically asked if there was any sign of Ron Abish. The answer was no. If he wasn't on Hangman's Hill, someone must be hiding him.

"Just remember," said a man leaning into Dad's space. "'The Lord loves discipline.' Can't get enough of that shit."

If Dad was offended, he didn't show it.

"'For the Lord disciplines the one He loves,'" he said, quoting Hebrews 12:6, "just as a father, the son he delights in.' Thanks, by the way, for reminding me of that last part."

Parishioners chatted and ate cookies, the last of those from a packed coffee hour. Courtney served them with a large grin while Brandy devastated old men by playing with her hair.

They ignored Dad and the man with a white beard, leather jacket, and potty mouth.

"That's why you don't got to get anxious. He *delights* in you the way you delight in your own boy."

"Now you're in Matthew," said Dad, covering his mouth. "'Therefore *I* tell *you*, do not be anxious about your life.' You come all this way to bust my balls? Or to threaten . . ."

Brandy pinched my arm for something, but I wriggled away.

"I'm here to help, Lewie."

"No." Dad softened his voice. "That won't be necessary."

"I can get these people to listen," said the shape. "But we're going to need what you owe. The Hilltowns haven't made you forget, have they?"

"I don't forget nothing."

Soon the man was a smudge in the light.

Dad clapped our members' hands in both of his. He grinned in their faces. After they left, his expression soured. I hesitated, having never heard Dad speak like that. A double negative?

"Sometimes I feel like I'm talking to an empty room." Dad shook his head and saw me watching the smudge get into a Lincoln. "You remember Uncle Toby, don't you, darling? One of Daddy's oldest friends?"

The police were already gone, their boot prints evaporating on the lot. Uncle Toby's Lincoln rolled over them, so shiny compared to the dull ones, then disappeared behind a switchback. The note clearly stated the kidnapper drove a black truck, not a town car. But why would Uncle Toby threaten Dad? Why wouldn't he help search for his nephew?

CHAPTER SIXTEEN

July 26, 2021

The commission adjourns for the day. Bradley Reeves and the white-haired man quickly pack and head for the door.

"Never mind the expense, Walter," says the chairman. "We have to exhaust all possibilities, no matter how implausible. Even if the evidence against Jay Nolan appears strong."

"It's been eighty-four days," says Walter. "If Nolan was going to cooperate, he would've by now."

I watch them leave. What do they have on Jay Nolan? And what is Walter's last name?

Packing up takes a few minutes, especially when I pause to jot down a few notes. Odinism, Courtney said, though I don't remember finding much there. And anyway, the Brotherhood didn't call him Odin, but rather Wodan.

My phone has a news update. *Earthquake in Western MA . . . 1.4 on Richter scale.*

They're hungry for you, said Scott. *You feel it in the tremors.*

I can't wait for Henderson anymore. I dial the 559 number, which I memorized, and get an automated response.

Please enter your voicemail password.

They're communicating through that number, leaving voicemails. Then I hear an automatic *click, click, click*. I'm trying to figure out what it means when the lights go out.

"Hey," I call.

The men murmur in the hallway. I follow.

And smack into darkness.

"Hello? Chairman Reeves?"

The benches are empty. Flags folded. The only lights are amber squares every twenty feet or so. Notices glow from the shadows as though floating. A flap of something from the ceiling leaves me on edge. I hold my breath, listening for the sound to repeat, and jump when my phone rings.

"Hey, it's me," says Henderson, his voice gruff.

"Hey," I say, breathless. I make sure no one's behind me, then head for the elevator. My suitcase rolls like a tank.

"Crusher Group is a subsidiary of Vulcan," says Henderson, "based in Fresno. I guess you knew that."

"I guess."

The elevator won't work. Its lights are off. You need a keycard, I think, leaving me with the stairs. The door booms. Each step takes my suitcase down to crash against my heels.

"I was granted access to the Crusher Group's assets." Henderson means he hacked it. His initiative is why I hired him. "Seeing how it's three dozen vehicles, loaders, bulldozers, and personnel vehicles, it was an easy list to go through. I'll send you an email."

Crusher Group's assets are some vehicles? That's it? "What about their voicemails?"

A door booms above. I look up the staircase, my throat dry. *Boom-boom-boom-boom.* Someone's tumbling downstairs.

Toward me.

"Sixteen-digit password," says Henderson, "double verification. Very difficult to bypass, but get this. Two days ago, Boston Police cited a 1987 Dodge Ram for running a red light. Crusher Group lists that Ram as a company car. Never heard of a twenty-year-old company car before. You still there?"

"I'm here."

Someone's in town. Maybe Trevor Fleming himself.

Maybe he's in the building looking for me.

I'm almost to the first floor when I see a shadow gliding down the stairs. Third floor. Second floor. It's a blur almost on top of me. By the shape, I say a man, though nothing about his movement makes sense. *He's running full speed, and doesn't make a sound.*

"We just want to go back to how it was in the old lands, Daphne."

The words echo from halogen lights. From the Fire Exit sign. Everywhere. So familiar, yet I can't say if it belongs to a man or to a woman.

The door's right there. Every nerve fires for me to escape, yet I can't move.

"You are a Drane," says that strangely blank voice. "Your blood must commune with the Elementals."

My traitorous legs take me up three steps. No. I dig my nails into my wrist. Like the one my little sister buried a razor in. The one a classmate's mom damn near pulverized.

The pain explodes, and so does my cry. Yet my steps take me to a dark space between the harsh lights. Foul breath lands tender on my neck.

Someone's there, dressed in black.

He grabs my arms. I can't scream.

"We got our intruder," says a voice. A *man's* voice.

I snap awake with him locking my elbows. Lights glow monstrously bright. I shake off the fist-to-the-temple dizziness as blood pumps back into my legs. I gain control over them again. And I reclaim my voice.

"Let go of me," I yell, and he does, telling me to *calm down*.

The man isn't wearing black but dark blue. He has a shield on his chest. A security guard in his late forties with a curly gray mustache.

I look back to the stairway door ajar, my suitcase preventing the door from closing. No one else there.

And I pull my hair back.

"Intruder?" I say. "I was being deposed by the CARD Team Commission. Ask Bradley Reeves, the chairman." I try to walk back to my suitcase, my heels wobbling like I've never worn them before in my life, and pull out the envelope that arrived two weeks ago. "The letter they sent?"

The security guard asks for my license. He calls it in. Less than a minute later, my heart making quick *tap-tap-taps*, his radio responds, something garbled I can't understand.

"Okay, ma'am," he says, returning my documentation. "Proceed to that door." He points to an Exit sign. "And head straight for your car." Back into the walkie-talkie. "Zulu, I'm headed up the northwest stairs. Let's see if we can pin him down."

"Who's up there?" I ask, uncertain on my heels. "How did someone break into an FBI building?"

The stairway door swings to a close, it and my question booming. Something else swings. On my suitcase handle. A mottled white ribbon.

I stare at it, my wrist shaking, drenched in sweat. Could it be an old luggage tag?

No. It's not paper. The ribbon's made of silk. And it definitely wasn't there before. Only a few times in my life have I seen a ribbon like that.

I'll drink and you'll drink, and you'll tell me, won't you?

Drink and exchange dark secrets.

"Eileen," I call out. Rusty's Mom. "Eileen Rahall, are you here?"

Holy hell, would I appreciate an answer.

Nothing.

I cut off the ribbon with my keys, and kick it into a corner. Thank God, I have an exit. The distance across the dark lot stretches for miles. I run, feeling like the closer I get to my car, the closer I am to someone grabbing me by the throat.

Then I'm in my car, and out of the security gate.

It's only six p.m. The sun is shining. The day is pleasant and warm. Children play outside. A few blocks down the road, and the FBI's stairwell feels like a dream I can barely remember.

"Henderson?"

"Still here. Everything okay?"

Of course he is. He'll keep the meter running as long as his phone has batteries.

"The Ram that ran a red light," I say. "Who was driving? Was it Eileen Rahall?"

"Uh, that's weird." Henderson rummages. "The police report doesn't have it."

"How can the report not include the driver's name?"

"Well, if you want . . ."

Henderson's saying he can reach out to his BPD contacts, but what's the point? The driver paid off whoever gave the ticket or, more likely, a higher-up redacted that crucial piece of evidence. Those assholes.

"I'll get back to you," I say. "Thanks."

I pull over to read Henderson's email. A black 1987 Dodge Ram. License plate 831-ARC. Here we go.

Whoever's driving that truck—Eileen, Trevor . . . it's got to be Trevor—but *whoever's* driving has to be here to testify before the CARD Team. Get his word on record. I'd be ready for that.

If it's Trevor.

I have three missed calls. Karl and I agreed to FaceTime at five thirty before Karl's parents took the kids out for pizza, and I forgot. Now it's seven. FaceTime shows the unflattering curvature of my sagging neck.

"They're asleep, Daphne," says Karl.

"Already?" Usually, good luck getting Zachary and Stephen in bed before eight.

"Why don't you call for breakfast," he says, "if it's convenient. If you're not too busy playing detective when the police have all the documents they need to solve this thing."

My stomach churns. Karl's mocking me, though I never told him about my dreams to be an amateur sleuth.

Something else, too. The eerie parallels between Mom and me. No one believed her either.

"There's something about New Minton," I say, "the documents can't tell you. You wouldn't believe what just happened."

A voice cuts into the phone. "Stephen can't have no orange juice."

"Who's that?" I ask. Immediately, I'm suspicious of the woman's double negative, the same speech pattern Dad tried to hide. And why is Stephen asking for juice? Didn't my husband just say the boys are in bed?

"I hired help, Daphne," says Karl.

One with hair exactly my shade? "So you hired a replacement wife," I say. "That's great. I'm gone three weeks."

"I can't believe you're coming at me with that. Who's the one out all night with this kid Gerard?"

"Please." In the rearview mirror, I see my lips quiver, remembering people whispering about Mom's transgressions. "Gerard Gedney's the only decent one of them. Poor kid was shut in half his life. The only time you'd see him is after chemotherapy, banging on the glass."

I still remember being eleven and running for my life from the Rahalls' house. Gerard was at a window on the second floor.

"Huh," says my husband. I'm annoyed he snaps my memory, even more so that he's apparently over our latest argument.

"What?" I say.

"It's just that." Karl sighs. "Gerard'd be sleeping all day, Daphne. If you're sure he just came back from chemo." His voice softens. "Just leave it there, Terry, and I'll grab it later."

When the chemo was at its worst, I dreamed about a boy, my older self, telling me I would survive. But . . .

Gerard had said more, leaving me dumbfounded. Then who did I see in the Gedneys' house?

What had Gerard been trying to tell me?

"I got to go, Daphne," says Karl, then he's gone.

The plunge from terror to confusion leaves my insides hacked out. Traffic blares by, blurry through tears.

How come you care more about two boys you never met than your own children?

Nothing's more important than them. Nothing.

Yet I'm in Chelsea, being chased by phantoms. On my phone, calling Gerard three times, replaying what he said about an older boy. What did Gerard mean?

Then I scroll through a list of all the hotels and motels in a ten-mile radius of the FBI Field House. During a holiday season, most of them would be booked. No such luck now. A weekday in late July leaves two hundred twenty-four possibilities.

If I find an old Ram with those plates in any of those parking lots, I'm one step closer to finding Grant and Roderick Nolan.

CHAPTER SEVENTEEN

July 27, 2021

Nothing.

Until dawn, I spiral out from the FBI Field House. Parking structures, pay lots, even nearby street parking. No Dodge Ram, no license plate 831-ARC.

I go back to the hotel long enough to brush my teeth. I need to get moving, but instead play the 9-1-1 tape. It works fine. Mom crying. Kids slamming things. Nothing obviously suspicious. Maybe Bradley Reeves was right. Maybe it was just another technical glitch.

Or maybe someone didn't want the CARD Team to hear Mom's voice in a sympathetic light.

A FaceTime call to Karl quickly gets rejected. Unavailable.

Then I head back to the FBI Fieldhouse, and sit on bench alongside grieving parents, waiting for the CARD Team to call my name. No sign of Gerard.

Behind the conference doors, the chairman asks a question. Someone answers.

I lean forward, and the chairman booms, "Did Derek Robinson ever tell you anything about Bill Abish and why he broke into your home?"

Derek. That was my sister's "gumdrop," what we used to call our crushes. No sooner do I think of her name than Courtney answers.

"No, sir." On the other side of the whitened glass, Courtney sounds more nasally than normal.

"Did he ever discuss the Brotherhood of the Raven?"

"No, sir."

I excuse myself through a group of three, realizing the conference door is ajar. It opens with a clang.

Of the fifty or so sitting in chairs, those nearest turn, exaggerating surprise. Day two of the commission has already convened with a splash of light on the FBI seal. The sun grows from a long window to my left, sharpening the men's cheekbones. Just like yesterday, Bradley Reeves sits in the center of the U-shaped table, hand up as though he's shooing away a waiter.

"Your testimony, Mrs. Sullivan," he says, "contradicts your sister Daphne Gauge's on a number of details." My stomach gets a zap. Courtney's married name. The stenographer follows the read out, mouth agape.

I move along the edge of the room, where aides stand with clipboards, stretching my neck to find Courtney over the seated crowd, when a groan begins in my stomach. Last thing I want is to have the same argument my sisters and I had in 2010, especially in front of the FBI.

"Daphne has a very overactive imagination," says Courtney. "Mom and Dad indulged it because they built this elaborate fantasy world for us to live in."

I won't let myself blush, which is difficult when a few dozen people notice me slip past the American flag. There, I halt at the empty witness chair. The committee seems oddly absorbed on the chairman's desk. I don't understand. Where is my sister?

"They never had real jobs," says Courtney from all around, "yet lived in a mansion. Owned hundreds of acres, an entire mountain, practically. How could they afford to build a giant church in the middle of nowhere, which just happened to be Mom's hometown?"

The speakers. Courtney's on a video call. The men are staring at a laptop, its back to us. Someone lowered the projectors, but they're black. At least the audio's working finally.

Vikki sets up enlarged photos of the Nolan boys beside the commission. When she sees me, she drops Grant facedown, and all but rolls her eyes, giving me another visitor's badge along with a note.

Last night there was a security breach. Exhibits A thru D stolen. Please keep this info to yourself.

Exhibit D was the Book of the Brotherhood. Whoever was in that stairwell with me last night was after the book. They wanted it from Scott. I intercepted it. Now they have it back. Whoever sent those postcards has them back.

"Tobias Halpern," says the chairman, "was the chief financier for the Second Unitarian Church."

"The Uncle Toby who wasn't our uncle," says Courtney.

We're going to need what you owe. The Hilltowns haven't made you forget, have they?

I scan the crowd behind me. Of course, it's absurd to think whoever stole the book would be sitting there, when a wrinkled old lady leans into my face.

"Just wanted to say hi, Daphne," she whispers.

Eileen Rahall's black-and-white hair is long and stringy, clipped with a raven's broach. This close, it breathes of almonds. She's swaddled in a ratty wool cardigan that looks like a nest. If her head hadn't shrunk, I would think her fiercely wide eyes and open mouth were botched surgery, the sparrow look from like ten years ago.

Except not a sparrow. Eileen Rahall resembles a raven.

The more you use the power, the more you become like them.

Eileen Rahall looks like a raven because she's using the Elementals' power. I guess the Brotherhood isn't as chauvinist as I thought.

"Caretaking," she says, eyes on the photos of the Nolan boys. "Brings one so close to children, don't you think?" The chairman questions Courtney, but I can't understand them. "Before the dad said I was stealing things."

A python wraps around my gut. "You babysat the Nolans?" I say, loud enough to irritate a member of the committee.

Eileen pats my shoulder. "All those hotels you visit," she says, "you'd think you'd be better rested. Take care of yourself."

Rusty's mom's spying on me. Why tell me that? Why tell me she babysat the boys?

"Because Eileen told the Brotherhood to take them," I say.

Time came for a new batch of unspoiled, and Eileen offered up Grant and Roderick. Jay Nolan pissed her off for some reason, so they cast blame onto him.

The chairman glances at me. Belatedly, I hear his tone, winding things down. "We appreciate you taking the time to speak with us today, Mrs. Sullivan."

"No problem," says Courtney. I can't help but rush to the committee, wanting to show my sister that I'm here, when I catch a glimpse of her, now light blond and riddled with split ends. They cut the feed. The lights grow brighter.

"Ms. Gauge," says the chairman. "Since you're here, um . . ." The awkwardness of his pause makes me wonder if I've cut the line. "Why don't we follow up on a few things?" He gestures to the witness chair. "Your sister mentioned the initial meeting with Sheriff Colquitt on April 1."

"Mr. Chairman," I say, sitting, hands shaking on my briefcase. "May I request a private meeting in your chambers? My sister Courtney wasn't present at many of these events."

Those around me laugh at my request. *In chambers. Do you see any chambers?* Nor is my sister's testimony the only thing to talk about. I search the room for Eileen's iron hair.

Bradley Reeves offers a paternal smile. "We're trying to gather statements from all parties," he says. "Was April 1 the first time your mother, Chastity Gauge, mentioned the possibility that she, or anyone else in your family, might be suspects?"

The question spins me. "Is that your purpose, Mr. Chairman?" I say. "To dig up dirt on my parents?" Just like they're digging up dirt on Jay Nolan now.

Bradley Reeves lies against his chair, an unflattering sound of flatulence. "Ms. Gauge, I'm trying to ascertain your mother's emotional state during this time. As I stated yesterday, we have a confession, do we not?"

"Neither Mom nor Dad confessed, sir," I say, resisting the urge to look back. Maybe Eileen's here to intimidate me. After leaving the ribbon on my suitcase last night, she wants to throw me off my game. Though how could an old lady outrun at least two security guards? "I'm in the middle of explaining how we tried to find my brother amid a morsel of clues. Clues that were clearly tampered with. They had us looking down the road, instead of under the bridge."

"Ms. Gauge, can we back up? Are you saying there's a connection between the Door drawings you made behind the elementary school and the star you saw under Lincoln Bridge?"

"The Book of the Brotherhood had a drawing," I say, unpacking my briefcase for the relevant file. "Of a star inscribed within the Door. I can't say for certain, but my best guess is they depicted the second Blót."

Soon as I say the phrase, *can't say for certain*, I wish I could take it back.

They're going to think I'm a hysterical woman. I can tell by the way Bradley Reeves partially closes one eye.

"So under the pretense of searching for your brother, some townspeople erased a diagram of Blót and removed evidence from the crime scene, is that correct?"

"Yes, sir."

"But you didn't recognize any of the men in the search party?"

I feel my cheeks reddening. "Not until the arrest, Mr. Chairman. As I said, it was very dark outside."

"Which brings us to Ron Abish," he says, reading. "The prime suspect you allege abducted four children for 'ritualistic purpose.' You believe he wasn't acting alone."

"They weren't."

"Why before and after those abductions would Ron Abish hang out on Hangman's Hill?"

"I can ask the same question Dad asked the sheriff in '88," I say. "Mr. Chairman, have you ever been up there?"

Bradley Reeves passes to Walter black-and-white photographs of a monolith on the Hill's bald summit. A funnel of black mass over the tree line. Homes reduced to nothing but stone foundations and broken sticks.

"You're alluding to the Idol," he says. "We've heard testimony about it. Could you explain in brief what the Idol is?"

"Only the most awful thing in the world."

"It's a landmark, is that correct, Ms. Gauge? Or it was. Erected in the late eighteenth century, believed to resemble an 'ancient hörgr in Gamla Uppsala, Sweden.' Am I saying that right, hörgr?"

The chairman's quoting Grandpop's article, published in 1958. It's never been entered into a database. You can't find it on Google. Harvard said they don't have any surviving copies, but I scrounged one up in, of all places, the main branch of the New York Public Library.

A white tower leaps from Grandpop's illustration. Composed of mottled stone, each slab is estimated to weigh half a ton. *Sixty-eight alens in height*, Grandpop wrote in the margins. Since an alen measures distance from the bend in your elbow to the top of your thumb, your average hörgr rises to approximately one hundred fifty-three feet. Steps are carved in the back for the *gothi* to ascend. A rectangular chamber flows into the hörgr's four corners, each representing the elements. Earth, air, fire, and water.

"A hörgr is not just any landmark, Mr. Chairman," I say. "It's an altar, considered sacred, used for sacrifice until 1953."

"What happened on June 7, 1953?"

"About an hour before the infamous Worcester tornado," I say, "an F3 tornado struck New Minton. It killed six people, injured eighty, and destroyed over three hundred homes and businesses, including the Idol."

Bradley Reeves's face crinkles. "What's strange," he says, "is the kind of buildings the tornado hit. The oldest Catholic Monastery in Western Massachusetts."

"Where in the 1700s, three nuns were executed for practicing witchcraft."

"A Lutheran Church, a Unitarian Church." The chairman waves his arms. "In every other city in America, the first thing that gets rebuilt is a church. But from 1953 to '78, New Minton did not have a house of worship in town limits. That's hard to believe."

"Some held service in their kitchens," I say, "those who were Christian. Others had the Idol, and now it's back. First thing the town did with a little extra money was bring it back."

I feel the people behind me, their heat. They may not be consciously moving their mouths, but something's going on in their throats, a collective growl. They don't like me talking about the Idol.

Especially not to the FBI.

And Eileen Rahall's among them.

"Exhibits G, H, and I," says Bradley Reeves, oblivious and cheery. "Could you take us through them, please, Ms. Gauge?"

"New Minton was old," I say. "By the time the county seat of Pittsfield was incorporated in 1761, New Minton had graveyards. Unlike the other Hilltowns, New Minton predates the county that presumes to govern them, and globalization only enhanced the divide. Most land was unsuitable for farming. No big rivers, so there's no mills. Railroads built around them. Maybe the plan was for the town, and the people, to be self-sufficient. Blót where no one can see you. Then comes Dad."

My last conversation with him replays in my head. *You know what it's for, right*?

"Dad was young, ambitious," I say. "He thought with enough help, he could change bad people to good. That's why he built the church on Hangman's Hill. That's why they wanted to tear it down."

"Who wanted to tear it down?" asks the chairman. "Who were your suspects, besides Ron Abish?"

Pinned to the wall of my hotel room is my list, men and women the New Minton Boys would trust, someone who could be strong enough to betray that trust. Someone that all the boys, from Paul to Grant and Roderick Nolan, would see on a daily basis.

The list has eighty-nine names and counting, including a woman sitting in the conference room.

"Ms. Gauge?"

"The fifth," I say, "marked the first time I met Trevor Fleming and Eileen Rahall, Rusty's Mom."

CHAPTER EIGHTEEN

April 5, 1988

My sisters argued in the bathroom. Because I was the first one ready for school, I read the newspaper, whose front page featured an article about Billy Rahall.

He disappeared sometime between 2:30 and 3:30 p.m. three days ago. They didn't know exactly when because Billy's mother, Eileen Rahall, called the news before the police. Sheriff Colquitt was quoted venting his frustration. *She let fifty journalists muck up the backyard*, he said.

I stared at the crack in the patio door, wondering why Mrs. Rahall would do that. Instead of an answer, something bright winked through a break in the fog. A white figure floating until I lost it in the trees.

"Oh," said a voice from the kitchen. Our neighbor Mrs. Leeds, far too young to be a widow. Everyone thought her milky, voluptuous figure and amphibian smile was the prettiest. She bent over some dark boiling pot. "You're so precious at this age. All sandy from last night's sleep."

"Good morning, Mrs. Leeds," I said, not having any tender feelings for the white crust on my eyelids. This was the third time she'd visited in three days, cleaning the house and warming the platters. I appreciated her help, but each second I stood here, that white figure got farther away.

"I can see why he gushes about you," said Mrs. Leeds.

What? A kettle screamed. Something was ready, and it reeked of jasmine. Taking advantage of the distraction, I galloped down the stairs and went outside.

A town car idled at the end of our driveway, its rear covered in fog.

Now would be the perfect time for the spy camera I ordered from *Boy's Life*. My first snap would be of a fuzzy blob wagging from the town car's passenger window like an excited dog, the windshield green and foggy. Except the blob revealed herself surprisingly quick. Mom.

She withdrew from the window and the back of my hand flamed with pain. I examined the oozy insides of a mayfly I'd vivisected with a swat.

"Hey, wait," called the driver, waving something. He slid off the driver cushion, standing almost as tall as Mom. "The date."

A date? Why would Mom be talking to a strange, shrimpy man about a date?

"Oh, sorry," said Mom, as though British, and bent over the roof.

The man slid his sunglasses to the edge of his nose. "Make it out to M.N.," he said.

I didn't like this, not at all. Especially not since I noticed the van's brake lights scuttling down the driveway at two in the morning. It returned just before dawn, headlights off. I made a mental note to check our van's odometer.

Headlights clicked on and the car rolled back. Had Mom been looking up, she would have seen me. But she reserved her frown for dark thoughts scrolling across the driveway, waddling with a cardboard box pressed against her belly.

"Donna Leeds and her perfect body," Mom mocked. "Donna Leeds and her stinky tea. Snooping through our things."

She slammed the front door, and I sprinted up Hangman's Hill's Road, each breath clouding the way.

The trees folded behind Mrs. Leeds's house, where she lived alone in a large but uninspired colonial manor, a wedding gift from her in-laws. I remembered how many months it took for them to build next door.

Mrs. Leeds's manicured property gave way to black markers of wet stone. Unlike Clai, Dad never took me on a hunt, so I had no way of knowing if, one, this tunnel of underbrush was a path, and two, this was where the figure had gone.

Then it rounded a tree and grabbed me.

Sparks of heat shot down my legs. A man. A man with a platinum ponytail so close in shade to Paul's he could be a twin, except older.

But with my slicker on, the man found no purchase. I socked him in the chest.

My actions surprised me, but they were even more surprising for the ponytailed man. No match for gravity, he fell into watering jugs hanging from Mrs. Leeds's garage. The jugs tottered as though on a seesaw, scratching a long black line down the white paint. Over the last three days, I saw levers everywhere.

You'll know the Day Star is coming when they wet the Fulcrum.

If I could just figure out what Grandpop meant. If he meant anything at all.

Maybe this man knew. He was pale, dimpled. In that moment, he was probably cute too.

I also thought he was dangerous, which was why I stomped on his toes.

"The hell, man?" The ponytailed man's voice cracked, and I realized that he wasn't a man at all. "Do you have any idea who I am?"

"No," I said. "Who are you?"

"Clocking me from behind is gonna get you in big trouble, man. Oh, my dad . . . it won't matter why I was here, when he hears about this." I kicked a jug at his knee and the ponytailed boy flinched. Apparently, he thought it, or the mud, would do more damage than it did.

"I'll do worse to you, the most hurtful things you can imagine." I tried to think of how to follow the threat, when I remembered how Cindy

Temple from *Mystery of the Midnight Message* always knew the perfect question to ask a suspect. "Do you know Ron Abish? Do you?"

"He-he uh. Drove sometimes. For my dad. And book studies on Friday nights."

"Who's your dad?"

"Thomas Fleming. He owns Lumber and Construction." He flinched. "I'm Trevor."

I fell back at the name. Like a hammer striking my knees.

"You're Trevor," I said, "who uses knives on squirrels?"

"Yeah, so?" he said. "Everyone was practicing for Lammas Day."

He continued whining. Trevor Fleming, in-laws to Mrs. Leeds, who was in our house right now, who sat behind us in church. In a matter of seconds, my list of suspects tripled.

"So Abish would drive your father's trucks," I said. "Any of those trucks black? Was he driving on March 31?"

The ponytailed boy wiped mud from his face. Rain caused his black eyeliner to run.

"You're like a girl," he said. "A little girl."

Vaguely, I sensed my grip slipping on a power I'd possessed for the first time, the ability to intimidate. "Is Ron Abish your accomplice?"

"You Jesus freaks. You have no idea who you're dealing with." He groaned to a sitting position. "Listen. You can't tell anyone I was here. I mean it."

"Just tell me where my brother Paul is," I said. Blood thudded in my temples. "Before they wet the Fulcrum."

The ponytailed boy massaged the back of his neck. While I sacrificed the last of my advantage by stepping backward, I summoned enough courage not to bolt when he stood.

"I'm a Raven now, you understand that?" When I didn't answer, he assumed the inflection of an adult. "Soon I'll be as strong as my dad, and if I want, I can demolish your daddy's church like that." He snapped his fingers. "Now you better not follow me. Woods are no place for a marked girl."

I fumed that he bossed me around, that a trusted neighbor like Mrs. Leeds betrayed us. Mostly, that I was getting nowhere with these suspects. I needed the boy who got away. The one who maybe saw the kidnapper and lived to tell about it.

I needed to talk to Clai Denton.

He would sit next to me all day; the "Ds" were always paired with the "Gs" for some reason, like my name. He'd tell me everything about Ron Abish, his hideout, and who was his accomplice. And maybe Clai would know what Trevor Fleming meant when he said I was a *marked girl*.

CHAPTER NINETEEN

Except Clai couldn't.

"Clai has poison oak," said Mrs. Patowski from her desk, a fleece vest making her look masculine. "Out two more weeks."

She shuffled papers, leaving me with nothing but Clai's empty chair. I'd been staring at it all day, though I didn't remember asking about him. I remembered talking, to myself, I guess, about what Chief Boyd said, what the sheriff said. If they had any leads.

Things Mom said.

Had Mrs. Patowski asked me something about it?

"Oh," said Mrs. Patowski. A warm hand guided me out of class. "I wouldn't ask anyone else about the Door or Blót. Just an old folktale. Okay, Daphne?"

"Just an old folktale," I said, my eyes swimming down the hallway. I bumped into Mr. D. bent over, revealing a plumber's butt.

"Keep getting stuck in the vents," he said, trying to yank something out of the air duct.

Kids gawked, but I didn't see the sizzling stick figure as a dead bird until Mr. D. laid it beside another two. My stomach tightened, but I couldn't look away. With their feathers cooked, they looked more like bats, except for the black tongues hanging out.

In the middle of the group was Ellie, speckled in neon paint, trailing her signature odor of ham and peas. The smell and her clicking a flashlight roused me. Red. Blue. Clear. Red. Blue. Clear.

"Hi, Ellie."

My sister acted as though we'd never met.

"What are the red and blue lights for? *El*?"

"Uh, red's for the Germans? Blue's for the von Trapps? Like, *duh*." The other girls erupted in giggles as they entered the auditorium. "I'm, like, so sorry, guys."

The door closed, revealing Rusty embroiled in a drum solo, with the lockers as his snare. My stickers escaped the worst of his rhythm, but my neighbors weren't so fortunate.

I stopped next to him, and he dragged a zipper up and down. "Oh, uh . . . hey, Daphne," he said. Copper hair tumbled into his hooded sweatshirt.

"Hey," I said. My patience burned.

"The other day, uh . . . the game was stupid. And it wasn't cool."

"No, it wasn't," I said, and tried to leave.

"Can you just wait a minute? *Geez*. I'm trying to, like, apologize."

The lockers absorbed his weight with a *thunk*.

Rusty saying sorry was unthinkable. He never liked me and never would, not after I got him suspended.

I didn't mean to be a rat. I just wanted to solve the mystery. It was the first time I felt good at something my sisters hadn't already taken. Okay, I picked up reading from Courtney, who considered every page with quiet dedication. But Courtney moved on from mysteries after, like, a summer.

The boys quickly slapped me out of my newfound confidence. The memory cocked a snarky comeback on my tongue.

But Rusty stunned me with glowing eyes. The typical arrogance was gone. A haunted misery took its place. "I told Billy he was too young to play Blót," he said. "But he went to the quarry with a knife."

"I know it's tough, Rusty," I said, "but you can't blame yourself."

Part of me wondered what the quarry had to do with Billy's disappearance in his backyard. Another part saw Mrs. Patowski joining the kids at the vestibule. They wore ponchos like me, sounding like tents when they moved.

Mr. Corwin was in swift pursuit, slipping into a coat, a secretary scuttling behind him. "Varsity teams' search is canceled," he said. "Inclement weather."

The news chilled my heart. I couldn't question Clai, I couldn't search. Now what was I going to do?

"Billy was just goofing," said Rusty. "But he ran away. Billy was telling him it was okay, when he stopped short, and . . ."

My eyes snapped to Rusty. I missed something he said. "Billy was telling who?"

Rusty glared at the group, leading me away. "Paul," he said.

I shook my head, my balance untethering. "Paul was at Lincoln Bridge. With Dominic."

"Paul got hit in the back of the head," said Rusty. "It was an accident."

"Billy did this?" I didn't care who heard me. I didn't care if raising my voice went against school rules. "*Billy* did this."

I meant to charge, but the tile pitched my balance down a sudden decline. Rusty caught me. His skin exuded an odor of onions and chocolate milk.

My hope that this whole thing was some big misunderstanding, that Paul got lost and maybe had amnesia while some sweet old lady took care of him—all that got ripped away. Tears burned my face. To think of how scared Paul must've been, at the quarry with an older boy like Billy Rahall. A boy he knew not to hang around.

"Sh, it's okay, Daphne," he said, still holding my shoulders, "it's going to be okay. We'll solve this together. Like those books you like?"

"Solve? Solve Paul's accident?" I batted Rusty away. "How'd they get all the way to the quarry without being seen?"

"There was like a van that just showed up out of nowhere. And Billy's supposed to do what an adult says."

Something was wrong. I just didn't know what.

"Are you sure Billy said *van*?" I said. "Not a truck?"

A black truck with dark windows.

A fireman told the boys they shouldn't be out without their parents.

"The man said the boys shouldn't be out without their parents," said Rusty, and my blood ran cold. That matched M.N.'s note word-for-word, all except the truck part. "Paul's like bawling, so the man said he'd bring him."

My question was breathless. "Bring Paul where?"

"To the hospital, Daphne."

"Did Billy recognize the man?"

"The homeless guy." Rusty squinted. "What is it?"

I finally understood the horror of the situation. "That was Ron Abish," I said, and followed Rusty's nod. "Six days, Rusty, and you're just telling me now? Billy could have identified Ron Abish and his van." Who, according to Trevor, sometimes drove for Trevor's dad. "The police could've put an APB on it." Just like they do on Dad's favorite show, *Dragnet*.

"The police ain't got a clue," said Rusty. "I was trying to get Billy to tell Mom and Dad. He was scared to get in trouble."

The part about the police rang true. No wonder all the information seemed illogical, absurd, even insane.

"Ron Abish took Billy to take care of loose ends, Rusty. If you'd said something before..." My voice broke, and Rusty wiped my cheek. For some reason, his touch didn't feel that bad. "At least we'd be looking for Paul in the right place."

Ron Abish could've taken Paul anywhere by now. Paul, who needed to see a doctor.

"Rusty," I said, "I need to know everything about Blót. What a marked girl is. And wetting the Fulcrum."

Rusty nodded as though submissive to a presence I couldn't see. "We'll go to my house."

Lights flicked off at the end of the hall. I couldn't see Mrs. Patowski or the other kids anymore.

"Okay," I said.

Rusty led me out of the school. We passed through the basketball courts and entered the woods, not far from the path where we played Blót.

"The Fulcrum is the quarry," he said, crunching twigs. "That's how the Wheel turns and keeps us safe." His eyebrows lowered. "How do you know about wetting it?"

"Heard it around," I said, not wanting to give up my source. The sky mixed into pallets of white. It would be the last significant rain of the spring.

EXHIBIT K

DATE 11-13-2023 **BY 90505/AUC/DOH/CARD/LCS Derivative**

Department of Justice
Federal Bureau of Investigation
Special Commission of the
Child Abduction Response Deployment (CARD Team)

Sworn Testimony
Deponent: Reginald Rahall
July 27, 2021

Q: We'd like to hear from Reginald Rahall. Of course, if you prefer, Mr. Rahall, we can send you right back to MSP.
A: What? I'm being good.

Q: When did rumors begin about "witchcraft" being the cause for the New Minton Boys' disappearance?
A: That's just it, Boss. A rumor don't really, like, have a beginning? *(Laughter)*
A: Bitch ruins my life, and that's funny to you guys, huh?

Q: Did you begin the rumor, Mr. Rahall, and afterward tell Daphne Gauge that your brother, William, struck Brady Paul Gauge with the handle of a knife?
A: Don't say his name. I told them guys already, I won't talk about my brother.

Q: Will you talk about Blót, Mr. Rahall? Tell us what it is and how it was introduced to you?
A: I don't remember much. I got this addiction now.

Q: What are you addicted to, Mr. Rahall?
A: Like painkillers. The other guys beat on me 'cause I was hanging with a twelve-year-old allegedly.

Q: Let the record show that in 2016, Reginald Rahall pled guilty to indecent assault and battery on a child under the age of fourteen.
A: Why you gotta go and do that with my mom here? I thought we were having a conversation.

Q: And received a ten-year sentence. Mr. Rahall, at five p.m. March 31, 1988, witnesses saw a truck or van leaving the area near Lincoln Bridge.
A: Doesn't sound like much of an eyewitness. Can't tell a truck from a van?

Q: At 6:15, another witness says a matching vehicle was "driving reckless" leaving Fleming Quarry, this one without working headlights or taillights. Mr. Rahall, do you recognize this vehicle's description?
A: I know you want me to say it's the Rett van, but no.

Q: Can you identify the driver?
A: Sorry, man.

Q: Mr. Rahall, was the Rett van the same van that allegedly transported Brady Paul Gauge from the scene of his abduction under the pretense of bringing the boy to the hospital? Did Martin Abish drive, or was it someone else? Perhaps your father, Marvin?
A: This is bullshit. I'm done here.

Q: Mr. Rahall, will you answer this, please? On April 5, 1988, did you convince Daphne Gauge to come to your house promising to explain how Blót was responsible for your brother William's assault of Brady Paul Gauge?

A: Don't say his name. Don't say his name.

Q: Mr. Rahall—

A: There's a lot of shit they ain't telling you. They put me in a mental hospital. They used electroshock therapy on me. I grew up in foster homes.

Q: What were your intentions of bringing Daphne to your house, Mr. Rahall?

A: You're talking to a dead soul, all right? I don't remember nothing about Billy. I don't remember nothing about my parents. It's like I was born in prison.

Q: Was it to hurt Daphne, Mr. Rahall? Was it to hurt her?

A: I don't remember.

CHAPTER TWENTY

April 5, 1988

Through the walk, I regained my sense of self. And I pelted Rusty with questions.

Did Billy mention if Ron Abish had an accomplice in the truck? A guy with a white mustache? Why would Clai have to wait in the earth three days, but for Paul, it's been six?

Still the behemoth remained unanswered: how did Paul get to the quarry two and a half miles from Lincoln Bridge without anyone noticing?

Rusty wasn't detail oriented. He either said, "No idea," or shrugged like I was Mrs. Patowski. Once in his house, he dropped my backpack on top of his. Particles of dust swooped around us as if on the hunt for one another. Copper mold ringed the ceiling. The television looked like someone had filled it with root beer.

"How come Abish called our house," I said, "but not yours?"

"Are you coming?" asked Rusty from the cellar door.

Why was he just standing around? I clapped my hands. "We're trying to find our brothers, aren't we?" I said. "You were going to show me Blót."

"They're not going to find him," he said.

"Find who?" I said. Rusty's eyes swam, then he descended the basement stairs. "Find who, Rusty?" I tried to follow, but fell into Mrs. Rahall, a woman with large ears and a smile like a shark.

"That looks nice on you, hon," said Mrs. Rahall, fixing a white ribbon around my wrist. "Are you thirsty?"

"Yes, ma'am," I said, my stomach churning. Who weren't they going to find? I wanted to tackle Rusty and shake him until he answered, but etiquette trapped me. Mom would be furious if she found out I was rude to Mrs. Rahall.

I'd never seen Rusty's mom before. People joked about her having social phobia, but she had a cool dress. Long flowing sequin in the style of Victorian ruffle, even if her hair was a bit tangled.

"Daphne." I was late to toast with Mrs. Rahall, though her glass was empty. "What would you do to see your little boy again?"

My eyes snapped back from the basement. "My brother, Paul?" I said. "Anything." My love for him pounded in my heart.

"You mean that?"

"Yes." I would do everything I could. That was why I was so determined to be a junior detective.

As I gulped, the effort to get here caught up to me. My vision zoomed out. A headache landed like a fist into my temple. "What. Is it?" I asked, holding the glass. Maybe Mrs. Rahall was out of practice being a good hostess, because the aftertaste was acidic. Maybe the orange juice was bad.

"So would I." Mrs. Rahall slipped a tin into a drawer with surreal slowness. Stenciled on the side were interlacing tridents I didn't recognize. "I think any mother would."

Oh man, my stomach was killing me. I swam to the wall to anchor myself. And in my clumsiness, I accidentally flipped a crucifix upside down.

It was a giant one hanging shoulder high. Mom's conniption would be a mushroom cloud if she heard about this.

The crucifix wouldn't budge. I pulled hard as I could, but someone nailed it that way. Didn't I just flip it? Two more crucifixes hung from the other side of the room. They were upside down too.

I stumbled into the bathroom, skin crackling, and ripped open the toilet lid. Black stains crawled up the bowl. I gagged. Sweat poured down my face. But I couldn't cough up the juice.

"If the Brotherhood took those children for Lammas Day," said Mrs. Rahall from the kitchen, "they would lie in the earth three days. They'd be washed clean, and kept unspoiled at the base of the hörgr until Blót. But they're not at the hörgr, are they?"

"Hörgr?" Acid clogged my throat. "You mean the Idol."

Next to the church. On Hangman's Hill.

I opened my eyes in the Rahall's bathtub, amid a hundred curly hairs. They crawled over my skin like worms. Part of the shower curtain was in my hand, the rest had a long rip. I must've grabbed it while falling. Though I couldn't remember the fall. Nor could I figure how long I had been lying here. Vertigo spun the yellowed ceiling.

Mrs. Rahall appeared at the bathroom door. *Good*, I thought. I had been out only for a second or two.

"Calling us savages," she said. "Like I'd Blót my own son and burn his bones. I think this was something else, but the Knowing never came clearly to me. I can make you drink, drink something much more powerful than the sedative I gave you, but I'm giving you the opportunity to be truthful. Can you do that, Daphne?"

"Make me drink what?" I said, too dizzy to understand. Mrs. Rahall poisoned me with something. And if I didn't give her the answer she wanted, she'd give me something worse. I flexed to pick myself up when I noticed a hole under the showerhead. The wall was hollow; through the hole, I caught the faintest pinprick of black light.

A passageway.

What would the Rahalls want with a secret passageway from the bathroom to elsewhere in the house? Mrs. Rahall had another question in mind.

"Your dad didn't try to save my Billy, did he? Because no one would think twice of a Christian pastor talking to the boys. Ripping children from mothers, social services declaring us unfit all over again."

"Dad? No."

Wires threatened to slice Mrs. Rahall's skin from underneath. "The boys were last seen getting into a van, Daphne. Your dad drives a van, doesn't he?"

Mrs. Rahall's facts were wrong. The day Paul disappeared, Mom had the van, we were visiting Grandpop, and Dad was wherever he was. Who I'd describe not as a Christian pastor but as a Unitarian minister, and no, he'd never do anything like that.

I saw the back door through the mirror's reflection, but I couldn't move forward, couldn't scooch back. It was like a hot string kept me in place as the room swooned.

"No, Daphne." Mrs. Rahall held up an index card of a large horse with so many legs I couldn't count. Under it was a bunch of weird circles and tridents. "You don't want to leave without me taking it back, do you?"

"Take. Back?" The ribbon tightened around my wrist and somehow drew me to my feet.

Panic became snakes under my clothes. *Clai, Clai, Clai, Clai, Clai.* Rusty said that very thing to Clai, and no one helped. Just like no one helped me now, trembling in Mrs. Rahall's shadow.

"I gave you the choice, didn't I?" she said, holding up a glass. "Now I'll drink and you'll drink, and you'll tell me where your father took my son. Because the Elementals of our church won't let there be secrets between us."

Elementals. What the heck were those?

Instead of answering, Mrs. Rahall inserted her pointer finger between her front teeth, and bit hard. A cloud of blood spurted from her mouth. The sound was wet, as though she'd bit into an apple. A dark river dribbled down her wrist.

"Mm," she slurped, as though I had to try it. She curled her vampire lips into a grimace identical to Rusty's. "Now you."

Every strange word she muttered turned me numb.

I couldn't measure time, let alone in seconds. Yet somehow I knew when to give her my ribboned hand, ready to repeat what Mrs. Rahall had done on my own finger, and drop my blood into the glass she offered. To drink and to join their church. Her eyes on the horse picture, Mrs. Rahall's teeth clicked on my middle finger's nail.

That picture. On a wave of intuition, I knew Mrs. Rahall needed it for the same reason Rusty needed that old book from the tree to do his freeze spell.

I tipped into her, mangling the card, momentum stealing my finger from Mrs. Rahall's grasp. On the tile, I tore it up.

The numbness didn't vanish. It still felt like angry bees were under my skin. But at least I could move.

I ducked Mrs. Rahall's arms and dragged myself to the front door, out of breath, sure Mrs. Rahall would catch me. She didn't, but her voice did.

"Make sure your daddy prays *real* hard, honey, okay? See if that brings our boys back."

CHAPTER TWENTY-ONE

The Rahalls' front yard rippled like an ocean of black oil. They were ravens fluttering shoulder to shoulder across the lawn and up a crooked oak. Dozens of them, a hundred.

As I ran, unable to slow down, the birds exploded upward. They cawed in my face, smelling of death. Talons ripped my hair. One sliced my forearm.

I punched my way to the end of the driveway. Soon as my shoe struck the street, the ravens disappeared. A few feathers skittered along the pavement.

My eyes darted to one on an oak branch, a truck on cinderblocks. Not until I looked up did I understand.

The rest had taken flight. They swirled overhead, the path of their flight an unmistakable shape. A circle.

Or Door.

Many of the houses' windows were boarded up, their lawns overgrown. Growling dogs sprang from junkyard cars. I ran down the road, holding my forearm, until I heard someone calling.

"Come inside, child." It was an aproned woman I needed a second to recognize, a baby in her arms.

"No, don't," said a man behind the screen door.

The woman turned. "George, she's scared."

"They're already at the quarry," he said. "I don't want the children here if they come for us."

I froze at their stone brown porch. There I saw the family crest, the Gedneys, unable to shake the numbness spreading up my arm, unable to speak. As mute as Clai, who couldn't speak for three days.

Something knocked on my skull. On the Gedneys' second floor, a boy banged the glass. Gerard, who I wouldn't see for another thirty-three years, looked like something out of Brandy's scary movies. Tubes up his arms, surgeon's mask, curl hanging from a white cap, cloaked in a greenish haze. I shivered at the end of the driveway, hand pressed against my arm, trying to stop the bleeding.

Dad stopped the van at the Gedneys' driveway. I needed a few tries to slide open the door. My sisters stared ahead.

"The sheriff called," said Dad, but he didn't explain, ask what I was doing there. He barely acknowledged the dried blood on my arm. The whole way home, I floated in a bubble, observing but not participating.

Courtney helped Dad load books from the back of the van. *King James Bible* and the *Gideon Bible*. Eugene Albert Nida's *God's Word in Man's Language*, Kahlil Gibran's *The Prophet*, and Vincent Bugliosi's *Helter Skelter*. Handwritten notes accompanied them, hieroglyphs circled in triplicate.

I followed them into the house, my legs on autopilot. At the sight of Sheriff Colquitt and Deputy Bixbee, hats tucked under their arms, Dad stopped so quick I ran into him.

"You found Paul? Is he . . ."

Dead? Alive?

To say one way might make Paul the other, or both, or neither. Wrestling with the dilemma exposed the flaws in his mask. This was the first time I ever thought Dad wore one, and I wondered if what I saw fill the cracks in his face was fear.

Lie in the earth three days.

Which didn't make sense. All the boys were saying the second Blót wasn't until Lammas Day.

"Go to your rooms, girls," said Mom, rocking so hard the chair crackled.

"We recovered a body," said the sheriff from the kitchen, "at the bottom of Fleming Quarry. A young boy's."

We had Grandma Charity's armoire halfway from the wall where the secret vent was located when the news flattened us. Paul had been at the quarry, but we were searching near Lincoln Bridge. If only that first night Dominic Gedney had told the truth.

I collapsed into bed. Air moaned through the room as it spun.

"I told you to find Ron Abish," she said between sobs. "Didn't I? Didn't I say?"

"When Brady was abducted," said Sheriff Colquitt, "Mr. Abish wasn't in New Minton, Mrs. Gauge. He'd checked himself into a detox facility following a relapse." She wailed, and Dad comforted her. "I'm sorry. We were too quick to fix on Abish because of his record; we own that. Six years ago, he took his surviving son across state lines to get him away from his alcoholic wife. He should've been charged for 'custodial interference' rather than kidnapping."

The news stung deep. Then who did Dad see on the Hill? Who tied up Clai, if the rumors were true?

What, if anything, was true anymore?

Something hammered the floor. "Let's go."

"Hon?"

"Someone needs to ID the body, Brandon," said Mom. "The skin will blister. I saw a boy they pulled from the lake once, when I was ten."

"Honey, we don't know if it's Paul."

"I *know*, goddamn it." Her voice broke. "'Wait for the police.' I should've done something. The boy's skin was greenish black."

"Ma'am," said Sheriff Colquitt. "We already have Brady's dental records. We have William's and David's as well. Forensics is comparing them as we speak."

"God," said Dad, "I didn't even think. It's going to be Paul or Billy Rahall or David Gedney, isn't it? Or some boy from some other family. Let it not be Paul. God forgive me, but please let it not be Paul."

"I'm so very sorry," said Sheriff Colquitt. "But right now, what would be the most helpful is if you could answer some questions."

"You questioned Thomas Fleming, didn't you?" asked Mom.

Courtney wiggled her purple finger until the knuckle popped. I opened my eyes. Brandy dismissed her with a stern shake of the head. No matter how hard I fought, each voice pushed me farther away.

"We spoke to him," said Sheriff Colquitt. "We know all about the feud since you purchased his ancestral property in '75. Lawsuits. Accusations of intimidation. Him plopping his son's house next to yours."

"Did you ask about the sandy area that looked like someone might've raked over it?" asked Mom. "About a mile from Lincoln Bridge that goes right by Fleming Property? Or why his son Trevor owns a copy of something called, *Codex Sacrificium*?"

I knew Trevor was bad news. Prowling around our house.

"Ma'am." Who was that? Bixbee? "On March 31, Mr. Fleming and his son Trevor were at the bank. With George Gedney, closing out a loan, about an hour before Brady's disappearance."

"Even after George's son disappears . . ." Mom sounded both mocking and bitter. "And may be dead in a quarry, he's still covering for them."

"We requested timestamps of the loan application," said Deputy Bixbee.

"I'm sure it'll all look very official," said Mom.

Deputy Bixbee continued on. "Might take a couple days," he said, "because Mr. Gedney's youngest son has been real sick with radiation treatment."

Gerard Gedney. He spiraled with me, banging on the window, eyes wide. How alone he must feel, never seeing any kids other than his brothers.

"Maybe it might be more helpful," said Sheriff Colquitt, "if we talk about the black van you saw earlier, Mrs. Gauge."

Your dad drives a van, doesn't he?

A white one.

All the boys went willingly with their captor.

No. It couldn't be Dad. I just needed to figure out who all the boys would trust, besides him.

"Think we could show you a few pictures and you could pick out a make and model?"

A shadow stood over me. "I think she has a fever, guys," said Brandy.

"I want to be left alone," I shrieked, hardly believing how angry I was, though Brandy was right. I felt like my head was boiling. "*Leave me alone*."

"If Daph had friends," said Courtney, "she wouldn't always talk like a book. Thinking a crumpled note's going to lead her to a secret hatch, like she's Beatrix B."

I couldn't point out that everything Courtney predicted had come true, except for me finding a hatch. Nor could I tell the sheriff about Trevor. In the other room, he assured my parents they'd wait all night for Forensics.

"Ew, what is this ratty thing?" I forced my eyes open one last time to see Brandy with a pair of scissors over Mrs. Rahall's white ribbon. My instinct was to pull away, take them from her if I had to, but I had no strength.

Brandy snipped.

I fell a great depth.

That night, I think she saved my life.

Sometime in the early morning, the phone rang.

My sisters ran to the kitchen. I stumbled after them, weak and shivering, a headache making the walls breathe.

"This is she," Mom said, wiping her hair, though she didn't have bed head.

She didn't have pajamas either, but jeans and a maroon sweater.

"Is it the kidnapper again?" Ellie whispered.

"Or maybe Grandpop?" asked Courtney.

Brandy crossed her arms. Her eyes ticked down, then widened as though stressed about a surprise quiz.

"They're going to say it's Paul," I said. It got so late, the sheriff and deputy had to go home, and they were calling to inform us our brother was dead.

"What?" said Mom, spiking my panic. Spiking Dad's, too, as he fumbled with the recorder, shaking his head as Courtney shook me by the collarbone.

"They told us yesterday it was Billy," she said, her hot breath in my ear. "If you didn't spend all day in bed, you'd know."

My eyes rolled like they were in a waking REM state. Billy Rahall, not Paul or David? What—

The speakers squealed. We covered our ears.

"We got the bastard," said Sheriff Colquitt on speaker, "he was just where you said." Dad stood back as though God's voice thundered from the recorder. "My deputy almost lost him because his brake lights weren't working. We'd like you to positively ID him once he gets to county for the interview."

The news, so much news, bolted over us.

"I'm happy to help, Sheriff," said Mom, hanging up, her face stone.

"Mom," said Brandy, the only one to smile, "so is it over?"

Mom kept rubbing her throat, kept trying to clear it, her expression blank. The only things moving were her eyes, darting left-to-right as though zipping through an article. My heart beat so fast I felt it in my neck.

"What bastard did they get?" asked Ellie.

They arrested someone. Mom said she should've done something, and she did, and whoever abducted Paul was now in jail. Everything was happening so quick.

"We're." A flush went all the way to the bald spot on top of Dad's head. "We're going to pray. For forgiveness for our trespasses, as well as for all the souls who trespass against us."

My sisters held hands, heads bowed. As we recited the Lord's Prayer, their fingers probed the pink callus burned into my wrist.

CHAPTER TWENTY-TWO

July 27, 2021

I keep having these out-of-body experiences, the unending river of my past spilling forth, until Bradley Reeves hooks me back.

"Can you clarify a discrepancy for us, Ms. Gauge?" He has his hand raised as though I might call on him. "A body was found on April 5. It was identified as William Rahall's on the sixth, official cause of death ruled drowning. Everett Ford was arrested on the seventh, was he not?"

It wasn't drowning, but the dates press in my skull until I go cross-eyed. The midmorning heat builds in the conference room. It's busier outside, taxis honking, tires chirping. They're calling my name.

"You're absolutely right, Mr. Chairman," I say, or yell. "I apologize. I must've combined those memories."

How could I do that? I was messed up in 1988, not now. I keep scratching my neck. They're looking for any excuse to discount me, and I give it to them. The memory of Eileen Rahall poured out so fast, I didn't make the connection to Ellie until too late. When Mom dragged Ellie into the bathroom, did Mom bite her finger, too, and try to combine their blood? Did

Mom and Ellie share dark secrets, ones that Ellie lives with on the streets of Boston?

"How about we take a break?" says the chairman. He nods at the committee. "A fifteen-minute recess?"

"No, please, sir," I say. "I'm fine. Ask your questions."

My phone buzzes. I wish it was from Ellie, but no, it's another text from Henderson.

Hotel clerk ID'd Eileen Rahall, but not TF. Maybe he didn't stay in hotel?

Eileen's in town. Thanks for the heads up. After she's harassed me twice already.

As far as Trevor goes, he could have an apartment in Boston, or a friend with a spare room. If that's true, how am I going to find him?

The white-haired Walter doesn't have an answer. He's already out the door. So are a lot of the others behind me. That makes me feel better. Like it's just the chairman and me.

"You allege that on April 5," he says, "shortly before William Rahall's body was discovered, his brother Reginald Rahall lured you to his home."

"Then his mother," I say. "Who's here now." I point to where Eileen was, but the space is empty. She must be in the crowd filing out.

"Then Eileen Rahall 'poisoned and hexed' you, is that right?"

"It's called a binding spell," I say, "used in black magic to cause harm to someone. Mr. Chairman, Eileen Rahall just told me she was the Nolans' babysitter."

"Just now?" Bradley Reeves cocks his head as though Eileen should materialize beside me. Of course, I don't mean right this second, I've been blabbing for well over an hour. "Ms. Gauge, I thought Reginald froze Claiborne Denton."

"Freezing is part of the Binding family." I hold up my right hand. "Doctors say the muscles deteriorated to the point I have a ninety-year-old's wrist. Sometimes this birthmark, which I never had before and which is where Eileen Rahall tied the ribbon, goes numb, and I can't hold my children. If Exhibit D were here, I could show you."

If someone hadn't stolen it. If I had only said *right away* that Eileen Rahall practically admitted she knew something about Grant and Roderick.

I can already hear Eileen's retort. Is it a crime to babysit?

"I have to be honest, Ms. Gauge." Bradley Reeves drops his glasses on the desk, where they wink. "And I think you have to admit as well, there's a credibility issue here. The Rahalls accused your father of abducting their son, William. And if your intent is to undermine those accusations—"

"And what?" I say. "Make up something outrageous? Dad never owned a black van. Exhibit Q proves who did."

"Eileen Rahall touches on an important point. Earlier, Ms. Gauge, you testified that Scott Wilson told you the Brotherhood of the Raven abducts outsiders. First, your brother Brady, now Grant and Roderick Nolan. But in between that, this group goes after David Gedney and William Rahall? Their families have been in New Minton since its founding. It makes no sense."

Defensiveness pricks up my spine. He agrees with Eileen, that since no one in the Brotherhood would attack their own, Dad must be responsible.

Thankfully, I calm myself. "If you read on, sir," I say, "you'll see that the Brotherhood is as fractured as any religion. The prime suspect apparently disagreed with abandoning old practices deemed too brutal. That's why this Blót was very different."

Bradley Reeves sighs, picking up his glasses, examining Exhibit Q. "I suppose that brings us to Everett T. Ford Jr.," he says. "Who wasn't homeless, a neighbor, or a firefighter. And who seemed to have no connection to any of the missing boys."

"Actually, Mr. Chairman," I say, "it was Clai Denton who told me about Ford's prayer meetings. The day before Billy Rahall's funeral, we were at the library—"

"Before we get to that, Ms. Gauge, can you clearly establish why county sheriffs targeted Everett Ford? He was a teacher fired for not disclosing his criminal history, is that correct?"

"Everett Ford was a convicted sex offender," I say, "with a long history of violence against children. Police suspected him of being the getaway driver in a botched robbery where an off-duty officer was shot in the leg. Before he was fired, he was a high-standing member of the community the boys would recognize and trust, and a known member of the Brotherhood of the Raven. That might be why Ford later got a job working night security at the Fleming Quarry."

"It says here," says Bradley Reeves, "your mother identified Everett Ford as conducting Black Masses behind the elementary school." His scoff invites more amusement from the five or six people who remain. "And the sheriffs accepted her word, despite her mental history."

"That didn't come out, Mr. Chairman, at least not to me, until after."

"MC Flanders Elementary School," he says, "where behind it you claim is a pagan tree, or altar, with a square hole in the trunk. We've heard testimony and seen photographs, Ms. Gauge, that show not a tree but a stump."

"Whose testimony, sir?"

Names scroll through my head so fast, I barely hear the snickering behind me. Besides Courtney, who else is the commission interviewing? Speculating makes my cheeks hot.

"That stump, Mr. Chairman?" I say. "That's where Everett Ford was spotted before leading the police on a chase with a van that had no lights. That's also where police reports make note."

Bradley Reeves reads, his lips moving.

"Make note of 'strange lights in the woods,'" he says. "At 12:58 a.m. April 7, Deputy Harold Bixbee pulled over Everett Ford in an all-black van fleeing school grounds."

"That van, Mr. Chairman, was a 1971 Dodge Tradesman 200. Everett Ford installed trick wires that allowed him to flip off all the lights on that van, including brake and taillights. That's why Deputy Bixbee almost lost him, why no witnesses could identify it. He could've been at Lincoln Bridge the night Paul disappeared, following Paul, and we'd never know."

"Did you say *trick wires*, Ms. Gauge?" asks Bradley Reeves. "Because a month ago,"—he sorts through papers—"New Minton police asked for help in identifying a 1990 Buick Regal."

I lean into the microphone. "I am aware of that report, Mr. Chairman."

On June 29, NMPD located the vehicle abandoned on Hangman's Hill. Forensics determined that someone doused the interior with bleach to frustrate any finding of hair follicles or fingerprints.

The police didn't say they believed the Buick was used as an escape car, to perhaps transport Grant and Roderick Nolan from their tent to the Hill and then to another unidentified vehicle. But I suspect it was so. Bradley Reeves seems to confirm that now.

Had Henderson tied the Buick Regal to the Crusher Group, that would've been the ballgame.

"This Buick was found without headlights or taillights. They'd been removed. Hm."

Don't say it's a coincidence. I'm really tired of that word. "It's their MO, Mr. Chairman. Everett Ford driving the Tradesman. Another Brother of the Raven driving that Buick Regal."

Now would be a good time to tell the committee about the Crusher Group's '87 Ram. Walter's still on break, but I worry about how far his influence extends.

"I wish it were possible to depose Everett Ford," says Bradley Reeves, "because I also see here that on April 6, a day before his arrest, Everett Ford's parole officer cited him."

"For an extra three hundred miles on his odometer," I say, "that wasn't authorized and couldn't be accounted for."

"So Everett Ford could've taken the New Minton Boys a hundred miles away. Did Ford make any statements during his arrest, Ms. Gauge?"

"Just six words, Mr. Chairman."

I still remember the reporters mobbing Everett Ford. One microphone breached the police barrier before a hand slapped it away. The thud pricked our eardrums like a needle. But Ford's words were unmistakable.

"He said, 'The mills of God grind slowly.'"

I feel it building in the conference room, the beginning of a wave.

"Any idea what Mr. Ford meant by that?" asks the chairman.

I wish I had an answer. Bradley Reeves flips a few pages ahead. The headline is stained yellow, one of the few to survive the Flood of 2006, but I see the aerial view of a stone diamond plunging into black water.

"And when the bodies were discovered in the quarry later that day, Ms. Gauge?"

"I don't think the sheriffs were looking for them," I say. "They were searching for Paul and David. But beginning April 7, they pulled at least eighteen human remains from Fleming Quarry. The numbers kept growing, a mix of adult and juvenile males, along with three women."

"What your grandfather referred to as *Wetting the Fulcrum*," says the chairman. "Did the police suspect foul play?"

"Yes, they did," I say, "which led us to another problem. If Everett Ford dumped the bodies in Fleming Quarry, he wasn't the only one."

"What makes you say that?"

The wave crests, a surge for the answers I seek.

"According to carbon dating," I say, "many of the bones were decades old. Some had been down there for over a hundred years."

CHAPTER TWENTY-THREE

April 10, 1988

All morning, Dad rallied my sisters around the idea that a service for Billy Rahall would heal the town. *Come on*, he said, buzzing with nervous energy. *We have flowers to order, chairs to arrange, windows to drape.*

Brandy countered Dad's nesting instinct by crossing her arms. *Do the Rahalls even* want *our help*? In Dad's mind, the service was already confirmed. He asked Mrs. Reynolds, the church's organ player, to pick up my sisters. And he pressed me to join him at the Rahalls', hoping to secure their permission.

Mr. Rahall slammed the door in our face. Dad stood on the Rahalls' porch for several minutes, as though there was some mistake.

Then we traveled to the New Minton Public Library, a brick building with twin smokestacks. I didn't object. After two days in bed, I wanted to know where Mom was. She'd left cans of Chef Boyardee for Courtney to microwave, but no other trace of herself. Not since the police arrested Everett Ford. Because Mom saw Mr. Ford do something with his grody van. But I wasn't sure exactly. Before that, had he offered Paul a ride after Billy struck my brother with the back of a knife? Assuming Rusty's story wasn't an outright lie. Rusty overheard me asking about Ron Abish, and fed me a tale gruesome enough I'd go to his house. All so Mrs. Rahall could interrogate me about Dad.

And nearly kill me.

I suspected Mom's absence had something to do with the bodies they found in Fleming Quarry. Everett Ford squatted in a stone-walled grist mill, owned by Thomas Fleming, within half a mile of the quarry. Finding more about the victims and if when Mr. Ford said, *The mills of God grind slowly*, he meant there were more, might help me find her too. This morning, the news said they found ten more victims. And some weird brass belt a guy on the news said was stolen from a Boston museum in 1911. I wasn't sure what all of that meant, if there was a place I could find out . . .

"The library doesn't have information like that," said Mr. Mellinger before I could finish. A fan blew his cowlick behind the reference desk. He turned away and stamped books.

I burned with disappointment, wondering why Mrs. Thornberg, the assistant librarian, kept glancing at me. She had creepy pink eyes. When Mr. Mellinger was distracted, she led me up a wood banister, open like an old theater. This section was supposed to be off-limits to young children. She undid the padlock, her skin smelling like sandpaper.

"Thank you, ma'am," I said, late to understand she was helping me.

Wonder carried me like a balloon. Cobwebs linked the books, all bound in dark-brown leather. The smell of mildew was disgusting, but at the same time, I loved it. How many eleven-year-olds got into the Elder Room?

"If it's a history of missing children you're after," said Mrs. Thornberg, "you should try looking at the relocations."

That caused a spark up my back. "Relocations?"

Your dad didn't try to save my Billy, did he?

Mrs. Thornberg tried to keep her head steady. "The hill kids," she said. "Never formally educated. Never seen a doctor or dentist. But the raids did more harm than good. Made people distrustful of the outside world."

Pressure built in my ears as I pieced together the adult universe. The hill kids lived in the hills, where we lived? Mrs. Thornberg and Mrs. Rahall must be referring to the same thing, social services raiding people's homes and separating families. How hateful she'd been toward Dad.

"All this boiled over at the Abish-Drane trial," said Mrs. Thornberg. "The couple was tried for shooting that poor boy."

I ran cold. Just when Sheriff Colquitt ruled out Ron Abish, there his name popped up again.

Actually, I found the articles quickly through the blur of microfiche, but didn't act like it until Mrs. Thornberg went to help a young boy, about four, find a book he had no business reading or knowing anything about, *The Twits*.

I felt bad, for Mrs. Thornberg had been super helpful. She led me to other victims. In 1889, a young girl was found burned to death in a chicken coop, believed to be age seven to nine. No birth record, which was unusual, though not unheard of.

In 1922, two thirteen-year-olds ran away, never to be seen again, but that seemed a pretty big stretch. A tent revival or carnival always attracted teenagers in a tight-knit town like New Minton. That's what they said happened to Rusty's sister three years ago, Amy Rahall.

Mrs. Thornberg also led me to Donnie Sobaski.

In 1969, Martin Abish and Charity Drane, then seventy-three and forty-seven, stood trial in what had been ruled a hunting accident fourteen years prior. They adopted ten-year-old Donnie in 1949, but five years later, Abish and Drane reported that the boy ran away. The following September, police found Donnie shot in the temple right on top of Hangman's Hill.

Police linked the bullet's caliber to a rifle Abish owned, but he and Drane were acquitted when witnesses later came forward, including a Lutheran minister, who established their alibi. According to the article, once news about Donnie broke, the transcript vanished, along with all forensic evidence.

What news about Donnie?

Someone had blacked out five paragraphs. But if I held it to the light, I caught snippets.

Ligature marks on wrists. Clothes burned. Possible hypothermia.

How did Donnie Sobaski get hypothermia, when he was shot?

Dad's quiet voice wafted from the stacks. "Our Society is endowed with a small trust," he said. "In times of crisis, we can absorb the cost."

Their photograph was strange, though, snapped on courthouse steps. Clearly a May and December couple, Martin Abish needing the support of his younger ladylove, who leaped from the page like Mom's mirror ten years in the future. Of course that couldn't be. I probably just thought that because Charity was my grandmother's name too.

"Marvin Rahall refuses to have a wake for Billy," said someone else. My interest piqued. Not Uncle Toby.

"Well," said Dad, "I'm a minister, not a priest."

"Marvin will not understand the difference, Mr. Gauge. Nor will he care."

I peered around a stack to see Dad speaking with Mr. Denton, tall and lanky, the man Clai would become. Dad froze in frustration, a frog-like smile that instantly made me doubt he had anything to do with kidnapping Billy. And make him Unitarian? The Rahalls may believe some strange things, but that was the craziest.

Wait. If Mr. Denton was here, might his son be here too? The stacks blurred as I half-trotted until I found him in the sci-fi section. "Clai?" I said. "Are you okay?"

He looked paler now. Angry red dots ran down his neck. I couldn't believe it was really him. No one had seen Clai in a week and a half, but it felt like a month.

"A mustache dragged me through a tunnel with goat horns," he said. "Broke my glasses. Stripped me. Told me to lie until I froze to death. Every time I screamed, I smelled my clothes burning. My mom's so freaked, I'm not allowed back to school. Okay is all I am."

"You must've been so scared," I said. *Clothes burned.* Like Donnie Sobaski's. A tunnel. Goat horns. "That's Lincoln Bridge, Clai."

Where Paul was last seen. I had placed a Band-Aid over the need to interrogate Clai about Ron Abish once police exonerated him. Now the old wound in my brain sprung a million questions. How had Clai made it so far, fumbling blindly the whole time? What did the police say?

And the big one, which flew out of my mouth: "Clai," I said. "Did you say *mustache*?"

"Brother Everett," he said. Everett Ford, the man Mom implicated. "You know what he does behind your house, don't you? It was supposed to be book studies. Trevor asked if I wanted to go, and at first, my parents were okay with it."

"*Trevor Fleming* invited you?" I said. The kid creeping around our backyard with the *Codex Sacrificium* while knifing squirrels? "What happened on Hangman's Hill?"

"It was sick, Daphne." Clai scratched his head. "Smoking pot and practicing on house pets. Learning to Blót 'the right way' with the original families. My dad's so pissed. The Brotherhood's more chill now. It's about prayer and family. But they want to revive all these ancient traditions. Quarter Moon. Marking girls."

I shivered, wondering if it had anything to do with Badger's sudden disappearance. I never quite believed the story of a farm in upstate New York.

Clai shook his head. "Me, David, and Billy decided enough was enough," he said. "We weren't going to go to Brother Everett's groups anymore."

"Then Everett Ford kidnaps you three," I said. "Why Paul, then? He wasn't going to those book studies."

I didn't hear Clai's response. My mind made the connection.

Back on March 31, Clai escaped the mud, and the firemen found him around 4:15. Maybe Everett Ford was still searching for Clai when, an hour later, Paul and Dominic Gedney decided to play near the Little Housic River under Lincoln Bridge.

Paul fell right into Mr. Ford's trap. Something else Clai said bothered me. "What did you mean," I said, "*Blótting the right way*? How many other families?"

"Pumpkin?" called Dad, lifting his eyebrows. "It's time."

Just another sec. I looked back, but Clai's mom was leading Clai away, staring me down as they left the library.

Dad liked no radio for the drive. Without a sibling to object, I watched the scenery roll, hand on my cheek. And I turned over everything Clai had said. How except for a few extremists, the Brotherhood of the Raven was more "chill" now. I wondered if it was the same for Unitarians.

"Dad?" I said. "How do you pray?"

"I think the key." Dad paused, his face intense. "To understand God is to understand His language."

"Like how He talks?"

"Sort of. What's the closest Word we have of God's?"

"Uh, the Bible?"

"Very good, Pumpkin." I scooted up the passenger seat, happy to receive a compliment. "So I take a passage. Any passage. And I write it down. Then I write another passage. I keep doing that until I hear His message. That's how I write my sermons."

I looked out the window. "Huh," I said. "I never thought of that." His words from the night of the heat lightning came back to me. *God tires me out sometimes*. Guess writing a lot could tire a person out.

"Pumpkin." Dad frowned at the scenery. "Have you noticed anything unusual about Mom? Has she purchased anything expensive lately?"

"She picks her face," I said.

Dad nodded like a doctor. He didn't notice the other car. A town car, that same short goateed man I saw in our driveway, now with Mom in the passenger seat. Neither of them waved back.

"Hey, isn't that—?"

"One more stop before the church, Pumpkin," said Dad, pulling up beside the General Store.

I knew I didn't imagine her, nor did I imagine how fogged up the windows were the first time I found her with that man. Asking about a date. With her son missing, Mom was having an affair. And she didn't care who in town saw her riding with him.

Then we headed home.

This time of year, the forest of Hangman's Hill was a tumble of the canopy's bones, a pale collage of red and brown terrain. From the cracked earth sprang Dad's church. Its windows broadcasted holy light across the downtown caldera.

We pulled into the parking lot, and Dad frowned at my sisters and a powder-headed Mrs. Reynolds milling about.

"They can't be done already," he said.

Normally, nothing would make me happier than to have the church's chores complete in advance of my arrival. But Billy's service was off, wasn't it? And if Trevor replaced Everett Ford as the leader of this rebel Brotherhood, then I had to stop him before he could hurt anyone else.

Dad popped the door and Mrs. Reynolds scuffed over in a wool blanket. "I didn't want them to go inside," she said. "I didn't know what else to do. I'm sorry, I know it's blustery out here."

Brandy sat on the curb, clutching her stomach. "We called like a *ba*zillion times, Dad."

"Oh," said Dad in a high and absent voice.

Ellie hopped off the stones of the Fountain of Life which, according to legend, once formed a triangle with the Idol. Where once Donnie Sobaski was found with a bullet in his head.

"Daddy?" she said, full of enthusiasm and short of breath. "What's a *war*?"

Dad moved his lips as though to repeat Mrs. Reynolds's words, but she was too hysterical to understand beyond, "Awful, just awful." He stomped to the church doors only to flinch.

"War, war," said Ellie, "what's a war?"

"Oh my God," Dad said.

My sisters ran to Dad. I chased after them, dropping my thoughts about Trevor only to pick them up again. He'd been here sometime in the night. I knew it.

Our posters, the ones we made to find our brother, had been defaced and rearranged to form a pentagram. Above it, swathed in orange coils across the front entrance, was a word. It wasn't "war." It actually spelled *whore*. Followed by *Blót*, and *cunt*, broken plates and glassware.

CHAPTER TWENTY-FOUR

July 27, 2021

This late in the afternoon, the crowd thins. The conference room echoes every cleared throat, every sigh. While Bradley Reeves waits for the ever-reliable Vikki to retrieve a file, others on the commission prop their heads with closed eyes.

"I see desecrations have increased," says the chairman. Men blink, taking in sharp breaths. "Up eighteen percent after a thirty-year low. Including a church in Revere earlier this week, just north of us. Some sentences were scrawled on the walls."

He distributes a memo I don't need to see. I know exactly what it says.

Nolan Boys are New Minton Boys.

The Nolans, Grant and Roderick.

On Lammas Day.

"Lab tests confirm," says the chairman, "it was written in goat's blood."

Revere PD had almost no choice to but to release the information. Someone leaked it to the Associated Press. Within an hour, teenagers flooded the internet with memes. Many thought it was a joke.

What must the boys' parents be thinking, seeing their children reduced to a hashtag?

"Ms. Gauge, when is Lammas Day?"

"Anytime between August 1 and September 1, depending on which calendar you use."

Which could be as soon as four days. That's all the time left before the Nolans are gone forever like the others. If only the CARD Team could've analyzed the Book of the Brotherhood.

"Ms. Gauge," says the chairman, "for the record, who desecrated New Minton's Second Unitarian Universalist back in '88?"

"Trevor Fleming, Mr. Chairman," I say. "Jeremy White, Brandy's boyfriend. A few of Trevor's friends."

"Mr. White recently confessed to his part."

"Though with the church burned down," I say, "what good does that do us now?"

Bradley Reeves winces.

"I'm sorry," I say.

"I think we all understand why you're upset." Though he appears less confident, soliciting sympathy from the other men on the commission. "Claiborne Denton's account suggests that Everett Ford was grooming Trevor Fleming, among other boys."

"Using Exhibit B," I say, "the Initiation, as gospel to advance Blót beyond one victim. Trevor wanted more. 'The Elementals will shower them with riches,' he told the Brotherhood."

"Can we get back to something Reginald Rahall said, please?" asks the chairman. "If Reginald lied about his brother William assaulting Brady with a knife at the 'Door's fulcrum,' then your brother was never at the quarry, is that right?"

"Paul had to be at Lincoln Bridge," I say. "That's where his sock was. That's where he and Clai were made to lie in the earth."

"Ms. Gauge, according to Reginald Rahall's statement, he denies telling you William assaulted Brady with a knife."

My knee bumps the underside of the table. They spoke to Rusty? Did they get him out of jail or did the chairman speak to him in Framingham MSP?

That's why Eileen Rahall was here. She wanted to see the son the state took away in 1990, due to allegations of gross child neglect.

"Reginald claims Billy Rahall was the victim of your family."

"Rusty Rahall is a liar and a criminal," I say. "He's distracting you, sir."

"Ms. Gauge. We're trying to sort through—"

"Whoever attacked Paul," I say, "whether it was Billy, or someone else, whether it was at Lincoln Bridge or the quarry, there was a fight and Paul got injured. Why else would they have to sweep up? Maybe Billy called his dad, Marvin Rahall, or Trevor, or Everett Ford, and Ford transported Paul in his Tradesman. No one got a good look because it was dark."

Though something bothers me. At five p.m., March 31, 1988, there'd be an hour of daylight left. That's why eyewitnesses saw Everett Ford's van at both the bridge and quarry.

And with everyone on alert about Clai Denton, how could people miss Paul? He was the reverend's son. He didn't belong with the Rahalls.

"Ms. Gauge?"

I look up.

"I was asking when you found out NMPD dropped all charges against Ron Abish?"

"On April 7," I say, "the same day as Everett Ford's arrest, they cleared Ron Abish of wrongdoing. The next few weeks were tense. We were on *Sixty Minutes*. Under questioning, Ford incriminated himself. His arraignment was set for early May."

"How did your mother react to all this, Ms. Gauge?"

Heat breaks out all over my skin. Each second I don't answer, the question grows wings.

"On April 20," I say, "Mountains with a View called to say Grandpop died in his sleep."

CHAPTER TWENTY-FIVE

April 25, 1988

Half a dozen cars creaked to a halt beside Northland Cemetery. Doors clapped off the rolling hills.

The procession clutched Courtney's and Ellie's elbows on the way to the casket where our parents stood. Grass broke under our feet, brittle as a desert flower.

Already sweating under the relentless sun, Dad smiled as though we were late but he didn't mind. His robe had caught on his belt, revealing the bottom half of checkered golf pants.

Only a handful of the elderly attended, and almost none of the regulars, those shackled to the hope their presence at every funeral might convince God to grant them a little more time. No Flemings, Rahalls, Dentons, Gedneys, or Patowskis. Grandpop's passing had made the papers, or so I was told.

Mom even waited five days, in case Everett Ford finally confessed to where he hid our brother. She had been here for hours, having driven herself, dressed in black, wobbling on heels.

"Some daughter I was," she said, adjusting her veil. "I stick him in a home where they abuse him. You heard what he said, Daphne. They beat him every night. But I didn't listen."

For the last two weeks, Mom conducted surprise inspections. She turned out our pockets, leaving behind yellow fingerprints and tobacco. *No one wants to admit what she did?* she screamed in our faces, frying pan over her head. Answering only got us in more trouble.

My sisters became pragmatic, avoiding trouble whenever possible. Mom and Dad argued about a lot of things including how Everett Ford stated details that only the kidnapper would know, where Brandy stayed the night, and if Grandpop died of natural causes.

I wondered what I could say to make Mom stop. What conspiracy could we confess to that would restore her to the mother we recognized?

"They need to do an autopsy," said Mom. "Then they'll dig deeper."

Brandy, who hadn't come with us either, sidled next to Mom, arms crossed. I hadn't seen her in a while. She hardly ate at the house anymore, and she'd flip out for using her hairbrush, if she talked to you at all.

"I know I've been screwing up," said Brandy, without moving her lips.

"I told you not to come today," said Mom, the veil implacable.

"To my grandfather's funeral?"

When the oldest and slowest found the chairs set for them, and Dad saw that no one else needed help, he unfolded a piece of paper.

"It is the secret of the world that all things subsist and do not die," he said, quoting Emerson, "but only retire a little from sight and afterwards return again."

A pussy willow mixed us in webs of shadow and light. Beyond that, a tarp blew off the mound of dirt they'd use to bury the casket. That, too, looked dry. Like beach sand.

"He'd be ashamed," said Mom. "Truancies, absences. Staying out all night for a boy."

"I'm seventeen now, Mom," said Brandy, her chin quivering. "It's my choice, and I choose to be in love."

"Then go with your choice," said Mom. Brandy looked into Mom's veil.

"Nothing is dead," said Dad. "Men feign themselves dead, and endure mock funerals and mournful obituaries, and there they stand looking out of the window, sound and well, in some strange new disguise. Jesus is not dead; he is very well alive; nor John, nor Paul, nor Mahomet, nor Aristotle; at times we believe we have seen them all, and could easily tell the names under which they go."

Swaddled in a yellow dress, Courtney scuffled to a point above the casket. Its waist gave her trouble, as did the violin she wriggled under her chin. Extra skin drooped over the instrument, the beginning of what would be her own scars. At Dad's nod, she drew the bow.

Over the last week, I'd nearly memorized Frédéric Chopin's "Funeral March." Courtney had practiced with a tape, so I frowned at the subtle changes, the moments she borrowed from the missing piano, and the muted undertone throughout her play. Many of the old people closed their eyes. When the bow screeched, Courtney hesitated. At the song's conclusion, Dad nodded.

"What a truly, just, ambitious undertaking," he said. "My daughter's been taking lessons with Mrs. Vonns for, oh, about five years now, and it's really, really paying off." A few chuckled. "Grandpop would've appreciated that, String. Just wonderful."

Courtney lowered her head, but her humbleness was a facade. Each time she missed a note in practice, we heard Courtney berating herself, *You're a stupid girl.*

"This next part is for anyone who wants to share something. Anyone can speak. About the deceased, about what he meant. To you."

The wind brought no relief through the trees. It was like a hair dryer.

Dad looked to us.

"I'll miss watching cartoons with Grandpop," I said.

"I'll miss his stories," said Brandy, sounding stuffed up. Against the sun, she scrunched her red face.

"I'm going to miss sitting on Grandpop's lap," said Ellie.

Dad nodded.

"My father wasn't really into classical music," Mom said. "He would've liked something fun, like Sinatra. I know Show-*pin*'s technically brilliant and all, but it's just *so* repetitive." The old people looked up at her. "I don't know. That's just me."

"Thank you, everyone," said Dad with one eye closed. "Thank you for coming." He winced when Courtney bawled, loud and unbroken.

The procession disbanded, with people whispering. "You found him, huh?"

"Physically, he was strong," said Scott's grandfather, Grandpop's roommate. "Mentally?" He drew circles around his skull.

An old couple nodded sorrowfully. "Blessed be," they said.

We paused on the hill.

A woman blocked the van, half in shadow. She wore a violet silk nightgown, one strap tantalizingly flung off her shoulder. I almost didn't recognize her as Mrs. Leeds.

"Where am I to live now?" she said, holding up some papers. "Where am I to *go*?"

Microscopic holes burned my face. Why was Mrs. Leeds staring at me?

"Loretta Gedney's sister is getting foreclosed on," said Mrs. Leeds. "Charlie Kouts's facing jail time? How does breaking up marriages help find your brother?"

"That's what happens when you break the rules." The veil obscured Mom's eyes but not her tightly pinched lips. I needed a few seconds before I realized that Mom was being smug.

"It was *you*?" Mrs. Leeds lunged. Dad and two other men held her back. They escorted Mrs. Leeds to her car, though we could still hear her shouting. "I looked after you. Took care of you and your family."

The men put Mrs. Leeds in her car. After a moment, she peeled out, honking, giving all of us the middle finger.

I looked down. The papers had fallen to my feet. *Notice of Foreclosure*, they said.

Ellie crimped the back of her neck. "What rule did Mrs. Leeds break, Momma?"

"I know she looks unhappy now," said Mom, her veil pointed toward the road, "but it was the right thing to do. That Trevor is Brandy's age, and you see that they're incapable of adult decisions. What do we say to you girls? If you don't confess when you get the chance, you might not get another chance. Look what happened to us. Right?"

I mulled Mom's tone. Much as we suffered, wouldn't Mr. Ford's confession make it all better? He would return Paul, and we could turn back into the people we were before he'd been taken.

Mom pinched my shoulder.

"Come, my babies. Let them work. The men have a lot of houses to clean."

On the car ride home, Mom didn't explain what she meant. She didn't talk about the coming days when every station frothed at Hollywood-caliber tales of disgrace and intrigue with local flair. Neighbors exposed for insurance scams. Parents outed for rehab stints. Police suspended, including Deputy Bixbee, who will face a "trial board" for an unspecified offense. Who knew, but our town had secrets. Once the land dried, and the wind unburied one, it wouldn't stop until all of them were uncovered.

Instead, she lectured about adult things we were old enough to understand now, like how even in the pursuit of God, we can be selfish.

The last I saw of Brandy that day was her whispering to Dad, lips popping, followed by a childish moan of denial.

Dad responded with a denial of his own. He said that nothing was wrong, that we must love each other and stay strong, that no one and nothing was changing forever.

CHAPTER TWENTY-SIX

July 27, 2021

I cram in a walk, breathing in dust from a construction crew, when trees writhe with birds. The Brotherhood's familiars crowding so they can unleash their power on me. One lands on a nearby park bench.

"Shoo," I scream. "*Shoo.*"

The raven flaps away with an angry squawk. I'm about to turn when I see what it left behind on the bench's backrest.

A rusty talon print. In dried blood.

I hold my throat and burst into the lobby, passing people who gawk at me.

"Mrs. Meraux?"

I turn at the sound of my outdated name. Or at least ambiguous. Am I still "Mrs. Meraux?" Am I "Ms. Meraux?" Or "Ms. Gauge?"

The hotel clerk is a pretty Asian woman with a bright flower clipped to her hair. My phone buzzes in my face before I can complete the call to Henderson. Right on cue with my existential crisis about who I am is a missed call from Karl. Great. Another problem.

We haven't spoken since the comment about Gerard probably sleeping all day after chemo.

"Yes?" I say.

The clerk pushes my mail across the counter. One, a manila envelope, is way too fancy for me. The writing is so elegant, I can't even read it.

"Delivered this afternoon, Mrs. Meraux," says the clerk, with a tiny bow.

The envelope is scented. My thumb takes a nasty cut tearing it open, thank you very much, either because of the patchouli oil or something else. Wouldn't be the first time someone thought poison would keep me silent.

"Thank you," I say.

Another buzz. The text's from Henderson.

Old black Ram. Plate 831-ARC. Econo Lodge. Revere.

More thinking dots.

Driver matches photo of Trevor Fleming.

The Brotherhood's leader is shacked up in Revere, Massachusetts. And my guy has him. Finally, some good news, though from the letter I see it'll be the last bit I'll hear tonight.

The letter's from Courtney.

Of course it is. I send a certified letter. After throwing me under the bus to the committee, Courtney responds with something Maid Marian wrote to King Richard.

It's ornate calligraphy and even looks like she wrote on a ruler, ensuring each word stays within imaginary lines. Who has she become, besides a lab tech at a pharmaceutical company?

My eyes find a two-sentence paragraph in the middle.

What you are doing here is really wrong.

Like a hatchet to my chest.

Safe in the room, I read Courtney's unnecessarily extravagant letter:

Daphne,

You are an aunt! A great-aunt to Claire, my oldest Kristen's daughter. Claire's two years old. She's beautiful, Daph. She has Dad's dimples.

I was hoping to soften you up for my apology. I didn't mean what I said at Dad's funeral. It's not like you dragged me into that kitchen. I am truly sorry.

And I'm sorry about undermining you to the committee. I know you think you're doing the right thing, but what you are doing here is <u>really wrong</u>.

I will not say her name. But everything they said about her is right.

The woman who said motherhood was "blood on our hands." Even if you tell them everything, including Mother's Day, you'll get hurt. Either by the answers or the things you won't be able to answer.

Or it'll suck you in. Just like it did with her.

I love you and I always have.
Courtney

I keep wiping my eyes when the phone's going again. I don't know why I'm crying. For seeing Courtney in the kitchen still. For her love, forgiveness, her rejection of all the things I think are important. Her insistence that justice is impossible.

Blood on our hands.

And thus portals to the chasm are paved with blood.

Or is it that Courtney's right? Too late, I'm realizing that my need for a justice I can live with has transformed me into a spider in a web. Three decades blow by, and I'm standing still, waiting for one more hapless clue to buzz by. I knew this week would be draining, defending my family, exposing our secrets to the world. But I'm sure that finally, one will. It has to.

"Ms. Gauge?"

"Yes." I part my hair as if I haven't been weeping. Even though the caller can't see my red eyes. Can't read them like Sheriff Colquitt could.

"Ms. Gauge, this is Chairman Reeves. How are you doing this evening?"

"I'm fine, Mr. Chairman," I say, rummaging in my briefcase for Henderson's notes on Bradley Reeves. Ivy League educated. Before entering the FBI, he was a US attorney for the Eastern District of Michigan. *Be careful*, writes one friend of Reeves. *He was born to prosecute a case*. "Thank you for asking."

"Well, the CARD Committee greatly appreciates your assistance. You've provided us with some wonderful insights." A tennis ball bounces, followed by the quick breaths of an excited dog. Bradley Reeves says something, *Go to your pillow*, and I can't help but smile at what the man does when he's not the chairman. "I wanted you to know, the FBI has concluded their fourth dredging of the Fleming Quarry. They discovered three more human remains. Juvenile males."

You'll know the Day Star is coming when they wet the Fulcrum.

Arcturus is set to move back to its original position in a few days. The end of the Hunt, and the coming of Lammas Day.

"Is it the Nolans?" I ask, trying not to cough, my voice tight. Grant, Roderick, and someone else?

Bradley Reeves answers in a rush of air. "They're too decomposed to be that recent," he says. "They think the bones have been down there at least thirty years."

The tightness slips like a blade into my chest, where it twists. "One of them could be David Gedney," I say. The Gedneys could finally have their child found.

"Ms. Gauge," says the chairman, "I'm afraid I have more bad news."

They're folding the CARD Team Commission. Shutting me down.

Walter. How much you want to bet he had something to do with it?

"Earlier this morning," says Bradley Reeves, "Boston police responded to a 9-1-1 hang-up at the Kenmore Inn. It's one of those cheap hostels around Fenway Park."

I can't keep my eyes still. They bounce from my wall of suspects, to the TV, to Courtney's letter. I have no idea where the chairman's going with this.

"There they found Gerard Gedney unconscious and unresponsive. Looks like he died of an apparent overdose."

No. I kneel on the coffee table. Not Gerard, the one who set this whole deadly thing back in motion. Haven't the Gedneys suffered enough?

I try to keep myself composed, wondering how much I should say. There's a conspiracy to squelch any talk of the New Minton Boys, even after thirty years. I can't afford to push away the CARD Team Chairman with crazy talk.

"They're sure it's suicide?"

"Well, no," says Bradley Reeves. "BPD won't be sure of anything until they complete their investigation. They did find a letter next to Gerard. He wrote an apology to his mother. And I'm afraid that's not the only death. The body of a middle-aged woman was found in an alleyway a block from Kenmore Inn. Eileen Rahall's. I've ordered enhanced security for tomorrow. And should you wish, I can have an agent escort you to the deposition."

"That's not necessary, Mr. Chairman," I say, then it hits me. Two people from New Minton dead within a city block is a heck of a coincidence. "Are you saying Gerard's and Eileen's deaths are connected?"

"She was apparently attacked by animals," he says.

Revelation strikes me cold. Not animals. Birds. For whatever reason, someone didn't want her transforming into a familiar after a lifetime of overusing the Elementals' power. They summoned the ravens to take her out after she took out Gerard.

Then the same ravens followed me, her blood on their claws.

"I also wanted to inform you," says Bradley Reeves, "that I can't depose everyone you requested."

"You can't get everybody?" My back tightens.

"Some are dead, Ms. Gauge. Others are concerned for their safety." Please. They're the ones killing people, not the other way around. "Of the two you wanted most, Reginald Rahall demanded furlough as a condition, Trevor Fleming immunity."

"Fine." I didn't see Rusty during my break in testimony, only the entourage of deputies. Even with nothing better to do than sit in a cell, no way would Rusty appear out of a sense of goodwill.

At least Trevor's acting as I hoped. For weeks, I've been matching wits with someone I haven't seen in over thirty years. The strongest impression I have of Trevor is the time I caught him sneaking out of Mrs. Leeds's house. Trevor was so humiliated he threatened an eleven-year-old girl with all the power he'd soon have after the second Blót.

Trevor's New Minton pedigree instructed him to feel superior to anyone he met, yet he was insecure and afraid.

Then he grew up to be a Harvard-educated snob whose only preoccupation was to expand Blót so the *Elementals will shower us with riches.*

Of course, that kind of person would want immunity. Protection is something Trevor's craved his entire life.

I hope I'm right.

"What about the issue of disclosing financial assets?" I ask.

"Well," says Bradley Reeves, "Mr. Fleming has already turned over documents of this nature. But, of course, I cannot discuss confidential matters."

"Can you tell me how much he got from the sale of the construction company?"

"Ms. Gauge, you know I can't."

"Can you tell me where he has properties?"

"What exactly are you hoping to find?" he asks. "Forensic Accounting reviewed Mr. Fleming's documents, Mr. Rahall's, everyone's. They found nothing unusual. And they found no connection to anything related to Crusher."

"What about Vulcan Inc.?" I ask. "And their office in Fresno?"

My free hand spreads Gerard's postcard, the Office of the Inspector General's report concerning the postcard's PVI strip, and junk mail samples that were mailed last August or September. Also in there for some reason is

Courtney's letter slapping me in the face. *What you are doing here is really wrong.*

Maybe I'm not just wrong in that I shouldn't do it. Are my facts wrong? All the hope I pinned, sure I'd get a lead, wasted.

". . . even has large donations to Sisters of Mercy."

I cough. One envelope is from the Catholic Women Religious Congregation. I turn it over. The Sisters of Mercy outsource their literature to PPMPrint. "Excuse me, sir?"

"Not quite the miscreant you say, Ms. Gauge."

A hundred tiny threads converge at once. Someone in the Brotherhood slipped the postcards into the Sisters of Mercy bulk mail so that they couldn't be traced. They can lie to our faces for thirty years, but I feel it, my life's work, my Dad's life's work, reaching fruition, that clue buzzing in.

"Ms. Gauge, why don't you get some rest, and we'll figure out this whole thing tomorrow morning?" He sighs. "If you're still willing to come in?"

"Good idea, Mr. Chairman. Yes, absolutely, I'll look for Vikki again." I thank him and hang up. My fingers blur along the keyboard.

There it is, on the About Us page. The institute director is a smiling white-haired woman named Sister Judith Abish-Ford. That name sort of jumps out. She thanks the Crusher Group, among others, for their donations. How did the FBI miss the connection? I'll let the chairman know tomorrow.

Sisters of Mercy is located in Los Angeles, California, a four hour drive from the Crusher Group's headquarters in Fresno. The organization specializes in providing care and housing to homeless teenagers. Vulnerable boys and girls who disappear all the time without anyone to miss them.

Just like the girl who burned in the chicken coop, Patricia Olsen. The runaways, Adam and Michael Cordon. Donnie Sobaski. Then came my generation, Paul, David, Billy, and Clai.

Most recently, the Nolans.

I go back to my Exhibits and open up P, which deals with all those awful years I spent tracing the relocations Eileen Rahall mentioned. In 1937, state police arrested two dozen New Minton men and women, including Thomas Fleming and Harriet Rahall. All were released without charge.

In 1954, the FBI repeated the raid, this time removing fifty children who suffered "gross neglect." Among them was Donnie Sobaski, then sixteen years old. Court records show that shortly thereafter, my grandmother Charity Drane divorced Grandpop, married his best friend, Martin Abish, and adopted Donnie.

I never learned why Charity made such an abrupt life change. The raid, divorce, and adoption happened so close to one another, but I can't see what connects them.

Now with state-recognized parents, life should've turned around for Donnie. He had a girlfriend, Jessica Ford. Shortly after filing a report claiming that Everett Ford threatened the couple because he was jealous, however, Jessica allegedly ran off with a visiting carnival in 1954. Jessica never made any attempt to contact her family, and Donnie ended up with a bullet hole in the back of his head.

Twelve years later, investigators trace that bullet to a rifle registered to his foster parents, Martin Abish and Charity Drane. In 1969, they stood trial until a transparently fake alibi allowed them to escape justice. Maybe the Brotherhood thought all the articles about Blót would attract too much attention.

I think that Donnie's murder was an initiation similar to the one Rusty, Scott, and them did in 1988, a reviving of some old tradition. Everett Ford was only too happy to suggest the friends who, in his view, betrayed him. Like Billy Rahall, they sacrificed Donnie and Jessica during that initiation, though only Donnie's body was ever found.

What did I want here? What did I see in the files?

I'm tapping the year of the FBI raid, 1954, and the trial, 1969. On top of each folder are the years Olsen, Cordon, Sobaski, and my brother disappeared or were found dead.

1954 seems like it should fit, but doesn't. Same with 1969. Then I remember: the Abish-Drane trial took place in 1969, but the hunting accident occurred in 1955. One year after the FBI took New Minton's Hill children. I write down the years of each death on a fresh piece of paper.

1889. 1922. 1955. 1988. 2021.

Ellie was right, the precious, snarky little sister New Minton ruined: it was *so* obvious. So obvious I missed how the years line up.

It's happening. It's been happening every thirty-three years.

I have the web. Now all I need is the spider.

CHAPTER TWENTY-SEVEN

July 28, 2021

And that spider is Trevor Fleming. It has to be.

Trevor and someone I've overlooked. He or she is left-handed, and likely the author of the postcards. And is so squeaky clean no one ever entered their fingerprints into a database.

The need to speak with Bradley Reeves is nauseating, especially when once again Jay Nolan makes headlines for the wrong reason.

Under his sister's Facebook Live account, Jay was caught selling his children's clothes and furniture. Jay's sister claims it's to raise money for a legal defense.

We ain't made a money, she told WBCZ. But the article includes Twitter responses bashing Jay Nolan.

Definitely guilty.

Scott Peterson flashbacks.

That last one is disturbing.

A parent would only sell his children's possessions if he knew they weren't coming back.

Jay Nolan doesn't need to sell his boys' things. I have proof of a pattern that goes back over a hundred years.

My plan is to revisit Exhibit I, Grandpop's illustration of the Idol: *sixty-eight alens in height,* he wrote, but the dimensions always nagged me as too tall. What if Grandpop meant *sixty-eight feet*?

That math would work out to be thirty-three alens. A number apparently sacred to the Brotherhood of the Raven.

In the conference room we watch the clock. The red second hand whirs around and around. The white-haired Walter sighs every time I glance his way. Vikki's ankles swing. Ten-thirty ticks by, then eleven.

Great, another distraction. I have a missed call from someone with a 713 area code. Not a number I recognize, which is always unsettling. I point to my phone. Do I have time to make a quick call? Vikki shrugs. I step out.

The corridor still has blue light, but half the people. They perk until they recognize I'm like them. Heels clack, their owners nowhere to be seen.

"'Sup, Daph!" I need a second before I recognize the voice.

"Brandy?" Ever the valley girl.

"It's been a super long time, huh?"

I find a nook where corkboards sport pinups of regulations and opportunities for advancement. Is Brandy being coy or vague on purpose? It's been eleven years. Of the eighteen birthday cards I sent her daughters, Stephen and Zachary got maybe three in return. She's fifty, works in Houston, private insurance. I guess I should be happy she actually called back, even if she couldn't be bothered to leave a voicemail.

"Get this, Daph, Dory and Keri? Like basketball. Yay! Of course, *Mark* is too busy. He's got a hot new young thing, and isn't it great they're expecting?"

Just as when I was eleven, I have trouble getting my voice in. Once again, I have to hear about how lousy her ex-husband Mark is. Interns float by, chuckling about something, which sobers Brandy.

"But that's not why you called, is it. Yes, I received your letter, Daph. Thanks for sending it certified, but . . ." Brandy sighs. "There's no way I'll make it to Mass."

"It's okay, Brandy," I say, my lips tight. "It, the commission, actually started Monday." At least only one sister bothered to refute my testimony. "But I could really use your help with something. You know the Ford family, right? You were friends with Elizabeth Ford in high school. Didn't an aunt run away in the mid-1950s?"

"There you go, Daph," says Brandy. "Thinking you have an obligation to Mom and Dad."

Even though no one can hear her, I cover the earpiece for a moment. "I don't," I say.

"I don't know why that makes me the angriest..." Her bitterness all but leaks through my earpiece, bitterness at being burned by every man in her life. Every woman too. "But you know what? You have to do what's right for you. Your kids, practice, movies, tournaments. That's all that matters."

Ah, the Gauge girls' mantra. Not everyone can make it, so salvage who you can. Who cares about other people's children.

"You don't have to be numb anymore, Bran." Though we both know Mom would say the opposite. And she'd scoff at this: "It's okay to feel again."

"Listen," she says, "I have to run, but stop by if you're ever in Southeast Texas. I miss you, Daph."

I stare at the phone long after the call's gone. The letter she referred to, I sent it May 8, a family anniversary of sorts, six days after I read about the Nolans in the *Boston Globe*. Brandy had two months to get her deadbeat husband to step up and get her ass here. Or do what my husband did. Hire a replacement wife to mother the children I haven't spoken to in two days.

I wish we could band together. Just this once. Show the world they were wrong to judge us.

If we had, the moment we truly understood the evil in that town, how many lives would've been spared?

"My apologies," says Bradley Reeves, a washout of beige. He looks at me with kind blue eyes as though we weren't just on the phone last night.

I nod, keeping my eyes down until confident they're clear. He escorts me into the conference room. We take our seats. The stenographer nods.

"Mr. Chairman," I say, Brandy's words still stinging me, "I have a theory about some cold cases. The first was in 1889."

"Sorry to interrupt, Ms. Gauge," says Bradley Reeves, gesturing to the television. "Can you turn that up, please? I'm afraid we have a tragic update on Jay Nolan."

"Yes, sir," I say, "I heard about Jay Nolan's ill-advised selling spree online." Though I'd hardly call that a *tragic* update.

A reporter stands in front of a hospital. ". . . and is in critical condition. Jay Nolan, father of two boys missing since May 2, has suffered a stroke while in police custody."

My heart, stomach, everything drops. The pressure that he was under. Who could take everybody thinking you were guilty?

My eyes go to Exhibit R. Maybe it was something else.

"Obviously, this is a terrible development," says Bradley Reeves. "I move to reconvene tomorrow."

"Mr. Chairman." I rise, a little faster than I intended. Not until I hear the bang I caused echo am I aware, and I shrug off a flush. "I respectfully request to go over Exhibit R."

Bradley Reeves grimaces. "Excuse me?"

"This." I point at the screen, which plays an iPhone video of Jay Nolan being lifted into an ambulance, feeling out of breath. "Has happened before. In 1988. The arraignment of Everett T. Ford Jr. for violating his parole."

Bradley Reeves leafs through a few papers in the file, reading slowly while the other members of the commission give him the same anxious frown. While I silently beg him not to adjourn, they clearly favor the opposite.

"May 2." The chairman clears his throat. "1988. Berkshire Superior Court."

"Yes," I say. Now my throat's scratchy too.

"It says here, the state intended to file additional charges against Everett Ford, including for the abduction of your brother. At this point, how long had Paul been missing?"

"One month and one day."

"What plea did Mr. Ford's lawyers enter?"

"None, Mr. Chairman."

Bradley Reeves raises his eyebrows. A sigh winds through the people behind me.

"And why not?" he asks.

"Because he died," I say. "In front of me."

CHAPTER TWENTY-EIGHT

May 2, 1988

A fuzzy bailiff peeked from the judge's private chambers. Everyone was eager for the show to begin.

And it would be a show.

The courtroom was almost large enough to be Dad's church, full like it was jury duty. The bony elbows of unseasonable heat denied us relief. We creaked under a torrent of light, the principles of justice towering over us like pagan gods.

Per Mom's orders, my sisters wore matching long socks and ribbons. Brandy had the lone custom accessory, a straw hat she tilted to feel the bumps on her chin.

Mom repeated her funeral attire, except now she had on white gloves, ready to serve as the state's star witness against Everett Ford. Every now and then, I caught her glancing back at the goateed man, last in a long row of townspeople.

Dad seemed uncomfortable in a suit and tie, brightly conspicuous out of his ceremonial robe. Before we left the house, he combed his hair into a swirl of shaving cream so that it wouldn't, in Mom's words, look like a mohawk. *Please* don't lose the judge's sympathy, too, she said.

A hush spread through the courtroom. Heads turned to the main doors.

We'd endured motions and continuances. The revolving door of court-appointed defense attorneys (three in the last two weeks). More concern for Everett Ford's loss of appetite than for Paul's welfare. The prosecution's insistence that while it hadn't linked the forensics of Billy Rahall's death to Paul and David's abduction, it would soon. Finally, the waiting was over.

The first man was Alfred Chandler, the Berkshire County District Attorney. "Can you see film on my lips?" he said to an aide. "I'm thirsty as Christ on the cross." As I was almost directly behind him, I saw that all he had in his briefcase was a single thin folder.

Next was Ben Hermann, Mr. Ford's defense attorney, shaking the DA's hand.

The heads of security officers appeared, which we took as a signal to stand. Outside the room, cameras clicked like machine guns. In the haze of townspeople and light, I spied a prison uniform, the urgent flash of neon red. As it approached, something like awe escaped people's lips, which the walls absorbed like they did all the evil and outrage released into this chamber over the years.

Our first glimpse of Everett T. Ford Jr. caused us to cringe and Mrs. Rahall to sob. Chains tinkled against his legs.

They warned us he would look thin, but God. He was a skeleton. His white tongue worked against his lower lip with unthinking insistence, a gesture that reminded me, inappropriately, of Grandpop.

The mills of God grind slowly.

What had he meant by that? Who would receive divine justice?

Everett Ford never looked at our side as he shuffled like a man much older than his age. When he sat, I saw shiny holes in his wild hair.

The bailiff called, unnecessarily, that all rise. Judge Plucho put on his spectacles and spoke to the stenographer as though finishing a conversation from earlier in the day. Something about a case number. The DA raised his hand, followed by the defense. The judge frowned at each man, looking constipated, and read the charges.

"MGL Chapter 127, Section 149A," he said, "the defendant's parole officer attests to a reasonable belief that the defendant has lapsed, or is about to lapse, into criminal ways."

Calls to shush silenced the crowd enough for the first row to hear.

Ask about Paul.

"We have an affidavit, Your Honor," said the DA, "where a witness claims she saw the defendant on public school grounds, which is in violation of his parole. We also have a transcript of the interrogation where the defendant gets a striking number of details correct regarding the abduction and disappearance of two children. Given the extenuating circumstances, we petition to file a detainer for the maximum fifteen days allowed by law to gather more evidence."

"We object to this so-called confession, Your Honor," said the defense.

Ask Mr. Ford about Paul.

"Patience," said Courtney, pausing at the bruises on my wrists. "What's that?"

The mills of God grind slowly.

My legs kept swaying, yes, we'd been patient. But now it was time for some damn answers.

We hoped that Ford would answer, and those answers would be honest and direct. We were here for revelation, for surely it was at hand.

"I'll tell," said Everett T. Ford Jr., rising.

". . . Murder in the first degree," read Judge Plucho as though Mr. Ford said nothing.

My eyes darted around the courtroom. The Rahalls sat opposite, as would our family's dark reflection, directly behind the defense counsel's table. Their noses were pointed down, they were asleep. Many I recognized too. David's parents, George and Loretta, just watched, eyes fixed on Ford in hate, no baby this time, Mr. Gedney almost bald now.

Shouldn't they sit with us? Didn't anyone else hear Everett Ford speak?

"And the abduction of two children," concluded the judge, and he looked up. "Mr. Ford, do you understand these charges?"

Sheriff Colquitt leaned to the DA's ear. "He damn well better."

"I'll tell you where to find the boy." Mr. Ford coughed wetly. "But I want my book."

His raspy voice prickled my back. Mom was right. Mr. Ford knew where Paul was.

Judge Plucho's spectacles slid to the tip of his nose. "Excuse me?" he said.

"The Book of the Brotherhood." Mr. Ford's voice grew hoarse. "I need it."

Wires wrapped around my chest. People moaned. The bench creaked like forests crumpling under a glacier.

"He's running out of food." The words came out a strangled whisper. "I don't know how long he'll—"

Mom exploded. "*Where's my son, you monster?*"

She got halfway around the prosecutor's table before the bailiff grabbed her shoulder. Dad tried to hug her. The men didn't notice Everett T. Ford Jr. raise his chained wrists and gag. Not until his larynx bulged as though some pink worm had slithered into his throat.

Is he choking? one asked. Mr. Ford's face blanched. *Did he swallow something*? asked another. His eyes rolled into the back of his head. *Can you see an obstruction*? He spouted like an ashen cherub, but nothing came out. Confusion and horror churned in my stomach.

The mills of God grind slowly.

"This man needs help," said the defense.

The DA was more specific: "Get the damn paramedic."

Ben Hermann could've caught his client's head before it struck the table's edge. He just froze; half of us did at the worst time.

The others rose. Hands lurched us forward. My sisters yelped. I couldn't get air. Despite pleas from the officers, pandemonium swept the courtroom.

Sweaty men trampled the lady who bagged groceries. She begged as her bones broke, but no one listened to our screams. They pried my hands from Brandy's and Courtney's grips. Caught in a riptide, I barreled into emergency responders who were helpless to stop me from arriving face-to-face with the dead man they tried to revive.

"You need to look." I gagged on the world's most foul white liquid bubbling down Mr. Ford's chin. "You need."

I reached for him, as desperate to listen as he was to speak, when a great blow rocked me back. Maybe an EMT accidentally kicked my head, maybe it was the gurney. They tried to explain later, *mild concussion*, each word roaring in a seashell.

I couldn't stop thinking about Mr. Ford's glazed-over eyes and boiled skin before they covered him with a white blanket.

And I couldn't forget his last words. I repeated them like a prayer, hoping that the next time they would make sense. *You need to look in the box.*

EXHIBIT R13

How will I know God's word? How do I know His words from others? Please. Please, God.

WE ARE ONE. FOR IN ONE SPIRIT WE WERE ALL BAPTIZED INTO ONE BODY AND ALL WERE MADE TO DRINK OF ONE SPIRIT.

~~I thought being 'made to drink' was the problem.~~ I will know God's word when I cannot tell it from my own?

WISDOM IS BETTER THAN RUBIES. ~~A FARTHING~~

Money makes us blind, truth makes us see, I know that from Revelation, but I fear . . . that in my heart I will always feel the pulse of two men, and right now the fire of the man I was is pounding through.

REVELATION IS NOT SEALED.

How is . . .? When . . .? ████████████████

We are always waiting for answers, for newer ones to replace the old ones, and sometimes I stare into the pit of . . . what else can it be but my soul?

. . .

After all these years of being all one ever-continuing, all tangled up, and still I cannot speak. I am as deaf to my sons as I was when I had all the rubies one could want.

~~GODLINESS IS. CLEANLINESS IS.~~

Please. Tell me plain.

WITH THE LORD ONE DAY IS AS A THOUSAND YEARS, AND A THOUSAND YEARS IS AS ONE DAY.

I try as hard as I ever tried at anything, but I can't. They're just words. Will God speak in words? Does He even have a voice?

I AM THE LORD THY GOD, AND HIM ONLY SHALT THOU SERVE.

REVELATION IS NOT SEALED.

AMEN.

—Surviving pages from the journal of Brandon T. Gauge, date unknown

CHAPTER TWENTY-NINE

May 3, 1988

I didn't understand.

Clues led one way. Mom implicated Everett Ford and the police arrested him. With the suspect found, the story turned to the last page. Always.

I'll tell you where the boy is.

That was how Trixie Belden found Jim Frayne. Okay, Jim had run away, not been kidnapped, but Trixie made *The Red Trailer Mystery* look easy. Same with Encyclopedia Brown, the boy who closed his eyes and asked a single question. Well, Mr. Brown, Boy Detective, for twenty-five cents, could you answer this: the prime suspect was dead, so who could tell us where our brother was now?

He's running out of food.

Every time I closed my eyes, I thought of Paul starving in Everett Ford's dungeon, miles away. No one would know where to look because Ford used a fake name.

The mills of God grind slowly.

Everett Ford knew he was going to die. He knew someone would kill him to shut him up.

Who?

You need to look in the box.

What box? I had no idea. And why hadn't M.N.'s notes even mentioned Everett Ford?

Questions churned and so did my stomach. I checked the clock for the thousandth time: 1:58 a.m. At this time yesterday, Everett Ford was still alive, waiting in his cell for the arraignment. Nine hours later, the Berkshire County coroner would pronounce him dead, though he'd been gone for well over an hour. An autopsy would conclude Mr. Ford suffered a thrombotic stroke. Back then, coroners ran for election, and ours was campaigning forty miles away in Northampton.

Every few seconds, Dad and Courtney's snores rattled the walls. Even they seemed farther away than they really were. I felt their distance, me to them, and them to me. I couldn't let that happen. Not any more than it had already. I would solve Paul's case.

How?

First thing when she got home, Mom piled a dozen books beside the fireplace. I asked why she was doing chores while still in her black dress. She didn't see that her white gloves were filthy now. She couldn't see much of anything, with her gaze distant and unblinking. Instead, she had lighter fluid in one hand and a box of matches in the other.

Then Dad came home. He was chatting with Courtney about great violinists. Mom rolled the veil down her face and told us that the books were Dad's journals, and under no circumstances were we to touch them. She brushed past us on her way out the door.

How could she wheel temptation before us and, with a straight face, expect us not to be tempted? The truth was Mom never suffered from irony or subtlety. This morning, she left a tampon on the toilet seat. When meeting the DA, she slobbered with enough compliments to make him uncomfortable, which she interpreted as rejection.

But God knew where Paul was, right? And Dad talked to Him. Then he wrote down the conversation and put it in the boxes Mom left in the living room. What if something in there could be that last clue that told me where?

The flashlight wavered over our parents' wedding plates, which occupied the countertop of an antique Japanese cabinet until the journals displaced them, their surface littered with yellow fingerprints. Now there were cardboard boxes.

You need to look in the box.

I dropped one on the kitchen table and opened it, and while I did not uncover Dad's transcription of the Word of God, I did uncover a revelation of a sort. I discovered Mom's boxes of surveillance that hurt so many in town.

First was a summary list of assets, police reports, insurance policies and claims, mortgage applications, check stubs, credit scores, tax returns, and bank account information. Something about Endicott Regional Savings and Loan issuing a suspect loan to A–F Collision Repair, but I didn't bother with those.

Remembering my earlier plan to snap pictures with a spy camera (which never arrived, actually), I looked at the photographs. Someone had thought the same thing, but on a much wider scale.

The smaller ones were in color, stamped with dashes, "---- - -," I recognized from an AE-1 camera. Dad, who had no interest in technology, also never filled in the date stamp.

They showed horizontal slabs of a farm. A gray-haired woman dressed in denim, a bucket in her gloved hand. Everett Ford's arrests. Mr. Mellinger walking a dog. Mr. Scofield, the high school band teacher, taking out the garbage. Doodles of tornado funnels. Mom was trying to find the other families, just like me.

And when she couldn't, Mom used all the intelligence she gathered to hurt our neighbors. It didn't make sense to be so vindictive.

More questions about financial records, which soon gave way to "M" answering.

Then, "Morty." Under receipts from some charity, I finally found a full name on a leather-bound pocket journal. "M.N." was Mort Norton.

Mom was cheating on Dad with the guy spying on everyone?

Stored at the bottom of one box, I found a list of Dad's assets. As the sole trustee, Tobias Halpern commissioned the sale of the marina and an undeveloped island in the Nantucket Sound, to . . . the trust of Brandon Gauge. Hadn't Dad donated the property to the Church back in the seventies? Why would he sell it back to himself? Could he own the property, as a trustee?

Next were newspaper clippings: an upcoming trial of Howie Winter would feature the DA's star witness, Lewis Pampel, in regard to a "suspected maritime cocaine drug ring." Apparently, Howie Winter was the boss of something called the Winter Hill Gang, a name I didn't recognize until *America's Most Wanted* broadcast the exploits of James Bulger, a man who would be on the run for another twenty-three years. Its edges had been cut only to include the text and the year, 1974.

Another article, dated April 19, just two weeks ago. *Plymouth Police recovered the remains of Tobias Halpern from a shallow grave.* Two shots to the back of the head.

Before he disappeared, Uncle Toby was the subject of a federal investigation for possible ties to the Winter Hill Gang.

I'm here to help, Lewie. But we're going to need what you owe.

Why had Uncle Toby called Dad *Lewie*?

Gradually, I became aware of my escalating breath and the hard beat of my heart. The moment I realized they weren't coming from my body was the moment I realized that someone was behind me, shoulders rising and falling.

I whirled, bit into a scream.

Mom's face glowed like bone.

I was prepared to drop the light the millisecond she snapped not to shine it in her face, but she didn't complain or even wince. Her eyes had rolled into the back of her head. Dozens of bloody Xs crisscrossed her cheeks. Then she turned.

A button trailed the wall. Mom had disappeared.

I lit Dad's desk, the kitchen. The fissure turned the light orange, irradiating Mom.

"Ugly," she said, though she was looking at the church, glowing white. "It has no place beside the Idol." She disappeared again.

Shadows padded across the kitchen tile quicker than I could track. I smelled Mom's soap and heard her breathe, but couldn't find her, only to watch her curl on the couch.

Almost instantly, her snore became smooth.

I swallowed bile. Then it occurred to me that I should take advantage of the reprieve. I ordered the remaining files without any attempt to remember where I found them, all but the photo of Trevor and bird heads. At my stealthiest, a pen rolled with insane glee across the table, and Mom snorted.

"Brady, is that you?"

The silence increased Mom's panic.

"Brady? *Baby*?"

"It's me, Momma," I said. When I knelt, she smeared my neck with hot tears. "We'll find Paul, Mom. I'm sure of it."

Her breath was like well water, but it sank me into the blissful quicksand of infancy. My fingers traced the ridges along her bumpy face.

"He was an angel in my arms. But Momma said he had a demon in him like the one in me. 'Have him slip and hit his head, spare him the pain of Blót,' she told me over and over, but I was onto her little game by then."

I saw it, too, though it wasn't Paul's head hitting the toilet. It was Mr. Ford's hitting the table. And the others, watching.

"Mom," I said, "when did Grandma Charity say all these things?" Because I thought she died long before Brandy was born, let alone Paul.

How could Grandma Charity know Paul would be kidnapped for Blót?

Mom's grip folded an eyelash into my eye. Rather than hear her words, I felt the thud of her inflection hammer the back of my skull. I hoped she couldn't feel the photograph, because my fingers found a bottle of pills in her robe.

"See, they always tell you the opposite," said Mom. "Call the truth a lie, and good evil until you think up is down."

A nocturnal animal scampered across our roof, or maybe it was the heat dragging me into the swamp of my love for her. I struggled to keep up, but time crumbled, as did her hips in my embrace. I forgot about her heartbeat, forgot about her lap, forgot to ask about the photographs from the boxes. Her voice remained, kind enough to escort me to oblivion.

"I'd like to flip it back on them." She sniffed. "Because if Mom . . . If she's right about Brady and Blót, I don't know how long I can keep going on."

CHAPTER THIRTY

May 4, 1988

Ellie's sheets were gone, but I knew why she was up early: the salty odor of ham sparkled in the recesses of her den. Since quitting drama, all Ellie would do after school is nap until dinner. She spent so much time there now, no wonder she was always wetting the bed.

I kept turning over a photo from the boxes. Trevor circled a fuzzy white monolith, where dead animals lay. Gross. Everett Ford's study groups continuing after his death. On the back, M.N. marked the place, *the hörgr*.

Where was that place? And how could I find it? When I opened the door to fumigate our room, my sister's door chirped. Brandy was teasing Courtney.

"Your boyfriend, Derek, is *he* why you like fishnets now?"

"Shut up," said Courtney. When she blushed, her birthmarks stood out like nipples. "We haven't even done anything yet."

Before Brandy could retort, Mom thundered from the kitchen.

"You want to talk crazy? How about I get drunk and go downstairs and babble on, 'I will serve as God's voice, if He doth choose *me*.'"

Papers zipped off one another like a match across a striker. Then a book toppled onto the landing, one I recognized as Dad's journal; I'd been looking for that.

"Boxes of photos," said Dad, "sifting through garbage. You've intruded on countless people's privacy, Chastity. That's goodwill. Have you thought about what happens after? We still have to live here."

"Do we?"

"And suspecting everyone won't bring Paul back."

"Why aren't you listening to me?" Mom hopped up and down on her toes. "You're committed to drivel. I tried to go back, you know. I offered them."

"Chastity?"

Sunlight faded as though the hallway closed its large pale eye. Something happened, I wasn't sure what. "I'd do anything to find my son, Brandon," said Mom. "But the Elementals don't speak to me anymore. That's why I took all those pictures. I'm trying to *do* something. And you're still looking for answers in that stupid pet project of yours like God speaks like it's still medieval times."

"This is God's will, honey. We're—*I'm*—being punished, and you know why."

"Get on your fucking knees, then," said Mom. "And *suck* on your God's will."

Silence struck my bedroom door.

"You don't know what you're saying," said Dad.

"When I was a girl—"

"You don't know what you're saying, if you're talking like that."

"We used to sing songs that made fun of all the Psalms. We'd laugh at the lions on Ignatius, and not just the kids. We flip everything you hold sacred."

"That's why we moved here, Chastity. Why I built the church. And you're shitting all over it."

"You weren't supposed to take it this far. 'Witness Protection in a far corner,' that's what you said. You left the money, and the people who worshipped you."

I scampered to my sisters. The heartbeats of three pounded as one. Mom's and Dad's shadows were scratched in charcoal along the hallway's wall.

"Maybe I haven't done a good job of being a husband," he said, "a listener."

"Nuh-uh, Brandon. Speaking God does not grant you a license to be a counselor."

"I think you forgot all the good this move did for us. If you could just look at yourself, see how much weight you've lost in the last month? It's not healthy."

We listened to her pant.

"It all comes down to my weight, doesn't it? *Maybe* I liked being skinny and I put it on so you would take me back."

"You can't rewrite history, Chas," said Dad. "You put it on because you chose to. You chose the pounds so you wouldn't be tempted anymore by flesh."

"Look who's talking, Mr. I-never-ever-make-a-mistake. The Mob knocking on our door with a baby in my arms, but I'm the one who has to atone?"

"Denying what you identified as the cause for seeking Charlie, and Jim, and Toby, *is* a mistake, Chastity. It's an error in judgment."

"*I only went with them because you couldn't be a man to your wife*," said Mom as though being strangled.

"So you turned to those friends. The ones who worshipped me."

The comment was the bitterest Dad would get. Fighting with him must be as unrewarding for a wife as it was for a daughter. He couldn't be rattled. He considered his family's sharp words as one tasted fine wine, peeling back projections, making us feel stupid for exposing our resentments and fears.

Worse than his all-know-it-ness was the tingling sense we couldn't shake, that nothing offended him because, ultimately, nothing was sacred.

Not his love for his wife, for his children, even for his God. Surely, if we could wound him, he cared about something, and it would make him weak.

Dad stopped at the landing to pick up his journal, his irises smoldering from the white sun. If he looked to his right, he would see three daughters huddled in the hallway.

Perhaps his aloofness prevented him from glancing over; perhaps it was the reason his shadow slid off the wall and we heard the floorboards narrate his retreat. Perhaps he didn't realize that sometimes all we really needed was for him to hug us, no matter how much we protested, and to tell us he understood, even if he didn't. Perhaps he didn't realize how comforting we would find this message, especially since we had nightmares about the dead man.

Perhaps Mom, in her indirect way, asked for comfort as well, for her shadow lingered above the stairwell.

A globe flashed. We screamed before we heard the crash, but we were silent as the wedding vase, the one that once caught the light on the mantel, lay in shards on the rug.

Dad was gone. The door to his study clicked to a close.

I shed tears of necessity, for the sand on our faces turned the world into prisms. Mom raised her robe so as not to step on the broken glass. As if overnight, her hair grayed. Her scabs resembled tiny crosses stamped along her cheekbones, the approximate width and length of a fingernail. Either she'd aged twelve years or was a deranged aunt, but one thing struck me:

Mom looked just like the black-and-white photograph of Charity Drane.

"Don't you look at me like that," she said when she spotted us. Like she read my mind. "Ungrateful daughters. Things are going to change around here. You can be sure of that."

Primordial light flooded the stairwell. Mom hesitated, halfway out the door. She watched the basement floor with a hand grasped around the brass knob.

We craned to see what she'd do next, which was why to us, she screamed, "I hate you all," and slammed the door.

CHAPTER THIRTY-ONE

July 28, 2021

1889. 1922. 1955. 1988. 2021.

I repeat the years like a mantra, finding the stained chair the last available. For everyone else, it's standing room only with more waiting in the hall.

Karl's left ten voicemails and sixty-five texts, though nothing specific about an emergency with the kids. Maybe my husband called about Jay Nolan, who's undergoing a thrombectomy for a clot in his brain. Even if I'm successful right now and the chairman declares Jay Nolan to be innocent, it'll be months before he'll comprehend it. He might not even remember that his boys are missing. I put the phone away.

Why thirty-three years?

We flip everything you hold sacred.

An answer is just at my fingertips, but Vikki dispels it by dropping off a package. An intern twirls a rod to close the blinds, blocking my light. Now the conference room is all wrong, like we stayed in a bar until dawn. Compounding the sense of wrongness is the white-haired Walter. He looks pleased with himself behind the semicircular table, tongue on his lips, the chairman conflicted. Still, my stomach doesn't drop.

Not until I see how thick the package is, how many packets they stapled and stamped *Copy*.

And the crowd quiets. The packets fill me with horror.

"Around this time, Ms. Gauge," says the chairman, "you recovered some documentation we mark as Exhibits S, T, and U."

A furious blush feels like cigarettes are burning my face. My eyes are like rocks skipping over a lake. I can't read whole sentences, just occasional phrases.

THE TRIAL COURT.

PROBATE AND FAMILY COURT DEPARTMENT.

"I never asked for these to be entered into evidence," I say. I'm blushing so hard I'm gushing.

"Would you tell the commission what you hold there in your hand, please?"

"I'd really prefer not to. It's personal."

"You see the date on Exhibit S, Ms. Gauge? You see only one parent signed the document."

Mom's and Dad's full names. My sisters' birthdates. I leaf through the packet. Copies of the Clifton officer's testimony, my health records, and, oh God. Even the tabloids.

I can't believe it. They ambushed me. They invited me here to ambush me.

"Which means it has no legal authority," continues the chairman, "yet it speaks to a topic you've consistently avoided, despite our clear and direct questions. Chastity Gauge's state of mind from as early as 1976." His sympathetic eyes are perfectly moist. "Yours too."

The committee of men stare. Again I'm reminded of the exhibits of the Salem Witch Trials, all the hysterical colonists towering over helpless old women. Where do I fit in?

"Let the record show that in 2011, Daphne Gauge was involuntarily committed to Southcoast Behavioral Health Hospital for three months."

"I see what you're doing." I say this directly to Walter. Though they're right. Ellie wasn't the only sister who had to spend nights in a padded room.

"For what doctors described as 'delusions and hallucinations following years of alcohol abuse.'"

"It was a secondary symptom."

"The alcoholism?"

More snickers, which makes my response more forceful.

"The hallucinations, as you call them, Mr. Chairman," I say. "I was drinking too much. I wasn't getting the nutrition my brain needed to function normally, and I thought I heard voices." I take a moment to look each member of the commission in the eye to let them know I'm not ashamed. "No one could stay sane after seeing the things I've seen, but I got my life together. I went back to school, got licensed, and became an ethics investigator. I got married and had two children. I'm a good mother."

The rage tears me up. I hate giving them the satisfaction of seeing me wipe my nose.

And no, I think too late, *the wine over this summer isn't a regression. I can have one drink.*

"Ms. Gauge," says Bradley Reeves, "the commission is simply trying to gather all relevant information, including evidence that as recently as Monday the twenty-sixth, you lapsed back into self-harm."

Lapsed. Karl's favorite word. I look at the bandage on my wrist. It's skin-colored but not camouflaged well enough. Yes, I harmed myself because I thought I could break free from whoever stole the Book of the Brotherhood. Not a compelling defense, but I push on.

"Whoever gave you that is trying to discredit me," I say again to Walter. "So you can draw this neat line from Mom to the accident, but they killed Everett Ford from across the room. To keep him silent or divert suspicion—"

"If half of your allegations are true," says the chairman, "why would Chastity Gauge return to New Minton? Why would she knowingly put her children in danger?"

Okay, they want me hacked open and on display, the greedy bastards.

"I think Dad had a conversion planned," I say. "For Mom. She rights her sins in their marriage, she rights her sins against him. His money and innocent girls were his leverage."

Bradley Reeves sits back. When he does, a chain rolls onto the desk, then a pocket watch. "That doesn't sound very Christian, Ms. Gauge," he says.

The pocket watch has faded from the years of thumbprints on it, but the back's design is unmistakable. Three interlocking triangles of Wodan.

A tingle crawls up my arm. Bradley Reeves isn't my friend. He never was.

"I know this is painful," says the chairman, "but maybe your mother was simply in an unhappy marriage. Her 'obsession with smells and cleaning' are clear indications of dissociation. She was breaking down and saw no way out."

"Sir, if I may." I'm not sure if I say it or just think it.

The law should be on my side, but I see it isn't. The Corwins and Gedneys, Salem judges who caved to fears that witches could eat them, now lend their names to residents of New Minton.

The family trees are twisted, their roots hopelessly entangled. They've infiltrated everywhere, even Bradley Reeves, a man who grew up in Pennsylvania. Can you imagine what would've happened had I told him about Trevor Fleming's relationship to the Crusher Group?

"We have medical reports," he says, reading. "Dated May 8, 1988, 2:13 a.m., that document Chastity Gauge's history of violence against her own children."

"No." Some are chuckling. Some are howling. Make them be quiet. Make him stop. The floor rumbles like Boston College is about to kick off. May 8. Mother's Day.

"Young female arrived at Saint Vincent's Hospital," he says, "with multiple stab wounds along the flexor region of both hands. Attending wrote that the wounds were deep enough the blade struck bone."

I put my head down, unable to shut out the chairman's words, the crowd's mayhem, and Courtney's letter.

The woman who said motherhood was "blood on our hands."

"Ms. Gauge, can you answer this?" Sweat beads above Bradley Reeves's lips. "Did you find Exhibit S before or after the evening of May 7, 1988?"

EXHIBIT S

COMMONWEALTH OF MASSACHUSETTS
THE TRIAL COURT

________ Division   Docket No. 07-P-127

PROBATE AND FAMILY COURT DEPARTMENT
JOINT PETITION FOR DIVORCE PURSUANT TO G.L. C. 208, § 1 A

Petitioner A		**Petitioner B**
Chastity Pauline Drane	and	Brandon T. Gauge
14 Millbury Ave		3321 Simmons Drive
(Street address)		*(Street address)*
Worcester MA 01605		Hyannis MA 02601
(City/Town) (State) (Zip)		*(City/Town) (State) (Zip)*

1. Petitioners were lawfully married at Saint Pius in Hyannis Port on May 30, 1970 and last lived together at 3321 Simmons Drive, Hyannis on June 11, 1976

2. The minor or dependent child(ren) of this marriage is/are:

Brandy Gauge	Courtney June Gauge
January 21, 1971	March 1, 1973
(Name of child / date of birth)	*(Name of child / date of birth)*
____________________	____________________
(Name of child / date of birth)	*(Name of child / date of birth)*
____________________	____________________

3. Petitioners certify that no previous action for divorce, annulment or affirmation of marriage, separate support, desertion, living apart for justifiable cause, or custody of child(ren) has been brought by either against the other except: ____

____

____

____

____

4. Cause(s) given for irreconcilable differences:

Petitioner A	**Petitioner B**
Irretrievable Breakdown of Marriage, 1B	Adultery
Gross and Confirmed Habits of Intoxication	Postpartum Depression (clinical)
Impotency	

5. On or about 6/~~04~~11/76, an irretrievable breakdown of the marriage under G.L. c. 208, § 1A occurred and continues to exist.

Petitioner A signature: Chastity Drane______ Date: June 14, 1976________

Petitioner B signature: __________________ Date: ________________

CHAPTER THIRTY-TWO

May 7, 1988

On Mother's Day Eve, Mom, Brandy, Courtney, and Ellie honored the tradition of a home-cooked meal for the last time. They chopped vegetables, slid the roasting rack into position. Brandy and Courtney shed layers like drunk Romans about to roll in the snow. Ellie wrinkled her nose at Mom's jacket, who must be in the bathroom, cleaning up.

"Smells like gas," she said.

I watched the sun smoldering behind dragon scales, on hold with New Minton Boutique.

"Sorry, hon," said the clerk after like fifteen minutes. "No one's purchased or rented any crow skull or black crow masks in the last six months."

"Okay, thanks," I said, and hung up. Darn.

If Trevor was going to Blót, he'd need the Raven-head costumes, right? If I could connect Trevor to the costumes, then maybe Sheriff Colquitt could arrest him. That morning, I had followed Trevor's path behind Mrs. Leeds's house until I happened upon some big random Victorian in the middle of nowhere, but turned up nothing.

"Daphne," said Brandy, gesturing with the butcher's knife. "Do your chore, please."

Right, set the table. The boxes were cleared, but under Dad's chair, in five women's tangled hair, I discovered a leather-bound journal. *Property of Mort Norton*, read the cover. Mom's boyfriend.

Any minute, Mom would be here. And she'd expect me to be a full participant. But I had to know what kind of love letters Mort Norton and Mom were exchanging, so I crawled down the stairs to the basement, out of everyone's sight.

An apparition flickered from the darkness, freezing me.

"I need to pick up some tools," said Dad. "The furnace has been running hot all day."

I nodded coolly while he closed the garage door. Because I had a secret of my own, I didn't question Dad's need for a bulky winter coat on a mild spring evening. I hated lying to him, so I reserved the action only in cases of extreme self-interest.

The phone station was a mahogany antique Mom found at a yard sale. Sitting on it, perusing Mort Norton's neat block-shaped print, I didn't find love letters.

I found copies of checks Mom signed. Hours Mort logged. More surveillance notes of the dates, times, and routines of the same townspeople in the boxes. Mort Norton wasn't Mom's boyfriend. He was a sleuth. He had my dream job.

And he was working for Mom. That confirmed Mom was the architect of all our town's secrets. The true sleuth in whose footsteps I would follow one day. A scribble blurred by:

> *Dominic claims the truck was driven by a <u>foreman</u> who told the boys "they shouldn't be out without their parents."*

No, that was wrong. Back on April 1, Mort Norton delivered a note right before the kidnapper called. I remembered exactly what it said . . .

> *According to George Gedney's initial statement, a black truck with dark windows followed Dominic and your son Brady to Lincoln Bridge. Dominic claims the truck was driven by a fireman who told the boys "they shouldn't be out without their parents."*

Mort had typed *fireman*. But in his notes, he had handwritten *foreman*.

No wonder the lead about a fireman never went anywhere. Mort Norton picked the worst possible time for a typo.

We had to look for a foreman. Any dads I knew fit that description?

Only one name popped into my head, but I flipped back a few pages to make sure Mort Norton was referring to the same person. Here it was the whole time, not under my nose, but under my head. The note I hid in my pillow until it got lost.

The note that implicated Marvin Rahall. A foreman recently laid off from A–F Collision Repair. He practically advertised it in Dad's church. He was the last adult to see Paul before he disappeared.

The phone was in my hand and my fingers dialed. My heart thumped, but instinct made the plan simple, inevitable.

Everything, *everything* fell into place, like it did in the stories; just took a little longer, was all.

Soon as Rusty heard my voice, he got very excited. "Hey," he said, "I was thinking about what you said, and I think I *do* know the homeless man you were talking about. He's one of my dad's friends."

I shook my head. Why would I care about Ron Abish anymore? "Rusty," I said, "I was wondering if I could come over and, you know, hang out or whatever."

Something thudded on the other end of the phone; somewhere in his house, Rusty fell.

"Really?" he said, sounding genuinely surprised, arrogantly pleased. "Th-that-that'd be awesome. But we're getting up early tomorrow. Me and Dad are going hunting."

I rolled my eyes. "Sounds charming."

"Clai's going too," said Rusty, his voice squeaking. "So's his dad. The Flemings. Gedneys even."

Gerard's dad looked so old last time I saw him. Still, what did it matter? They wanted to shoot innocent creatures, let them.

So long as I got to search their house first, and find where they were hiding my brother.

"It'd be after dinner," I said. "You'll have to sneak me upstairs. Your parents can't . . ."

I stiffened. A month ago, Mrs. Rahall wanted to know what I would do to get my brother back. I could tell her what right now. I was ready to crawl back into the abomination she called a home.

But no way could I face her again. One hex from Mrs. Rahall could immobilize me at the worst possible time.

"Don't worry about Mom," said Rusty. I held out the phone. What was he, psychic? I thought the Rahalls couldn't divine. Or maybe just Rusty's mom? "She can't charm when hitting it hard."

Hitting it hard. Boozing? Mom's shout scattered my thoughts.

"Stop answering the *goddamned phone.*"

For a moment, doubt crept in. Just because Marvin Rahall was the last known adult to see Paul didn't mean he was guilty of abducting my brother.

But he was . . . what did Sheriff Colquitt call it? A person of interest.

A *big* person of interest.

He owned a truck that matched an early description of a suspicious vehicle. He had a lot of free time, being out of work. He spent many afternoons at the Commoner's Wealth, a local tavern four blocks from Lincoln Bridge.

He spoke to one of the kids at the time of the abduction.

And he had that weird black light in his bathroom.

A peephole where the walls were hollow. Not a hatch like Courtney said, not a Door like the kids said, but a passageway leading from the bathroom to somewhere deep inside the Rahalls' house, where anyone could be transported in secret.

Goosebumps stood out on my forearms.

The Rahalls were one of the families. Along with the Fords and the Flemings, they would Blót. Unless I stopped them.

Courtney carried a steaming platter of mashed potatoes, topped with her signature twirl, into the dining room.

"The secret," said Courtney, "is to season the potatoes while boiling, and again while adding milk, cream, and cheese. Right, Mom? That's what you said?"

I saw that all the sides were ready too. Mom was ready to sit, and I still hadn't set the table. Sweat ran down the windows, smearing the night.

"Means so much to me that my girls still like doing stuff like this," Mom was saying, her smile slow and fragile. "So many changes. The eldest getting married."

Brandy held up her left hand. "I'm en*gag*ed."

Courtney examined Brandy's ring finger the way Grandpop regarded strange food. "How come Jeremy only gave you a ring with half a diamond?" she asked.

"It's a quarter moon ring."

Courtney's expression remained skeptical. "When did this happen, Brand-o?"

"Apparently," said Mom, "weeks ago. And Ellie was the only one Brandy told."

"I didn't tell anyone," said Brandy. "You're only finding out 'cause someone outed me. She's always skulking around, and if you look around right now, you probably won't see her."

Not true. I folded napkins, waiting for their collective attention to wander from me. Then I would return Mort Norton's pocket journal without anyone being the wiser.

"Who would be the maid of honor?" asked Courtney.

Mom and Brandy laughed. "Someone's inserting themselves into your wedding plans." Courtney blushed. Mom's puffy face appeared feline.

Thank you, Big Sister. I dropped the journal at the bottom of the Japanese drawer. Closing the drawer made no noise, yet Mom's eyes flicked to me behind oval rims, then to my unfinished chore. I remembered the napkins but not the plates, which cradled reflections of the overhead lights. I forgot something else: the journal wasn't in the drawer, but under Dad's chair. When I looked up, Mom's jawbone flexed.

"Where are my things?" she boomed.

I shrugged as I laid out each plate. But my fingers became clumsy at the worst possible moment, compromising any attempt to project all the naivete I could muster.

"My property, Daphne. Where is it?"

"What," I said. "The boxes?"

Brandy whirled back to the oven. Courtney needed a few tries before she could set the cinnamon candle on a glass holder because her hands shook. After lighting the wick, she dropped the match in the sink. The smoke drifted to me.

Mom and I were kindred spirits, but now was the wrong time to make my case. So a remarkable strategy occurred to me: appear to consider her words, let her conclude that the forthcoming lecture would be well-contemplated, then escape from my bedroom window. With Paul found, and her life's work realized, I figured she'd forget about the need to punish me.

"Your father stole my things," she said, smirking as though she knew every thought I ever had in my life. "First, my home, my dad, my son, *my pills so I can sleep*. Now my papers, which I was using to find him."

"Dad didn't take Paul away," said Courtney.

"And you helped?" Mom wiped her face. "All of you helped."

I couldn't see what Mom picked up off the countertop, but Brandy dragged Ellie out of the kitchen as though a tiger had slouched into the house.

"You girls never hurt me as much as you have today," said Mom. "Now I want the truth."

Something flashed across her chest, something long and slim that caught the light so fast it winked. I only noticed because the air had turned black.

Mom fixed me first, my legs too heavy to move, but Courtney had laid her glasses next to the sink, her right eye drifting from its normal alignment. Only when she put them back on did Courtney seem to realize that she was pinned into the corner where the counters met, alone with Mom. Alone in the kitchen.

"Put out your hands, Courtney. It's time to confess."

The wink was a blade, one that would fit into the slots of the electric carving knives, the same blade that would motor through the tanned, supple exterior of the turkey.

"You never wanted to do this, did you? You were playing a trick. A trick on your mommy your father put you up to, isn't that right? 'Make a big show, play pretend,' *use* my girls to distract me."

Courtney did not answer, nor did she obey Mom's instruction, but when she scratched her cheek as if to buy herself time to think, Mom rapped Courtney's knuckle with the flat side of the blade. Courtney examined her hand in a panic to make sure it didn't have any puncture marks. Then she gazed upward in horror.

"Mom," said Brandy from the landing.

Over the bobbing flame of the candle, Mom blistered. "To destroy my work, so he can keep covering up for this awful town? *Look* at Mommy."

She grabbed a lock of Courtney's hair, which had fallen from behind her ears. Courtney's chest hitched. Beads of sweat formed on her upper lip.

"This hair. It's your father's, you know? 'Course you never part it like I said to, so it keeps falling in your stupid fucking *face* the whole time."

Impersonating an electric buzzer, Mom sawed through the lock still in her grasp.

"There." She grunted. "Now you can look Mommy in the eye for once."

Courtney touched the bright calico stump where her bangs used to be. Her fingertips came away with blood. A whine squeaked out of Courtney's mouth. The candle was unblinking.

"Mom," said Brandy.

Mom waved the blade. "Want me to get the rest while we're at it?"

Courtney burrowed fingers under her glasses.

"*Mom*," repeated Brandy. "Stop."

"What?" said Mom. "Not like it won't grow back. I was teasing. Can't take the joke when it's directed at you? The know-it-all who can't get up to pee?"

That description matched Ellie, sort of, whom Brandy shielded on the landing, the cords on her neck tight. The blade was still inches from Courtney's trembling face.

Courtney, who had done nothing wrong, who was the most obedient of all of us, who just happened to be in the kitchen at the wrong time, forced to participate in Mom's joke, which we all did, I guess, after finding out that's what it was.

"Or," said Mom, turning. "How about Daphne, Daddy's little accomplice? Momma can fix that crooked nose in a jiffy."

I hadn't moved from the dining room. In many ways, the girl I was still stands there, frozen. I wish I could point to the moment when I couldn't go back to her, but my brain didn't store the memory. It was before smoke chugged from the oven, before a protest bulged in my throat, before the screams began.

I blinked and Courtney was up Mom's back, reaching for the blade. Mom squatted like a hockey player about to absorb a big hit. A gray film coated them, both stocky and bulbous, in anonymity. I was sure that it was still a game somehow.

They were easier to hear, stomping across the kitchen, snorting like pigs, spinning until their dizzying, manic dance threatened the safety of my voyeurism.

"Guys," said Ellie.

"*Stop it*." Brandy bounced on her toes as if she wanted someone to pass her the ball. Maybe they'd been shouting the whole time.

Courtney relaxed in midtackle. Mom threw an elbow.

The fire alarm sounded, and we covered our ears.

Courtney shrieked before coming to rest.

Mom rotated again, realizing late that on the last revolution she'd been alone, and stumbled over Courtney's leg.

"What'd you do that for?" shouted Mom. "You big dummy. *Huh*?"

Courtney slipped to her knees, her gold rims bent. Oil coated her fist. No, not oil. It was maroon, not black. Something else. Something worse.

"Oh God," said Brandy.

Mom flinched at the dark blade in her hand. She flung it into the sink, and its edges shrieked against the chrome.

A wet stain expanded down Courtney's pant leg, too dark and in the wrong place for her to have a toddler's accident. It turned red only when it spattered squares around her. Seeing it, Ellie blubbered as though she was a baby trying to say her first words.

Mom bent over. "Let me see," she said. "What, did you cut your hand?"

Courtney bawled. "My fingers, my fingers, my fingers."

Maybe they both had their hands on the blade. In the fight, it sliced Courtney's fingers. Mom didn't mean to.

"Why didn't you stay still, Courtney? You shouldn't have moved."

Cradling her hand, Courtney moaned like a cat, abused too long, about to strike. Ghostly imprints of pink swathed her sweater. The fire alarm screeched as though it, too, needed breath.

Keeping her lips pinched, Mom dragged a chair to the location under the smoke detector. She used her fist to club it off the ceiling, then stomped it on the floor. Brandy's eyes flicked to the front door, and I followed them. Mom's scabs throbbed, violet holes bleeding into the pale contours of her clumpy face. Sweat dripped from her hair until, with an enervated beep, the alarm cycled to silence.

Ellie couldn't stop stuttering. "Shu-shu-shu-shu-shu?"

Mom slapped Ellie across the nose. Hot needle pricks boiled on my face. Droplets of blood spattered our cheeks.

"You nosy brat," shouted Mom. "You want to know why I took all those photos? What this town is really about?"

Ellie felt where the welt whitened, a dull hiss squeezing out of her mouth. She sounded like a tire deflating, unable to understand how anything so unexpected and painful would happen to her.

"I didn't want you to end up like Billy." Mom grabbed Ellie's arm. "But you're the age I was when my mom showed me."

Ellie's legs were too slow for the pace Mom set down the stairs, so they tumbled. Ellie screamed for someone to help. She was so loud her pitch pricked my ears, then the bathroom door slammed.

Mom's voice shook the house. "I'll drink and you'll drink," she said, "and I'll be a little like you, and you'll be a little like me."

Outside, a storm raged. I went to the patio to see the trees swaying. Silver leaves thrashed.

Rocks struck the patio door. I fell back with a scream. Three, six, a dozen.

They weren't rocks. They were black birds.

They struck the patio window headfirst, though I couldn't see how they got in. Now they writhed on the floor, croaking with their tongues out. I covered my ears, and backed up until I tripped over Courtney.

"I think they're severed," she said, rocking and whimpering on the kitchen floor.

That broke Brandy's trance. She went to the phone and dialed.

"Hi, this is Brandy Gauge. I live at One Hangman's Hill. My sister's hurt. We need an ambulance now, please."

"What are you doing?"

A cold breeze whooshed behind Mom. Somehow, she'd ascended the stairs without anyone hearing. That's when I realized the black birds had stopped croaking. A spider web of cracks emanated from the long one Ron Abish left there months ago. Behind that, their bodies looked like small stones.

"Give me the phone, Brandy."

Mom wiped the corner of her mouth, and held out her hand. Her pointer finger was wrapped in a makeshift bandage. Brandy's lips quivered. The operator asked if the caller was still there.

"Now, Brandy."

Brandy stepped away and left the phone.

I wiped the dark drops off my nose, tasted the copper in my sister's blood. Mom's voice was cheerful and apologetic on the phone, as though girls will be girls.

"Oh, no need for that," said Mom. "Probably a teenager's prank."

Then, click. Mom left bloody fingerprints on the phone's handle.

Courtney rocked herself. "I want my dad. I want my dad. I want my dad."

"Your father isn't here, Courtney. So you better go to your room and get dressed, all of you."

We didn't dare ask where we were going. Or why we had to leave.

Mom had blood in her teeth. She'd bitten her finger, just like Mrs. Rahall. Did she pour blood in a cup? Did Ellie too? Did they drink?

"The man who took your brother," said Mom, "wants all of you."

The muscles in my heart tightened. I looked to Brandy, who ducked her head as though hoping to refuse the order by not acknowledging it. Mom's stale cigarette breath filled the landing and blocked any last chance we had for escape.

"But I'm not going to let that happen," said Mom. "We'll all join together so the Elementals will protect us. We can't do it here. We have to go pray on the Hill. That's how we flip it back on them." Mom appeared lost in thought. "But how can something be sacred, if the person who built it is corrupt?"

Courtney was the first to move, breaking the stalemate, revealing a blotch of blood on the back of her sweater. Perhaps she sensed, much more than I did, that if we didn't obey, Mom would slice through all of us until none was left.

Mom stomped after us, making sure we headed straight for our rooms. The door slammed, leaving me alone.

I felt like, somewhere inside me, a baby tooth wasn't ready to be plucked, but unthinking, relentless fingers wouldn't stop twisting until it detached the last copper roots from its jawbone. My entire body was numb.

EXHIBIT T1

SPECIAL COMMISSION OF THE CARD TEAM

Sworn Testimony
Deponent: Ethan A. Gilpatrick
July 29, 2021

Q: Mr. Ethan Gilpatrick. What was your job title from 1981 to 2004, sir?
A: I was a police officer in Clifton, Massachusetts.

Q: Clifton. How far away is that from New Minton?
A: About twenty miles.

Q: Approximately from April 3 to May 7, 1988, your department received three reports of quote "strange lights" in the Clifton woods, is that correct?
A: And I responded to each one.

Q: Was there any connection between the lights in the Clifton woods and those behind New Minton's elementary school?
A: Not that I'm aware.

Q: We have your report here, sir, marked "Exhibit T2." Would you take us through it, please?
A: On two of those three occasions, April 15 and May 4, I observed what appeared to be a five-foot tall person running away from me. I shouted for her to stop. I tried to track her. But the woods are very dense in Clifton.

Q: A person.
A: Yes.

Q: Not a werewolf or a Bigfoot, as some have suggested.
(Laughter)
A: No, she was bipedal. Clothed in rags. About three hundred yards away, I called, and got a brief flash of her face. Then she ran.

Q: Where exactly did this occur, Mr. Gilpatrick?
A: Along the Little Housic.

Q: The river, sir. Which runs from New Minton through Clifton. About twenty miles more or less due south of the last known sighting of Brady Paul Gauge. Mr. Gilpatrick, why do you say *her*?
A: Mostly because of the long hair, the hunched way it ran. A little short for a man, but a woman sounds right. I lost track of her about a mile in. I reported it. That's it.

Q: You consulted a sketch artist, is that correct, sir?
A: I did.

Q: And subsequently, you compared your sketch to a photograph of Chastity Gauge?
A: Like I said, I got a flash of her face.

Q: What was your conclusion, Mr. Gilpatrick?
A: The woman I saw in the woods on those days was Chastity Gauge.

EXHIBIT U

WEEKLY WORLD
NEWS
March 31, 1989
30599
Vol. 7, Issue 16

MY WHOLE LIFE IS A LIE!

GAUGE FAMILY TURNS ON ONE ANOTHER, REVEALS DARKEST SECRETS IN TITILLATING FREE-FOR-ALL!

POLICE:

SATANIC CULTS IN OUR VERY OWN BACKYARD?

DEPUTY:

SHERIFF HAD DRINKING PROBLEM DURING NEW MINTON BOYS INVESTIGATION!

LEARN THE SHOCKING TRUTH!

CHAPTER THIRTY-THREE

May 7, 1988

Every time furniture toppled, Courtney whimpered through the walls like a rejected sow. Mom stomped up the hall. "You have five more minutes," she screamed, "then I'm dragging you out." Farther away now. "The Bad Man's almost here."

What was Mom doing out there? Why was she taking us to church on a Saturday night?

Time glowed in place: 8:08, 8:08, 8:08.

It was all my fault. I had snooped through Mom's things, lied about where I was going, gotten myself entangled with those responsible for Paul's abduction. I should be punished, yet Courtney saved me. Now her fingers might be cut off, and Ellie was downstairs suffering through God-knows-what, which was nothing compared to our brother's plight.

Paul and David were somewhere in the Rahalls' house. A room whose door was blocked with a bookshelf, a hole without windows. If I was right, the lone access point was the hollow wall in the shower. I had to find some way across town and hope Rusty stayed up late.

But first I had to withstand the irrational cycle of Mom's rage.

The time was still 8:08. I aged in a crevasse of anxiety.

Behind the armoire, pipes ticked with the urgency of forgotten prisoners begging for food.

Finally, salvation. Brandy cheered the headlights rolling up the driveway, but the engine idled for a long time. Mom paused in midbellow. I waited at the window. The van's lights flicked off.

Inside, an expectant hush welled.

Outside, the unhurried footsteps of someone clacked up the walkway.

I lost line of sight in the silver glint of leaves. A drop of acid plunked my stomach.

Pressure against the bedroom door.

"Is anybody home?" called Dad.

With his presence restored, we felt secure enough to open our doors. Picture frames lay in fragments, torn from the nails they'd hung from in the hallway. Courtney crunched through broken glass, blubbering in a tone too high-pitched to be language.

"String," he said, "what the heck happened?"

Dad accepted Courtney's bandaged hand and turned it over. The blood, which had turned maroon, flaked at his inspection.

My first instinct was to warn them that Mom was behind him, *right behind him*, an impulse part of me laughed off as absurd. The kitchen had been chaotic, and the situation got out of hand, but anyone could see, as I saw now, that Mom was more or less back to normal. She'd never do us *real* harm, would she?

With her eyebrows up and a towel slung over her forearm, the answer appeared to be no. Mom's eyes were clearly, glitteringly blue. In fact, she was alert to Dad's concern, and needed to see Courtney's hand for herself. She was even taken aback when Courtney jerked away. If I hadn't known better,

I might believe that we'd interrupted her washing dishes. At Courtney's reaction, Dad escorted Courtney through the hallway, his nostrils flaring. He didn't look at Mom or her hopeful expression as they passed.

"I didn't realize how bad it was, Brandon," she said. Her voice was different. Hesitant, unsure of herself, perhaps a touch of fear underneath. "It-it didn't *look* like that when she first cut it." More forceful now. "She must've been picking at it."

"*You're the one who picks.*" We held our breath at Dad's outburst. Electricity buzzed in the house. Seeing Dad lose control made the panic real. "God, Chastity, have you looked at yourself in the mirror lately?"

Brandy whooshed me into my bedroom and closed the door. Despite caring for Courtney over the last hour (or so I assumed), she'd found the time to change into a pullover and jeans, and to fix her hair.

"I know this might sound crazy," I whispered, "but I know where Paul is."

Brandy embraced me. A hum began in her chest.

"Paul's dead, Pumpkin," she said. "Mom killed him."

"You can't say that," I said, and pulled away. "You can't even think it."

Brandy grabbed my wrists, reigniting the old pain.

"You know what they're saying, right?" Wires tightened behind her face. "Mom ran away when she was sixteen 'cause her mom was like a psycho who hurt kids. Our grandmother was obsessed with Mom the same way Mom's obsessed with Paul. That day at Mountains with a View, she left you with Grandpop, right?"

I shook my head like I was tasting bad food. "For like a second?"

"Hm." Brandy narrowed her eyes. "I bet it was longer, Pumpkin. I know because Mom used to do it to me too. Have me read to Grandpop for an hour. Meanwhile, she takes off to hang out with some disgusting guy."

I looked down, trying to remember. Mom got Grandpop to bed, but the rest was strangely blank.

"Then Mom slipped out," said Brandy. "She went to the school first, but Paul was already gone. Fortunately, it was only a few minutes to Lincoln

Bridge. Dominic didn't hear signs of a struggle because what boy would be alarmed by his mother?"

"This is crazy."

"But maybe Paul wanted his father. He stopped cooperating, so she killed him. David and Billy too."

"No, Bran."

"Or else she's hiding him." Brandy shrugged. "She's gone almost every night, all night."

Here, I thought I was alone in putting the puzzle together. Mom had done it. So had Brandy. They had the same puzzle pieces as me, yet both of them reached different and disturbing conclusions.

"You're describing yourself," I said.

"You really think someone else could take care of Paul for the last month without giving it away by now?"

I wanted to tell her that Rusty Rahall *did* give his father away. Mort Norton's journal confirmed it. But I noticed chocolate on my pants.

"There's so much to tell you," said Brandy. "Our last name isn't even Gauge. I used to have a monogrammed towel with like 'Brandy Pampel' on it."

"Pampel?" I backed away, trying to remember. Mom's box had an article about a Lewis Pampel mixed up with drug smuggling. And Uncle Toby called Dad *Lewie*. Lewie, short for Lewis.

"Dad is really Lewis Pampel?" I said. "He was involved with drugs?"

An open flap of Brandy's jeans mirrored my stain. She must've transferred it when we hugged. Except on her jeans, it wasn't chocolate. Angry red blood oozed from slices on her thigh.

"You're bleeding, Bran," I said.

Brandy's face changed. She grew more feline, more like Mom.

"It's not a cry for attention," she said. "I never told anyone, but the *power* of it. It's better than anything I could describe, like *anything*. Like I'm outside myself and *focused* and, mm . . . it's just the best."

"You did it to yourself?" I shook my head. "Why?"

First, Mrs. Rahall. Then Mom. Now Brandy. It was like everyone had lost their minds.

"Kids?" said Dad from the hallway. "We're going to Saint Vins."

"Soon as I can," said Brandy. "Soon as they're distracted, or . . . Maybe I'll create a diversion. I'll light the hospital on fire if I have to. But I'm leaving, Pumpkin. And, if you want, I'll take you with us."

"*Us*?" I touched her shoulder, hoping Brandy could hear herself. The cutting, a teenage runaway just like Mom. "Who's *us*? Jeremy? What about school?"

"Sh. That's all done with now." Brandy cocked her head to listen, then slipped into the hallway.

I didn't, and probably couldn't, say anything in return. I was oddly flattered that Brandy chose me over the others. Was being special so important? I feared it might be, just as I feared my sisters would carry the baggage as well. As I feared they would build something just to become frustrated with flaws in the design and crush it. They would weep to watch it crumble, but in part they would be glad, savagely glad. Like Mom, the sisters would inflict wounds on others. Cuts that became scars.

Unless I found Paul.

"Oh, I'll take them to church," said Mom. "You can meet us there."

"Why would they go to church *now*?" Dad breathed through his nose, Courtney in his arms like she was a newborn calf. "Bean? Where's Pumpkin? *Peel*. Oh Jesus. We're *leaving*."

"I didn't mean—"

The decision to leave, not after the hospital, not after learning Courtney's fate, clicked the moment I saw Ellie swaying in the foyer, one eye glowing under a red welt in the unmistakable shape of a hand. The other iris glittered as blue as Mom's. Her lips were red as though from a popsicle.

Mom stood over broken picture frames, trophies, and ribbons, glassy eyes seeing the wreckage as though for the first time. In that moment, I saw Mom the way Brandy did. As a kidnapper.

A murderer.

"You're not taking them, are you, Brandon," said Mom. "You're taking me. You don't want them here when you call the police. You want to spare them the sight of their mother hauled away in handcuffs. Just like they did to my mom. And I begged you not to move us here. I begged."

My escape route blossomed with rapid clarity. Sneak out the patio. Get my bike in the shed. Dad would be driving, so take the path behind Mrs. Leeds's house. All I had to do was walk past Mom, her heartbeat bending me like a magnet.

My feet tingled all the way to the patio door. The fissure crackled as I opened it, the sound of bone against bone. No one noticed.

I couldn't see Dad, but I heard his keys jangle and the door pop open.

"Blood's on your hands if you leave." Mom's voice was tight, but faint. "You'll be sorry. So, so sorry."

That was the last I heard of my parents' exchange. I sprinted down the patio stairs, dodging raven corpses curled into the fetal position, lightheaded enough to lose all color but lavender. Even at night, the humidity was an anvil.

The route to the shed should be clear, but I tripped over some rocks. Small boulders more like, forming a circle in our backyard.

The heck? I never noticed them before.

The stone circle contained some dying embers. Maybe the chimney spewed some; Mom had been using it almost every night, but I couldn't think of a single explanation as to why there was a lock of hair in there too. Blond hair, too long to be Paul's or Ellie's. The hair was pinned to a card.

My vision adjusted to poles springing from our lawn. Their tops smoked as though someone had extinguished them just minutes ago.

I wiped off the card. Not until I held it up did I see the card was actually a photograph.

A Polaroid of Mom.

The quality was grainy, but it was definitely her. Mom wasn't facing whoever took the picture, and she wasn't smiling. Someone had erased her eyes.

"Long blond hair," I said aloud, my stomach bubbling.

Just as I knew the red hairs under Mrs. Patowski's desk belonged to Rusty, I knew the lock belonged to Trevor, I *knew* it. Even before the surrounding darkness rose like a funnel. Towering over me. My heart beat so hard I couldn't draw air.

Then it turned. Something grew out of the night.

The dead eyes of a raven mask.

CHAPTER THIRTY-FOUR

May 7, 1988

Earlier today, I'd phoned New Minton Boutique to see if anyone in town rented any black crow masks. They were no help, but now I had an answer. Of sorts.

One that was terrifying.

Someone with one of those masks stood over me. The rest were along the dark perimeter, halfway in the woods, at least six of them with their bug eyes fixed on me.

Definitely people but with heads of ravens.

The Brotherhood of the Raven.

"Trevor," I said, my voice hoarse. "I know it's you. And I know who the other families are."

The Raven cocked its head. A dozen whispers echoed off the trees.

"Ford," I said, "you, and the Rahalls all getting together for two more Blóts. Take that stupid mask off."

"Only one family has Blótted so far, Daphne," said the Raven. "And it wasn't ours." Wait, the mask was garbling him. "Whores."

I took a step forward. "What, Trevor?" *Whores*. That was a mean word someone spray-painted on the church.

Sparks shot from the Raven's hand. If all the house lights didn't go on when they did, I don't know what would've happened. Would Trevor have burned me?

Thankfully, they did. The Raven shielded his eyes and scuttled away.

"Daphne?" called Dad, followed by Brandy. "Pumpkin, where are you?"

The Ravens were arguing, their voices panicked.

"She's looking right at us," said one. "We're busted."

I turned to my bedroom window. Mom stared out.

"She's blinded," said the one I was pretty sure was Trevor. "I'm telling you, it's going to work."

What did that mean, that Mom was blinded? I didn't have time to think. Dad and Brandy kept shouting my name, sounding closer. I made a run for the shed, gulping the odor of burned plastic. The door's creaky ruts rolled an inch at a time. *Come on.*

A hand fell on my shoulder. I yelped, but it turned out to be a glove from the shelf. Like I needed another heart attack.

Also not helping was my bicycle wheel caught on something. A strap.

A strap from a backpack.

With so many lights on, the fabric glowed. I had no trouble seeing. No trouble smelling either, the foul odor in its pockets.

The backpack's zipper had a name tag. *David Gedney*.

Horror sprung spider legs from my navel. Inside were burned clothes in plastic bags, though I recognized the orange sleeves of David's Pac-Man T-shirt. Last was a bloody knife. What was this stuff doing buried in our shed? How long had it been here?

Whores replayed in my mind, and I realized it wasn't right. *Only one family has Blótted so far*, said Trevor. Not whores. *Yours*.

Our family Blótted David?

No, it was impossible. No one in our family would murder a twelve-year-old boy or our brother. Mom and Dad didn't know anything about

Blót, except when somehow Grandma Charity told Mom about Blót after she died. That was why I had to do so much investigating.

I'll drink and you'll drink, and I'll be a little like you, and you'll be a little like me.

We'll all join together so the Elementals will protect us.

Mom acted like she never heard of it before. Yet she said nearly the same thing as Mrs. Rahall when she wanted me to drop blood in an offered cup.

The Elementals of *our* Church. Not the Unitarian one Dad built, but the one for the Brotherhood of the Raven.

No, no, no, *no*. Trevor planted David's backpack. He was trying to confuse me. Confuse everyone. Marvin Rahall killed Billy and locked Paul in his daughter's room. Soon as I got to the Rahalls', I would prove it.

Just so no one would get the wrong idea, though, I hid David's backpack under tarps. I'd tell Dad about it later, after I rescued Paul. They weren't going to blame our family.

With my bicycle finally free, I pushed through the woods until I reached Mrs. Leeds's stone markers, my head on a swivel, a voice warning that *at any moment* Trevor would leap out and ravage my corpse in the anonymity of twilight. Dad's and Brandy's voices grew faint.

I hopped onto my bike and pedaled out of the neighborhood. At a right turn, an acorn popped. At first, I couldn't tell what the white thing floating behind me was. A shark, but of course that made no sense. Then the street lamp lit up the hood of a car.

A car was following me.

A car driven by the Brotherhood of the Raven.

Its lights flashed with hypnotic power. I dug in to pedal as hard as I could, but the chain broke.

My front tire locked. Momentum flung me over the handlebars. For one moment, I was weightless.

Then the pavement rushed up. A flicker of black. Barrel rolls until my back found the sharp roots of a tree. When I came to, I saw my shirt was ripped open at the belly. A dozen places on my body burned, all cuts and scratches.

No time to nurse my wounds. The vehicle's driver door opened. I watched the dark figure exit, praying for another car to come. Anything so that I could escape. I was so scared, I didn't recognize the blue felt as a uniform even when the figure offered his hand.

"Little lady," said Chief Boyd, "what're you doing out here alone this late at night?"

CHAPTER THIRTY-FIVE

July 29, 2021

"At approximately 10:45 p.m. on May 7, 1988," says Bradley Reeves.

He clears his throat, and I chug water. The chairman's posture has diminished through the week. Now he resembles what I imagine his grandfather looks like, too small for his suit.

"Chief Randall Boyd logs detaining you," he says, "for violating curfew."

One last swallow, and I cough. "Brandy ratted me out," I say, failing to blunt the wryness in my voice.

The late morning sun crawls across him and the other CARD Team members. Rectangles burn their suits and skin, breaking the men into living cubist art. That might explain why everyone's wincing in my general direction. Everyone except Walter. The autopsy is nearly done. My insides steam at their feet. Mom's abuse, Dad's aloofness. Good old Walter is engrossed in a report, and we haven't even gotten to Mother's Day yet.

"She told the police," I say, "that her sister Daphne was about to get herself in big trouble if they didn't go to the Rahalls' house right away.

Then she eloped, and I didn't see her for seven years. Not until Jeremy was long gone."

Bradley Reeves nods thoughtfully. "You told Chief Boyd that you believed David Gedney and Brady Paul Gauge were being held at the Rahalls' house. What was his response?"

I uncross my arms, not sure when I crossed them. "If you have his report," I say, "you can see he referred to me as the nutty girl."

Laughter from the crowd. The brightness of the front of the conference room casts the others in shadow. They're tufts of hair and shining scalps, their faces difficult to see.

"Marvin Rahall," says the chairman, reading, "belongs to the Brotherhood of the Raven, who believe they can open a door to another dimension." More snickers. "Did Chief Boyd conduct a search of the Rahalls' premises?"

"No. I begged him to listen, but he took me home. Tried, at least. No one was there." Which wasn't exactly true. Chief Boyd acted like he didn't see Mom passing from window to window, so I pretended not to see her too. "So we went to the hospital, where I learned doctors reattached the tendons and ligaments to Courtney's three digits. She'd never play the violin again."

The conference door opens, and Vikki clacks to the CARD Team in an inappropriate pink swing dress.

"So how was Marvin Rahalls' guilt ever definitely established?" he asks. She slips a paper to Bradley Reeves who squints at the message.

"Later," I say, "he admitted to unloading from Rett's van. Served five years for human trafficking."

"Which suggests Mort Norton's intelligence was valid, at least on this point. Did Marvin Rahall ever confess anything specific about your brother, Brady Paul Gauge?"

"As part of his plea," I say, "his confession was sealed. If my brother or David were in his house, I never had the chance to prove it. By morning, it didn't matter anyway."

"I'm sorry, Ms. Gauge," says Bradley Reeves, removing his glasses. His knees strike the table before he stands. "We have an unexpected closed-door session that begins at noon."

My stomach boils and I glance at the clock—five minutes until. The CARD Team packs with unexpected efficiency and heads for the exits.

An unexpected closed-door session would have to be with someone important. Someone on the FBI's wish list of invitees who has yet to agree to appear before now. I have one guess who.

"Mr. Chairman," I say, chasing him through the traffic of men in suits. He takes one turn down the hallway, then another. "May I ask, are you meeting with Trevor Fleming? Mr. Chairman?"

Bradley Reeves stops in front of a door marked Restricted. "We will have to excuse you until eight a.m. tomorrow, Ms. Gauge," he says. "For the witness's safety."

I catch a glimpse of an older blond man with an arm in a sling, then the door closes in my face. Yes, the age is right. It has to be Trevor. The chairman's nonreaction was also a tell. Otherwise, he would've acted surprised.

Trevor accepted the chairman's offer of immunity in exchange for his testimony. He's on the other side of this steel-reinforced door. And the FBI has no intention of letting me anywhere near him.

Dozens obstruct any last sight of the commission. Heartburn spreads to my throat.

All my planning to get in the same room as Trevor, enduring the commission's intrusion into every aspect of my personal life, and the CARD Team will have to excuse me for the remainder of the day?

I could forget about the Ford family's special power of blinding and go home. Give Karl's replacement wife a break, kiss my boys, and be back in time to conclude my deposition tomorrow morning. Everything rides on it, especially after Walter outflanked me.

Instead, I put on a hat and fill two gas cans. I keep my head down and pay with cash. In the parking garage, I fill three dozen Molotov cocktails, breathing so hard I think I'll pass out.

The CARD Team Task Force is compromised. I was stupid to trust them. Trevor's going to get away, and years from now, someone will find bones in some overgrown field that belong to Grant and Roderick Nolan.

A certified letter's taped to my hotel room door. It's from Murphy and Brahmin LLP, at least ten pages thick.

Dear Mrs. Meraux,

Our client, Gerard Gedney, asked that in the case of his death, you should be copied on a sworn deposition he gave on July 27, 2021.

That was two days ago. Lawyers deposed Gerard a day before BPD found him dead from an overdose at the Kenmore Inn.

My necklace is choking me. I rip it off. The visitor's badge got caught on it. Not that I need the thing now anyway. The line of Gerard's deposition knocks me to my knees.

I tried to tell Daphne the truth a thousand times, it reads. *Paul stayed at our house the first week he went missing.*

My chest burns. I can't get the words out.

When the chemo was at its worst, Gerard told me back in April, *I dreamed about a boy, my older self, telling me I would survive. But it wasn't a dream.*

The deposition continues. *Dad*—George Gedney—*dressed Paul up like me. Snuck Paul past everyone. We played in my room, and he took care of me. Until one day, Brother Everett picked up Paul, and I never saw him again.*

"The boy knocking from the second floor," I say to myself, palms tingling. I feel like I'm looking at myself from the top of a chasm. The day I ran from the Rahalls, I didn't see Gerard on the Gedneys' top floor. I saw Paul, my brother Paul. He looked so abnormal, greenish behind the window, the curl hanging from his white cap.

Oh God.

The horror of it. Paul trusted the Gedneys to help him when he got hurt. Instead, they held Paul against his will.

The time was five, an hour before sunset, and Everett Ford's Tradesman was useless, so George Gedney improvised. He disguised Paul as his sick son to get him past everyone. Who was so valuable that George had to protect them?

"Why didn't you tell me, Gerard?" I say, wiping my eyes. "When you were still alive, and your words could carry weight?"

While I can never make up for the lie I carried for thirty years, says the deposition, *I hope this is a start.*

Gerard refers to an enclosed envelope. I open it to discover Crusher's financials, including payoffs to George Gedney and New Minton Police officers. Everything about his family, the Rahalls, and Flemings.

Which means I can take them all down.

I stop, listening to the click of hotel locks and farther away, a vacuum cleaner. I can hear again. Smell again, too, the odor of gasoline seeped in my clothes. Acid reflux burns in my throat.

What the hell was I about to do?

Thank God the letter arrived when it did. And thank Gerard too.

Let Walter have his cheap shot. It won't matter if Bradley Reeves has a strange pocket watch, or if Gerard can't corroborate his testimony because he's dead.

They can't ignore the evidence. Tomorrow, I'll play it cool. Take them through the rest of the case. Exhibit Y is my bombshell.

Finally, the guilty will be named in a federal document for the first time.

EXHIBIT V

SPECIAL COMMISSION OF THE CARD TEAM

Sworn Testimony
Deponent: Trevor Augustus Fleming
July 29, 2021

Q: You are Trevor Fleming, raised in New Minton, Massachusetts, though you have not lived in New Minton since you were sixteen, is that correct?

A: I live as far as I can without swimming. I won't say where exactly.

Q: In May of 1988, New Minton Police suspected you of a crime.
A: I vandalized their stupid church because the Gauge girls ratted out me and Donna, but why's that matter now? I thought you said I have immunity.

Q: You were having a relationship with Donna Leeds, your brother's wife, after he died?
A: Yeah, and Donna's still a registered sex offender. Tell me, is that right?

Q: And on April 1, 1988, you prank called the Gauge residence, claiming you were going to Blót Brady Paul Gauge, is that right?
A: It was a stupid thing to do.

Q: Mr. Fleming, how did you know so many details, such as Baja Buggy?
A: Man, every kid had that toy.

Q: The commission is curious as to whether you had another motive for vandalizing the Unitarian Universalist Church, Mr. Fleming. We've heard testimony that you studied under Everett Ford. And while under the influence of drugs, Mr. Ford would encourage you and other boys to stab animals. He would teach you ancient, outlawed traditions of the Brotherhood of the Raven, such as the Quarter Moon Ritual.
A: As a kid, I did a lot of stupid things. Chose the wrong role models.

Q: Your close friends, Jeremy White and Derek Robinson, corroborate the allegation that Mr. Ford also impressed the idea that you should expand the practice of Blót to include four children: Claiborne Denton, Brady Paul Gauge, David Gedney, and William Rahall. Kidnap and prepare them for ritual sacrifice. I'm sorry, Mr. Fleming, is something funny?
A: Chastity Gauge. Or was it Pampel? Killed those boys, and she abducted her own son because she was nuts, just like her mom and just like her kids.

Q: Just one more question, Mr. Fleming. On the night of May 7, 1988, did you, as a member of the Brotherhood of the Raven, participate in a pagan ritual in which you drew pentagrams and Baphomet behind One Hangman's Hill, the Gauge's residence?

A: Who, by the way, never apologized to the families of those four firefighters.

Q: On the night of May 7, Mr. Fleming, were you at the Gauge residence?

A: I was asleep probably. Now are we done here? I'd like the papers now. I answered your questions, and I have immunity.

CHAPTER THIRTY-SIX

July 29, 2021

My hotel room has a stack of take-out boxes on the couch, a tangle of clothes on the table. I'm shaking out what I wore on Tuesday, hoping I could recycle the pants for Friday, when the Teledex rings. I answer it without thinking.

"Daphne," says my husband, "why do bank records show you've withdrawn twenty-seven hundred dollars over the last five days?"

Dad's money didn't go as far as I hoped it would, not that I want that conversation. I'm in the bathroom with no memory of how I got there. I avoided Karl all week, really all month, because he makes me pace. He tricked me, calling from a number I can't screen.

"You promised you'd take your name off the account, Karl," I say, my head thudding.

"Please, Daphne," he says. "I know you're determined to prove Jay Nolan innocent because you couldn't do it for your mom, but come home."

He knows about Mom. Her history of being quick-tempered and emotionally fragile was going to come out.

I was deluding myself to think otherwise.

"I have proof of their guilt," I say. "Gerard's deposition implicates Trevor, Rusty, and George."

"Did you tell this to the FBI?"

"I was so blind, yes, of course I will tell them, Karl. Today was a train wreck. I couldn't see how Chairman Reeves played me." I shake my head, unable to block the image of him checking the time. "With his vintage pocket watch."

"He played you with a pocket watch," Karl repeats. "Daphne, I hate to play this card."

"So don't play it."

"But it puts things in perspective," he says. "How you sound, sometimes? I might've hid that too."

"Who do I sound like, Karl?"

I know whose name my estranged husband will say. Except I can't prepare myself for the comparison.

"Your mother, Daphne. How she couldn't admit she was wrong. Too headstrong, refusing to listen to reason."

"I sound like a murderer," I say. "A kidnapper. The prime suspect so iron-clad, no one looks seriously at anyone else. That's great, Karl. Thanks for that."

I wish I could remember Karl's voice the day Dad died again. I wish I could recapture the feeling that he was the one. Last time I really saw him was when he was handsome in a tuxedo and I was eye candy for his bosses. I don't even know if Karl got the job or promotion or whatever he wanted.

"I'm sorry," says Karl. "I didn't mean it like that. It's just, the boys are sick, babe. They're asking for you."

Despite everything, I get a spark from him calling me *babe*. Like we're dating again.

"Talk to Mommy." Cough, cough. "Talk to Mommy."

"Oh," I say, "what is Zachary doing?"

We're the kind of parents who let our kids interrupt us. I think Karl likes using them to bring me back from Planet Weirdo. He doesn't realize how my heart, already beating at a good clip, now races.

"Tell Mommy what you did, Zach."

"Mommy, I saw the ball, and the ball." He sneezes, the most adorable little sneeze. "And I, the soccer." He sneezes again. "And I *kicked* it, Mommy."

"Wow," I say, "good job, Zachary." I'm so glad to hear him, enthusiastic and inexhaustible.

"He's gone, Daph. Now he's wrestling with the ball."

I laugh, wiping my eyes. "Is Stephen there?"

"Want to say hi to Mommy, Stephen?" Pause. "He's very into his anime, apparently."

Makes sense. Stephen's only gotten more aloof and more like his mother.

"Daphne," says Karl. "You're not going to do anything crazy, are you?"

"Course not," I say, pulling a line of thread off my forearm. It's from a T-shirt I tore when capping thirty or so homemade bombs. "I have one more exhibit to show the committee." Which will clear Mom of charges and lead to Trevor Fleming's arrest. "Then I'll come home."

Something tells me as I zip up the locksmith equipment—maybe it's that sense Trixie and Genny had, even if I don't believe in those things anymore—that if Trevor Fleming is allowed to go free, he'll set out in his vintage Ram, license plate 831-ARC, and head west.

The destination will be somewhere in the Fresno hills, where the postcards came from, where only the locals know the roads. A place where Trevor continues his work. Consecrating new ground. Teaching a new generation, as Everett Ford taught him.

I can't let that happen. Henderson will have to deal with Trevor's travel plans, but my other phone says Henderson can't meet. Bryan can, whoever that is.

Basement, he texts. *2 hours*.

I'm so pumped that for once I do as Karl begs me to do. I forget, and before I hang up, what comes out of my mouth is the free, pure version of my greatest hopes. My thoughts as Daphne Meraux, age forty-four, mother of two.

"I love you, Karl," I say. "The boys too."

"She sounds like a monster," says a pale woman on TV.

I look up from my phone's blank screen, my heart thumping, convinced for a moment she's in the room, talking to me. It's some documentary on Mom. I snap off the television, wondering when I turned it on.

Tears come, pouring down hard.

I never told Karl to call me. Zachary's coughing and sneezing, and I never said, if Zachary's cold gets worse, let Mommy know. Why didn't I say it, and what if Zachary gets pneumonia? Or his TB and whooping cough immunizations don't take? I didn't ask because I'm a bad mother. I don't deserve to live with them. I belong in hotel rooms like these. Among a dozen Styrofoam containers that stare at me, their jaws unhinged.

Until the money runs out.

As I get myself together, I do two things.

I imagine even more gruesome scenarios for Zachary.

And I wonder if I'm about to do the worst thing of my life.

Only resentment allows me to focus. Not once, in all the years Karl got called in to perform orthopedic surgery, did I guilt him with sick kids.

Then I go downstairs and wait for Bryan.

The elevator dings at the parking garage, where the valets tap their phones. It's dank here, and dark. A man waits by my car, face in shadow. Even in the summer, the man wears a heavy green coat and a black beanie.

"You're early," he says.

"So are you." I fumble in my purse. "Are you Bryan, recommended by Chad?"

The man smirks, maybe because I slur the name, his breath steaming.

"I think my brother's name is Henderson. I get a first name, he takes our last name."

I don't like how sloppy he is. Makes me remember how much Zebra Investigations was a joke, and how naïve I was to think that nonetheless, Mom's idea to use a PI was sound.

"What have you been doing this week, Bryan?" I ask. My fingers find the bills. They find the Beretta too. Depending on if this guy's creep meter rises or not, I'm ready to pull out either one. See how he likes a pistol shoved in his face.

"I've been following a black Ram with Mass plates 831-ARC. It's stayed in Saugus and Revere. Now it's in Allston. After I bribed the hotel clerk, he ID'd the guest as, uh . . ."

Allston, of course. West of Boston. Easier to cut through the afternoon commute.

"Trevor Fleming," continues Bryan. "Who will check out tomorrow."

"Bryan," I say, "this two hundred is for you."

How long does it take to count four fifties, but Bryan's slow. His fingers shake.

"Another two hundred if you do two things. First, he needs car trouble tonight. Something that makes him stay in town until Friday afternoon, no sooner. And you tell me when he leaves Allston."

I hold out Courtney's envelope, now with the extra money. Bryan appears skeptical.

"Is anyone going to get hurt, Miss?"

"Excuse me?"

"This is your Prius, isn't it?" he says, pointing to my expired Wellfleet beach pass. "I thought you might've had a problem with the gas line. But you've got lots of bottles banging in the back. And sorry, Miss, but your clothes are drenched in gasoline too."

Smells like gas.

If only we listened to Ellie. If only I listened.

I'm so close to repeating the same mistakes.

"No one's getting hurt, Bryan," I say, forcing a laugh, forcing myself to relax my grip on the pistol for this nosy sleazeball. "Our lawn mower leaks. And those empties in there?" I take the chance he can't tell. "They're for my children's bottle drive."

Bryan's thick eyebrows cover his eyes. His hair must be brown or black. "I thought Henderson said you had no family."

"I have a family, Bryan."

Bryan studies me for a long time. "So," he says. "Car trouble that'll take a day."

"Friday afternoon. That part is very important."

"Then call you on this phone when he checks out." Bryan shakes a disposable phone I passed to Henderson weeks ago. All these Samsungs and Huaweis in my purse, any one of which could ring at any second. "That's it?"

"That's it."

"And no one's getting hurt."

"So long as you don't screw up," I say. "If you do, I won't forget."

Bryan laughs until he sees my face. The smile fades. And he nods. "Yes, ma'am."

I make sure he doesn't follow me, the dirty, disgusting man. The door slides, the elevator lifts. Brandy's perfume is in here. Likely I'm imagining it. Then I'm back in my room.

Yes, I understand the consequences of my actions. I am in full control of my thoughts. I know full well that I may go to jail for what I'm about to do.

But I'm different from Mom. How?

I will be more selective.

Make sure children, especially the Nolan Boys and whoever else they're holding, aren't inside any of the houses Trevor visits on his way to Fresno.

For the sake of our children, the Door must remain open.

For our children's sake, I can't give any quarter. I think Stephen and Zachary will understand that.

"That's a backup," I say to the empty room. "Only a backup."

With any luck, Trevor will incriminate himself, and I'll keep my word that no one will get hurt. Either way, he can't leave tonight. Because tomorrow morning I have to tell the committee about the last awful time I saw Mom, and I can't do it on another two hours of sleep.

EXHIBIT X1

SPECIAL COMMISSION OF THE CARD TEAM

Sworn Testimony
Deponent: Randall A. Boyd
July 29, 2021

Q: Mr. Randall A. Boyd, you were Chief of Police of New Minton from—

A: I'm going to go on ahead and skip to the part that matters. I got the nutty Gauge girl in the back seat . . . and I says, "You know it wouldn't be the first time Mort Norton made it all up." He was a sleaze. But the Gauge girl "We can't be accusing another innocent man without evidence."

Q: Marvin Rahall.

A: Right, "We can't accuse Marvin Rahall without evidence." She says, "We have to hurry, because the Rahalls are hunting the next day." And I says to myself, "Gee, we got a tip about a hunting cabin in Clifton." Owned by Lynne Sobaski, about twenty miles from where Brady Paul Gauge was last seen.

Q: In fact, your department knew of this cabin for weeks, Mr. Boyd. Seems like an awfully good place to hide a young child.

A: Which was Number 499 on a list of . . . you're right. Apparently, Flemings used that place, even Dranes. Second hunch I ever had in my life, both on this case.

Q: And what happened after you dropped off Daphne Gauge with her father at Saint Vincent's Hospital?

A: Nutty girl wouldn't let me go. Kept raving about if a false accusation makes her a liar. And if Mort Norton did make up a foreman, "who else would suffer the consequences of making Mom paranoid?" Her dad was doing his best to calm her down, but all the girls were in bad shape.

Q: Excuse me, Mr. Boyd. Daphne Gauge asked you, "Who else would suffer the consequences of making [her] mom paranoid?" What did you make of the question?

A: I should've thought on it more. Now I know. But all I was thinking was, I got to get to the cabin and check it out.

Q: 39 Wahl Lane, Clifton, MA. What time did you arrive?

A: 4:30 a.m. The residence looked abandoned enough. Looks like kids partied there at one point, with all that Blót graffiti nonsense.

Q: Did you enter the premises?
A: I was real nervous, mind you. I forgot my weapon. We were required to carry one, but I thought I'd be out for just a minute.

Q: What did you see, Mr. Boyd, when you looked inside?
A: First thing I saw was a body.

CHAPTER THIRTY-SEVEN

May 8, 1988

"We're going home," Dad said as he loaded us into the van. I imagined Mom alone in the house, wondering how the night had escalated from unmemorable to one where she stabbed her own daughter. Could she see how far she'd gone?

Without eyes, she couldn't see anything. Because Trevor blinded her.

No. I told myself that we'd roll back Mom's disintegration. Find a way to heal.

I'm not sure how long I dreamed, but I woke between the van's creaky cushions, too day-whipped to pull myself out. An unclasped belt dug into my back, but what kept me from falling back asleep was a red shadow dancing across Ellie's fuzzy cheek. The driver door was open, but no one occupied the seat.

"Dad?"

Flames chugged up the stone wall of Dad's church. The van had been parked only twenty feet away, close enough for black bubbles to form on the windows. At my touch, the door handle melted like chocolate.

"Guys?" I said. "You need to wake up now."

Courtney wiggled into a corner, and covered her eyes with the bandage, looking like a bloated frog made out of oatmeal. Her poor hand would never be the same. When I pinched it, her eyes blared open.

"What the hell, man?"

"Fire," I said. "We've got to go. *Fire*."

"Oh, Jesus Christ." Courtney startled as though I'd dropped a spider on her lap. She slithered over the back seat, onto Ellie, and out the driver door.

I had to drag Ellie by myself. She didn't scream when I wrenched her around the driver seat and onto the church's gravel parking lot.

There we hunkered, speechless and unsupervised. Were we safe now? Where was Dad?

Fear gave way to horror as flames shooed higher up the stone. And finally, the lump in our throats, the acceptance that everything we'd committed to would soon be gone, and we could do nothing but watch it turn into ash.

The end of the church Dad built to save New Minton. The end of his life's work. His last shot for communion with God in His language.

Because I failed. Even though to find Paul I worked the hardest I ever worked for anything, like Dad, I would be denied. The clues had ended.

They were nothing but a house of mirrors anyway, a demon echo that whispered for us to satisfy vendettas. Ron Abish. Donna Leeds. The Rahalls, so Mort Norton said. It wasn't my power of deduction that led me to believe that each was guilty, it was my irrational certainty that somebody was responsible, so it might as well be whoever they thrust in my face first. And what was left, the Mob somewhere in Hyannis?

"Who's that?" said Courtney, pointing with her bandage to the other end of the lot. The hair Mom cut bled white, sprouting from her dark bangs like a weed.

I barely had the energy to look over. Glinting around the bend was a car, light pastel blue. It disappeared behind some trees in the time it took to blink. We probably imagined the car—but then it rolled through the entrance, unhurried, crunching each acorn from last season, the grille bouncing toward us. It was an LTD, the lights off. Just when it would strike Ellie, Chief Boyd cut the wheel. At the sight of a toothpick in his mouth, and how rude he'd been hours ago, accusing me of lying, I balled my fists.

"Paul?" said Courtney. Dimly, I was aware of her squinting.

Perhaps with his sunglasses, Chief Boyd's eyes could be anywhere. He might not be smirking at Courtney, Ellie, and me still tingling from the fire that had leaped to the van's hood, seeming to ask, what the heck are you girls doing out here? He might only be staring over my head, his expression transmuting from smug to confused, and I could see why.

The squad car's windshield reflected the gust of heat I felt breathing down my neck. It was heavy as a dragon's breath, which only made me angrier that Chief Boyd chose, *after* my family was forever torn apart, to get off his lazy butt. When he got to me, I'd crush those stupid glasses under my heel. Take *that*, and I'd spit.

"Oh my goodness," cried Courtney. She pounded Chief Boyd's window with her good hand, not the least bit angry he happened up Hangman's Hill. "Oh my goodness, *oh my goodness*."

My first thought was Mom's attack caused Courtney to lose her mind. I actually considered picking up a rock and putting Courtney out of her misery. It felt perfectly, coldly logical. The only reason I didn't was Ellie looked to me as though waking from a long nap.

"Is. He. Real?" she said.

I realized Ellie looked to me as I looked to Chief Boyd, but he wouldn't or couldn't confirm, let alone explain.

Courtney was sure for all of us. She dented the car door, screaming Paul's name, raising the hair on my arms. Through the dim blue tint of the squad car's windows, I saw a shadow in the back seat.

He had long hair, brown not blond. But his forward slump and chapped lips were unmistakable. Years could pass and I'd recognize them puckered out no matter what.

"It's Paul," said Courtney. "It's Paul."

His name welled in my throat, strong enough for me to tear open the front passenger door and worm until I could unlock the back.

We cradled him on the parking lot. We closed our eyes and rocked and cried. *We have Paul back. We can actually bring him home.*

"It's Daphne, Paul," I said. "I've been looking for you, brother."

"He's so bony," said Ellie.

We lifted his dark rags until we found him, dirt smeared all over his exposed ribcage. No cuts or bruises. That wasn't Paul's blood on the knife.

"And he smells."

Like a sour old dog, but Courtney echoed what I thought: "I don't care." She hugged him. "He's the most perfect little brother."

Paul didn't react. He looked like Dad did in baby pictures, but his grumpy tired look came only from Mom.

"I searched everywhere I could, Paul," I said. "You remember those stories I read to you, Trixie Belden, Ginny Gordon, Beverly Gray, Donna Parker? I used what I learned from them to *find* you. And I did. I risked everything, I even thought I was coming apart, but I wouldn't give up. You're my brother and I would do anything for you, you understand?"

We held each other, holding in the familiar stink of parmesan cheese from his oily hair. We were a family, and we were never letting go.

Except I didn't find Paul at all. All the stress of the last six weeks crushed me on the parking lot. Every day replayed as slowly in my mind as we lived it, from the many who told me he was dead, to the hours worrying if, despite our spoiling him, he had learned in seven short years to care for himself. For the darkest, loneliest of moments, I feared they would be right. But Paul in my arms proved them wrong. I would watch Paul grow up and I'd protect him when he couldn't defend himself. Chief Boyd may have found him, but I'd get to be his big sister again, now and forever.

"Where have you been, Paul?" said Courtney. She shook her head, laughing and crying in her good hand.

"I mean, like, someone clearly took you, right?" said Ellie. "I wonder who?"

Under any other circumstance, I would've rolled my eyes. I was close, watching Ellie pat Paul as if he was a suspicious neighbor's pet, one of her eyes still red.

Paul's eyebrows went down. His eyelids danced as though he might be dreaming.

"Ehnnnnnn."

"Paul?" I said. "What is it?"

My fingers caught on Paul's wrist. He had a white ribbon around it, similar to the one Mrs. Rahall had fixed onto me.

Paul's ribbon was a little different; it had blond hair braided around it. And three raven feathers were attached. One of them pricked my hand.

Trevor Fleming.

Before I could say his name, Paul let out a sound somewhere between a sigh, a growl, and a cry. I never heard anything like it before. At the time, I thought he might be calling for Mom.

"I saw you," he said. "*I saw you, I saw you, I saw you.*"

"Paul, honey. Stay still."

I forced Paul's eyes open. He had blue irises like Mom, but not that day. They were white. His eyes were dancing in the back of his head.

Immediately, the need to bolt into action caused me to jump up.

"What happened to him?" I said. "What did Trevor do?"

"What's, ah." Chief Boyd patted his hip. A look of fear flashed across his face, and he looked as though he forgot what he was doing there. "Going on here?"

"*He needs a doctor*," I shrieked. Chief Boyd tripped over his two feet. The old panic crawled up my throat. Despite our bout of good fortune, something was wrong with Paul, horribly wrong.

EXHIBIT X2

SPECIAL COMMISSION OF THE CARD TEAM

Sworn Testimony
Deponent: Randall A. Boyd
July 29, 2021

Q: A body, Mr. Boyd?
A: Mort Norton's.

Q: The private investigator that Chastity Gauge hired to probe her son's abduction. Why do police logs record you stating that a young boy was found?
A: Norton was so slim, at first I mistook him to be a child buried under them clothes. Still don't know how I didn't hear the shot, but I found Norton with a self-inflicted head wound. He must've just finished his confession when he heard me rolling up and decided to take the coward's way out.

Q: The confession was a letter, Mr. Boyd?
A: Norton and Chastity Gauge were in love. They were going to run away together, but she couldn't leave her son behind. So they decided to fake kidnappings. Figured the town would go crazy over satanic cults while they holed up somewhere in Clifton. First, Brady Paul Gauge. Then David Gedney. Guess she didn't care too much about her other kids.

Q: Did they intend to murder David Gedney and William Rahall?

A: Norton expressed a lot of remorse about that. No one was supposed to get hurt, but I guess things went sideways when Billy wouldn't get in the car.

Q: Mort Norton's town car, not Everett Ford's van?

A: Right, but the boy got killed. Norton panicked and dumped Billy's body in the quarry so it looked like the Flemings had something to do with it. David was a witness, so he went in the quarry too. Never found him, though. Just some of David's belongings in the Gauge shed.

Q: Daphne Gauge-Meraux claims a handwriting expert proved that Mort Norton's so-called confession was made under duress. Is it possible that someone coerced Mr. Norton?

A: That nutty girl can say whatever she wants, but you know two words I never hear from her? Thank you, Mr. Boyd, for saving him.

Q: To be clear, sir, saving who?

A: Brady Gauge. I found him not twenty feet from Norton, chained to the fridge.
(Rustling in the conference room)

Q: Was he alive?

A: Yes.

Q: What was his condition?

A: I'd say pretty good for a boy eating field rations for six weeks. He was emaciated. Almost feral, too, like I couldn't get him to talk to me. Brady seemed to be suffering some sort of epileptic convulsion, so I took him home.

Q: Not to a hospital? The boy is having an epileptic convulsion, and you bring him home?

A: I was just a police chief, how was I supposed to know his own mother done all this? Not even taking care of him. Poor kid was eating those rations raw.

Q: Was anyone at the Gauge's house, One Hangman's Hill Road?

A: Nope. That's when I looked up and saw the fire.

Q: When did you suspect arson, Mr. Boyd?

A: It wasn't until after we put it out and had time to think for ourselves, that Charlie Kouts, who used to own the General Store, told me, "Gee whiz, I seen her filling up a dozen cans the morning of." Then, to answer your earlier question, I was really thinking about what Daphne had said about paranoia.

Q: Early on the morning of May 8, 1988, is that correct, Mr. Boyd? For the record, who did Mr. Kouts name?

A: Chastity Gauge. Who else?

CHAPTER THIRTY-EIGHT

May 8, 1988

Courtney pleaded for us to remain together, but I didn't think, didn't turn around; after I tore the ribbon off Paul's wrist, I scampered across the withered lawn. And even though I didn't have to, I leaped over the dry Fountain of Life.

While the fire had consumed much of the church's rear, it had yet to reach its front. And the service door was open where black feathers lay in a circle.

Inside, the faucet's arc twinkled. The countertops were spotless. Except for the overwhelming odor of charred wood, the kitchen was just as we left it following Dad's would-be service for Billy Rahall.

"Mom, Dad," I yelled inside. "Paul needs help. *Now*."

As it had for all the Sundays I'd lived, Dad's voice filled the church. "We don't know it's Paul," he said.

"I heard it on the CB," said Mom, her voice panicked. A loud slam echoed through the church. "They found a boy's body where we used to play as kids."

No, Mom was wrong. I had to find her. Tell her about Paul.

I stepped into the hallway where tomorrow, parishioners would hang their coats. Black birds flapped from one empty hook to another, unable to dispel the smoke. I covered my mouth, trying not to cough.

"Aw, hell," said Chief Boyd from behind. He'd followed me most of the way, but stopped well short of the door, sweating and gasping. "I ain't dumb enough to go in there. You just run on in, then, silly girl."

Dark light pulsed from the vestibule. For the first time I could remember, the main doors were locked. On the other side, what sounded like pine logs tumbled from a tractor trailer. More birds were here, dead, feathers burned to a crisp. I quickened my steps.

Because I had taken the long way around, I entered the sanctuary from the rear. Anyone standing behind the pulpit would have her back to me, as Mom did now. She stacked the pews in her mourner's dress, which didn't make sense because it isolated her on the pulpit. If she wanted privacy, she almost had it, but I guess she overlooked the entrance to Dad's private office.

"But it's not too late," said Mom. The blue murals lit her greasy face and eyes. "We can offer the Elementals something. Something they wanted for years."

"Offer what?" asked Dad.

Mom held a red can over the pews. Water poured onto them and pattered the altar. Three more cans stood next to the pulpit.

"And he'll bring him back," she said. "If I flip it."

"Who?" said Dad. "Chastity, it's just us."

The Brotherhood took the opposite. Defiled Christian teachings to please the Elementals, which caused their magic to work. Mom wasn't performing Blót, but she was doing something like it. A ritual that would counter whatever deadly magic Trevor had set in motion.

Mom wetted the floor to make the shape of a large circle, similar to Scott and the other kids that day behind the school. Perhaps recognizing the pattern, Dad looked angry. "You want to burn down my life's work?" he asked. "Fine. We'll go together, if that's what you want. But I'm not leaving without you."

On his side of the pews, Dad had his own red can, which he sloshed across his belt buckle. The odor of gasoline stung my eyes.

"I'd say burning down this lie of a house is a pretty good act of heresy . . ." Mom saw Dad dousing himself and scoffed. "*No*, Brandon. That's not how you do it. I still have the whole house to finish and you're—"

She ripped out a chunk of hair.

"It would be just like you, wouldn't it, to lay down your life like it's some noble gesture instead of helping your wife *with this one last thing*."

Behind him, a shadow bloomed roughly the size of a fishing boat. The organ's pipes smoked. Velvet curtains burned bright, and their braids swung limp. The soot rained and Mom cocked her head as though listening to something we couldn't hear. Somewhere farther back, ticks and thuds snapped at the walls. The fire was knocking, asking to be let in.

Dad was about to say something when his eyes flickered over Mom's shoulder, then back to her.

"Come quick, Dad," I said. "Paul's hurt. I don't know what's wrong with him."

"You can't be here," he said, without any emotion.

Drops of my sweat steamed on the floor, but Mom didn't turn. She overlooked the nave as though the congregation was there. Between them, white dots sparkled in the air. Ravens combusted from the pews, yet they didn't fly away, stoic as self-immolating monks.

"Not until all your wrongs are out in the open."

"Why won't anyone listen to me?" I shouted. All of Mom's craziness was because of Paul, but it was like she was deaf to any mention of him.

The moment I stomped, a beam shuddered to a terrible crash. Something snapped behind Dad's eyes, some decision that he made. He dove onto the pews, where they creaked and groaned.

Mom raised a lighter. "Brandon?" she said, as though speaking to a child. "I have to destroy the monster he built on Hangman's Hill, his pride."

Dad clawed onto the platform. "Don't take another one," he said. "Please. Not another."

In spinning from his reach, Mom knocked over the red cans. The dozen or so surviving ravens rose in a circle overhead. The cans glugged arms of water across the platform, filling the circle she had made. Mom's shoes squeaked and she staggered to keep her balance with her right hand still held high.

"*Look* what you made me do," she said. "And, ugh, it's here already. I'm running out of time."

Arms raised, panting, the shoulder of his flannel soaked, Dad circled, and Mom mirrored him. From her fist, a long, thin flame like a cobra rose, keeping him at bay. Except he didn't appear committed to outmaneuvering her or the lighter. Every few steps, he glanced at me. Mom's gaze snapped as though I caught them role-playing in the bedroom.

"Or is that what you want?" she said to the pews, "One for one? An unspoiled."

Unspoiled. I'd heard that somewhere. Or maybe it was in one of the library books. *And thus portals to the chasm are paved with blood.*

Wind blew back Mom's hair. Her mask bent down to my level, grotesque in its misshapen grin. The scabs on her face glowed.

"Not much time, Daphne Girl. Momma needs your help, okay? Come. Come to Momma? He's almost here."

The air boiled as I glanced from the glittering madness in Mom's eyes to the paralysis in Dad's. If I chose her, Dad couldn't stop me. But why did it have to be one over the other? My feet might as well have been stuck to the floor.

Mom's eyebrows strained. She slammed her forehead and again turned away, taking large, panicked breaths.

"Chastity," he said softly. "Come back to us. Come back."

"Come outside, Mommy," I said. "Come see Paul."

Mom cried into her hand. "You have to get her out, Brandon. I told you to keep them away." Behind her, a scorching bright rainbow rippled across the sanctuary's floor.

Still Dad didn't move, not until we watched a bug, about the size of a black fly, land on Mom's forearm. She frowned, and I thought of Trevor's blinding of Mom. Perhaps he hadn't meant a literal blindness. Perhaps . . .

Mom's sleeve erupted in holy light.

Dad smothered me in his embrace of gasoline and sweat. He tried to navigate me into his armpit, but my neck popped with the effort to keep my eyes on her and her futile attempts to shake off the flame.

Fire unfurled across the pews, climbed the walls, raced to banners, exploded windows. Into the shape of hands, they leaped onto Dad's clothes.

More hands, gloved hands, grabbed us by the shoulder. At the sight of the firefighters, I screamed. Their puffy coats and gas masks made them look like alien opportunists come to abduct us.

They stripped where Dad smoked until he had nothing on but pants and shoes, explaining something muffled I couldn't understand. Dad pointed to the sanctuary and hollered back.

A pair broke from us. Though I couldn't be certain with the haze distorting her, Mom looked like a woman waking from a dream. She appeared lost, even disoriented, in the bend of color and smoke. Some plea found her eyes but not her voice. When she saw the firefighters approach, her expression turned bitter and she shook her head as though, once again, we disappointed her.

"*No*," she screamed and stumbled into the piano. Over the fire, it cranked an atonal thud. "I can't leave yet. *I have to get my son*."

With all my might, I tried to scream that Paul was outside right now and in need of a doctor, but a firefighter elbowed me. Ravens dropped, their corpses sizzling, suffocating us with the awful smell of charred sewer meat.

Mom slapped off one flame on her elbow only to fend another crawling up her knee. With the firefighters' hands outreached, she shimmied up the organ. Perhaps she screeched or perhaps the burning wood screeched for her.

"After all he's done?" she screamed. "*After all he's done*?"

"You have to save her," cried Dad.

He reached out again, me clinging to his slick ribs. Despite him begging them not to, they dragged us out of the heat and into the cold sunshine. On the field, overlooking the town, they burned us with icy water and cloaked us in wool blankets.

Paul fell into Dad's arms.

He patted my brother absently, still blinking the smoke from his eyes. He didn't realize it was Paul until he pulled the boy off his chest. His eyebrows went down as he pulled Paul close. As it had for me, the smell convinced him his son really lay in his arms, and Dad wept.

"Thank God," he said, looking up. "Thank you, God. Thank you for answering our prayers."

He spun to the church.

"Chastity, Paul's *here. He's with me.*"

From somewhere, a walkie-talkie crackled: "WXZB88-niner, this is Unit 2. We got a Class B fire out of control and no available flow up here on Hangman's Hill. Two, repeat, two recovered safely, but another's still inside. Victim appears incapacitated, trying to pull her out now. Over."

The smoke had swollen my eyes, too, so I couldn't see when Courtney pointed to the steeple's collapse. "Did you get my *mom*?" she shrieked. "Did you get my *mom*?"

"*Chastity.*"

Dad tried to stand, but with Paul's weight, he fell over. Blisters formed a red path running down his back.

"*Chastity.*" Dad's call stretched until it snapped. "*Chastity*?"

Firefighters trotted by and the walkie-talkie continued: "Jesus, we got half a dozen men in there. What's taking so long?"

"Garson, this is Carmine. Lady's nuts. She-she." Static. ". . . up in the rafters, *she's kicking at us when we get close*. Garson, what do you want us to do? Over."

"WXZB88-niner, where the hell is F.C. Decker?"

"The building's falling down around our ears. Incident commander requesting a bus and an additional engine. Dispatch, respond. Over."

Courtney demanded to know when they'd bring out Mom. Chief Boyd stood over us, quietly recounting his heroics to the old firefighter with the walkie-talkie. When Courtney tapped Dad's shoulder, he curled into a ball and wouldn't lift his head from Paul's. What could I say? The last I saw, a fuzzy white light pounced on Mom's back and dragged her across the coals.

CHAPTER THIRTY-NINE

Chief Boyd gunned down the winding road, Ellie, Courtney, and I squished in the back of the LTD. No placemats below our shoes, just a stripped gray space where muddy crumbs still held the shape of Paul's bare feet. He and Dad were in front of us, in the ambulance, the siren roaring. Last was the fire engine. Men clung to its sides, ducking the long branches that threatened to knock them off.

We screamed by our house, surprised to see the living room on fire, then feeling its heat, though I guess we shouldn't have been. On Chief Boyd's radio, we heard Deputy Chief Tom Garrison order the fire department to evacuate Hangman's Hill.

The wind blew from the west, so that was where they headed. From the Cheshire Turnaround, we rode the long way to North Adams Regional, my family's second hospital in twelve hours.

Doctors diagnosed Paul with idiopathic seizures. He must've always had them, said the doctors, and we didn't notice. He still gets them to this day if he has, say, a high fever.

There we stayed for three days, resting much of the first two, our wounds hardening into scars. When he woke, Paul had full memory of going to soccer practice and deciding to walk home with Dominic Gedney. But he couldn't remember going under Lincoln Bridge or staying for six weeks in the Clifton cabin.

He couldn't remember if Mom was there, if she fed him. For the first year, he'd forget she was dead.

In our first examination of Paul, my sisters and I missed something. Doctors found damage done to Paul's occipital and parietal cranial bones. Blunt force trauma to the back of the head, they determined, though they couldn't explain the burn scar under his hair.

They theorized perhaps this was responsible for his memory loss. When Paul was thirteen, Dad encouraged him to undergo hypnosis. The procedure triggered another seizure.

East of Hangman's Hill, the fire gained intensity. According to witnesses, flames rolled like waves across treetops. At its highest point, the fire was one long uninterrupted snake of six miles. With a water deficit of three and a half inches, it had plenty of fuel.

New Minton's phone service went down at 8:05 a.m. due to an overload of calls. But the town still had air-raid sirens, leftovers from World War II, which they repurposed in case the Soviets ever invaded their corner of heaven. Its echo off the hills alerted most of the townspeople to the fire. Except for a few fender benders, most made it safely down.

In New Minton center, as in neighboring towns, the hydrants were uncapped and the volunteers were ready to deflect any fire that came their way, lessons from Maine's Great Fires in 1947 sharp in their minds. But the pumps only went so far.

They also say the fire can bury itself in the ground. Emergency crews would move somewhere else more urgent. Dry brush would smoke, and they began again. Twenty fires ate through five miles of New Minton. It leveled roughly a third of the town.

Only in the wreckage did revelation unseal, at least in part.

Four firefighters perished on Hangman's Hill. Elsewhere, a family of five couldn't evacuate in time. Eleven died, including Mom and Mort Norton. Twelve if you count Billy Rahall.

The thirteenth was an elderly man I recognized right away, Martin Abish. He who refused to vacate his residence of eighty years. The man left behind a bewildering history, and not just because he was the second husband of my grandmother, Charity Drane.

For years, I struggled to trace his history from the records of rural town halls. In addition to being the town jeweler, Martin Abish and Grandpop copublished a few articles; that was how Abish met my grandmother. In 1943, Professor Abish discovered two incunables, books originally published before 1501. They're extremely rare, and each text had something to do with authenticating the Necronomicon, a book classifying the dead.

From that point on, the government funded Professor Abish to write about Adolph Hitler's obsession with the occult. He wrote many books on the subject, none of which exist today in print. Twenty-six years later, his last public appearance would be at Berkshire Superior Court. The basement fire destroyed all his work, including any journals and family photographs.

No one questioned Mom's guilt. She was an unfaithful wife who turned Mort Norton from lover to henchman. Norton's confession proved it. *Star-crossed Killers*, *Dateline* called them.

They never recovered Mom's body. Tales spun that in sacrificing herself she was now a vengeful spirit haunting the hill where, for the first year, the remains of the church gleamed like a lion's tooth. Some wouldn't speak her name for fear she might rest on their neck while they slept. Until they built the memorial, necking teenagers brave enough to make the trip would be caught in the stony hulk of the chamber where Dad once preached the Word of God.

For weeks, we couldn't accept Mom was gone and Paul was back. Why couldn't she wait another day? Why did she believe that sacrificing the church, and herself, would bring him home? We asked so many questions, we forgot to eat.

Before leaving for the church, Mom dumped gasoline on the living room carpet of our house. But after a short time, the house fire whiffed out.

Investigators couldn't figure out why or how it happened. Winds pushed the main fire east, sparing One Hangman's Hill. Originally, Dad determined this as a sign we should stay.

Using her notes, I retraced Mom's last movements. Occasionally through Mom's looking glass, I caught a glimpse of her whole and unbroken.

Those late nights snapping photographs. Logging the town's activity. Bribing police. The lifetime of resentment that disappeared the day her only son vanished because suddenly she had purpose.

That everyone else thought Mom was crazy made her sure that one day she would be vindicated. She'd always been obstinate and paranoid, but these characteristics became assets when they made her committed like few others, even though they also translated any vulnerability into an unforgivable flaw. The reflection of those insecurities in her daughters distorted them to lethal proportions.

At night, I checked up on Paul only to find Dad rocking on his heels, asleep while standing. Every noise made my palms sweat. I was convinced that whoever abducted Paul would try to reclaim him.

A week later, June 3, 1988, the New Minton Police and Berkshire County Departments held a joint press conference. They closed the case, citing a chain of "incontrovertible evidence" that Mom had planned to abduct Paul and start over far away from her two-faced husband: knitted clothing and C-rations found in our van, the same ones she allegedly asked Mrs. Reynolds about the day Paul vanished; Officer Gilpatrick's testimony; Baja Buggy recovered in the Clifton cabin; and David Gedney's backpack, which the tarps preserved. Everything but the bloody knife that was never found.

To divert suspicion onto Thomas and Trevor Fleming, she murdered Billy and David and dumped at least one body in the quarry, another possibly somewhere else. Their biggest regret is for the Gedney family, they told the world, whose oldest boy, David, may never be found. With David officially listed as "missing," the count stood at thirteen.

To accuse the Flemings or Rahalls of anything made us sound as crazy as Mom.

CHAPTER FORTY

June 24, 1989

Until the summer of 1989, Dad determined that we would stay in New Minton.

After all, he was a sentimental man. He wanted to dote on Mom's tombstone. He wanted us to remember Mom in the rooms where she used to read. He probably thought it would help Ellie and Paul with their nightmares. He also wanted to rebuild the church.

But the town council revoked Dad's building permits, citing the adverse impact his new church would have on the environment. They declared that all nonresidential areas in the hills receive special protection for the next one hundred years so the wildlife could have a chance to regenerate. And the vandals denied us peace.

One morning, a rock burst into our living room. No one gasped. Dad nodded at the ribboned obsidian (no doubt, some pornographic note affixed).

"Well," he said. "If New Minton's seen enough of the Gauge family, perhaps the Gauge family's seen enough of New Minton."

We left a day later in two moving vans. People gathered at the town center to watch us go. Hands shadowed their faces, then the hills flattened, the sky got bluer and the cars shinier.

Until we were grown, Courtney, Ellie, Paul, and I swam in the icy green waters of Cape Cod. We finished the last of our youth in the anonymity of the affluent. The kids at the academy didn't care about why our pictures had been on the news. They accepted everything with composed faces. In many ways, they were more sensitive than we were.

I got cut like a surfer and just as tan. I finally had even legs and a body that wasn't Brandy's or Courtney's. Except for my dark-blue eyes, I don't look anything like Mom.

From then to 1991, Dad's money went to a legal team. The district attorney couldn't make arson stick, arguing that in admitting to pouring the gas on himself, Dad confessed to being an accessory. But eventually the DA dropped charges of neglect and child endangerment against Brandon Gauge.

Eventually, the FBI softened. They acknowledged that they never found forensic evidence of any kind linking Mom to the cabin in Clifton. Yes, they were willing to accept new DNA evidence, provided we absorb all costs related to the otherwise closed investigation. What no one tells you is tests take years to petition through the courts, months to confirm that nothing can be concluded. Possibility becomes our lives. Plausibility denies us relief. How do they expect us to live like that?

For years, we tried.

CHAPTER FORTY-ONE

July 30, 2021

The conference room smells of stale sweat and foul breath, like a locker room after a muddy game. My head's killing me. I've spoken for so long, my tongue feels caked in clay. It's like for each hour that's passed I've aged a full year.

"Last," I say, "is Exhibit Y."

Bradley Reeves's lips aren't moving, though I hear his voice as he packs up. "Jay Nolan has woken from his coma," he says. "And has been charged with the kidnapping of his children. So I guess that's it. Ms. Gauge, the commission would like to thank you for your contributions this week. We, too, are troubled by the thirty-seven percent rise in child disappearances in Western Mass."

The crowd loudly exits their seats, scratching chairs, complaining they never got a chance to speak. Now it's three p.m., and only nine of us remain, those dedicated to seeing the end of our fatal dance.

The last of the chairman's committee have elbows on their briefcases, like students with five minutes left in class. More talk outside as though it's some after-party. As though they won. The white-haired Walter is their leading man, speaking to reporters in the hall.

"I think what we've seen," he says, "is how conveniently vague the defense is. Was Chastity impaired by some influence, or 'blinded,' when she attacked her daughter or set a fire that killed thirteen people?"

This time, Bradley Reeves's lips do move, but not until halfway through. "Though I should point out," he says, "many of these disappearances involve human trafficking, and have nothing to do with witchcraft."

I open Gerard's deposition, handling the papers as though drunk. Vikki raps her fist on the door, then I hear the knock. Like my eyes and ears are out of sync. For the first time, I notice how bright it is. Something's buzzing.

Also for the first time, an armed police officer is in the conference room. An officer with a bandage over her nose. She goes straight for my copies of Exhibit Y.

"You can't do this." I look for the chairman on the left, but he moved to the right. "Gerard Gedney's deposition proves Trevor Fleming paid off George Gedney and three police officers through various shell companies of the Crusher Group."

Bradley Reeves's voice comes from behind me. "I'm afraid those documents could interfere with New Minton's internal police operations," he says. "Just having them in your possession violates state law."

My nose sneers. "That's a lie," I say. "Gerard's lawyers handed over this information."

"The commission shall hold a private hearing on whether to allow Exhibit Y into evidence." Even though he's across the room, Bradley Reeves's breath tickles my ear. "Two weeks from Monday. Ms. Gauge, the commission would be happy to hear your input on Exhibit Y at that time."

"Once Trevor Fleming and everyone else are far, far away," I say, hearing the scratch of the tape before the officer scoops my stack into a cardboard box and seals it.

Just like that, my exculpatory evidence is gone. Like we live in a totalitarian state. But they can't suppress my memories. The buzz gets louder.

"Gerard also implicates his brother," I say, "Dominic, along with Everett Ford, Trevor Fleming, and Rusty Rahall. Remember when Rusty said Billy hit Paul with a knife? That happened, though it wasn't at the quarry. It was at Lincoln Bridge. Dominic lured Paul there. Trevor and Rusty were waiting."

Somehow, the distance between my chair and their table lengthens. I'm getting dizzy.

"Paul fought for his life. Rusty hit Paul with the knife, knocking him unconscious, and that's why Paul gets seizures now." I try to keep my voice steady. "And they called for help."

Tap. Tap-tap.

"Ford ran covert transport, but there was a problem. Rusty acted too early. He attacked Paul at around five p.m., about an hour before the sun would set at 6:09. Ford's van was spotted twice, searching for Clai Denton because it wasn't dark enough outside yet. So they had to move Paul through the last hour of daylight. Just before he died, Gerard wrote a letter admitting that his father disguised my brother as his own son so that he could imprison Paul for a week."

Tapping on the glass tears me back to the Gedneys' stone porch.

Paul wailed on the windowpane for his life, and I didn't recognize him. It still haunts me. Yet the chairman shows no reaction.

"Have you been listening to a thing I said, Mr. Chairman? Paul stayed in Gerard's room. He was the one I saw in the Gedneys' window with a curl hanging from his cooling cap. Paul had hair. Gerard, who was going through chemo, didn't."

The taps are from birds. A dozen birds are ramming the window.

"I think they rotated Paul from house to house," I say. "At the Gedneys' for a few days, then the Rahalls'. Everett Ford transported Paul to the Clifton cabin, or it was Marvin Rahall, and David they killed even after all he'd done for them. Then they tampered with all the scenes so police would think the boys knew and trusted their kidnappers. That is, my mom or dad. It's all in Exhibit Y."

Orioles flap wildly, along with blue jays, and, of course, ravens. Their colors are blinding.

You'll get a sick feeling in your stomach. Then you're paralyzed.

Your crucifix won't stop it. Neither will prayer.

Until they clamp my mouth shut, I won't give up. "1889," I say. "1922, '55, '88, 2021. Every thirty-three years this happens. They cursed Mom to drive her insane, so she'd be blamed for the boys' deaths. Just like Jay Nolan now."

The buzzing is in my ear, wriggling like a bee. They're saying something to me, a deposition from Gerard Gedney that contradicts everything he told me. That's not possible.

"And that officer," I say, "Gilpatrick, he didn't identify Mom until June 3, 1988, after he saw her on the news. In his initial report on April 21, he claims he caught an obstructed view of 'someone' in the woods."

For a moment, the buzzing recedes, and the lights dim closer to normal. Bradley Reeves is talking, his tone gaining clarity and an eerie calm. Maybe he's been talking this whole time.

"By your own admission, Ms. Gauge," he says, "your mother has no alibi. If she was out all night, she wasn't surveilling suspects, Mort Norton was. I sound like a broken record, but we know from his confession. Just like we know your brother Brady was eating rations taken from the basement of your father's church. The government still has the receipts from when they donated the rations in 1983. During the Hilltowns Famine. Not to mention, the forensics recovered from David Gedney's backpack. You even established a clear chain of custody of Baja Buggy from your brother's room to the Clifton cabin."

The light returns, whittling the men to toothpicks.

"Except for the bloody knife that conveniently disappeared," I say. "Didn't you think it was convenient that Chief Boyd happened to locate my brother the morning I happened to suspect the Rahalls? We were getting too close, so Chief Boyd 'found' Paul. Just in time, except it wasn't. It wasn't before Mom lost her grip on reality."

My instinct is to dig my nails into the chair as though they might throw me out.

"I know my brother refused to appear today, but have you ever been struck by a rock in the head, then kidnapped for six weeks? Has anyone here?"

Through the light, I see the committee rise. One drags a rolling chair until it lets go of his coat. They're talking, a murmur underwater. They're talking golf.

"Drive through New Minton," I say.

"Ms. Gauge." Only Bradley Reeves remains, pinching his nose. No wonder Bradley Reeves is divorced, if he talks to his wife like this. "We're sorry if you feel disappointed, but our purpose was never to retry the case."

"You can keep the visitor's badge," says Vikki, her voice rising cutely. "As a souvenir."

"Cook's Meat Packing Plant," I say. The stenographer closes her laptop, making my voice race. "The Antique Restoration, the bank, all decide to up and go? Population down by half. Why would they leave, unless they were found out? And for thirty years, they lay low."

The stenographer scurries past Vikki. Now it's just Bradley Reeves at the door, the mouth of my carry-on open, all my stupid exhibits littering the table like beer cans after a concert. And they are stupid. I thought . . . I don't know what I thought.

Why won't the FBI listen?

After a minute, he shrugs, keys swinging in his hands.

"They waited until we forgot about them," I say to the empty room. The blinds grind. "But they're right back at it with these postcards written by an unknown left-handed person. The families who escaped justice for over three decades. How else do you explain the Nolan boys?"

CHAPTER FORTY-TWO

Not until I'm a few minutes from the hotel does the fog lift. I wake in the middle of the road to find drivers honking and pedestrians filming me.

They remind me to check my phone. I have an email from Paul, sent early this morning. Three words long.

To: dmeraux@comcast.net
From: Brady Pampel
Subject: CARD Deposition

Let this go.

I lock myself in the hotel room, push the piles of take-out containers off the bed, and lie down, trying to identify the echo crashing within my chest. This week, Paul waits until the last day of the deposition to get back to his sister. And no one, not even the boy who was abducted, supports me.

Yes, Paul's back. If you call this being back.

He lives in Washington, DC, and lobbies for various child activism issues, lately focusing on human trafficking in Central and South America.

I don't want to sound ungrateful, but he's not the same boy whose hand I held on March 31, 1988. Sure, he has a girlfriend (finally), a kindergarten teacher who's very patient during the nights he stares at the wall. I remember how scared we were, him ignoring us for hours, saying, *I can't talk right now*. It reminds me of how Mom was the night before she died. When she planned for us to be a little like her forever.

Sometimes Paul disappears too. He won't get back to anyone for months, *clearing his head*.

I've been on a few benders, but Paul's last much longer than mine. This one I'd say since Christmas. At least now I know he's okay.

The hotel front desk keeps calling. "Do you intend to stay for another night?"

If not, get the hell out.

I'm waiting for Bryan to call. He'll tell me when Trevor leaves his hotel. I'll tail him to wherever he's hiding Grant and Roderick Nolan. Then everyone will see. They'll see.

What if I didn't have Trevor Fleming to tail?

I'd have nothing to do. I wouldn't have a place to stay. I'd be just another mumbling old lady smelling like pee wandering the streets of Boston.

I'd be Ellie.

A text from Bryan. *Walter Denton*, reads the front, image attached. I have to keep turning the phone and magnifying to read Bryan's report. It doesn't say much other than the white-haired Walter is Walter Denton, and he holds no official position in the FBI.

Yet Walter Denton sits next to the Committee Chair. An uncle of Clai's perhaps? He was the only one of the commission to call him Clai. Everyone else referred to him as Claiborne, though I'm sure the chairman would say his colleague's last name, like his pocket watch, was a coincidence.

I put down the phone.

Accept it, I tell myself.

Find solace in that while Mom is gone, we have Paul back.

Let go of the pain.

If only we had Paul back.

It was a truce I rationalized to myself, broken the day I read about the Nolan boys, the latest chapter in the New Minton Boys, no matter what the CARD Team thinks.

But I don't feel pain right now.

I don't feel anything other than detachment.

CHAPTER FORTY-THREE

May 8, 2010

I withheld one part of the story, one of the last times I spoke with Dad.

On May 1, 2010, he sent a chainmail about the following week, not that I needed the reminder. May 8, I drank myself numb, then followed stone fencing to Dad's house, faded Cape paneling attached to a red chimney. Just like the shingle home in New Minton. I hardly believed I made it.

Dad stood in the driveway, his beard scraggly and off-center. He had large freckles on his crown because Dad never applied sunscreen to his head.

"You hear from your brother?" he asked. The wind pushed his khakis against his body, revealing how bony he was.

I turned off the engine and shook my head. Paul's latest bender would last another five weeks.

Dad gave a pained expression, smelling my breath. "Your sisters?"

Seagulls cried in the harsh salty air. Dad called for the five of us, and I was the only child to respond. He led me to the atrium, where I spent high school and college studying. It stood over the harsh metal of the Atlantic. Nantucket was a black triangle thirty miles away.

We went through the business; then I was still listed as the company accountant. "Payroll's a little high," I said, "but accounts receivable has us at a sixth solid quarter in a row." I shrugged. "Profits are good."

Dad crinkled the top page that read *Gauge Marina, Hyannis*. He kept his name but for the last twenty years returned to his old passion, selling yachts to millionaires.

"I was a better businessman than a minister," he said. "She always said that. So." He rubbed his eyes. "You have a boyfriend you're going to introduce me to?"

"*Dad*," I said, trying to make myself blush. I'd meet Karl in a few months, though that May I hardly felt like I had to get married. Brandy had been there, Courtney still was. Ellie was engaged to a guy who opened credit cards in our names.

My chest was heavy, Dad trying to joke like other families, my heart beating the alcohol from my system. Refusing to acknowledge the cancer eating his liver. Just as, for years, we blinded ourselves to Dad drinking again, though not heavily. Just a glass or three after dinner.

Not that I could talk. Maybe Dad was drunk as I was, though he rarely showed it.

A skiff cut a white line through the ocean. It was the kind of boat Dad could convince a Boston lawyer to buy in five minutes.

"Housic Waste Management." Dad watched the waves crash. "Has a charity, HWM Cares. I have paperwork for you to sign naming you executive director."

He waited for me to say something. I didn't.

"Never withdraw more than ten every few months."

Ten *thousand*?

A selfish need flickered in my belly. Withdrawing $9,999 at that rate would make me debt-free in three years. Grad school was something on the horizon, though super expensive, and I had other debts too. Dad's quiet expression pushed my becoming an ethics investigator until two years after Karl and I married. By then, I was in recovery.

"Dad, the business with Uncle Toby," a board member of Housic Waste Management shot twice twenty-two years ago. "I heard a rumor about *barrels of cash* on Hangman's Hill, millions in drug money the government never found. They wanted to charge us with tax evasion, but without the money, and Uncle Toby's word, the case was dropped." I shook my head. "Was Toby murdered over that money?"

Now I waited for Dad to speak. He didn't. The eastern sky darkened, a storm approaching quickly.

"May sound like a lot to us," he said, "but HWM is small beans, Daphne. It's more like an arrow that, if found, points to them. Our friends in Hyannis."

Something flicked between Dad and me. Just like that, I wasn't Pumpkin anymore, I was an adult. I could be trusted with how the marina and places like Housic Waste Management really worked. More than anything, I regretted being so drunk I might say the wrong thing.

"They didn't like Uncle Toby acting out," I said. "Thought he might blab about HWM's money laundering."

"They'll leave us alone so long as we protect that old connection," Dad said. "But hell, I have regrets. I do. Toby had seven kids, for Christ's sake."

Rain pelted the sand on its way to the atrium's roof. *Christ's sake*. Heck of a way for a minister to talk, one who hasn't had a flock in twenty years.

"Dad, I'm not judging."

"But how did I get mixed up with Irish gangsters?" The fading light made Dad's beard semi-transparent. "My delivery boats were carrying an extra five hundred pounds a week for eight years, and I was like, so what? I wasn't hurting anybody, the money was easy. I had all the excuses, Daphne. Then I saw this story. A two-year-old who overdosed on forty-percent pure powder cocaine. She found it tangled in her father's car keys."

Dad sighed between his legs.

"That's the age kids are stuffing things in their mouths, you know? This little girl, the same age as my girls, and I know that forty-percent pure came from my boats. We were the only ones whose quality was that high, and your mom says the strangest thing." Dad's right eye pinched. "*You think that girl's sad, you should see where I came from.*"

A tingle crawled up my arms. "What did she mean?"

"They always seemed like campfire stories. A Blót on the Idol in America? Couldn't be true." Dad took a long time to finish. "After what your mother said happened to other kids happened to Paul, I realized, no one knows what people do in dark corners. I couldn't deny my sin anymore. I wasn't the man I wanted to be, I wasn't the father, I was so far gone from God. And suddenly, I remember having the strongest, like earth-trembling thought. The police can bust drug dealers. But what could they do about the children in New Minton? I could right that wrong."

Dad couldn't bring that two-year-old girl back. But if he saved New Minton, he could save himself. For the first time, Dad's commitment to his faith made sense to me.

He never said how much his failure to save the town hurt him. Maybe he hid it so he could raise his daughters as well as he could by himself.

"For so many others," he said, "it cost everything. But all I had to give up was my name. Who wanted to be Lewie Pampel anyway?"

Lewis Pampel. It was the first time I heard Dad say the name his father gave him.

"And some of the money," he said. "I kept my family together. I got to do something important. Something that really mattered."

A few minutes later, Dad came back with tumblers. Whiskey, his favorite. I downed mine in two gulps.

"Using drug money to be a Unitarian Minister." I thought to be light, even as darkness came over us. "Pretty original."

"Daphne." Somehow in the twilight, I saw him as he was before the fire, saw the dimples of a boy. "Your mother said there was a pattern. Every generation or so. If there is, you know what it's for, right? The money?"

I nodded, though I wasn't sure. Not until May 2 eleven years later, New Minton's deadly pattern finally uncovered, and I'd have to protect us once again from threats on both sides.

Dad would be dead by Christmas, December 14, 2010, unable to dispute the official account that his wife murdered two children and abducted her only son before killing herself. His liver didn't kill him, his heart failed. He was fifty-seven.

CHAPTER FORTY-FOUR

July 30, 2021

My phone's buzzing. On the hotel rug, out of reach. I'm so tired that I keep hoping it'll stop and whatever it is will go away. Let me space out until I can feel again.

Bzz, bzz, bzz.

Finally, annoyance wins. I get up, my suit now wrinkled, and check to see Karl's called eighteen times in the last twenty minutes. On the phone, he's furious.

"You signed out our children at noon," he screams, "to take them on a carnival ride? You conniving bitch. My lawyer says I should file charges."

I clutch my chest, the air difficult to take in. *Conniving bitch.* It's the first time Karl's ever sworn at me. The mention of a lawyer drags me under. What lawyer? Our separation is nowhere near that.

"Karl," I say. "I was with the CARD Team at noon. They let us out an hour ago. Call the FBI if you don't believe me." The clock reads four-thirty, the exact time any reliable adult saw Paul in 1988, and too late, I finally understand. "Are you saying the boys aren't at daycare?"

"The school said it was your signature." Though Karl sounds doubtful. "You have to show an ID every time, Daphne."

I run in circles around the table, tossing my clothes and files into my luggage, when my vision goes black. One reason I chose Tadpoles Daycare was for its security measures. Cameras at all entrances. A parent has to wait to be buzzed in. A sign-in sheet. One woman was a retired police officer. Discharging children to anyone but their parents is exactly what should not happen.

And who could the staff possibly confuse with me?

"Karl," I say, "hang up the phone." The hotel door slams into my carry-on, and I have to fight it off before I can step into the hallway. "Call the police. You remember what Zachary and Stephen were wearing?"

"I don't just rely on Terry's notes," he says.

"Terry?" The elevator dings as the name prickles the hairs on my arm. So does something else Karl accused me of. *Take them on some carnival ride*?

"We argued about Terry the other day. The woman I hired. She gave me your card this morning." I'm immediately jealous again, which I hide from the cleaning ladies who shake out trash bags. One of them arranges a neat stack of Wi-Fi Access instructions, which stops me.

"What card, Karl?"

"Uh . . ." he says. "'Meraux boys keep the Wheel from turning, so the Door stays open.'"

The world drains of color. I don't know how long I see nothing, and for how long I think nothing. Long enough that the empty elevator is closing before I stop it.

"Not a Ferris wheel, Karl," I say. "The Wheel, with a capital *W*. Does the postcard have a picture on the front? Is it a crow?"

The reception gets spotty. Acid pings my stomach. Then Karl's back. "Yeah, a bunch of them," he says. "Why?"

Thirty-three years of experience with these people, but nothing prepares me for this moment.

My children were taken. By the Brotherhood of the Raven.

By Trevor Fleming. He found out where I lived. He found out where we dropped off our children at daycare. Somehow, he forged an ID.

And now the Brotherhood is going to murder my boys.

Once in the Prius, I floor it out of the hotel's dark parking garage. A hard turn, the glass clinks, but instead of burning rubber down Spruce Street, I slam on the brakes. Traffic runs eight cars deep to the light. Hondas, Jettas, and Audis gathering at 4:50 on a Friday night in Boston. I should've known. Damn evening commute.

Bryan. I need to speak with Bryan Henderson.

He answers on the first ring, sounding gruff and skeezy, nothing like my husband. "I was just about to call you," he says. "Uber picked him up five minutes ago."

Picked up Trevor from his Allston hotel. "Did he have two boys with him?" I ask, tapping the speaker button, holding the phone with my left hand while I steer. "And a woman with shoulder-length brown hair?"

"A couple hours ago," says Bryan. "A brunette showed up briefly. I think there were kids in her car. Why?"

My fingers tighten into claws. The driver behind me honks like, *What the fuck, lady*? And I see the light has turned green. I try not to stomp on the gas. We might as well crawl. Not even five cars go before the light flicks red.

"Did she leave the kids with Trevor?" I ask.

"She opened the door to take 'em out," he says, "but he stopped her. She got real upset."

Emotions burn through my skin, and I lose it. "Who has my kids," I scream, "Trevor or this woman?"

Bryan pauses. "*Your* kids?"

My heart pounds. Bryan's going to call the police. If they catch him with Zachary and Stephen, Trevor will not be captured, and he will not leave this earth alone, I promise you. If he doesn't have my boys, he won't cooperate with the police. He'll stall long enough for another Raven to complete the sacrifice.

So I laugh it off. "The phone cut out," I say. "Her kids. The kids. What happened?"

I practically hear Bryan shrugging. "He sent her off with a map, I think, and I was like, who uses a map anymore when everyone has GPS?"

Because they're low-tech. They rely on postcards and maps, which don't leave digital footprints.

"So she left with Zachary and Stephen," I say, thinking it through. The woman was delivering my boys to Trevor. But I had Bryan sabotage Trevor's truck so that it wasn't available. Trevor had new instructions. An alternative drop-off, is my guess, which apparently frustrated her. Because she's not a willing conspirator? Trevor has leverage over her, though I can't think of what.

I need to know who this woman is.

"Bryan," I say. "Tell me you took her picture."

"I already uploaded it," he says. I swipe to my email and check three times, but nothing new is there. "Uh, his truck's ready. You got fifteen minutes tops." The traffic light turns green, and now we're moving. "Sure you don't want me to follow him?"

My pocket buzzes. Massachusetts police write tickets for talking on the phone, and now I have two, one in each hand, because I was too lazy to set up Bluetooth. I'm also speeding with my knee keeping the steering wheel straight. Still nothing from Bryan.

"Daphne," says Karl, "the police are here." Through the phone, I hear the security beep. "I'm really sorry about before. I don't know where that word came from."

Words, actually. *Conniving bitch.*

My first phone finally beeps. An email from Bryan Henderson with three attachments. While Karl explains to the officer, I click on the grainy picture of the woman who took my kids.

Adrenaline tightens my grip.

Black-framed glasses, feathery hair, lines around her mouth from a lifetime of pinching her lips. Of course, I shouldn't recognize the woman with a dye job and glasses that match mine. But I saw her on the news enough back in May.

"Terry is Theresa Nolan?" I say.

I can't talk to no writers. Stephen can't have no orange juice. Theresa talked in double negatives. The detail never seemed important before now.

Bryan's asking something. Karl's yelling. "Why would the woman whose children disappeared two months ago move to Quincy and nanny our kids for ten dollars an hour?"

"I don't know, Karl," I say.

Except I do. After our disastrous phone call, Theresa joined the Brotherhood. She changed her hair to look like mine. Maybe that's why Karl hired her.

He couldn't have one mousy brunette walking around the house, so he got a substitute, that replacement wife he could pay to stay.

Why would Theresa Nolan go from a stay-at-home mom fresh to New Minton, and a stranger like I was, to an aggrieved mother, to the abductor of my boys? And all in a year?

Mom turned in a matter of weeks.

Karl rants about how it makes no sense. The police officer repeats himself, "Sir, I need you to calm down, please." Bryan's elbowing in too: "He's driving out of the lot." I'm going to split in two.

Ahead is the exit for Quincy, which will take me into Karl's arms while we wait just like Mom and Dad waited for news that their missing boy would come home.

Like the parents who clutched picture frames and smelled their children's blankets, hoping sight and smell could bring them back. They've been waiting for decades.

No. I won't wait. I won't wait until the police show up on our door with hats in their armpits.

"*Daphne*," shout Karl and Bryan at the same time.

"The police," says Karl, "want to know when you're getting here."

"He's getting on the Pike," says Bryan. "Should I follow?"

The Mass Turnpike. I cut through three lanes of traffic. Horns blast. Brakes shriek. The guardrail sparks. I don't know how my decision to take a U-turn doesn't flip the Prius. I'm on I-93 North, and set to merge with I-90.

"Bryan?" I say. "I'm on my way to you, but I'm a few miles behind and in heavy traffic. Whatever you do, don't lose sight of that Ram."

"Got it," says Bryan. Before he hangs up, I hear the giddiness in his voice. *The overtime, the overtime.* I wonder how disappointed he's going to be when I might have to stiff him for a few months to pay other bills.

"Karl," I say, back to one phone. "I need to see someone." Or follow him. Trevor, who's going to be on alert for a tail, if he is on his way to my boys.

"You're not coming home?" Karl's voice booms with bewilderment. *"Why?"*

"No matter what you hear," I say, "I'm doing this for our boys. For all those boys."

"Daphne," he says, "the police can handle it. What if something happens to you, or—"

I hang up. Pulling out the SIM card is a little trickier with the car going, but I toss it on the passenger seat. Just in case Karl tracks me. I'm glad I didn't let him talk me into installing an anti-theft system in the Prius.

Thirty minutes later, traffic eases enough for me to weave through the cars and eighteen wheelers. I cry out in relief when I see Henderson's beat-up Celebrity.

I pass him, and he gives me a salute. Despite his brother Bryan, Henderson came through. He came through when my siblings did not.

After the sign for Framingham, I finally lock onto Trevor's black Ram.

The Prius roars up to his bumper. All I can think is, *Where are Zachary and Stephen, you son of a bitch*?

Then I stop myself. Back away. Hope Trevor didn't see me.

His Ram has a bench seat and an open bed. He clearly doesn't have my children in the vehicle. Theresa took them somewhere. Trevor knows where because he drew her a map.

Stick to the plan, I tell myself. Follow him.

An electronic billboard flashes overhead. Trevor's truck passes first, then mine.

CHILD ABDUCTION ALERT.

Theresa Nolan. Gray Hyundai Santa Fe. They include a photograph. I wouldn't say she looks like me. She looks more like Mom.

2 BOYS.
CALL 911.

CHAPTER FORTY-FIVE

Pentagrams and penises splash the walls where we once hung family photos. All the mirrors in my old house are broken. No smell of smoke like I remember, though the kitchen's tiles are charred black where my sister knelt, head bowed.

Why didn't you stay still, Courtney?

The girl I was is trapped here, unable to move on and be the mother Stephen and Zachary deserve. What is a woman, but a girl in suspension?

I didn't want to search my family home. I didn't want to see New Minton ever again. But Trevor aimed right for Hangman's Hill, where I found his black Ram parked in our old driveway. Lights on the Hill's bald summit burn like embers.

Something's going on up there.

Yeah, they're about to Blót my children at the Idol. They're not waiting three months, let alone three hours. Before that happens, they need a good hiding spot. The abandoned Gauge house seems like a good bet, though I find nothing but my mocking thoughts.

Did you really think you could use the CARD Team as a venue to take your best shot at Trevor without payback?

The desecrations in Revere were a warning. I embarrassed Trevor in public. So he responded the only way he knew how, hurting me in the most brutal way he could. The postcard from the Brotherhood of the Raven was Trevor bragging that I couldn't stop him.

Maybe I can't. Just like I couldn't find Paul thirty years ago. I should be moving. Racing up the Hill. Anywhere but on my knees in my parents' bedroom. The brown light gives it the ambiance of an empty tomb.

"Mom, Dad," I say. "You'll never hold my boys, never play."

The boys I left. The boys Trevor took.

God, it crushes me.

When Dad asked me to be executive director of HWM Cares, I still had fire in me. I wanted those responsible for kidnapping Paul and blinding Mom to pay for what they did. If I had to launder Dad's money to get them, I'd do it. I'd do anything for him. I had done everything for him.

That was eleven years ago.

I don't know if age is the reason, but lately, I hear myself creaking. I feel myself weak, tired. I'm slower, I'm duller.

All I keep telling myself is one more push, one more horizon to reach. But the sad truth is thirty years is a long time to have your claws out.

Outside, I hear music.

I wipe my eyes. Nothing remains of my parents, not even their voices, but I have to keep it together. One last push.

The walk up is filled with festive cheer.

Families and friends in garish costumes travel in herds. More than a hundred vehicles line the shoulder, hopped up onto the curb like a car show for antiques. Many have out-of-state plates. Oklahoma, Florida, Alaska, Utah. Red and blue tents hide behind the trees. If they're here for Lammas

Day, they're at least one day early. Or they're using a calendar I've never heard of.

Or kidnapping my children accelerated their deadly ritual.

I always thought Mrs. Leeds's house looked more like a museum, and that's what it appears to be now, converted into some kind of community center. Inside, people cook and talk. Any time someone asks if I'm lost, I say I'm looking for the bathroom. My jeans probably stand out, but I have a hood that kind of looks like I'm a Nordic archer. At least it covers my face. No sign of the boys here either.

"Blessed be Lammas Day, my child."

I try not to scream. She has gray hair and a wart on her chin, and she must've been hiding behind the door or something. Her outer layer is blue, widening from the chest all the way to Mrs. Leeds's driveway.

"Blessed be," I say, keeping my eyes down.

The woman slips her arm through mine. She gives it a *hmmm-m* like I'm her cat.

"My children loved this time of year," she says, her voice a croak.

"Mine too," I say.

Okay, we'll ascend Hangman's Hill together. While my palms sweat, every neuron alert to the friction in her dress and whiff of mothballs, hers remain dry. With her free hand, she waves at tall women and bearded men who give us a friendly cheer. At the perimeter of the summit, we pass signs.

LITHASBLÓT, 2021

NO PHONES OR RECORDINGS ALLOWED

It's like a Renaissance festival. They set up more tents, a stage where men play a fiddle and accordion. A singer slaps a tambourine against her thigh while others clap and dance. Now that I'm closer, the music sounds elemental, like wind passing through trees. The games are played with sticks bound together with rope. They're trying to corral a dark-blue stone. It all seems so innocent, until I see the banner.

We defeated the Nazis seventy years ago, but tonight their symbol ripples over New Minton, sixty yards wide. The ancient Indo-European symbol of the sonnenrad.

"The Sun Wheel. Beautiful, isn't it?"

"Yes," I say.

No one cares, and no one remembers.

Mom's words come back to me, what they did on the Hill for Lammas Day. Though I have more pressing concerns.

How am I going to be able to search all these places with a grandma slower than molasses on my elbow?

A police officer questions a group. He's got a wide neck, turning sideways as though it causes him pain. When the officer shows something on his iPad, the group shakes their heads.

He stops us. "Have you seen Theresa Nolan?"

"Why, no," says my escort, then puts on glasses to read the iPad.

The first picture is Theresa, the one identical to the Amber Alert broadcast. As I shake my head, keeping my eyes down so the officer won't see the image's likeness to mine, I find them burning at a photo I didn't expect.

Zachary with a big grin. Stephen twirling his hair like he's saying, *My bro is crazy.*

My boys. My baby boys.

"Miss." The officer winces to turn. "Have you seen them?"

"No," I say hoarsely, and he asks someone else.

My escort doesn't seem to notice how red I am, the emotion hammering through my body. She continues her endless monologue. I try to keep myself together, glancing at how easily the officer navigates the festival.

Mom always thought the local police were corrupt, either members of the Brotherhood or sympathizers. Yet they're here at Lithasblót 2021, trying to find Theresa Nolan and my children.

What does that mean?

"Gerard was set to be a captain like my late husband, George. Until he outgrew all this."

At the false summit, I see almost no evidence of the church left, just the foundation cordoned off like a Roman archeological site, which distracts me from registering the name. I've seen this old woman twice before now, I realize. Once after Mrs. Rahall hexed me, the second at Mr. Ford's trial.

"Mrs. Gedney?" I say, stopping her.

She looks up from a food cart, searching my eyes. "Were you a friend of my Sarah's?"

"Yes," I say, trying to breathe out the anger. Now I know why this woman clung to me ever since the Leeds' house. Buried under her dementia is recognition of Paul in me, the boy she hid in Gerard's room for weeks.

"One minute," she says, and approaches a food vendor. I watch her point to various knotted things, meats or bread, I can't tell, trying to suppress the urge to knock an old lady to the ground.

And I'm certain Mrs. Gedney only had three boys. Sarah must have been born after 1988, unless this is one of Mrs. Gedney's bad days. She certainly seems to think Gerard's still alive.

"What are you doing here?"

I can't afford to jump. Keeping my head down, and my archer's hood halfway over my eyes, I turn to the shadow. It's Clai Denton.

He may be forty-four, but Clai could easily pass for fifteen. He's tall and skinny, and looks like he works as a computer tech somewhere.

"No outsiders, Daphne. Please leave now."

Clai points behind me, blocking my path, angry at me for crashing his Lithasblót party.

"Clai," I say, keeping my voice low as crowds push past us, moving right to left. "Today, I don't give a fuck about what you worship."

Clai keeps pushing dark frames against his forehead. "You're looking for those boys?"

"I'm looking for my kids, Clai. Those cops have pictures of my sons. Theresa Nolan abducted them five hours ago."

"And you thought she'd bring them here?" Clai's voice is growing uncomfortably loud. "What kind of people do you think we are, Daphne?"

"I think you're the kind of person who could've told me about the cabin where my brother was, and you let everyone blame my mom." Or about Walter Denton sabotaging me to the CARD Team Committee.

"I didn't know anything about that," he says. "I was a kid. Besides, Blótting never made sense. The kind of literalist who thought he could actually open a Door would know that it would risk stopping the Wheel, which would destroy everything we believe."

"You really think a religious debate is what I need right now?" I say, leaning to Clai's ear. "I want my sons. Zachary and Stephen. I want Grant and Roderick too." Clai tries to pull away, and I grab him back, amazed by how frail he is. "I will burn this place to the fucking ground if I don't get them back. Do you understand me?"

Clai's body grows softer. He bows his head, and I let him go.

All my life, I heard the whispers about Mom being a kidnapper, arsonist, and killer. Whenever I spoke up, someone would compare me to her. *You're just like your mother*.

I learned to hide. I tried to run from myself.

But in my whole life, I've never wanted someone to be more afraid as I do now. And I see how easily I can become her.

More than that, I *want* to become her. If it means getting my boys back.

Mrs. Gedney returns. "Well," she says, "I'm glad you get to see each other again."

"I'm Sarah's friend," I say, raising my eyebrows at Clai.

He could holler that a Gauge crashed the party. *Get her*, and they'd pile all over me. The police might stop them, but I have to assume I'm a person of interest in my children's disappearance.

Instead, Clai nods. We're both angry at each other—me for his omissions, him for my invasion of their worship. I can see his point. He protected me from Rusty as best he could.

Maybe that nod leaves us with a stalemate.

If Clai wants to do one better, he can ask around. Inquire on my behalf. Someone at Lithasblót 2021 has to know something.

Maybe Clai understands, or maybe he's thinking everyone's right and I'm just like Mom. I can't tell. There's no time to process.

"Nice to see you again," is all Clai says, and steps into the moving crowd, which is growing thicker.

"Remember what I said, Clai," I say.

In another minute, he's gone, and Mrs. Gedney hands me food and drink. I'm late to recognize them. "Bread, bread!" she yells. "Wine, wine!"

The way Mrs. Gedney holds them, I know they're not to eat or drink. *Why* doesn't become clear until we slowly ascend the bald rock and smack into the new Idol. It's a thirty-foot eruption of stone, a giant's tooth pocked with black holes.

"We ask our King," says a man, "the provider of earth, fire, wind, and water, grant our gothi a seat in the great Valhöll." He's older and frailer, but completely recognizable as Mr. Corwin, who pours his glass on a wreath that drips onto an enlarged photograph. Thomas Fleming, 1934–2021.

"Gothi," echo the women and men around me.

I sweat, eyes darting through the crowd. If their eulogy is leading up to Blót, my boys have to be here. They have to be. I even remove my hood at the worst moment because I don't find them—I find Trevor.

He's not platinum blond anymore, not at fifty-three. His hair is gray and thin. He has a slight limp, probably from gout, and a belly like the one Dad had until the last year of his life. And his arm is in the same sling I saw at the FBI Fieldhouse. Trevor gives a weak smile to Mr. Corwin, whose eyes swim behind his glasses. He might be crying.

I squeeze closer, trying to see Trevor's free hand. In a crowd, children get swallowed, but if he's holding hands with anyone, with *my children*, I'm going to lunge at him. My hands are out, and they want to murder.

"Please, oh King. Take our sacrifice."

"Our King."

No. They're not going to sacrifice my children.

Whoever chooses the red candle guts the steer and drips blood on the Idol. And for another year, the Door remains open. They call it Blót.

I'm in midlunge when my neighbors' offerings pelt my shoes. I look down at the cheap red wine glistening before my shoelaces absorb it.

Throughout the eulogy, Trevor's free hand remained behind his back. No boys are near him. No children are anywhere close to the Idol. The eulogy is for adults only.

I don't understand. What are they sacrificing if not my boys?

"Empty your cups to Wodan, my Brothers."

The people hold up their glasses, and do just that.

"The Wheel turns every year, closing all doors and restoring balance to dark and light."

I still don't understand. That's exactly what Clai and the other kids said to me behind the school all those years ago, though they'd left out a few details.

Whether it's warring kings or a Wheel, almost every pagan religion believes that the summer solstice is the time when balance is restored.

Meraux boys keep the Wheel from turning, so the Door stays open.

The Brotherhood of the Raven never wanted to balance the dark with the light. They want power. The Elementals' power that each family learns to wield with the help of their dead loved ones.

I turn back, and Trevor's gone. A flash of him, hurried. Trevor came to pay respects to his father. Maybe, in ensuring he'd be a day late, I caused him to miss something important in planning his father's funeral. Whoops.

Now Trevor's leaving. He's upset. Is it about his father, or something Mr. Corwin did? Or didn't do?

Even Mrs. Gedney is teary. "It's so sweet," she says.

What's the nicest way to tell an old lady who conspired to abduct your brother you don't want her arm wrapped around yours anymore? I try my best.

"My dad lied about a lot of things," I say.

"Oh." Mrs. Gedney doesn't like the sound of that, and I definitely don't like the sight of Clai whispering to some men glancing my way. I guess Clai prefers to break our stalemate the other way, forcing me to talk faster.

"About his past and religion," I say, "but never his faith. Because he believed in the goodness of people, Mrs. Gedney." I give her the softest squeeze I can. "You talk about how special it was with your children, even though somewhere in that sick head of yours, you remember imprisoning my brother Paul."

"Sorry, honey. I don't." Mrs. Gedney shakes her head, eyebrows down. "What did you say your name was?"

"Don't the Nolans deserve that too?" I ask. "Don't my boys?"

Having been around Grandpop so much during his declining years, I recognize Mrs. Gedney's smile. The one where someone asks, *Can I help you?*, and you find yourself in the dairy aisle in your underwear.

No, Mrs. Gedney may not get it. But Mr. Corwin's fixing me pretty good, thanks to Clai, his eyes boiling with hate. And yes, they are black. Definitely not hazel.

More are staring, gathering.

"You don't remember me, do you, Mrs. Gedney? You don't remember Paul and Gerard sharing a room."

"You must have me confused," says Mrs. Gedney.

"We don't hurt children, Daphne," says Mr. Corwin. "You're the family who hurts children."

I have no reason to believe him, especially if he's going to protect Mrs. Gedney. I'm about to ask why I ever would when, again, my eyes follow the people pouring wine and leaving bread on the Idol.

Please, oh King. Take our sacrifice.

A symbolic sacrifice, not an actual sacrifice.

Which means . . .

"My boys aren't here?" I say. "Then, where?"

Mrs. Gedney's eyes widen. "Interloper," she hisses, pointing. "*Interloper.*"

Oh Jesus. Hot needles prick my legs.

It means I was wrong to ever take my eyes off Trevor. He was sentimental, paying respects to his father. Or he wanted to establish an alibi before Blót.

The real Blót where whoever picks the red candle will murder four children.

A drunk guy grabs my shoulder, breathing beer in my face. Acid fills my throat. I kick until he changes his mind. Others come to his defense, and I point behind the stage, feigning anger. "She went that way," I say.

Of course, all the Brotherhood needs is one raven to rat me out. Or have one Rahall cousin freeze me. But with my hood on, the crowd is disorganized, confused. I hop from one outraged search party to the next, weaving down the Hill.

Please let me catch up, please let me catch Trevor. My right shoulder is cold, and I see that the drunk guy ripped my clothes, the jackass. Somewhere behind me, Mrs. Gedney screams my name.

CHAPTER FORTY-SIX

Ten miles up Cheshire Street, I stop at a fork in the road. I should've caught up to Trevor by now.

A right takes me to 202 then the Pike. Trevor could be on his way to Fresno, and I only have two bars on my fuel gauge.

There's the Passerine Diner and a gas station, but both are closed. No streetlights are on anywhere downtown. The only movement is a poster fluttering from a telephone pole. "Have you seen me?" the Nolan boys ask no one.

Seconds tick before I snap the SIM card into my phone. Maybe the GasBuddy app will bail me out. Instead, I have five voicemails from Karl.

He begs me to come home. I'm about to press delete when I hear something about fingerprints.

". . . match the other postcards," Karl says. "The police are telling me you are putting yourself in a very dangerous situation. Please, Daph—"

Fingerprints on our postcard match the Gedney and Wilson postcards. It's been three hours since I left Quincy, so it's possible the crime lab rushed the results. Whoever sent those postcards is the same person. Trevor must be meeting him or her. Where?

I backtrack five miles, head thumping. Voices tell me I'm making a mistake. Then brake lights burn behind white mountain pine. A blink, and they're gone.

Out of the dusk comes a billboard, FOR SALE BY OWNER. A little farther is another one, its letters fallen off. Clean spots on the plywood are all that spell FLEMING QUARRY. I slow, and so does my heart.

"They have to wet the Fulcrum," I say.

Just like they did with Billy Rahall. This time they have four boys. I remember how Dad's first crack came that night he faced not knowing which boy was found in the quarry. I don't just push away the thought it could be Zachary and Stephen. I kick it.

Trevor must have a private road to the quarry. I'd be crazy to follow. Even if he didn't lay a booby trap, he'd hear my Prius long before I ever saw him. I scoot ahead, my headlights off, and park at an overlook, where a sign suggests I take a picture.

Five hundred feet below is the Fleming Quarry, a giant staircase of steps carved out of the rock that run all the way down to a bowl of silver where the water holds less than half its orange mark. A road skirts around the quarry's south side, leading to three buildings connected by shafts. The crusher towers over them, though it's been silent for as long as I remember.

If Trevor or my children are in those buildings below, I can't tell. The tree cover is too deep.

A voice of what sounds like reason thunders. Maybe he's here to check on his father's estate. Pick up a check.

Then I see the glint of a white vehicle beyond the parking lot, behind some trees. Someone pushed it there, and buried the car under branches. Cut recently too. An SUV, actually. A gray Hyundai Santa Fe.

Theresa's ride.

I almost forgot to pull out my phone's SIM card again. By the time my gear is set, all the light is gone.

In the dark, I plunge into the muck. My muscles burn. Branches double snap as though the forest crumbles around me.

When Mom compiled her surveillance of the town's suspects, she was thirty-five, nine years younger than me. Sure, Mort Norton snuck around a lot on Mom's behalf, but how'd she do it on his off days?

A floodlight winks on, orienting me about two hundred yards from a gravel road. I can hear Trevor talking.

"It says you need the Book," he says. "So do you have it or not?"

"Relax, Brother. It'll be fine. Now tell me what they said."

I hold my breath. Either they suck at divination as much as Eileen Rahall, or they're ignoring me. I decide the former. It's the only way to keep moving. Ahead is a sharp drop, a ravine where vines tangle over some rocks. I slip through them, slowing my fall. I'm at the edge of the woods, behind a wide slab of stone that should conceal me from their sight.

I pull out my Canon PowerShot SX620 HS. It can zoom from twenty-four to twelve hundred millimeters, 20.2 megapixels of crystal-clear photos admissible in a court of law. The quietest camera I could find at Target. I pluck off the cap. It beeps to power up, and I cringe. Can't believe I forgot about that.

"She's as crazy as her mother," says Trevor, and my knee jumps. "You should've seen how they rolled their eyes, soon as she walked in. Not even her family backed the bitch up."

You assholes.

The battery's at full charge.

"Daphne," says the man, mulling my name. "It's too bad the Brothers won't get their revenge."

"But her kids is worse, isn't it? She'll have to live with it."

"If I caught up to her the other day. If that old fart security guard was on the other side of the building."

Trevor's talking to the person who broke into the FBI Fieldhouse. To steal the Book of the Brotherhood. And get revenge on *me*. What for?

I can't think of a single reason why as Trevor rummages in the bed of his vintage company car Dodge Ram. "Can you believe Corwin actually begged me to come back?"

"Holding Lammas Day on the thirtieth, pouring out cheap wine. They're lost, Brother."

"The crowds are there. We just have to win them back, the old way."

Nothing immediately suspicious about tossing garbage bags onto private property, but I snap a few pictures.

My hands shake right before my finger can find the button. Most of the shots are blurry zigzags, but I get enough to establish Trevor and his sweaty T-shirt. What about his friend who knows my name?

"You know, Brother," he says, "the Druids believed metal drained you of your powers." Who is that voice? Seems so familiar. The lights bleach his face, but not his arms. The man holds up a bag in his left hand.

Left-handed author.

"Well," says Trevor, "we're not frickin' Druids, are we?"

I snap a picture, but I can't tell what he's holding up other than it's shiny and slim.

Move out of the light, I think. *Move out of the light.*

A few pebbles strike my heel, having rolled down the ravine, but I have my finger ready. The camera's screen grows hot against my cheek.

"I don't like this," says Trevor, shaking his head. "Someone's going to come around asking questions."

The boots close on Trevor. On reflex, I snap a dozen pictures, so loud that they turn. They look right at me. I bury my head in the dirt, cover my mouth. Can they see anything reflective—my eyes, the camera lens?

"The Book, the Calendar, they're all clear, Brother," says the man. "Wetting the Fulcrum must be performed before Lammas Day."

They're back to staring each other down. I wipe off the camera, scroll to the photographs. They're clear enough to leap into real life.

The man is about Trevor's age. Shrunken head, black hair, hawk-like nose that resembles Scott's. Despite his last known photograph being taken for School Picture Day in 1987, I have no problem recognizing the man next to Trevor Fleming.

It's David Gedney.

Of course. The Boy Never Found because he'd never been missing. Like Gerard, David could dim himself. That's how he broke into an FBI building.

For someone Mom and Mort Norton murdered thirty years ago, he looks pretty good in jeans and sneakers, just like any dad. Dark bags under his eyes though, as though he doesn't sleep well. A bolt of excitement begins in my legs, one I make myself repress.

I see it all now.

Mort Norton wasn't at the Clifton cabin because he was Mom's accomplice. Maybe he discovered something in the box of surveillance that broke the case open. He went to the cabin only for someone to kill him, but not before they coerced his confession. His suicide note sealed Mom's guilt. In truth, Mort Norton died trying to save my brother.

Once clear, Trevor and David communicated through postcards. Something low-tech that they knew postal workers would overlook. The postcard from last October to George Gedney was from David, warning his father that their ritual was about to begin again.

What does that mean? Trevor wasn't paying off George. He paid David to stay in hiding long enough to have an adult face no one would recognize. They buried all the money in Crusher Group and other subsidiaries.

Or David communicated with his parents over the years, telling them he was okay. That's probably why George and Loretta hid Paul when it was their turn. Though they felt awful, didn't they?

I got Trevor and David dead to rights. I could run into the light, Beretta in hand. Make Trevor and David lie on the ground. If they stonewall, I'll show them the Beretta is loaded.

Could I put a bullet in them?

I tap the question on the camera. Yes. If I had to. If they made me.

No sooner is that settled than Karl's question comes back with a resounding crash. *What if something happens to you*?

They could have a gun too. I could trip.

I could run out with all the speed of a sedentary forty-four-year-old, and even if I keep my balance the men could sprint in opposite directions. If I followed the wrong man, David or Trevor would have enough time to kill my boys before I searched all the buildings.

The camera.

One reason I brought the Canon PowerShot was for its mobile hotspot, which allowed me to automatically store all photos in my cloud. My thinking was that Karl might eventually check my cloud account (I changed the password two months ago, but last week I changed it back), see the photos, and send the cavalry.

The only problem with this plan is I didn't expect to be five hundred feet in a quarry in rural Western Massachusetts. I'd have to get back to the Prius, where I can get a signal, and upload from there.

What if they kill the children while I'm gone?

I watch Trevor and David unpack things from their car. They're still setting up. I have time. That's what I decide, so I pack up the camera.

No noise to power down, thank goodness. I can zip up the way I came, maybe even get Bradley Reeves on the phone, or his boss, who will send the FBI—they'll have to. With any luck, Trevor and David will have to explain themselves to a grand jury.

Too bad I won't be able to tell the pricks it was me who busted them, Daphne Gauge-Meraux, former junior detective. I'll have to imagine payback once I'm back in my car. They'll be in jail while my boys are in my arms.

Except I don't get to do that either. Pebbles rush down my intended handhold. I feel the heat of somebody and smell bad breath but get no farther when a sharp blow cracks me on the forehead. The cold earth rushes up to meet me, and I black out.

CHAPTER FORTY-SEVEN

Frayed tennis shoes poke me. Somewhere between them and the fog, pain gnaws on my skull. I can't turn; my wrists scream. My hands are bound behind my back.

I lie on a gravel road, my vision vibrating, the floodlight placed ten feet from my face. Trevor's pickup is here. So is David's clunker, the Chrysler, I presume.

The buildings are nothing but outlines of white shadow.

"You know, Daphne. I still own this property. I'm perfectly within my rights."

Trevor points a firearm legally registered to me at my head. His other arm is in the same sling I saw at the FBI Field House. How's he going to claim self-defense when I have ligature marks on my wrists and a head wound?

"Trevor," I say. "Where are my boys?"

"Which ones?" says Trevor, his eyes filling with demonic light. "The Merauxs or the Nolans?"

"I found Theresa's Hyundai," I say. Trevor's eyes darken as though he forgot about that loose end. "Are Zachary and Stephen here now? Trevor, please. Don't hurt them."

"Theresa? Huh."

Trevor undoes his sling on the way to the Chrysler, unrolling the bandage to reveal not a broken arm, which is what I assumed, but rather his calcified left hand. I gulp. His hand is hardening into a claw.

Then Trevor leans into the driver side to pop the trunk. Before he says anything, my stomach fills with stones. Why go to the trunk? Please don't have my children in the trunk. Please don't claw my children.

"Theresa," says Trevor, looking inside, "Daphne Gauge asked about her kids. Who was very eager to trade your kids for hers, by the way."

Trevor tugs. A limp arm flops onto the Chrysler's fender. I scream, not wanting to see my dead children, unable to look away.

He lifts a body. My vision darkens. It's Theresa Nolan.

Trevor has the body of Theresa face me so I can see the whites of her eyes, that frizzy hair unmistakable. Her lips are smooshed. My first thought is they suffocated her.

"Theresa?" says Trevor. "Oh, Theresa? She hasn't been very talkative lately."

"Stop it, Trevor," I say, the adrenaline causing me to shiver. "You already killed her. Leave her alone."

For months, I pitied Theresa Nolan. I thought about contacting her again and apologizing for pumping her for information instead of empathizing. Over the last few hours, my feelings for her have grown more complicated. But I don't hate her.

"You want to kill me?" I say. "Fine. Do whatever you want. But let my children go."

"Another unspoiled for the year's harvest," says someone behind me. "We're honored."

David walks around the light, his shadow bobbing across the vehicles. His hands are so arthritic they look like claws. Yet he has deep blue eyes that, in another circumstance, I might think were kind. The sort of eyes Theresa trusted before they killed her.

Hearing myself, I wonder what I would've done in Theresa's place. How I'd act if I got that desperate.

Would I cling to the hope that, after they strangled me, they'd leave my children unharmed?

"You have me," I say. "And I can help. Scott Wilson killed himself so he wouldn't be damned to eternity as a raven. Surely you know the consequences of your magic. I won't fight you. So what do you need my boys for? Grant and Roderick? The charities in California?"

David considers the question. "Soon," he says, "we will have many Doors all over the world. And the Brotherhood will commune with the Elementals as we did in the old lands. They will regenerate us."

"Trevor, David, please. Scott said you could use my blood, right?"

I feel myself tipping. There's no way I can break out of their handcuffs or zip tie, I'm just causing myself more pain, but I can't stop myself. I can't stop the tears from coming. They're an explosion of heat, these men breaking me.

Causing me to shriek.

"Please let my children go. They're innocent. Zachary and Stephen are wonderful boys who don't deserve this. Please. *Please. God damn it.*"

"Innocent ones are the best, Daphne," says David.

"I enjoy hearing her beg, though," says Trevor.

The outrage gushes out, black as bile.

I could've gone home at any point in the last two months, but I didn't. I abandoned my children, and Trevor arranged for Theresa to take them. Instead of calling the police, I was arrogant.

And now I'll watch them die.

Or they'll watch me.

God. They'll watch these men killing their mother.

"Yes, Daphne," says David, and my eyes flick to him. "You know. Talking won't make any difference. The Elementals will not be denied."

Eventually, I return enough from the brink to realize something. Trevor and David were both in my sights the entire time I took their picture. Who hit me from behind then?

Soon as the question comes, I see a shadow behind the lights.

"Let me see the piece," it says. "Fine, I'll trade you Daphne's camera with incriminating evidence for it. Come on, already, Brother." The shadow drops my camera into Trevor's hands and dissolves into a man squinting into the barrel of my gun as though he's looking for the bullet in the chamber. "Cool."

I blink tears until I see all the red hair he lost. Actually, he lost it the moment he turned skinhead, which makes him look younger than his friends. I also see three tattoos. A teardrop under one eye, another raven on his forearm. Even in corduroys and a rolled-up tan jacket, Rusty looks like he belongs in prison.

Rusty frigging Rahall. The boy who tried to kill my brother, then lured me to his house. Except it can't be him. He's only halfway through his ten-year sentence.

Brother or not, Trevor doesn't like a convicted felon holding the pistol, I can tell. He gives David a look as though he wants David to back him up, the three boys who formed a sick pact decades ago.

"How many conditions of furlough does this violate, you think?" says Rusty. "It's a nine millimeter, right? Nine millimeter Beretta. You guys were right. They stamped the request without a second look. I walked right out."

"You have to believe, Brother," says David.

Belief has nothing to do with Rusty's to-be-determined furlough, dumbass, not that it matters now. I practically begged Bradley Reeves to grant Rusty's request.

Anger doesn't stop me from sniffling, but I'm more in control now.

If they have my gun and camera, they must have my other stuff, too, somewhere. I roll ever so slightly onto my back. Upside down, I follow their legs to a dark pile. That must be my backpack there.

Tucked in a pocket is a relay attack, a device about the size of a large cell phone that copies the electronic signature of a key. Criminals use it to boost cars that are supposed to be theft-proof.

The relay attack can set off my Prius's alarm from a thousand yards away.

"Holy shit." Trevor holds the camera so David can see. "This whole week, this psycho's been following me. Taking pics of every place I slept. We gotta get rid of this stuff."

"Chuck it in the quarry, Brother," says David.

I hold my breath. If they do, I'm screwed.

"Are you crazy?" says Trevor. "Everyone knows who the Fleming Quarry belongs to. They find anything in there they can trace back to her, we'll be back in the shit again, and I don't have any more money to pay people off."

David takes the camera and drops it next to my pack, along with mace and a black box. It's twenty feet away maybe. If I was untied, I could just hop over and grab it.

Rusty plays with my pistol like he's in the Old West. "Daphne Gauge," he says. "Even at my brother's funeral, I had the biggest hard-on for you. The way Jeremy and Derek got your sisters, and gothi got your grandma, I'd get you."

"Why? Why me?"

"Why does a man want a virgin, Daph?" I can't see Rusty, only his forked tongue. "You still a virgin? Didn't think so. Too bad you're not a true unspoiled. Every thirty-three years, right, guys?"

David nods. "The Calendar of Christ keeps us blessed," he says.

The wind whips through the quarry. Rocks skip down the great steps, unseen.

Calendar of Christ. Every thirty-three years. Like the thirty-three alens of a hörgr.

"That's why they killed your mom, Rusty?" I say. "Because a calendar told you? Is that why Billy died too?"

"I'd never hurt Billy," says Rusty. His cheeks twitch. So convincing.

"Well, let's not keep her in suspense," says Trevor, breaking from the others. "Daph, is it? I wasn't at the quarry when Billy died, despite what you told the FBI." I don't remember saying that, but Trevor goes on. "There were three, though. Brother Reginald, Brother David." He's grinning again. "Speak of the devil."

A car rolls over rocks and stops. Strange that I didn't hear it. The driver door opens with a metallic cry.

Footsteps and dust.

There were three.

Three at the quarry the day Billy died. Rusty, David, and who else?

"Help her up, Brother," says Trevor. "So she can see."

David opens his eyes. While Trevor enjoys mocking me, I see David is more serious. It makes sense. Largely isolated for most of his life, the Brotherhood's faith is all David has.

He grabs me by the elbow. My ankles are bound, too, so I have to hop around one car to see the other.

Another beat-up POS, like the others. The driver door is open, the seat empty. In the back, I see two lumps, outlines of children.

"*Stephen*," I cry, and my chin strikes the unpaved road. I taste dirt and blood. David just let me fall. "*Zachary*." I crawl. Rocks bite my knees.

"They're asleep, Daphne," says David, picking me up with one hand. He's much stronger than he looks. "But they're not your children. Come see."

He takes me to the rear passenger window, rolled halfway down. Even in the dark, I see David's right. The hair is too black, a gene handed down from Theresa Nolan. Their mouths look nothing like Karl's.

"Grant," I say, at one puff of hair, "Roderick," to the other. One stirs, showing his face in the light before wriggling into a dark corner of the seat.

No dried tears. No red faces. No creased foreheads. The boys look untroubled, packed in sleeping bags, dozing in the back seat as though on their way home from a movie.

"What are you going to do to them?" I say, turning to David.

"It's so much worse for them if they're scared, Daphne," he says. "Don't you understand yet?"

"You're going to murder innocent children, David," I say, as he escorts me back a hop at a time. "For no reason. There's no Door. You've bought into a fantasy. Scared Theresa Nolan to buy in. Even the lunatic whom you made drive these kids to Fleming Quarry for Blót has bought into a *lie*."

My bag's only eight feet away. I'm about to dive for it. Then I see. Standing behind the generator are three men. Trevor, Rusty, and another man whose face is unmistakable.

"A family reunion," says Trevor with a smile.

"No," I say.

Once again, David lets me fall. The pain is like sharp glass on my kneecap. I hardly notice.

The third man is the same boy I spent weeks trying to find only for Chief Boyd to drop him off at a burning church. The same boy whose disappearance broke Mom.

"No," I say again.

The same man who earlier today told me to *let this go*. Forty now, he still has blond hair, just not any on the top of his head. His face hidden as though he prays with Trevor and Rusty.

I can barely get his name out. "Paul?"

CHAPTER FORTY-EIGHT

Half in darkness, Paul's features are as soft as Mom's. Her nose. The sad way she crinkled her eyebrows.

"I'm sorry, Daphne," he says.

This time I don't cry. I'm all out of tears. The agony is too jarring. All I feel throughout my body is the endless throb of numbness.

"You drove the Nolans here, Paul," I say. "You're going to be responsible for their murders. And my sons, your nephews? Why? Because of some stupid Wheel?"

Paul shakes his head. "Mom knew you'd never understand," he says.

Now the pain is lead inflating in my chest. "You don't remember Mom, Paul," I say. "You were too young."

"Mom told me I was a Brother," says Paul, though he smiles uncertainly. "And one day, I would be a Raven, and I'd never be afraid again."

I turn on Trevor. That soft childlike way in which Paul speaks. "What'd you do to him? You brainwashed him. In the Clifton cabin. Filled his head with lies?"

"Paul," says Trevor, "tell your sister what you did to Billy."

"When I cut Billy," says Paul.

"You did no such thing, Paul," I say through gritted teeth. "*Don't say you did that.*"

"I told you thirty years ago," says Trevor. "I told you, the first family to Blót was yours. Didn't I?"

"I saw Blót for what it is," says Paul.

"It's true, Daphne," says David. "Through the power of prayer, Paul opened a Door, and the Elementals made his seizures stop."

"I saw you looking for me, Daph," says Paul.

"And you'd never know he was there," says David.

"Paul," I say, "you saw me because the Gedneys had you in their house. You were banging on the glass from the second floor. Remember?"

"Just like Boyd walked past me," says David, "and went right for your mom's boyfriend."

"Mort Norton wasn't Mom's boyfriend," I say. "You framed them. Made him write the confession. Planted David's backpack at our house."

"Mind control doesn't always work out." David grins at Paul, and they share an inside joke. "Back in '88, we told Gilpatrick a million times to forget he found me and Paul."

Gilpatrick. The Clifton officer who identified Mom near the cabin.

"What does he do?" David shakes his head. "Tells the world he saw your mom. Guess the resemblance was too strong."

"No," I say. "Please, God."

It wasn't fear. Paul wasn't afraid of David and Trevor, he was . . . I can't even think it—*guilty*? Paul ran away from Officer Gilpatrick because David forced him to do something horrible. It explains all the odd behaviors, all the things we tried to ignore. To think how close I was to solving the mystery only to wrap myself in it.

"We prepared Billy," says Rusty. "We laid him in the earth for three days."

"As it is written."

"Written," I say. "Written by whom, Rusty, your father? A pathetic drunk?"

Cuh-click.

The Beretta shakes. Each time I breathe, dust kicks up from the road.

"You take it back, bitch. *You take it back.*"

There he is again. Under the Nazi tattoos is that trembling, white-lipped boy I defied during the Quarter Moon Ritual. Rusty will pull the trigger. He's too much of an angry kid, from the abuse to the foster care to prison. Violence is all he knows.

Not David, though, the calculating one. He places a hand on Rusty's shoulder.

"My father." Rusty wipes his mouth before turning to David. "Was a great m-man."

David nods. Takes the gun. He continues to pat Rusty.

"What of the pogroms, Daphne?" he says. "Were they evil? The Floods of '36 and '06? The Tornado of '53? The Irish gangsters at HWM your father hung out with. Yes, we know about them. The most sanctimonious are often the most wretched."

"Or our gothi?" asks Trevor. "Whom your mother murdered."

The hate they fix me with. Hot enough to burn, they're so certain. Even if the accusation's ridiculous.

"Who's your priest?" I say, my head pounding. The memorial, on the Hill. "Thomas Fleming died thirty-three years after my mom. You pinning that on her too?"

"My father was not a true gothi, Daphne," says Trevor. "Quint Abish, our grandfather, was. All of ours."

I try to find Trevor in the haze. "Martin Abish," I say. "And Mom's fire didn't kill him either. The basement fire he set did." Everyone knows that.

Paul says nothing. He looks ahead. Like he's waiting for someone to tell him what to do next.

"Martin Quint Abish, Daphne," says David, and that's right. After the Sobaski trial, he went by Quint. "He gifted your mom a priceless family heirloom, and she thanked him by burning down his house. She's responsible for his death."

The Victorian at the end of Mrs. Leeds's path. "Mom targeted him over a 'priceless family heirloom?'" Trying to put it together pinches my brain.

I'd say burning down this lie of a house is a pretty good act of heresy.

House, not church. I always assumed Mom meant Dad, but maybe all along she meant Martin Quint Abish's house. She tried to set Abish's house on fire, but got confused and burned down the church. It was another spell.

"Gothi's grandson," says David, "your own cousin, delivered the jewelry to make peace."

"Ron Abish," I say, shaking my head. The transient who broke in just before Paul disappeared. "Is your cousin too. He wasn't there to rob us? He left something behind?"

No, that's impossible.

"Get the robes, Paul," says David.

"Yes, Brother," says Paul, and disappears. I hear him rummaging through plastic bags.

"Freeze her, Rusty," says Trevor. "I don't want anything to go wrong."

Stay with your thought, Pumpkin. Focus.

A piece of jewelry. A priceless family heirloom.

"A tennis bracelet," I say.

Rusty kneels in front of me, stitches popping in his jeans. He extends a hand over my face, and I remember.

Mom wore it everywhere until she died, but it never made sense that Dad bought jewelry to pacify her after Martin Abish broke in. Revelation 3:17. "You say, 'I am rich; I have acquired wealth and do not need a thing.' But you do not realize that you are wretched, pitiful, poor, blind, and naked." One of his favorite passages.

Many pagan religions believe diamonds blind the person who wears them. The Fords had the power to blind, but the hefty diamond ornament arrived courtesy of her stepfather Quint Abish. Why she'd ever accept anything from them is something I'd like to know. Maybe the Brotherhood was skeptical, too, for they also erased her eyes in a photo burned in our backyard, pinned with Trevor's hair.

But I'm not wearing any jewelry. Just my—

"My visitor tag," I say. "Vikki? She's one of you too?" That bitch.

They're laughing, even more so when I put all my weight on my right shoulder. Rusty's hand is shaking. Again, I feel the heat coming off him, and smell his sweat.

"Vikki Harper," says Trevor. "Brother Everett's niece. We knew you couldn't resist. Not a badge from the FBI. Rusty, what's taking so long?"

I feel the pit in my stomach, searching wildly for birds. Trees caw. Then the pit is gone.

"I can't," says Rusty. He stands up and staggers. "Sorry, it's been a minute."

David scans the darkness over the quarry. "The Door must be closing faster than we thought. We must hurry."

If the Door closes, we'd be on even ground. Or as even as it gets when you're hog-tied and outnumbered three to one.

Four, if you count Paul.

No, I won't count him. I refuse.

I turn onto the crown of my thudding head, my neck feeling very brittle. The plastic cover slaps me in the face. I feel its darkness, its slimy rotten heart beating next to mine.

All the planning I put into today, and in my vanity, I kept... something they charmed?

Or cursed.

As Mom was blinded to her family and surroundings, I see that I was blind too. I was irritable, impulsive, the same woman who security cameras caught filling a few dozen bottles with gasoline.

And for those mistakes, my children will pay with their lives.

"For many years," says Trevor, "we wondered how it was your mom could know of our gothi." Paul hands each of them a cloth with the three interlocking triangles of Wodan, which they unroll with care. "That's why many went into hiding. Why they threw away their charms. Some feared the Idol could no longer protect them."

"Mom died trying to stop them, Paul," I say, forcing words out through the pain and nausea. "They cursed her to burn down the church, but somehow Mom was able to take out their gothi."

Paul blinks. For a moment, his features drop, giving him a more adult look. "Mom?" he says.

"She's telling lies, Brother," says David, then flashes a knife, its gold handle smudged with fingerprints. "Once you see Blót, Daphne, *yes*." He's pleased to see the knife terrifies me, the same one Rusty hit Paul with thirty-three years ago. "May be hard to believe, but this dagger is a millennium old."

"I'll do it," says Rusty, taking the knife. "Paul? Hello? You killed my brother, I kill your sister. This'll fuck you up like it fucked me up, but it's only fair, ain't it, Paul?"

"Yes, Brother," says Paul, his eyes downcast.

Seeing the return of that childhood look should crush me, but I hear Dad. Somehow in the storm raging in my head, I hear Dad's voice in mine. "Listen, Paul. Listen to that voice. That's Mom and Dad telling you to fight."

"I killed my father," says David. "He lost faith. So did my brothers. What a waste."

"After the first ten," says Trevor, shaking his head at the night sky, "you lose count." His shrug gives me chills.

The moment Rusty faces me, my brother bear-hugs him. They slam into a car door, grunting where I can't see. Trevor and David are slow to understand.

Joy leaps in my throat. Paul's playing them. He's going to free me, and together we'll find my children.

Except Rusty has thirty pounds of prison-fed muscle on my brother. After the initial shock, Rusty frees an arm and clocks Paul. My brother's nose snaps to the right with a sickening crunch. He crumples into a plume of dust.

"*Paul*," I scream.

A snort comes from the car Paul drove. I hear the rustle of a sleeping bag. The Nolans. If they're not hog-tied like me, maybe they can run away.

Rusty points the knife at Paul's neck. "We trusted you like a Brother, man," says Rusty, breathing hard. "You betrayed us."

Paul sucks in air, chest heaving, his neck smeared with what looks like a scarf of blood.

"Mom wasn't at the cabin," says Paul. "You were."

"Don't kill him, Rusty," I say.

David steps in Rusty's way. He holds out his hand toward the knife.

"You'd put your blood on the line for this halfie?" says Rusty.

"The Dranes are pure, Brother," says David. "Everyone loses faith from time to time."

"I couldn't do that to Stephen and Zachary," says Paul in tears. "They're my family. Ask me anything else. Anything, Brothers."

"They're not your brothers, Paul," I say.

Trevor and David exchange a glance. I read their look. *What are we going to do with him*?

"Run, Paul," I say. "Get in the car. Get help."

Paul doesn't move. "Yes, Brother," he says to David, as if I haven't spoken.

Jesus. What did they do to him? What have they done? It's like Paul has bouts of sanity, then slips right back in. Just like Mom. I keep turning, wriggling. The visitor tag's caught in my hair.

"Where are we?" asks a soft voice. It's Grant or Roderick. "I'm hungry."

Run. Someone who can run, frickin' RUN. God, my head pounds.

The others are thinking so hard they don't hear. "Pick him up," says David. He hands the keys to Rusty, who seems to understand right away. Rusty opens the trunk.

"No," I shout. "Not with Theresa inside."

Paul's eyes widen. Though I can't see Theresa Nolan's crushed face, I can't forget her. Paul looks like he feels the same way.

"No," says Paul, so hoarse he bubbles. "P-p-please. Brothers."

The men upend Paul into the trunk, and slam it.

The Chrysler shakes. Paul screams for help.

"I'm tired of screwing around," says Trevor over Paul's knocking and pleading. "Her first. Then the kids."

The chain lets go. I see the badge on the pulverized white stone. *Yes, I see it.*

Like that, the headache's gone, and so is the anxiety. Light floods in. The men snap into focus. Cars, knife, quarry, and buildings too. Trying to blind me, those assholes. The Ford special.

"Book says we can't skip steps, Brother," says David. "We need the red candle."

Trevor points past me. "You want to wait until the Door closes forever, be my guest."

No choice but to roll one final time, my backpack inches away, the heat from the floodlight rumbling in the gravel. I'm there. I push the button. Why won't it work? I keep pushing. We're well within a thousand yards. We have to be.

Finally, my car alarm sounds. White and orange lights flash across the quarry. Please someone hear it. Hear it and call the cops. New Minton may not be perfect, but . . .

Trevor flips me over. "What do you have there, huh?" he says like a tired father.

I have no intention of explaining what a relay attack is, but unfortunately, Trevor understands the concept pretty well. He pushes the button until the alarm stops. Then he smashes the box. Pieces of plastic spray the road and me.

"No one will save you, Daphne," says David. Rusty hands him a crumpled robe with red and gold insignia running down its center. Not silk, but close enough, I guess. The robe for each unspoiled. They can break every bone in my body, but I'm not putting on that fucking thing. David raises his arms. "Can't you hear it? Can't you hear the sound of true faith?"

The thing is, I can.

In the wake of my car alarm being silenced, nature responds with a deafening yawp. Owls thunder from the trees. So do the crickets, bullfrogs, and unseen birds flapping their wings. Either it drowns out Paul or it awes him too.

All together, it sounds like a hymn, as though just beyond my sight, the ravens congregate once more to watch these men fulfill an obligation to their dark church.

David holds up the dagger, chanting like the animals. Rusty and Trevor join him.

I close my eyes, trying not to cry. I'm on my own, as I've always been. Paul in the trunk. No Brandy to the rescue. With everyone on the Hill? Probably no one's around.

When I turn, something pokes my stomach, and I see Trevor's right. No one will save me. Maybe I can save myself.

It's a jagged piece of plastic from the relay attack, about the length of a finger. I let it fall to the ground so I can scoop it up. If I could just get it low enough, I might be able to cut what I think is a zip tie. They probably have a hundred of them in their trash bags. Muzzles and blindfolds, too, so they can restrain their victims, their unspoileds.

Three cuts, and my ankles break free. Now my wrists.

"For thirty-three years," says David, "the same years as your Lord Christ's life, the Elementals shall feast on your blood, and you will hold the Door open. Blót, as it's been done for centuries."

The damn plastic won't bite. All I've done is sharpen the point.

And made a shiv.

Trevor dusts off his Raven's head. Rusty has to stow my pistol in his waistband to check his. I roll until I bump into Rusty's shins.

He looks down, surprised I'm pawing the leather tongue of his boot. Rusty's indecision is more than enough time to lift with my hips, and drive the plastic blade into his foot with all my weight.

"Oh, *fuck*-stick," Rusty hollers, face in agony, hopping away.

Incredibly, the pistol lands on the rocks next to me. Too bad my hands are tied. I fumble for it, shoulder muscles straining, each blind finger pushing the darn thing farther away. My wrists scream, then I have the pistol by the slide. I roll onto my knees. Jesus, how am I going to fight three grown men when I can't even scratch my chin?

Someone grabs my shoulder for the second time tonight, which might be why the fabric tears right off. I stumble like a drunkard between parked cars, trying to turn the pistol without dropping it. Just when I grab the grip, hands shove me into the generator, knocking it and me over.

Light winks out.

The engine dies.

"Bitch fucking stabbed me."

"Where is she?"

I can't see shit. Thankfully, they're the same. It's a race to whose eyes adjust first.

The trees' frosty edges color in, as does the gravel. Buildings, too, then cars. Paul's banging again. Over that, I hear the men prowling.

With no way to see the pistol's sight, I keep my shoulder pointed where the shove came from. My hands sweat too much to get a good grip, which is only worsened by the sand on my palms. I pray my finger's muscle memory is correct; the safety switch is off when it's up. My wrist is a beacon of pain, twisted like this.

"We're going to fucking kill you, Daphne," says Trevor. Like I didn't know that already. My shoulder twitches. He's a lot closer than I thought, but still I can't.

Something dark shuffles right. My eyes follow.

Trevor charges from the left, the dagger at face level, whooping with his neck cords stretched tight. He comes straight for my front, where I'm most vulnerable. I fall and spin.

My shot strikes gravel.

I don't have time for another. Trevor stomps my head. I squeeze the pistol. My vision goes red.

The first stab wound is like lava drilling into my back. I cry out, but I don't feel the second or the third, just the pressure. I squeeze more shots, screaming until my throat cracks. I'm not going to die, I'm not going to die.

Trevor slumps onto me. He has to be two hundred pounds.

I shoulder him until I can wheel the pistol, which is just in time to catch David leaping with his arms wide out like wings. The bullet wound in his leg catches him like a wire. He strikes the road face first.

"Oh, God," he cries. "Oh, *it hurts so bad*."

As if being bound isn't hard enough, blood's gushing so fast I feel it weighing down my clothes. I don't know how I shake Trevor off, but he slumps over, allowing me to get to my knees. His throat rattles, his eyes half-closed. He's dead, or will be soon. If I knew how many bullets I had left, I might fire some more into his fat ass.

Instead, I twist to find Rusty, who tosses something into the darkness. Then he holds out one hand, keeps the other on his bleeding foot.

"You can't hit me like that," he says. "Not from behind."

"Want to test my skills?" I spit. This isn't good. I'm bleeding out of my mouth too. Blood's filling my lungs. "What'd you throw over there?"

"The keys," he says, looking over the cars, grinning. "For all of them, Daph."

Hard as I strain my ears, I don't remember hearing the keys land. Rusty could've tossed them all the way into the quarry.

Shit, shit, shit.

I replay the memory of Trevor opening the trunk with a button in the car, but David gave Rusty the keys. Had Trevor done the same?

"No," I say. "Trevor still has his keys to the truck."

In his pocket. What a relief, seeing how I don't know how I'll scale five hundred feet with multiple stab wounds.

"Rusty, get the knife," I say. "Slow. Place it on the ground."

Stop sweating. Go someplace safe. Be cold, be fierce.

Rusty grimaces at Trevor's body. "Bleh," he says before rolling Trevor.

"You go near his pockets," I say, "and I'll shoot you dead."

"You had to follow him," says Rusty, grabbing the dagger. "You understand?" I turn again so he can see the pistol, and he drops the dagger ten feet away. "Please, Daph. I had to watch your brother kill mine."

Rusty's words dig under my ribs. Guilt wants to drag me into the fetal position. Then I remind myself that even a beast can look innocent.

"You feel so bad about Billy," I say, "how come when the police had you for juvenile prostitution, you never gave up your Brotherhood?" He winces, and drops his eyes. "That's what I thought. Now back away. Lie down. On your belly."

I glance back to make sure David's still writhing on the ground, crying now about how the bullet is lodged right up on his thigh bone. Try getting stabbed. After the first one, you don't feel a thing.

"Face away from me, Rusty. Stay there. Don't you move until I say."

Each heartbeat pumps more blood out of my body. I feel myself getting lightheaded. But still I count to one hundred Mississippi. Then I go for their ancient dagger.

Soon as I touch it, the knife blazes. Like I pulled it out of a fire, searing my skin. My instinct is to throw it as far as possible, but I don't let myself. I keep screaming through the pain, refusing to stop until I cut my hands free.

On the ground, the dagger smolders and so does my dead skin charcoaled to it. My hand's a bubble of purple flesh. It won't stop shaking.

"Aw, Jesus," I whimper, picking up the gun with my off hand. Now it feels strange to line up the men so easily. "Oh God. What the hell is that thing?"

I recognize the wound pattern. It's the same as the one on the back of Paul's head. The curved lines of the hilt's design that baffled the doctors and police. They came from the same knife that Rusty used on Paul under Lincoln Bridge.

A knife that burns anyone who isn't like them.

No time to think about it. I find my bag, which is fine, but the phone's destroyed. I drop to my knee, pat Trevor's body. The Ram's keys are in my hand. Soon as I get my boys, we can drive to Mommy's Prius.

"I don't belong here," says David. "You know that, Daphne. I'm supposed to be dead. Your mom killed me."

"No, she didn't," I say, "and Mom sure didn't abduct you. Where are my kids, David? Where are Zachary and Stephen?"

Thank goodness, even cultists still bring iPhones to sacrifices. No idea what Trevor's passcode is, but the iPhone lets you bypass if it's an emergency.

"Damn it."

No dots, just the words *No Service*. A text to 9-1-1 fails, turning red. Dimly, I'm aware the chanting has stopped, and so have the crickets, but we're still far removed from civilization.

"We proved ourselves unworthy, Brothers," says David, his beady blue eyes staring into the night sky. "Now our crops will fail. Our families will be impoverished."

"If you don't know where my kids are, David," I say, pointing the gun at him, "you're not much use to me."

David slumps down. If he passed out due to shock, I'm supposed to tell him to keep his eyes open, but forget him. He's on his own. I need all my energy to keep my own eyes open.

CHAPTER FORTY-NINE

I find the trash bag of zip ties. I cinch Rusty, David, and Trevor, then I cinch them together. I also find the Book of the Brotherhood on David's dashboard.

Chasms of fire and ice, Elementals, opening a Door. I don't dare touch it. Not this time. In Paul's car, Grant and Roderick fell back asleep. At least I've got that going for me.

Fleming Quarry has at least three buildings. The first is a mobile home with an aluminum exterior. It looks like someone peeled the upper right half corner before giving up.

Someone's breathing behind me.

Two boys look up with wide blank eyes. "Blessed be, Sister," says the taller one. "Are you taking us to the Door?"

First reactions are always critical, especially when meeting children who say unexpectedly sinister things, so I manage not to scream.

"Not right now," I say, pausing to take them in. The boys shouldn't be creepy. They're filthy and shoeless, neglected if anything, their hair as long and as ragged as Paul's thirty-three years ago. Also like Paul, they sound brainwashed. Grant and Roderick Nolan in white robes. Paul probably dressed them. "Are you Grant?"

He nods. "Yes, Sister."

"That makes you Roderick?" I ask.

The shorter one doesn't say anything. He holds the same wide stare as though something's floating just a few feet from my forehead.

"Roderick," I say, "nice to meet you. Have you seen any other boys around?"

They stare blankly at me.

"When are we going to the Door, Sister?" asks Grant.

"Stay there," I say, "okay? We're going to get out of here in a minute, but I need to check in this building if . . ."

If my children are in there, but I don't finish the thought. My back got stabbed, yet my legs wobble on the slippery steps to the mobile home.

The door screams open. "Stephen?" I call in a husk. "Zachary?"

Must rushes out. I cover my face too late. Every time I cough, I feel my wounds squeeze out more blood. I shine Trevor's phone, my only light. A weak orange square that jerkily sketches a desk and filing cabinets.

I keep calling until the pain is too much. No answer.

Dust is a quarter of an inch high over the billboard notices. Behind the desk, water filled the wood, covering the ceiling with mold. No doubt I'm hallucinating, but the mold resembles a raven's head.

Water drips, despite the dryness of the winter, keeping one white wall shining.

There's nowhere to hide my boys.

Back outside, I see that behind the mobile home stands the ghostly outline of a four-story processing plant. Arms shoot out from the top floor, traveling to the ground floor at a forty-five degree decline. Those arms lead to other structures. My children could be in any of them.

There's no way I could search all of the buildings before bleeding out. I need help closing the wounds, or I need help searching.

The boys aren't where I left them.

"Grant, Roderick?" I call, shuffling to the cars. "Honey? Don't wander too far, okay?"

I see the top halves of their bodies on the other side of the Chrysler, only about thirty feet from where I asked them to stay put. Something about the cars is off, they're tilted up or down, but I can't think about that now. Nonetheless, I pause to watch how rigid Grant's and Roderick's backs are, the curious way their elbows are out.

Birds. They look like birds about to take off.

"Boys," I say, "you can't wander off."

The Nolan boys stare at Trevor's dead body. They watch with the fascination of morbid children, absorbing every detail.

They're already scarred. And I made it worse.

I reach for the boys, realizing my math is off. Trevor's body is still there. Rusty's sitting up, watching the children observe the body. I'm sure I tied his hands behind his back, but now they're resting on his stomach. David's gone.

"What did you do?" I say, spinning Grant. "Grant, answer me."

If Grant was my son, he would blink, act scared, and probably cry. But these boys only stare blankly. "What happened to Brother Trevor?" asks Grant.

"That one," says Rusty, pointing to Grant, "cut David loose."

I should've known. Bound or not, these men hold enormous power over the boys. To them, I am the interloper, the enemy. Just like I am every minute I spend in this twisted town.

"Cut with what?" I say without taking my eyes off the boys.

"Relax, Daphne. David took the knife with him."

"The thousand-year-old dagger that burns people's flesh? Very relaxing news, Rusty." I hold up my burned palm, the flesh brightly red and still steaming, which only amuses Rusty. "They let David go, but not you?"

Rusty shrugs. "They don't know me," he says. "Stranger danger."

Thank God for that. Though that's the last of the good news I see.

I scan the trees, the dark spot where the quarry is. Before disappearing into the woods or God-knows-where-else, David could've freed Rusty, but he didn't. Maybe David figured Rusty was a liability.

Or David didn't have time.

I see now why all the cars are cocked at strange angles. David was busy slashing tires. All but one, the Chrysler.

Now, wounded or not, David is armed and knows the quarry. He can find where Rusty threw the keys—Rusty could've told him where to search—and escape in the only working vehicle down here.

My eyes longingly search for an easy path to my Prius. Even after I find my Zachary and Stephen, how am I going to get up there? Each heartbeat sparks agony, and other possibilities of David's intent, but not a decision.

David can be hiding, dimmed to strike.

If David comes at me, and I miss?

Soon as that knife touches my flesh, it will burn. David can hold the blade against my skin until I drop the gun.

I can't take that chance. Not after how far I've come.

That leaves Paul.

I don't like the idea of getting Paul out of the trunk only for David to reappear and convince Paul to switch sides back to David. But I also don't like Paul stuck in the trunk with the body of Theresa Nolan. I don't see another choice.

"Boys," I say. "Stay over there, no matter what." I take a breath. "Paul? It's Daphne."

"Yes, Brother. Yes, Brother, *please*."

"Paul, stop that shit." I glance back and frown at the Nolan boys; between whatever they endured over the last two months and Trevor's body, I figure a little cussing's okay. "It's your sister who loves you, Paul. Trevor's dead and David's dying." At least, I can hope, right? "I need you. Do you understand?" Again, I cough up blood. It feels like fire splitting the skin on my back, dropping me to a knee. The darkness spins.

"Daphne?"

That sounds more like him, snapping me back. "Yes, Paul."

"Daphne, it smells like piss and shit and there's a woman, and she's—"

"You can get out any time you want," I say, wishing I could cover Grant's and Roderick's ears. Please don't say their mother's name. I'll tell them when all this is over, but not now. "Through the back seat. Do you know how?"

"I've done a lot of bad things, Daphne," says Paul, "but I only pretended to go along with tonight. You've got to believe me."

I do. I want to. Even though he dressed the Nolans in robes. And he was on one of his benders while they were missing.

But I don't have time to argue. I barely have the strength to stand.

"Look for a handle, Paul."

"Because of Stephen and Zach," he says.

"Or a trunk release." I spit a dark sickle. Grant and Roderick watch it with quiet amazement.

"I don't see one."

"Okay," I say. "The car's probably older than 2002. Go through the back seat. If you don't see a handle, just push your way through."

I hear a long rubbery squeak, agonizingly slow, like a shoe sliding across a basketball court, then a thump. Paul needs forever to get into position. He growls to exert himself.

"Do it, Paul." I have to place my hands on the trunk. I'm getting lightheaded. When I come to, Grant has three small fingers on the Beretta in my hand. He turns back, and I follow his gaze to Rusty, who watches silently.

Some metal spring pops. The back seat crashes down. And Paul's next to me in tears.

"Daphne, please forgive me," he says, trying to hug me. He almost knocks me over.

"It's okay, Paul," I say and turn my back so he can see.

Surely in thirty-three years, Paul is substantially more brainwashed than Grant and Roderick. If he wants to hit me over the head, jab my wounds, wait for me to bleed out, here's his chance. I hope the kindness of a big sister is enough.

"Oh God," he says. "Who did this?"

"Trevor," I say. "I need you to tear those robes. Press them against my back, no matter how much I scream. We have to stop the bleeding."

"I heard you screaming. I heard the shots."

"But Sister." Grant cocks his head. "Why did Brother Trevor hurt you? Was he mad?"

"It's okay, sweetie," I say. "The robes, Paul."

My brother runs away. Fuck, he's off to find David, but no, Paul's crashing through David's garbage bags. He returns with some proper gauze and tape.

Glad to know David's so prepared.

"Paul, are my children in one of these buildings?"

"I don't know, Daph," he says behind me, tearing packages open. "I swear. They only trusted me with small things like picking up the kids. This was my first time alone with them. I was thinking, they see me with the Nolans, they'll show me where Stephen and Zach are."

Picking up the kids. Transporting them. Like what Everett Ford and Marvin Rahall did for the Flemings. The new Brothers have to work their way up.

"Seven," says Paul.

"Seven what?" asks Grant, his hand again clearly out for the pistol.

Seven stab wounds. God.

"Can we help, Sister?" says Roderick. The first time he's spoken.

"Because when Brother Trevor says," says Grant, "we're all supposed to hold hands and jump. Like this."

Seeing Grant act out his last moments with such innocence drills into my chest. I shake my head at Rusty.

"You're monsters," I say.

"I'm a Raven," says Rusty, "and you're all worms. A bleeding worm who'll never find her boys. That place." He whistles at the processing plant. "Is a maze."

"Come on," I say, needing help to get up. Paul can take advantage of my dizziness and take the Beretta out of my hands before I realize it's gone, but he doesn't. I have no choice but to trust his shame is real.

Because Rusty's right. It's like trying to breathe through a straw. I don't have long.

Paul helps me down a gravel path a few hundred yards from the quarry's caldera, Grant and Roderick in tow. We descend into darkness, our shoes crunching over dead leaves.

At maintenance sheds, Paul stops. I lean against a light post. The pole and buildings have industrial light sources, but the power's probably been off fifteen years.

"Stephen?" calls Paul. "Zachary?" He rattles the doors but every building's locked. Bright blue-green mold runs along the doors, highlighting their steel frames. Paul tries his shoulder. They don't budge.

Paul calls again. We listen. Nothing. We move farther down the road, farther into the plant's shadow.

I fall three times before we reach the main entrance.

"Do you want to rest, Daph?"

"No, Paul," I say, "I want to find my children."

The processing plant is four stories that probably total 80 thousand square feet. Rusty's right. There's no way we're going to be able to search this whole place. It'd take police and dogs days to comb the plant.

A corrugated door rolls up what looks like a hundred feet, large enough for dump trucks to enter and exit. Signs have been graffitied with images of ravens. Under that reads, NO TRESPASSING. Another set of doors is next to that, but . . .

"There's a chain," says Paul.

"It's locked too?" I'm having trouble keeping my eyes open. Pessimism becomes smoke in my periphery.

"It's loose enough to slip through," says Paul.

I can't see anything beyond the doors and chain, only smell the overpowering odor of copper. My eyes won't adjust. They see sky, nothing but sky.

"Careful, Daph." Paul's holding me. Did I fall, lose my balance?

He sets me on the cold concrete.

The air presses on me, a force that wants to grind me into the ground.

"I don't think I can squeeze," I say, hearing myself gurgling. Drool's rolling down my chin. The color's pink, getting darker.

"I'll search, Daph," says Paul. "Just hold on."

"Go. I'll be fine."

Grant and Roderick's eyes glow like evil dolls. I can't think of anything to say to them. Apparently, they feel the same way.

On the other side of the mobile home, lights flash. At the gate.

The police are here.

Just ram it. Don't bother with the chain. I try to yell that, but instead I cough.

"Can we get up now?" asks Grant.

Hold on. Just hold on.

"Hold on," I say aloud, spitting some more. I'm losing the strength to sit up. My back feels like it got pounded rather than stabbed. "Zachary. Stephen. We're coming. We're coming."

An officer stands with hands on his hips, his name Patowski. Grandson of my old teacher, or great-nephew?

"No one's in those buildings, ma'am."

What? No. My boys are here. Rusty said so.

"Rusty says you killed your kids just like your mother killed his brother."

"*No*," I say.

Rage at the accusation powers me off the ground. I search furiously for the officer in the night.

"I'm not going to lose my kids," I scream. "They're alive. Bring in search dogs. Look everywhere. See if the cabinets have been moved recently."

"Daphne?" I'm being shaken. "Daphne, what's wrong?"

Paul snaps me back. I'm at the edge of a meadow. No police are there. No Patowski. Just camouflaged ravens flapping their wings.

Because a closing Door isn't the same as a *closed* Door.

Nearest I can tell, I'm about a hundred yards from the rear of the plant, which means I traveled all the way through pipes and piles to the moment I would plunge into deep woods. If Paul hadn't grabbed me, and I came to even five minutes later, I doubt I'd have enough light to find my way back.

"I've been trying to tell you," says Paul, "no one's there in the plant. Not that I can see."

"The same thing the police officer said," I say.

"Daphne, what?"

Or maybe that's just my evil thoughts leading me to get lost on the Fleming Quarry's private property.

"Did you search all four floors, Paul?" I ask, sounding as skeptical as Mom would.

"It's freaky in there," says Paul. "But everything's moved out."

A sliver of moonlight catches Paul streaked in white fuzzies. I touch a row on his chest.

"Miles of empty space," he says, "like a hangar. We can try the towers on the other side."

"The dust," I say, holding it so he can see.

Paul shakes his head. "What?"

"The first thing you look for is if the dust has been disturbed," I say, my thoughts heating up. "You walked through dust. You didn't see footprints on any of the floors, did you?"

"No, I don't think."

"Because the quarry's been abandoned for years," I say, and look back. "Except one place."

"Daphne."

I wrap my arm around Paul's neck. He's dirty, sweating, and hot. He must've raced through all the rooms, yelling while I hallucinated or some last remnant of Vikki Harper's curse tried to kill me. But they couldn't stop me from solving the most important case of my life.

"Back up there," I say.

The walk is excruciating. I can barely get my legs to take steps.

Rusty's trying to bite through the restraints. He stops when we pass.

Back in the mobile home. Toxins float over the littered desk.

"Where are we going, Daphne?" asks Paul.

"That wall," I say, pointing.

I assumed the wall was dark because of the water dripping down. Up close, I see the wall's not wet at all. It only looks wet because it's the only thing not covered in dust.

"Stephen?" I call. "Zachary?"

The wall breathes. With each knock, my vision dims. Vertigo flips the ceiling and floor.

"Careful, Daphne." Paul tries to keep me upright.

"They have to be here," I say, banging harder. Please. It's the last place left.

Darkness closes in. Paul's telling me I need to rest when I hear something muffled. "En," says the wall, then a thump.

"Boys?" I shout. "*Boys*?" Sweat rolls like eels down my back.

"Daphne, you have to pull," says Paul.

I don't understand why he's working against me. For a moment, I'm convinced Paul switched back to David's side.

Wood creaks and snaps in the gloom. Then the board—it's just a plywood board—gives way and crashes. Thankfully, I'm no match for my brother. Dust rushes over a sleeping bag. A lump in the shape of a head. Oh God. I fall to my knees, reaching for it.

"Stephen?" I say, shaking him awake. "Stephen? It's Mommy."

Red hair pops out of the sleeping bag. I'm so shocked, my mouth falls open.

"I'm Andrew," says the redheaded boy with a dark frown. "This is Johnny."

"Who's Johnny?" I ask, out of breath.

My heart can't handle any more strange children, but the light from Trevor's phone captures a boy in his underwear with scabs on his legs.

"Andrew," I say, peering farther into the false wall. "Where are you from? It's okay. I'm not going to hurt you."

"Milwaukee," says Andrew, still skeptical. "My dad likes that drink."

"Milwaukee beer," I say. The phone's light fades. "Is Johnny your brother?"

"I'm from Madrid," says Johnny.

"Oh, Madrid." I pat more lumps and nod, though I don't follow. Does Johnny mean *Spain*?

"That's in New Mexico," says Johnny. "But I haven't seen it in this many."

Johnny holds up all of his fingers.

"Ten?" I say. Behind Andrew and Johnny lie dozens more boys. Like Andrew, they look at me sleepy-eyed and afraid. "Someone took you from your home ten days ago?"

Johnny nods. "And I'm supposed to be taking care of my brother . . ."

I don't remember anyone named Johnny from New Mexico in the last ten days. Or an Andrew from Milwaukee. While I was getting ready for the CARD Team Commission, David and Trevor were sweeping the country. They went on a ferocious binge, abducting children, and somehow escaped any notice.

Claws dig into my kidneys. I have to find my children. I feel myself spiraling.

"Have you seen a boy with dirty blond hair?" I ask. "Named Stephen? Or a brown—"

"*Mommy.*"

I choke on my son's name. "Zachary?"

"Scared, Mommy, scared."

"Oh, baby," I cry. "Find Momma. Follow Momma's voice."

Andrew and Johnny part. From their shadows he comes. A magnet tugging my soul. The unstoppable force that draws Zachary like a torpedo to my chest.

Oof. I fall back. My arms are too weak to pick him up, my hands jelly. Is he really here? Is he really unharmed? Numbness tingles all over. We lie on the ground, everything spinning too fast.

"Zachary," I say, the only thing that's anchoring me. "Where's your brother? Where's Stephen?"

"Mom?" Stephen rubs his face as though he's not sure if he's dreaming.

"Stephen." Relief floods my chest. "Come here. Come see."

My children cling like an octopus, feverishly hot in my arms. Their smells blanket me, the milky smell they never lost.

"Miss Tee-Tee took me," sobs Zachary, "to bad men. Bad men. Bad."

"I'm so sorry, baby," I say. "Momma's so sorry."

"They wanted to drain our blood," says Stephen.

"Mommy's here now," I say, stifling a sob. Drain their Drane blood. What horrors did they plan for my boys? I rock them. "Mommy's here."

And I really am. No more being preoccupied with depositions and finding justice for Mom. Clawing through corrupt agents, curses, and knife-wielding murderers to get back my sons.

It's over, it's finally over. My sons are safe. I can hold them and love them and be their mother again. Soon as we get home, Karl will be with us, and we'll never be apart again. The four of us, an unbreakable family.

"Thank you," I whisper. *Thank you, thank you, thank you.*

When I look up, I catch Paul's face quivering. He never got what I have. Mom never got to hold him like I hold my boys now.

I reach out my hand, and Paul kneels to embrace us, a weight I'm grateful to share.

"Can we go home, Mommy?"

"Yes," I say, sniffing.

"Can we go home too?" asks Andrew.

I pull back, the shock of the question giving me a moment to process. Paul's eyes glitter with haunting silence. Finally, I arrive at the only answer.

"Yes," I say. "You're all going back."

Thirty-three. That's the number of children that surround the Chrysler, where in the trunk lies a mother to two of these boys. The children Trevor, David, and Rusty were prepared to kill to keep a Door open as part of their plan to franchise the Brotherhood.

These boys who, even in the dark, shimmer in white blankets. They go around the circle and tell us their names. Joey. Tony. Tim. Gabriel. I wonder if any of the people I saw in Chelsea, holding picture frames and toys, might have their prayers answered.

I see the rock I hid behind, the rock where Rusty knocked me out. Beyond that is the trail I used to climb down.

"Hold each other's hands," I say. "No one lets go. Not for any reason. Okay?"

"Yes, Sister," say a handful of them. I can't tell if they're drugged or indoctrinated. The others blink dully. Maybe David and Trevor abducted them more recently.

Paul's patting my elbow, rare real estate of available space considering Zachary and Stephen are hanging off me.

"I said, we can't get all those kids up the hill, Daphne," says Paul. "Someone's going to twist an ankle or fall."

I'm too lightheaded to argue. But my kids aren't.

"Why can't Uncle Paul carry you?" asks Stephen.

"Because Mommy's too heavy," I say, smoothing Stephen's bangs. He and Zachary look up at me, sucking in their cheeks, eyes large like Karl's.

The quarry's spinning. I can't get up that hill. I can't transport thirty-something children. Help has to come to us. How?

"How are we going to get out?" asks Paul, reflecting my thoughts. His panic stirs the others.

My eyes catch the generator, the one they knocked me into, and I overturned.

"Rusty." I have to stop coughing. "Do you have a lighter?"

His chin is red from the struggle to free himself, as though he ate a strawberry. "Yeah," he says, "why?"

"Leave it on the ground."

I'm not sure if Rusty will obey. Especially with me asking.

Either the memory of the gun or the sight of the children spurs Rusty to wrestle into his pockets. He holds it up before dropping it on the road.

"Stephen, honey, get that for Mommy, but don't get too close to that tied-up man. And don't open the lighter no matter what." He scoots for it, and I turn to Paul. "Open the tank."

"Why?" says Rusty over everyone. Just like he'd do to the teachers, *why* them to death.

"Just do it." *Hurry*.

Paul unscrews the cap. Who knows how much gasoline they put in that thing, but I hear it glugging, a long dark pool rolling down the hill and into the trees.

"Kids, stand back."

I click Rusty's lighter. A long flame unrolls, a demon's tongue.

Zachary latches onto my ring finger. He peers around me, watching the light. What must he be thinking?

Not much time, Daphne Girl. Momma needs your help, okay? Come. Come to Momma?

Probably the same I did when I was eleven.

Confusion. Fascination. The untethering of yourself because you never saw your mother like this before.

Mom's last words to me were asking to help, and I rejected her.

I left Mom to be consumed by her own madness. I'm sorry, Mom. I didn't understand then. Glancing at David's Chrysler, I wonder if I do now.

I drop the lighter. Blue light follows the stream. The orange whoosh pierces my eyes.

As it was in 1988, the spring was dry. According to the National Weather Service, they haven't seen a decent storm in weeks.

"The Fire Department's amped about another wildfire," I say, "they'll come."

Paul's face dances as though he's wearing a mask. He says nothing. The children gape at the rising flames.

I stagger to the Chrysler. The Brotherhood's book rests on the dashboard. Careful not to touch its binding, I cover it with a strip of robe.

"Hey," says Rusty.

I toss in the book too. Immediately, the smell is awful. Like burning hair. The children groan. The cover smokes. Papers curl. Whatever evil got released, I don't see it. Guess the next gothi will have to start from scratch.

Rusty watches in disgust. "You really are psycho, Daphne," he says.

Smoke floats to the stars. Are the flames bright enough? Is anyone looking down in the quarry? I stare through the trees, praying for blue lights.

"You don't know how many there are, Daphne," says Paul. His panic wants company, but I won't let it out. "They could rescue Rusty instead of us, and finish." He leans, his breath foul. "Finish the job."

My vision tunnels. I hear whispers from the tree trunks.

"No," I say, after a moment. Clai and Mr. Corwin were repulsed at my accusation. "They may spill wine on a Hill, but I don't think the Dentons and whoever are capable of abducting children. Trevor's dead. Rusty's going back to jail." Something clicks in the leaves, and I get dizzy. "David's face is about to be broadcast on the evening news. Mom's and Mort Norton's names will be cleared."

A shadow drops onto the rocks in front of us. A raven. Its luminous black eyes draw me in, but I snap from the haze. Vertigo. Loss of sight. It's another spell. David, or maybe Rusty. One last ditch effort before the Door slams shut.

"Paul, *watch out*."

A man-sized shadow knocks us down, the pain a hot pinch on my shoulder blades. Children scream. I reach for my boys, but I keep slipping farther down. The harder I fight, the farther I float away. I don't understand.

"Olsen. Where's Chief Olsen?"

"Here."

I know that name, Geoffrey Olsen. I recognize that snaggle-tooth too. The men ripple over a surface I burst through. Paul and the boys are gone but a cruiser's here. *Suffolk*, reads the car door. The town between New Minton and Clifton. Hallelujah. Fire trucks are red lights grinding down Trevor's private road.

"I got two dead males, Chief, and one unconscious." The man in black points to a prone body. I slap someone's hands, trying to see. It's Paul.

"The skinhead here was standing over the female, about to shoot. I had no choice."

Yes, I see Rusty dead on the ground. He broke out of his zip tie. He got the drop on Paul. If Suffolk PD hadn't arrived, Rusty would've killed me. Is Paul okay?

"Uh, Chief, Patowski just found a 2019 Prius parked on the side of the road with over two dozen incendiary devices."

Forget about that for now. Come quick. I need to—

"The kids are saying there's a third male." The officer pauses, staring down at me. "She snapped a picture, but her camera's busted. We haven't found anyone else so far."

"ID on the third male?"

"David Gedney."

"Has to be an alias."

Firelight burns the canopy, but I can't face it. I need the pain.

I need its needles to tangle with my skin and keep me awake.

They have to put out David's picture. Otherwise, none of us are safe.

"Look, she's trying to say something."

"We're looking for the Merauxs, right, Chief? Two kids. Who the hell are the others?"

"Blessed be."

With the last of my strength, I lift my head. The men gawk at the dozens taking tender steps across the gravel. Thirty-three boys, including my sons. The paramedics should be tending to them, but they keep holding me down, shouting something. I'm not sure at what point I leave the pain behind.

"Dangerously low blood pressure."

"Air medical's at least an hour away."

Pebbles rattle into a long shadow. My eyes follow the rocky limestone up to something impossibly large swinging over the quarry.

It looks like the spine of a dinosaur, like the one I took my boys to see last year in New York. The white bone is a jigsaw of lumbar and cartilage, and it blots the heavens.

Fangs curve from each heart-shaped vertebra. The spine's alive too. Flesh is the wrong word, but intertwined with the bleached white bone are yellow nerves and sweating veins that pulse as though it has a heartbeat. It's a living, breathing dragon's spine. Maybe the vertebrae are the source of the White Stone.

I see no beginning or end. The spine floats as though in suspension. Its joints grind and bend, curving as subtly as the earth before disappearing into the night. Either the men don't see it, or they ignore it.

My mouth goes dry.

The spine is the Wheel. It's got to be.

The quarry turns the Wheel, said Rusty. Why isn't it turning now?

It wants to. Giant tendons snap. Somewhere, some motor burns up, trying to make the Wheel rotate around its axis. The Wheel's caught on something. What?

The kind of literalist who thought he could actually open a Door, said Clai, *would know that it would risk stopping the Wheel, which would destroy everything we believe.*

I follow the darkness to where the road meets the quarry. There the night shimmers. A trick of the light, but it's not.

Strange that I never concentrated on that shimmer until now, the answer towering thirty feet away all this time. If I stare hard enough, a rough circle unhoods.

A circle they call the Door.

Milky-red light froths from the Door's corona. It's getting bolder. It wants me to see.

A gateway to life eternal, rotating over a heap of bones.

Somewhere on the other side of that bloody eye is a power these men sought for centuries. Murdering strangers and neighbors, even their fathers, to get scraps from their Elementals. Every thirty-three years, they delayed the Wheel's turn, creating in our little town a struggle downright biblical.

It should close. Why doesn't it? I denied the sacrifice.

There's too much I don't know. I don't know what Trevor does after he kills. How the heap figures into the ritual.

Not just any heap. A pyre. Mottled femurs and rib cages picked clean. Whoever built it locked the bones by stacking them crosswise. For hundreds of years, they lay around the Door, countless victims Trevor and his ancestors trapped. They hold the Door open.

"They hold it open with their bones," I say, then kneel. "Not anymore, they don't."

I grab a tibia protruding from the pile, and it bites me.

My eyes spring open. I'm on the ground again, my back on fire. The paramedics slip a needle into my arm. Any rational person would let them finish a blood transfusion, but I fight.

"Stop, Mommy," cries Stephen. "Please."

I lift my arm, shocked by the sight of the tibia in my hand. One of the paramedics disarms me, then holds it up to his partner.

"Where the hell'd she get that?" They look around, their questions traveling down a long well. Yellow splinters weep from my palm.

Somehow, I'm able to carry the bones. And return them to our world.

Then I'm back at the Door. It's still spinning, but I hear something grinding. And I get a distinct whiff of a charred laurel wreath. The Door's outer wall droops into a bruised lip.

Dark sky crackles. Like the air itself is splitting. My children's voices are muffled.

It's the Wheel. Leaning on the Door with a tectonic groan. Teeth swing.

Yes, turn. Close the Door, *topple it*. Crush the son of a bitch with your weight.

I remove more bones from the pyre and squeeze, my blood mixing with their marrow.

Wake up, I tell myself.

I have to get back. I have to bring these boys back. I have to bury them beside their parents.

The only illumination is the Door's bloody light, off balance now. Each gyration causes the portal to fall back on itself, like unbalanced clay spinning too fast on a pottery wheel.

My hands turn invisible, but I don't stop. I keep gathering them, cradling them in my arms, until the Door grinds to a dusty close, and leaves me in darkness.

CHAPTER FIFTY

May 12, 2024

"Daphne?"

Karl's steps cause my cup of tea to tremble.

I'm on the patio, smoothing the tablecloth. Ideally, the backyard would be in full bloom, but I'm still waiting for the wood anemones. At least we can eat in the shade and listen to the sound of waves. My back stiffens when I turn, which I hide with an expectant smile.

Karl blows past the chairs and tables. "Da—" He has the door handle before he sees me, face melting from worried to relieved. "Hey."

Over the last three years, Karl's beard has grayed. He never got the promotion for director of clinical apps, so along with a coworker, Karl opened a private practice in our home in Quincy. Now we live and work under the same roof. It's great, though sometimes I wonder if Karl volunteered our first floor to keep an eye on me.

"Think I made a run for it?" I ask. "Fat chance with Beepy here." I point to my ankle bracelet, courtesy of the state's Electronic Monitoring Program. Stephen and Zachary covered it with rainbow stickers so I don't have to see the green light that flashes every few seconds and beeps when the battery runs low. Yes, the DA was so appreciative of my saving thirty-three children, they only charged me with thirty counts of "making or possessing a destructive device."

Karl pulls me close and kisses me with his delicious prickles. "How's your foot?" he asks. Any time Karl has a question about my health, his lip wriggles.

Numb, but I don't say that. "This makes it better."

My husband is so calm and patient, he is almost superhuman. Through my probation, Karl made dinner, cleaned dishes, and picked up the kids until I got over my resentment, and he never complained. I hope that I show my husband that I love him like he loves me.

The bracelet comes off August 1, 2025. I can't wait, though as a licensed PI specializing in cyber security, I hardly need to leave home anyway. My upstairs office serves as the perfect hidey hole to solve wire fraud.

"Your sister's here," says Karl.

"She is?" Joy flutters in my chest. I straighten, groaning louder than I intended. Old wounds cinch as though someone's pulling strings woven into my back. The worst is standing after bending down.

"Honey?"

"I'm fine, Karl," I say, shooing his hands.

"Oh, you poor thing, having to do everything yourself. Come here."

Embarrassment jolts me. Who else saw?

Courtney did, her hair whitish blond now. She's still round and rosy cheeked, eyes squinting behind chic glasses. Mom without the scars.

"Oh, I love your house, Daph," she says, drawing me into a soft embrace. "So much room."

She twists me gently, her perfume transporting me to the moment I woke from a coma. Courtney's flowery smell roused me, as did her reading news from an iPad.

Before that, we hadn't seen each other in thirteen years. Not since our fight at Dad's funeral.

"The sun really lights it up," I say. "Thanks for coming."

Has it really been two years? We tried to coordinate a reunion, but Thanksgiving was no good because of Courtney's mother-in-law. Christmas 2022 snowed out. Now that Courtney's here, our place feels like a real home.

Courtney should have a dozen more compliments. Our stone garden, which is set up for badminton, anything the kids want to play. Instead, Courtney's fingers find the hard circles on my shoulder blades. If she wants to strip search me, there's a whole lot more where that came from. Seven circles, in fact. If the Gauges can do anything, it's skip the small talk.

"What did they do to you, Daph?" asks Courtney. When I pull away, I see her crying.

"I'm not going to break," I say.

Three of Trevor's stab wounds were deep enough to hit vital organs. Two were the most dangerous, a five-centimeter puncture of my left ventricle and a six-centimeter puncture of my left lung. I lost three pints of blood. If the paramedics hadn't administered a transfusion, I would've died on my way to North Adams Regional, like Rusty.

The amazing doctors performed a procedure called a left anterior thoracotomy. They opened my chest to repair my left ventricle. They also resected the injured segment of my lung. I did eighteen months of physical therapy right in our living room. Me and Beepy.

"Girls." Courtney sniffles. "I want you to meet your Aunt Daphne."

She gestures to three sets of families standing awkwardly at the doorway. A disheveled man, husband Randy, teaches geology at Emerson. Daughter Kristen, her four boys. Lots more names, but I hear chopping behind them.

"Welcome," I say, aware that I'm hunching. I can't straighten that last part out as I move between them. "It's so great having everyone here."

They part as though I'm yelling. Or royalty. Let's go with that.

For years, the only people in this house besides my family were the repairmen. Now my kitchen is filled.

Two girls sit at the table, faces buried in their phones. "Hello," I say. They ignore me. Tall, slim, brunette. I know who they belong to even before I hear the hiss of flames.

"Girls," says Brandy, turning from the stove. "Say hi to Auntie."

"Hi," say the girls. Dory and Keri, teenagers now.

"Hey, girl," says Brandy, her voice husky. "You look good."

Not as good as Brandy.

From behind, she still passes for twenty. Hugging Brandy is like putting your arms around a loving coat rack. One filled with coffee and spice.

"Make yourself at home," I say, raising my voice so Karl can hear. "Sis-*ters*, honey. Not sister."

"Sorry," he says, grabbing a platter wrapped in tinfoil. "People are coming in faster than I can track. I'll start the burgers." Courtney's sons-in-law follow Karl, eager for a chore.

Courtney and company are still standing at the door. I wish I could get them to relax. Did Brandy and Courtney see each other yet? The kitchen's temperature rises.

"You realize we got pulled pork and baked beans, right, Bran?" I ask. "Enough mac and cheese to feed the neighborhood." An opinion Karl was kind enough to share during yesterday's prep. "What are you making?"

"Lemon parm." Brandy's teeth are larger and whiter, or maybe she's tanner. "But don't worry. Everything's ready but the chicken. It didn't transport well."

I blink, then follow Courtney, who instructs her clan to bring the foils to the patio. Courtney's younger girls ask Dory and Keri what they're doing. "Mom's favorite," I say.

"It is Mother's Day, you know."

Ellie's voice squelches any response I might have. "You know, it is wicked cool," she says, as though picking up where Brandy left off.

Ellie enters the kitchen from Karl's practice. She fixes a beaded necklace that got tangled in her hair, which is long and dirty blond. Butterflies fill my stomach, even though Ellie looks good. Forty-four, and while unnaturally petite, she looks fifty. The scars pulse on her cheeks.

"Big sisters," says Ellie, spreading her arms for Brandy.

"We're not 'big,'" says Brandy.

A quick dance move, then Ellie's onto Courtney, heels clacking. Karl definitely won't be thrilled about all the holes Ellie's Neiman knockoff pumps are poking into the walnut.

When my turn comes, Ellie holds my hand. "Daph," she says, "I want you to meet my fiancé. Binh brought coffee because he's that sweet."

Brandy aws, embarrassing a handsome young man. Binh's jet-black hair is tapered on top. He's also at least ten years younger than Ellie.

"We met in the program," says Ellie, smiling to give Binh confidence. "Binh's three years sober. I'm fourteen months."

"That's great, El," says Courtney. "Congratulations."

Binh gestures to two coffee travelers. "Want some?" he asks. The smell immediately tugs me.

"I wish I could," I say, hating that I have to refuse the first thing he asks.

"Daphne can't drink coffee, honey," says Ellie.

I nod, blushing at the attention. Coffee should speed up recovery, but Trevor's blade found my liver. My body can't process caffeine or alcohol anymore. I'm strictly on herbal tea forever. At least what seems like forever.

"I had to cut out sugar," Ellie says. "Not good for recovery. Bitterness was my trigger. Then those FBI guys finally got it. They knew, Daph, about what the Flemings were doing, and they helped." She sees the girls at the table. "SOBs."

"Who?" asks Courtney's Kristen. Strange to see her mother's curiosity so flawlessly imitated.

"Bradley Reeves, honey," says Courtney, naming the former chairman of the CARD task force. "Remember, I told you? Your Aunt Daphne stopped bad men from hurting people."

Kristen asks for a follow-up while my eyes burn. Today marks the first time any of my older sisters acknowledged I had done anything, let alone solved a case. Last year, Bradley Reeves pled guilty to suppressing reports of dozens of child abductions stretching from Fresno to Boston. Johnny Bianchi and Andrew Solarsh were just two of those boys taken.

Walter Denton too. More than a dozen cases pending against local investigators and public officials who took bribes traced back to the Crusher Group. Many wondered how all these people could operate so brazenly. I think that once the Door closed, their charms couldn't protect them anymore.

"That whole thing is crazy," says Brandy. "Can someone please get me the salt?"

Amazing that Brandy's backside can shoot a mom look. Change the subject?

"Mom, Mom," cries Stephen, stomping into the kitchen, Zachary and five boys in tow. "Can we show everyone my new Prowler?"

"Stay in the yard," I say, patting Stephen's sweaty head.

"All *right*," they shout, and stomp. Everyone's smile lingers on them, but again I have to cover my eyes. Stephen's expectant look, wanting his mother's permission. Like he's a normal boy again, Trevor forgotten. Courtney's boys playing with mine.

Last is Paul, lugging a cage with an excited dog in it. In two years, he's put on at least thirty pounds. His eyes are Mom's, except sadder. A dent is a shadow above his right ear where Rusty pistol-whipped him. Due to a lack of evidence, the DA never charged Paul for the murder of Billy Rahall.

"Don't worry, Daph," he says, "I won't unleash him in the house."

I hug him, glad that he smells like Dad. "Did you go to the doctor's yet?"

Paul blushes. "It wasn't a seizure," he says. "I just got lightheaded."

Brandy yanks Paul and kisses him on the forehead. "And is this dog the girlfriend we've heard so much about?"

"We broke up last year," says Paul with Ellie hanging off him. Courtney has his right hand. Like when we were kids, I have no space to squeeze in. "This is a Tibetan mastiff. They're highly sought after."

Ellie snorts, patting his chest. "Whatever that means."

"Brunchtime," says Karl, which the kids are only too pleased to repeat.

"Before our bellies bust out," says Brandy, reaching into her purse, "can we get a picture of all of us?"

We gather on the patio. The sun rises, firing until the sky is brilliantly orange. I can't ask for a better contrast to the pink azaleas in my garden. The dots of violet creeping thyme are gorgeous. Today's high is supposed to be in the seventies.

"Let's get the Gauge kids together, please?" Brandy hands her phone to Binh, then bosses us around. "How about you . . . here? You, there. Oh, Daphne?"

My stomach knots. I'm a bad hostess if I let Ellie's fiancé assume the duties of a family photographer.

She doesn't seem to mind. Ellie wants to be dipped, a dance move that causes Courtney to breathe hard. I have to remember to get a picture with Binh and Ellie later.

Brandy packs Courtney, Ellie, Paul, and me together. Their breath brings me back to childhood Christmas photos. We were so grumpy in those, but now we're giggling the way we did before Paul vanished.

We touch the lines on each other's faces. Laugh at gray hairs.

"We're old ladies now," says Courtney.

"Speak for yourself," says Ellie, teasing her curls. Binh mimes a Vogue photographer, drawing more laughter. I'm glad Ellie found someone with a sense of humor.

This is how large families should be. Cousins playing in all corners, astonishing us with growth spurts.

"Definitely Mom's teeth," says Brandy, pointing to Courtney's granddaughter, then to Zachary. "Dad's shoulders."

Nephews share Ellie's chin. Dad's height. Mom's walk.

"Their faces," I say, trying not to be too emotional. "It's everyone I've ever loved."

Then we fit the whole group.

Brandy and her girls take center stage, no surprise. Courtney to the left. Karl, the boys, and me on the right. Ellie slides onto the floor, propped by an elbow.

"Have you been back?"

Paul's on the other side of Karl, whispering in my ear. I don't have to ask, *Back where*? New Minton.

"I've seen pictures," I say. Zachary holds my hand, reminding me of the time he watched Mommy set a town on fire, heart beating in my thumb.

"The devastation is unbelievable," says Paul.

At 12:49 a.m. July 31, 2021, the Weston Observatory at Boston College recorded an earthquake in Western Massachusetts. It measured 8.9 on the Richter scale, easily the largest on record. It also broke the record for shallowest quake, barely more than a mile beneath the earth's surface.

Ninety dead, four hundred injured, thousands homeless. Hangman's Hill traveled nearly four miles to bury downtown under a heap of rock. Now there's no more hill, just a bald dome.

No one will say that closing the Door caused the quake. Just like no one ever bothered to explain where the bones came from, the cemetery I happened to be lying on while the paramedics revived me. They prefer that explanation to mine, where in a space between this world and the Elementals', I plucked those bones from the Door's edge.

The only thing they say is that about ten square miles of land suddenly dropped 333 feet. It dropped despite being nowhere near a known fault line.

I wish I knew what that meant. Was it one foot for every victim? How long has the Brotherhood been sacrificing children in our town and beyond?

"They say it's God trying to tell them to change or get off His land," says Paul.

I smile at Binh, who motions for me to stare straight ahead. "What about David, Paul?"

"No sign," he says.

I don't know what to believe. Police located a blood trail only for it to suddenly disappear at a ravine on the south side of the quarry. Once again, they think David Gedney's body is in there. I won't be fooled twice. Someone helped him, a firefighter, an officer. Someone who escaped the purge.

"Thirty years from now," says Paul, "David's going to be in his seventies. All of us will. How are we going to stop him then?"

"Assuming David wants to wait." I look over the children joking and laughing with each other. "Someone has to take over HWM Cares. Finish Dad's fight."

Binh snaps more photos. Paul doesn't say anything. I'm glad. That's a conversation for later. Maybe when one of Kristen's daughters is old enough.

Brandy holds up a glass. "Happy Mother's Day, Mom," she says, slurring. How'd she get tipsy so fast?

"Happy Mother's Day," everyone says around me. I'm a little late.

The settings are ready, and so is the food. We pass dishes and silverware while Karl tells a funny story about the kids. Binh throws an arm over Ellie's shoulder.

Thirty-six years later, we finally finish a meal, all of us, together.

DISCLAIMER

Daphne notes that coroners ran for election, which is why a valid medical examiner was not immediately available to autopsy Mr. Ford's body. That detail was true in the 1960s in Massachusetts, but not by the 1980s. Also, Daphne misidentifies the sonnenrad as a Nazi symbol, but Nazi propagandists inverted the sonnenrad to make the swastika. And Daphne claims that the Canon PowerShot SX620 HS has a mobile hotspot, which it does not.

ACKNOWLEDGMENTS

So many thanks to Sue Arroyo at CamCat, and for THAT PHONE CALL.

Thanks to Helga Schier and to Christie Stratos, who drew my attention to hitting the manuscript's most important beats. Thanks to Penni Askew for her in-depth editing. Thanks to Maryann Appel for a rocking book cover, and to Maia Lai for a creepy family tree. Many thanks to Bill Lehto, Meredith Lyons, Laura Wooffitt, and to everyone else at CamCat for being such wonderful people to work with.

Thanks to the many readers who patiently read multiple drafts: Captain Frank Nolan and Kebbie Walker for their insightful early comments that radically changed my bad idea; Connor Chauveaux, whose penchant for internal logic might be the only reason this manuscript makes sense; Michael Walonen for his suggestion to find the right title; and Jessie DeLong, whose comment that "You have a lot of chase in the past, but you need a chase in the present," transformed the novel into its present shape.

Thanks to my father, stepmother, brothers, sister, and to the rest of my family.

And so much love and thanks to my wife and three sons, whose unwavering support kept me afloat through all the lonely years, days, and nights I typed out Daphne's story.

ABOUT THE AUTHOR

Brendon Vayo lives with his wife and three sons in Austin, TX. *Girl Among Crows* is his first novel.

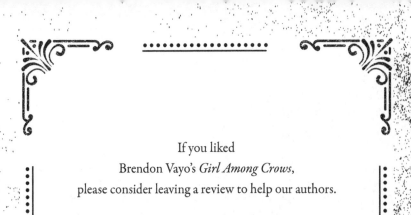

If you liked
Brendon Vayo's *Girl Among Crows*,
please consider leaving a review to help our authors.

And check out another
spine-tingling horror story from CamCat,
Valentina Cano Repetto's *Sanctuary*.

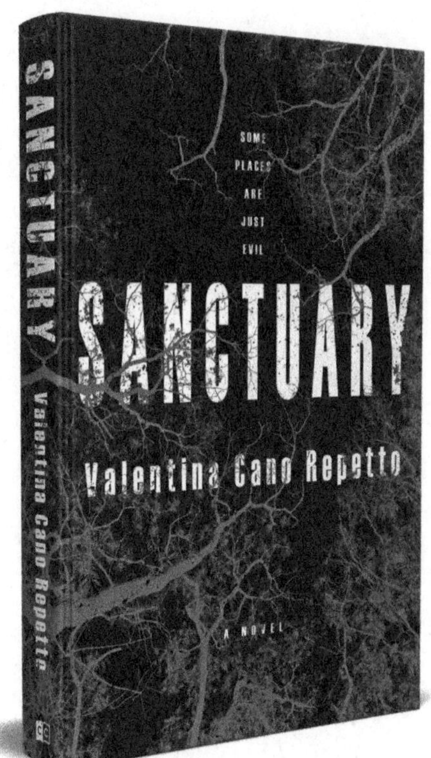

MADDALENA
1596

I dipped the silver spoon into the steaming dark liquid and filled it with death.

The dusky blue of the soup plate's painted lilies gleamed through beef and broth, flakes of chopped herbs swirling around the rim of the maiolica. I could almost see the enameled figure at the bottom, the maiden always bent of knee, the unicorn's head heavy on her lap. The empty forest around them as if the world had come to a hush.

I doubted I'd manage to reach the maiden with breath left in my body.

I took the first sip of the weak stew. There was a trace of bitterness, a tail end of it, but the rosemary and the basil had disguised it, faithful friends they always were. Even now, the herbs spoke to me, whispering warnings in their earth-soaked language that I blinked away as the liquid scorched my throat. I knew all too well what I was doing.

"It's too hot," Francesco said, his large eyes squinting at the steam.

I forced myself to smile. "Blow on it for a few seconds. Gently," I added as his cheeks puffed up with air.

I looked down the stone table at my other children, eating in silence, my eyes and mind attempting to fly over the empty seat and falling like shot birds. At the end of the table, Florindo sat staring at the walnut backrest of that chair, conjuring up the same tendrils of golden hair that I could almost feel under my fingers. His spoon hovered over the plate.

"Eat, *sposo*," I said.

He blinked and the tears fell but he did as he was told. A good husband and father. A good man.

I followed my own instructions and drank more broth, the vital part, my jaw too tight to chew through beef. The only sounds were the tapping of spoons against maiolica and the roar of the torrent behind the mill. But under layers upon layers of the noises that had filled my days since it had happened, there was that one sound. That crack. It ricocheted through me still.

A twist of nausea made me bite the inside of my lips. I looked up at one of the etched cornices that encircled the *sala*, focusing on a gold-leaf curlicue as I breathed and swallowed the bile down. If I became ill now, so soon, none of this would work. They would all stop, and they must not.

How I wished we'd never left *Genova*. That we'd never come to this place.

I did what I could to ignore the bite of sudden hot pain in my stomach and dipped my spoon back in the stew. My hand trembled. Candlelight contracted like a pupil.

Please let this be over quickly.

SIBILLA

1933

The car rolled over yet another stone, the thin and worn leather seat doing little to cushion the steel knobs and joints that had been knocking against me for the past half hour. My hands flew to my stomach. To cover the small mound that still didn't require much adjustments to my waistlines, the mound that was the first and last thing I thought about each day. All of this movement couldn't be good for him, for the boy I knew I carried. I felt his maleness like a bone ache. It hadn't felt like that before, not in the other two pregnancies. With care, I smoothed out my skirt, eyes sliding down to look for snags in the rayon stockings I'd bought especially for this trip. They were pristine.

The driver jerked the steering wheel, the car rattling as if it were considering spread-wheeled collapse as it swerved to avoid half a tree trunk. I winced and shifted again. We'd had the option of a better car at the station in Ovada, one with seats so cushioned and oiled they looked like sofas in those well-to-do clubs that pocked Torino, but Giovanni had insisted on this one. He had to have his reasons, of course, but it couldn't have cost very much more than hiring this rickety contraption, and we had the money now. Habits of the middle class, I supposed.

Yes, out of which his clever mind has lifted us.

Because we now owned a home, a villa, and not just that but a mill and hectares upon hectares of land. The thought was like a sip of brandy.

With a smile, I slid my hand off the mound and slipped my arm through Giovanni's. "Do you think there's much more to go?"

"Why?"

I didn't need more than that to know I'd said the wrong thing. Not an unusual occurrence in our five years of marriage but it still managed to yank me off-center when it happened.

"I was just wondering, that's all," I said, and forced a smile into my voice.

He smoothed out a crease on a trouser leg with a hand that I could have sworn had a small tremble in it. "You're sure you weren't thinking this is too far flung a place to be convenient? That perhaps I've made the wrong choice?"

How had he gathered all of that from my simple question? It was true, he hadn't consulted me before purchasing the property, placing the deeds on our kitchen table just three days before we were meant to take the train down here, but what good would my opinion have been in these matters? I knew nothing of mills or of purchasing land. Besides, he had bought it all with the money from his invention, his patent, money that was his and not mine. He didn't need to consult with me on its use.

The car gave another jostle, and I pressed a hand to my stomach once more, as if that alone could keep the child safe. A gust of cold worry swept through me. I didn't know what I'd do if I felt the cramps now, the red loss soaking into my rayon stockings.

"This is strategically smart, Sibilla."

"Yes, of course," I said, blinking, though I didn't know what he meant.

"What do you see?"

MORE HORROR TALES FROM CAMCAT BOOKS

Available now, wherever books are sold.